A
Pirate Treasure Weekend

By

Bob Hoelzle

Claudia has inherited a map of
pirate Billy Bowlegs' hidden treasure. Skip is
determined to win the Big Bend Saltwater
Classic Fishing Tournament. When their
paths collide, the next three days are
MAYHEM!

Dedicated to my wonderful son Zach, and my sister and brother, who have all stuck with me through good times and bad. And to the organizers and volunteers at local amateur fishing tournaments, who get the scales and fish slime all over them, but very little kudos for their time spent and hard work. Also to Margaret Trammel and Linda Solimine for their review and suggestions.

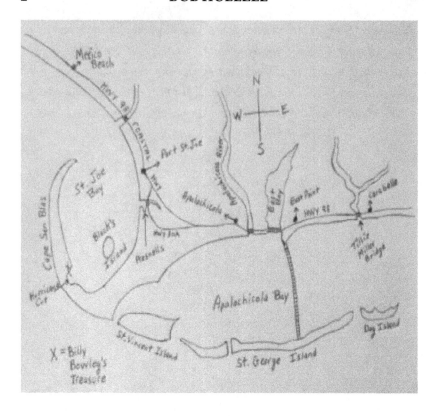

CHAPTER I
BROWN TROUT

S kip Walters should never have stopped at the BP gas station in Carabelle on the way to the coast that hot and humid North Florida panhandle morning in mid-June. His boat in tow, Skip parked the rusty old beige Isuzu pick-up next to the convenience store portion of the business. Nature called in a big, urgent way!

Fortunately, the men's room was unlocked. Yanking hard twice on the loose doorknob, Skip managed to get the squeaky, salt-air corroded door open.

Looking in the mirror at his tall, thin reflection, he noticed the invasion of gray hair mingling with the brown and red hairs of his neatly trimmed beard. As always he checked his fine brown hair to be sure the gray hadn't infiltrated there yet, and was satisfied that it had not. He wished there was some way to eliminate the small wrinkles fanning out from the corner of his hazel-colored eyes, but he knew that years of exposure to the sun took its toll.

Locking the door behind him, he looked around in the dim light provided by a bare bulb above the dirty sink. The toilet paper roll holder dangled from one screw on the wall next to the toilet bowl. It held only a few squares of cheap paper, but, to his relief, there was a full roll on the top of the chipped white ceramic tank. He took off his lucky fishing cap, placed it carefully next to the full roll of toilet paper, pulled some paper off the dangling fixture, and wiped the seat.

Whoever designed the bathroom never had to relieve themselves in the sweltering north Florida heat, and the heat wave during the summer of 1998 made things worse. There was no air conditioning duct, and the temperature in the cramped room must have been one-hundred-and-ten degrees. Skip flushed, reached for his hat, and then it happened! In a hurry for fresh air, he grabbed the hat in haste, which brushed the full roll of toilet paper. Wobbling as it rolled toward the edge of the tank, like a car out of control, it tumbled over the raised seat back and plunged toward the open bowl. He made a quick swipe at it with his hand, but missed.

Nasty water splattered his calves and sneakers before he could jump back to avoid the splash. At least his shorts had been spared the insult.

"Crap!" Skip shouted. Having spent years in the retail business, he had promised himself that he would never leave messes for others to clean up, like so many had done to him. "Do unto others as you would have them do unto you" echoed in his mind. On the other hand, he was not about to reach down into that God-forsaken bowl and yank the soggy mess out. Pondering several possible solutions, he finally chose one he would come to regret. He figured the best thing to do was return to his pick-up, get the stout grouper rod (he already had a big hook tied on), and catch a roll of toilet paper.

Unlocking the rusty restroom door, he rammed it with his shoulder, and it opened with a creak. Sticking his head out and looking both ways, he satisfied himself that there was no one in sight, and hastily continued with his plan. Grabbing the thick rod and heavy reel combination, quickly untangling it from light spinning tackle he had tossed in the pickup bed, he returned to the bathroom unnoticed. He freed the oversized hook from the eye of the pole. Holding the rod with both hands, he began the delicate task of setting the hook in the waterlogged roll of toilet paper. The round hole of the cardboard center became the game fish's mouth, and he adroitly dropped the hook in it on the first try. "This has got to mean good luck in the tournament!" he thought. He set the hook firmly, flicking the rod tip to the left and up. The end of the pole bent, and he had caught his first prize! Lifting the dripping glob out of the bowl, his heart sank as he heard the squeaky bathroom door opening. How he wished he had remembered to lock it!

"Someone in here!" he shouted.

Too late! A rough looking fisherman with a can of beer in his hand barged his way through the door. The moment he saw Skip, he stopped dead in his tracks, staring at the sight of the bent rod and the soggy roll of toilet paper dripping on the dirty floor. Skip froze, and stared back, horrified to be caught in the act.

"Hey, now, son!" said the large barrel-chested man. "You know the tournament don't start 'til the morning – whatcha doin' there?"

His slim, rough-looking companion who had been waiting outside looked over the burly fisherman's shoulder in disbelief. At that moment, the only thing that could have made Skip more embarrassed was if he knew those two guys. As he looked in their smirking faces, to his horror, he realized he did know them! Well, he knew who they were, casual acquaintances from past tournaments, and they didn't know Skip all that well.

The second one in the door, Lucas Millender, shouted, "Hey, Buck! I do believe that this boy has found himself a honey of a brown trout hole!"

They both started laughing so hard that beer began sloshing over the rims of their cans. "And look at that chunk of bait!" Buck Quigley blurted out between guffaws. "He's a-goin' fer the big-uns!" Laughing uproariously, they both stumbled back out of the bathroom in hysterics.

Now, Skip always said that people with a poor sense of self-esteem are usually the ones who can't take a ribbing, and folks with a healthy sense of self worth can roll with the punches. He tried hard to remember that, as he dropped the dripping toilet paper in the plastic garbage can. Resting the pole against the edge of the sink, he proceeded to wash off his line and hook, then his legs with soap and water. Outside, the roars of laughter continued, and he heard Lucas blurt out "brown trout!" as Buck slapped him on the back in glee. The two country boys were having a good ol' time.

Skip stood over the sink, shaking his head, wishing he were anyplace but there. Looking in the mirror, his face flushed with a mixture of heat and embarrassment, Skip wondered how he could turn the table on the two laughing hyenas outside. He washed his hands, reached for the handy cloth towel feeder, pulled down, hoping to find a clean place no one had used yet. But the soiled cloth wouldn't budge. He looked at one of those useless hot air blowers on the wall, and wound up drying his hands half on the used cloth and half on his olive khaki shorts. Taking a firm grasp of the rod and reel, he went out to face the music.

"Hey, did ya get any keepers?" Lucas asked between chuckles.

"You didn't run outta bait, did ya?" Big Buck chimed in. "Cause they got a special on that kinda bait at the Winn-Dixie. Four for ninety-nine cents!" More laughter. It was becoming clear to Skip that he would never live this incident down.

He shook his head, and curled his thin lips in a forced smile, and put the fishing pole back in the bed of the pick-up. Glancing back, he noticed their new, white seventeen-foot Grady-White center console, equipped with a powerful Yamaha 175 horsepower outboard. The expensive rig was being pulled by a late model burgundy Dodge Ram extended cab truck. Their outfit made his look like a toy. Skip's shallow sided fifteen-foot Lancer was powered by a twenty-nine year old 18 horsepower Evinrude, a gift from a friend. Fiberglass patches dotted the brown sides and the tan bottom of the small boat. It had been built years ago for use in rivers, lakes and tidal creeks. Lucas and Buck's boat would have done well in eight-foot seas, even though it was only seventeen feet long.

"Nice rig!" Skip remarked, hoping to get their minds off of what they had just witnessed. It didn't work.

"Thanks!" Buck said. "We got her all rigged up for brown trout!"

Skip realized their belly laughing would go on for awhile, so, deciding to save himself more humiliation, he headed for the cab of his truck. He had wanted to win the tournament pretty bad before this encounter with Lucas and Buck, but now he wanted it more than anything else in the world. He became obsessed with getting the last laugh on those two clowns, and made up his mind to go to any length to beat them. And when Skip was determined to do something, he would not let Hell or high water get in his way. Or so he thought!

The two hysterical fishermen stumbled into the bathroom, one after the other, laughing like two kids. Then an idea hit Skip – one of his inner voices shouted, "Don't do it!" Another voice shouted, "Go for it!" He ignored the better side of him, and acted on the spur of the moment. Quickly flipping the latch that held his boat trailer on to the truck's trailer ball, he threw off the rusty chains held to the bumper with "S" hooks, disconnected the trailer lights, and started the old truck. He carefully backed around his detached boat and trailer, and a few seconds later, the truck's back bumper made a smacking sound as it bumped against the men's room door. When the two men heard the loud thump of the truck hitting the door, they stopped laughing for the first time in ten minutes. They banged on the rusty door in an attempt to open it. The top corner of the door opposite the hinges buckled out as powerful Buck gave it a mighty, yet futile shove.

"Say, you guys wouldn't like to share with me where you caught that gator trout last year that won the tournament, would ya?" Skip asked in a calm voice. Buck had taken first place in the speckled sea trout division with a six-pound ten-ounce whopper. During the award ceremony, Skip had asked him where he caught it, to which Buck replied that they had discovered a mysterious hole while drifting in the bay. That told Skip nothing. He didn't know what bay they had been drifting: Alligator Point, East, Apalachicola, or St. Joseph's.

After a few seconds of silence, Skip heard Lucas say to Buck, "Go ahead, tell him, Buck. After all, we know where his brown trout honey hole is now!" More laughter. Skip knew it was getting hot in there, and he didn't know what kind of tempers those guys had.

"Tell ya what...at least tell me which bay you were drifting when you hooked that monster that won the tournament last year."

"Port St. Joe," Lucas said reluctantly.

"Shut your mouth, fool!" Buck shouted at Lucas.

"Thanks! See y'all out there!" Skip said, jumping into his pickup truck. All ready to speed away, Skip realized his get-even plan had one minor flaw; his boat was sitting bow-down in the parking lot! He couldn't just blast out of there as he had hoped.

Rolling up the windows and locking the doors in case things got ugly, he pulled away slowly, and drove the truck alongside, then in front of his boat and trailer. As the bathroom door burst open, Lucas popped out, his gaunt, bony face flushed from the heat and the laughing. Skip heard him say "Go ahead, Buck, but hurry! I'm about to bust a bladder!"

Skip quickly hooked the boat trailer to the truck, and took off. Looking back, he waved good-bye to Lucas, who just stood there grinning and shaking his head. Skip punched the accelerator to the floor, and thought "Let's see you smile as I hold up the winning trout on Sunday, sucker!"

Driving away, he had the feeling that, over the next three days of the tournament, he would be seeing those two again, and he'd be less than subtly reminded of his rendezvous with the brown trout.

CHAPTER II
GETTING AWAY

"**B**ig Buck" Quigley wasn't about to let any jerk from the city beat him at the game he began playing when he was two years old in 1956. His daddy put a cane pole in his hand and walked him out to the catfish pond on the farm near Blountstown, baited his hook with an earthworm, and Buck began pulling catfish out of that pond like he was born to fish!

"Lucas, I'd be awful angry right now if I thought that city boy knew how to fish. Why did you tell him where we caught that gator trout last year?"

"Hell, Buck, everyone whose worth their salt around these parts knows the biggest trout come from St. Joseph's Bay. Besides, that's a big darn bay and he has no idea where you caught it."

"Well, if that jerk starts following us around, I'm gonna introduce him to my friend Smith and Wesson!"

"No need to get upset, big guy. You ain't gonna win the tourney this year anyhow. I'm gonna catch a trout so big it won't fit in the dad-gum cooler!"

Lucas Millender was no novice at the game, either. Born in East Point, right on Apalachicola Bay, he was the son of an oysterman. One day in mid-May, 1958, his father put him aboard the oyster boat at the ripe old age of four, gave him a closed-faced Zebco reel, a short rod, tied on a green-bodied jig, and taught Lucas how to cast. As his callous-handed father went about the business of raking delicious shellfish from the choppy, shallow waters of the bay, his son amazed him by catching twelve speckled trout. Lucas Millender was known by the folks in East Point to be one of the best sport fishermen around, and was constantly stopped and asked for advice on where to fish. Being a convivial and talkative sort, he never minded obliging. On the other hand, Buck had the attitude that you put in the time finding good spots, and when you finally find one, you keep it to yourself 'til your dying day.

They had met in Vietnam, Buck pulled Lucas out of a downed, burning chopper and saved his life. They became best of friends, and, when the war ended, both went to work in the paper mill owned by the St. Joe Paper Company. When the mill shut down a couple of years ago, Lucas scraped a living out of the bay, like his father before him, harvesting succulent oysters. To supplement his income, he occasionally filled in for local light-tackle fishing guides, if he was lucky enough to be asked. Being single, and living in the same home he grew up in that his father left him when he died, Lucas was able to make ends meet, but didn't have a lot left over.

Buck, on the other hand, was doing quite well for himself. He managed a marina on Alligator Point, which provided him and his wife a place to live for free next to the marina, and a decent salary. He supplemented his income by doing boat repairs for the clients of the marina, and his wife worked as a bar maid in the Blue Lagoon lounge in Apalachicola. Buck purchased the Grady-White brand spanking new, and paid cash.

Buck and Lucas had been fishing the Big Bend Saltwater Classic every year since its inception in 1989, and not a year went by without one or the other of them taking a first or second in the speckled trout division, they were that good. However, the one thing that eluded them was winning the whole tournament. In order to win the grand prize, you had to have the most over-all points. That usually meant you had to catch other species of fish and win a first, second or third in those divisions, and have the most points of any of the fishermen entered in the tournament. Rarely, if no one fisherman caught fish that placed in more than one division, someone would win by their first place fish being a larger percentage heavier than the second place fish in that category.

Winning the grand prize was always a tough task, as there were a lot of talented offshore fishermen in the tournament each year, who would put together a winning combination of such species as grouper, amberjack, wahoo, kingfish, and cobia. Buck and Lucas fished for inshore species, and, although they consistently placed in the speckled trout division, they only occasionally placed in the flounder, gaff-top sailcat or Spanish mackerel divisions.

SKIP PULLED OUT OF the gas station heading west on U.S. Hwy. 98, known locally as Coastal Highway. Glancing to the left as he crossed the intersection of Marine Street, he strained to see if old Riley's Bait and Tackle shop was still in business. Ancient Mrs. Acres, the melancholy, yet talkative, gray-haired widow of the original owner had told Skip one of the most useful fishing tips he had ever heard. She said her husband, Riley Acres, had been a long time local fishing guide, and fished the Carabelle River, Crooked River and the New River with his clients. When Skip asked where her late husband did most of his fishing, she replied that he fished up and down all three, but mostly stopped by the steep banks near curves. "Why there?" Skip asked.

"Don'tcha know, honey?" she asked. "I thought everyone knew that's where you find the deeper holes! And the fish."

Well, maybe everyone else in Carabelle knew that, but Skip sure didn't. Fishing the New and Crooked Rivers later that winter, he found some of those deep holes by bends and scored nice catches of redfish and speckled trout.

Skip attributed his fishing success, which was fair, to one thing – his penchant for listening to folks and asking a lot of questions. And he wasn't particular about who he asked. It seemed to him that every person who fished knew at least a little something he didn't. Skip figured that the more you knew, the more likely you were to catch fish. So he would query anyone: young boys, gray-haired women, wrinkled veteran fishermen and owners of fancy boats, if they had managed to catch some nice fish. He gleaned knowledge about tides, lures, times of day, locations, live baits, techniques, water depth, and wind conditions, then stored it away in the back of his head. It would have taken him two lifetimes of fishing every day to gather all the information he learned from other people by asking questions, and another two lifetimes of fishing every day to accumulate all the information about fishing he picked up by reading books, and magazines like the *Florida Sportsman*.

Being very grateful to every person who shared their knowledge with him, he felt it was his duty to share all he had learned with others. "Knowledge is nothing if it's not passed on" was a motto Skip coined, and he applied that principle to knowledge gained in other aspects of his life as well.

As the north Florida morning sun blazed down on his slow moving truck, he looked to the right and noticed the smallest police station in the world. The locally famous police station consisted of a lone phone booth next to the curb on Coastal Highway. If you needed to report a crime, that's where you would go. Or that was the idea. The smallest police station was also the most useless police station, as the last time he looked inside, the wires to the phone were dangling in the air.

For the quaint seaside town, which still had no direct mail delivery, change was brewing. The stores next to the smallest police sta-

tion, old brick buildings, once housed a general store and a veteri-
narian. Now they were the offices of Apalachee Bay Properties and
Carabelle Realty. The "forgotten coast" had been remembered – discovered by wealthy folks looking to build retirement homes by the
pristine Gulf shore.

North of town the landscape turned to swamps, then pine forest,
and the pinelands stretch (with the exception of a few farms and villages) all the way to the Georgia border, some one-hundred miles to
the north.

To Skip's left the Carabelle River, with its brackish, unpolluted,
yet tannic acid colored water, gave a scenic backdrop to several small
seafood restaurants nestled between Hwy. 98 and the river. The
Carrabelle also provided a deep haven for commercial fishing boats
that were moored in back of oyster-shell filled lots and dilapidated
wholesale seafood buildings. Skip recalled the story of a seven pound
sailcat that had been caught off one of the docks he was passing, that
had won first place in the Big Bend Saltwater Fishing Classic tournament a few years earlier. The unusual thing was that the lucky angler
caught the winning fish within a hundred yards of the weigh-in station and tournament headquarters. Wiley fishermen had fished their
favorite spots from the Aucilla River to the east, to Mexico Beach to
the west, and the prize winner was caught right there off the dock.

Skip knew the tide was low because the sandbar that mysterious-
ly rose from the middle of the deep river and paralleled the shore
was visible. He wondered how many inexperienced captains ground-
ed their craft on that particular bar.

Just before crossing the concrete Tillie Miller Bridge that would
carry him over the river, he glanced at the large Carabelle Marina
complex, host of the Big Bend Saltwater Classic. It consisted of
eighty-seven slips filled to capacity with fishing boats, pleasure vessels, and sailboats. He noticed two men hoisting the thirty-foot plastic banner that boldly announced "Big Bend Saltwater Classic" over

a street entrance to the marina. They had their backs turned to him, and he could see fish swimming in a circle of blue water on their tournament T-shirts. One of the nicest things about entering this tournament was, with the payment of the forty dollar entry fee, you got a shopping bag full of goodies. It reminded Skip of getting a stocking full of surprises Christmas mornings of his youth in the once quiet town of Tallahassee. Now each year he looked forward to opening that complimentary bag of fishing accessories with the open-eyed delight of a child who still believed in Santa Claus. The bag was filled with products donated by merchants and manufacturers. He loved to pull out one item at a time; lures, floating key rings, caps, hats, tooth brushes with "Quill Turk, DDS" stamped on the handle, elastic sunglass bands to keep your sunglasses from falling overboard as you tried to boat a big game fish, can openers, hooks, plastic jig bodies, and much more. The finest thing in the bag, year after year, was always the beautiful Big Bend Saltwater Classic T-shirt. The contents of the bag were not all fluff items to be eventually discarded. Skip's friend Todd Wiggins, who had fished the tournament with him for the past several years, had taken second place in the speckled trout division using a plastic jig body he found in his bag of odds-and-ends. He wished Todd had been available to fish the tournament with him again this year, as it had become sort of a tradition. But Todd apologetically explained that he had previous commitments.

The road rose under him as Skip ascended the small bridge that spanned the Carabelle River. The concrete railings stood sentry for those enjoying the sights too much, and ensured that their vehicles stayed on course. Looking north, to the right over the guardrail, he caught sight of a man-made island that split the river to the north of the bridge. It consisted of sand dredged from the riverbed when they deepened a too-shallow channel. Further to the north, he could see small tidal creeks that divided marshes of spartina grass, fertile areas so necessary for the continued proliferation of the abundant sea life in the area. Looking south, he saw rows of boats in the Carabelle Marina, and beyond them the tall riggings of commercial shrimp boats and net boats that sat at the docks awaiting their crews. Further south, he could see where the Carabelle emptied into Apalachicola Bay. Across the bay he caught a glimpse of Dog Island, which sheltered the harbor from big waves that occasionally rose in the Gulf of Mexico. When the wind howled from the southwest, choppy waves pushed their way through East Pass and across the three-mile wide bay, making the mouth of the river a dangerous place for small boats. The Dog Island Ferry traversed the bay twice daily. It was the only way to access Dog Island, unless you were lucky enough to own a boat or a small plane. Fifty or so beach houses dotted the remote island; some were vacation homes, others year-round residences. It seemed like the perfect quiet haven from the always-too-much-to-do life Skip was leading, raising a young son, owning a house, and working for the State of Florida in the Public Assistance program. But Skip knew better than to allow his mind to ponder the stresses of his job when not at work.

One of the most refreshing things about fishing was that, when he floated in the middle of a beautiful saltwater bay, and the breeze was blowing and the waves were rocking his boat, and he just knew that the next cast was going to produce a vicious strike, all the troubles and worries and responsibilities in his life were a long, long way away. Taking a deep breath of fresh salty air, looking around at the distant shore, and gazing at an osprey circling overhead, his mind was totally in the present. It was moments such as these that he came to realize just how blessed he was to be alive on such an awe-inspiring planet, and thanked God for the beauty of it all, and for having the time to enjoy it. When he was in that state of mind, he could fish all day without a bite, and still have a really good time!

On the right, the Hobo's Ice Cream Parlor sign beckoned him to stop and partake of their smooth, cold treats. But Skip was starting to get excited about the prospect of casting some top water plugs as the sun set over St. Joseph's Bay. A thin, attractive woman raced by him in an old forest green Fiat spider convertible, her light brown hair blowing in the wind. She waved as she passed, and Skip waved back, but he wasn't sure the woman saw him wave, as she was obviously hell-bent on arriving somewhere in a hurry. Skip wished her luck getting to her destination, as he recalled the reputation of those sports cars – fun to drive, but hard to keep running. He wondered where she was going in such a rush, and if their paths might cross sometime during the weekend.

Skip passed the little municipal beach area, with its picnic tables and grills protected from the heat of the sun by a concrete overhang built to withstand tropical storms. The beach was narrow, and had tannish-brown sand, and Skip for the life of him couldn't understand why anyone would stop there, a beach on the bay, when in another twenty minutes they could be spreading their blankets on the powder-fine white sand of St. George's Island. "Oh, well," he thought, "each to his own."

He daydreamed about an article he read in the *Florida Sportsman*. Two fly fishermen had spent years experimenting with different color combinations while fishing St. Joseph's Bay. They discovered the fly pattern that worked best in enticing fish to strike; yellow and orange. Yellow and orange! Bizarre! What the heck were those fish thinking? Skip could not recall anything he saw swimming in those waters that was yellow and orange. He visualized one fish saying to another, "Hey, Joe! Look at that! Have you ever seen anything so stupid looking in all your life? I feel sorry for it. Let's eat it and put it out of its' misery. Gulp!!"

Skip had heard some folks say fish can only see shades of black and white. He heard others say fish can see colors the same as we can. Skip believed they could – he had no other explanation for why some colors produced more strikes than others. He had always heard that it was wise to match the lure color to the color of bait the predators were eating. Although he had found that to work well sometimes, other times the fish seemed to prefer hot pink, and, yes, maybe even yellow and orange combinations. He intended to find out for himself, as he had just bought a yellow and orange-bellied top water popper with a green back by J & W Lures the night before at Wal-Mart. The lure was called a Tootsie Pop (yeah, some fisherman are suckers!) and Skip was convinced that no one would believe him if he told them he'd been catching fish on one. Skip could resist ice cream, he could resist gambling, he had the willpower to resist drug and alcohol addiction, and he could resist all kinds of material enticements, but he was a weak person when he found himself amidst hundreds of fishing lures that he had not tried yet. One voice inside him said "You can't afford any more lures!" Then another voice reasoned "But that might be the one that wins the tournament!" The second voice always won, much to the chagrin of his meager bank balance. That's why his tackle box looked like a condominium! The chagrin on his friend's faces told it all when he showed up with his huge tackle box. "You're not bringing that thing aboard! Where am I going to stow that?" Anticipating their question, Skip mentioned the fact that, if the boat sank, they could paddle the tackle box to safety. They were usually less than amused. To confirm their suspicion that they made a big mistake inviting Skip fishing, he would pull seven rods out of his truck. After a few words, and several hints, such as, "You know, man, this ain't the Queen Mary!" Skip would whittle his selection down to five, and his friends begrudgingly stowed them. Maybe, Skip thought, that's why he was fishing the tournament alone this year.

As he approached the tiny town of East Point, he could see the seafood wholesaler's tin framed warehouses sitting quietly on the shore of Apalachicola Bay. Not much happened on Thursday afternoons in Eastpoint. The old pickup's exhaust system had rusted away from the frequent launching of his boat in salt water. The noise of the

diesel engine echoed through the peaceful fishing village as he accelerated. It was louder than the refrigerated sixteen wheelers that sat
idling next to the warehouses, waiting to be loaded with oysters and
fish, and driven to major cities in the East and Midwest. Black hood-
ed seagulls glided above the piles of oyster shells bleaching in the sun
between the highway and the narrow, man-made harbor. Forming
the 50-foot wide harbor on the south was a small rock barrier that
sheltered the oyster boats docked behind the seafood retail stores
and warehouses. Choppy waves from Apalachicola Bay lapped at the
rock jetty that ran parallel to the shore, as a southerly breeze blew
across the wide expanse of water that stretched from St. George's Island to the mainland. The bay came within ten feet of Coastal Highway 98 in places, the erosion of the beach causing 98 to be vulnerable
to being wiped out by tropical storms and hurricanes. Looking out
toward the two sections of bridge that spanned the four miles and
connected the mainland to St. George's, he could see at least forty
small oyster boats bobbing in the waves. The strong-armed oystermen were grinding their tongs on the submerged oyster bars, opening and closing the tool like a big pair of scissors, reaping shelled del-
icacies from the shallow, fertile waters of the bay. Skip envisioned
sheepshead and black drum cruising through the murky sediment to
feed on the shrimp and crabs disturbed by the oystermen's rakes. A
thought of fishing close to the oystermen came to mind, as he recalled an article he read about someone fishing in the Great South
Bay of Long Island, New York. The fisherman noticed schools of bait
being blasted in the middle of a loose ring of clam boats. Casting into the commotion, his rod was nearly jolted out of his hand. Fighting the fish for fifteen minutes the lucky fisherman finally prevailed
and boated a beautiful, huge eight-pound weakfish; a close relative to
the speckled trout. Yet Skip had not explored fishing near oystermen,
and resolved to try that some time soon.

One of Skip's earliest memories came back to him. He recalled the first time his father put a cane pole in his hand, baited the hook with a cricket, and, sitting on a dock on Lake Talquin, helped three-year old Skip swing the bobber and bait into muddy water. He recalled his excitement when the pencil bobber stood on end, then vanished beneath the water, and his father and mother shouted "Pull it up!" He yanked with all his might on the long, thin cane pole, and, to his surprise and delight, out of the water came a red-breasted shell cracker, which he managed to swing up to the dock all by himself. He remembered shaking, just shaking with excitement, as his parents cheered his success. That was how his life-long love affair with fishing had begun.

Across the bay St. George's Island's white outline emerged on the hazy horizon. The barrier island stretched its rolling sand dunes, scrub brush and pine trees across the Gulf, and offered East Point and Apalachicola some protection from the raging seas during hurricanes. The fine white sand beach, created by the waves rolling in from the Gulf of Mexico, appeared in his mind. How nice a quick dip in the warm Gulf water would feel on that humid ninety-five-degree North Florida afternoon, Skip thought. His daydreaming was rudely interrupted by someone blasting their horn behind him. Looking in his rear view mirror, he saw Buck and Lucas tailgating him, the sun glinting off of their fancy burgundy truck. Buck flashed his headlights, and blew his horn. It sounded like a siren on top of a lighthouse. Skip decided it would be prudent to let them pass. So he pulled off the road into the parking lot of Fisherman's Choice Bait and Tackle store. As they roared by, Buck yelled out the window "Get that trash off the highway!" Skip was tempted to give him the peace sign minus the index finger, but figured he'd already annoyed them enough for one day, and didn't want to push his luck. But their rude, king-of-the-road behavior stirred an anger deep inside Skip. "We'll see who has the last laugh!" He redirected his rage into a determination he had never before experienced in a fishing tournament. He knew he would do anything humanly possible to beat those guys this year. He wanted to win so badly, he could feel it from his head to his toes. Nothing would stop him, he resolved. He would do whatever it took to look down at those two clowns from the winners' platform at the awards ceremony.

Skip's new-found motivation to win the tournament, along with his addiction to fishing lures, made him jump out of his truck and enter the tackle shop. Most specialty tackle shops' merchandise was high-priced, but he had found some good deals on lures in Fisherman's Choice in the past, and they had a wide variety of tackle. The young man with big arms and a blue, beat-up baseball cap behind the counter greeted him with a "Howdy!" and "Can I hep ya find anything?"

"Nah, just looking around. What are the trout hitting now-a-days?" asked Skip.

"I caught some nice ones by the dry bar last week on that purple Mirror Lure." The clerk offered.

"Sinker or floater?"

"Sinker."

"Fast retrieve or slow?"

"Slow."

"What tide?"

"Incoming."

"Any size to 'em?"

"One was over five pounds."

"That's a nice trout! What time of day?"

"Late afternoon."

Skip put the purple Mirror Lure he selected on the counter. "Where's the dry bar?" The clerk tried to explain the location to him, but Skip was too preoccupied thinking of his run-in with Buck and Lucas to concentrate. He thanked the clerk for the tip, went to the bed of his truck, and managed to squeeze the lure in with three other colored sinking Mirror Lures in a compartment of his oversized tackle box that was only meant to hold one lure. He put his seat belt on, and cranked up the engine. He was really anxious to be out on the water. He wanted to get to St. Joseph's Bay as soon as he could, set up his tent, launch the boat, and try out some spots that afternoon before the tournament began the next morning. Even before his encounter with Lucas and Buck, he had decided to fish St. Joseph's Bay, as he knew the reputation it had for harboring oversized speckled trout.

The Big Bend Saltwater Classic is held each year on the Friday, Saturday and Sunday of Father's Day weekend. Skip's ex-wife used to get upset about the timing of the tournament. "You're supposed to spend Father's Day with your family!" she would complain. Skip explained to her that he looked forward all year to this tournament, how much it meant to him, and that, at 2 PM on Father's Day it would be all over and he could spend the rest of the day with her and their son. She never did get it – fishing this three day tournament was a bigger, more meaningful gift to him for Father's Day than anything she could buy. But that wasn't the reason for the divorce. She was a beautiful woman, used to the finer things in life, and he was the son of a state worker. She had a taste for filet mignon. He had a taste for fish and chips. She spent like they had a million. He worked overtime, and still couldn't make ends meet. She was a hairdresser in a fancy salon, and rubbed elbows with the most wealthy of Tallahasseans. He worked for the state, and determined eligibility for Food Stamps, Cash Assistance and Medicaid, and rubbed elbows with the folks that had the least. He bought clothes at the discount stores and yard sales. She bought her wardrobe from only the most expensive specialty stores in town. And he came home early one day to find her in bed with the owner of the salon she worked for, and his heart was broken and he couldn't find it in himself to forgive her, and she didn't seem to care that much that he couldn't. So they went their separate ways, each retaining half custody of the most precious little three-year-old boy in the world. He was the one jewel that came from the ill-fitted relationship, and Skip loved that boy more than life itself. He couldn't wait until Benny was old enough to fish the tournament with him. And now, at the tender age of six, Skip knew Benny didn't have the patience or the desire to be out fishing all day, and so he left him with his ex-wife for the weekend. She agreed to drop Benny off to Skip at the weigh-in on Father's day. Although he missed his son any time he was away from him, he was glad to have the freedom to fish the tournament this year without having to take care of the lad. And looking into Benny's smiling face at the end of the tournament after not seeing him for a few days would be so uplifting, it would make the end of the tournament a delight no matter what the outcome.

Back on the road, Skip's thoughts returned to the fiasco at the gas station, and his yearning to win the speckled trout division grew each time he recalled the brown trout episode.

CHAPTER III
THE GOOD SAMARITAN

"Thirty-five more miles and I'm there – paradise!"

St. Joseph's Bay occupied his thoughts. He considered it one of the prettiest bodies of water on the face of the Earth. Dreaming of the crystal clear salt water, he imagined himself peering over the side of the boat, seeing the sea grass flowing with the tide and the baitfish darting about. The water clarity made the bottom look so close it seemed you could reach out and touch it with your hand, even though it was twelve feet deep. He thought nothing could delay his much anticipated arrival at Presnell's Fish Camp, when he saw her standing, hands on her slender hips, looking under the hood of the green Fiat Spider – the same woman who had recently blown past him, hell-bound for who-knows-where.

Skip didn't want anything in the world to distract him from the burning desire he felt to win the trout division of the tournament. Yet his conscience couldn't allow him to simply wave and pass the stranded woman. It was just not his nature. Besides, she was awfully pretty. And that's when his carefully planned weekend strategy went askew.

A driver of old cars, he had been very appreciative of those folks kind enough to stop, seeing him broken down on the side of the road, and offering their assistance. He recalled the words of a South

Florida truck driver with whom he had hitched a ride when he was a college student. After the driver treated Skip to a steak dinner and took him from Tennessee to the Florida border, Skip asked him how he could repay him. The driver said, "Just do something nice for someone else – sooner or later it will come back to me!"

So like a reluctant Good Samaritan, Skip pulled his truck and boat into the parking lot of a small motel beyond the broken-down Fiat. Getting out of the pickup, he walked back toward the stranded woman.

"Hi!" he said in the friendliest tone he could muster, stopping ten feet away from her to let her know he meant no harm. "What's wrong with your car?"

"The hell if I know!"

"I'm no mechanic, but I'll take a look at it if you want."

"Sure – have at it. But if you can't get it going in the next ten minutes, I'm outta here."

He looked at the engine and mulled over what she just said. "How're ya gonna leave if I can't get the car started?"

Their eyes met, he noticed the green-gold flecked coloring of her irises, and his heart skipped a beat. There was something about her he found incredibly attractive. Her high cheekbones and the way she held her lips, in an I-can-handle-anything confident way, caused him to want to keep looking at her. She was very slender, and her small bra-less breasts made little creases in her white cotton, loose fitting sleeveless blouse. She wore blue denim cutoff shorts that fit tight at the waist but had a few inches to spare on the bottom, giving her sinewy, yet shapely thighs room to breathe. Perhaps she was a runner. Not the type of woman who would win a beauty pageant, but Skip was attracted by her natural, outdoors look. She wore no makeup, nor did she need any as far as he was concerned. His palms became sweaty.

"I'll hitch a ride, if I have to. I've got to meet someone at five o'clock!"

"Well, if I can't get this started, I'll give you a ride." As fascinated and taken by her as he was, he would have given her a ride to Texas and back, had it not been the weekend of the tournament.

"Thanks." she said, nodding toward the open hood.

He checked the spark plug wire connections, from the distributor to the plugs, then inspected the battery connections, looking for loose or frayed wires. Nothing seemed amiss.

"You have plenty of gas?"

"Yes!"

"What did the car do before it stopped?"

"Sputtered a few times, then just conked out."

"Hmm...that could be your fuel pump. Or the timing chain. Either way, I wouldn't be able to fix it."

"Then let's go! I only paid four-hundred for it anyway."

"You're not going to just leave it here, are you?"

"No, I don't want a ticket." she said in a tone that he took to mean, "of course not, you idiot!"

"How about pushing it into the lot of that restaurant?" She pointed to the Sand Bottom Barbeque parking lot.

"Not a good idea, unless you want to get it towed away. Let's push it down the road a little, just beyond the Motel parking entrance, and it will look like you're staying at the Motel."

"O.K."

Skip said, "Hop in."

She put the car in neutral. He closed the hood, and began pushing it from the rear. "My name's Skip!" he shouted.

"I'm Claudia!" He detected some warmth in her voice for the first time. "Thanks for your help."

She stopped the car on the sparse grass of the road's shoulder, just beyond Aaron's on the Bay Motel. He helped her get the convertible top up, and she locked the car.

"Shouldn't we let the folks at the motel know we are leaving my car here for awhile?"

"You can if you want, but what if they say you can't leave it there?"

"Right. Let's just get out of here."

While pushing the Fiat, he had noticed the Monroe County, Florida license plate and wondered what someone from south Florida was doing so far from home.

"Where ya from?" Skip asked.

"The Keys."

"Where ya headin'?"

"Treasure Bay Lodge."

Her tone of voice gave Skip the feeling his questions were making her uncomfortable.

She swung the pocketbook strap over her freckled shoulder. The small blue bag matched her shorts, and was embroidered with a tropical beach scene depicting the sun rising, or perhaps falling, over a palm tree island. She carried a black duffle bag that had compartments at either end, and was full to bursting with what Skip imagined to be clothes. Had this been Melissa, his ex, she would have been carrying three suitcases. They walked back to the truck side-by-side. At six-foot, Skip was only two inches taller than Claudia. He tried to glimpse her face again through the straight, sun-lightened brown, shoulder length hair. He unlocked the passenger door, and, to make way for her, threw his sleeping bag and tent in the bed of the truck. He slid the box of Cheezits over, brushed off some yellow crumbs from the seat, and she hopped in. He started the engine, and was embarrassed by the loudness of the old diesel blowing it's exhaust out somewhere below the driver's seat. They got a few miles down the road, and he asked, "So, where you meeting this guy?"

"Who said it was a guy?" she said in a playful manner. "I'm to meet this person in front of the Treasure Bay Lodge near St. Joe – do you know where that is?"

"Yeah!" he said, thrilled not to have to go out of his way. "It's just before Presnell's, which is where I'm camping for the next three nights."

Noticing she was looking north over the wide expanse of bay and tidal creeks visible as they made their way over the two long bridges that led to the town of Apalachicola, he said, "That's East Bay."

"Oh, no!" Claudia exclaimed.

"Yeah – it really is..."

"Can you go back?" she pleaded.

"I'd rather not, but I can," he responded, seeing the chances of wetting a line that afternoon dwindle. There was no place to turn around until he got to the island between the bridges. He looked at his watch and it was 4:14.

"I'm really sorry, but I left some stuff in the car that I'm going to need."

"What did you forget?"

"Just some stuff that I really must have."

"Can't this person drive you back to East Point to pick it up, and get someone to look at your car at the same time?"

"Not really!"

"O.K."

As the first bridge ended, Skip pulled over near a pair of sand palms, and waited for the lanes to clear before making a U-turn. Heading back East on Hwy. 98, he tried to place her accent, but couldn't. It was not a deep southern drawl, yet not a northern accent either.

"What part of the Keys are you from?"

"I was born and raised in Ft. Lauderdale. Lived in Key West recently." He got the feeling she was not a very talkative person.

"What brings you to this corner of the world, Claudia?"

"Personal business. Can we change the subject?"

After a long period of awkward silence, she pointed to the disabled car. "There it is. This will only take a second, I promise."

She jumped out of the truck almost before it stopped, keys in hand. Opening the trunk, and she pulled out a square cookie-tin, white with red writing, a wide-brimmed Panama hat with a leather strap to secure it in a wind, and a metal-handled spade that had been broken down into two pieces.

She tossed the tool into the rusty truck bed, and Skip winced as the digging end of her shovel clattered to a stop against his fishing poles. He had just spooled each spinning reel with new line, and he was not about to lose the prize fish because of a nick. He put on the emergency brake, got out, carefully lifting the spade and nestling it between her bag and the wheel well.

"What do you use that shovel for?"

No response.

"If it were mine, I'd use it to dig for sand fleas on the beach. Do you know what sand fleas are?"

"No."

"They're little white crustaceans that look like miniature armadillos, and make excellent bait for pompano."

"Oh."

"So, what do you use it for?"

"Ah, I'm into gardening."

"Gardening! I thought maybe you were going to dig for buried treasure!"

Her face flushed.

"Are you going fishing, or coming back?"

"Take a sniff. If I was coming back, you'd know it! I'm going. I fish in the Big Bend Saltwater Classic tournament each June, and it's this weekend. Ever heard of it?"

"No."

"Well, it's a big event in these parts. The tournament lasts three days, and there are several divisions. Recreational – that's the one I enter, Team, Commercial, Fly and Children's divisions."

"What kind of fish are you after?"

"Brown trout!" Skip giggled. She looked at him as if he was crazy.

"You had to be there!" Skip shook his head. "Actually, I'm hoping to win the speckled trout and flounder categories. I've been looking forward to this tournament for a long time. I began cleaning and lubricating my reels seven months ago, in December. And I'm so psyched that I had a hard time sleeping the last couple of nights."

"What do you get if you win?"

"Well, if you take a first place, you get four-hundred-and-fifty dollars, second is two-hundred-and-fifty dollars, and third is a hundred dollars. Then, in the Recreational Division, the one with the most over all points gets a five day fishing trip to Costa Rica."

"Oh, joy!" She rose slightly in her seat and pulled at the end of her shorts. "What if you don't like to fish?"

"Then you probably wouldn't have entered the tournament in the first place."

"True."

"But it's not just about the money and the trip to Costa Rica. I'm gonna fish 'til I drop if that's what it takes to beat those two clowns."

"What two clowns?"

"Buck Quigley and Lucas Millender."

"Why do you want to beat them so badly?"

"They think they're the greatest fishermen that ever walked the earth. They drive a new truck, have a fancy new boat with all the electronics and use only the best fishing gear. Besides, they just embarrassed the hell out of me."

"How?"

"I'd rather not say. But I want to win the speckled trout division so bad, I can taste it. Holding up the winning fish, and seeing the expression on their faces would be worth more to me than all of the prizes put together."

"I hope I'm not getting in your way – "

"No. Not at all. Like I said, I'm heading to St. Joseph's Bay anyway, and the Treasure Bay Lodge is right on the way. It's nice to have some company."

"What is the thrill of fishing anyway? I always thought it was pretty boring."

"It's all in your attitude. If you go out hell-bent on catching a load of fish, chances are you are going to be disappointed. But if you go fishing with the idea that it's a wonderful way to spend some time, relaxing by the sea and appreciating the beautiful surroundings, the sights and smells, and the feel of the waves rocking your boat, then if you catch a fish, it's kind of a bonus."

"But aren't you hell-bent on catching fish?"

"Got me there! But once this tournament is over, I'll be back into fishing for the peace of mind it brings. Ever catch a fish?"

"I've gone a few times, but haven't really enjoyed it. Waiting hours for something to happen, having to be quiet so you don't disturb them – I don't think it's my cup of tea."

"To me, catching a fish is one of the most thrilling things in the world. I cast these top water plugs about fifty feet away from the boat. Then I reel in the slack, twitch my rod, and make that lure pop on the surface. Sometimes, after a few noisy pops, BLAM! The water explodes as a trout blasts the plug. You jerk back and reel as fast as you can. The rod bends, and you hear your drag peeling out line as the fish races to get away. Sends adrenaline through my whole body!

I get so excited that, ten minutes after boating the fish, my tongue is still tripping over words, and my whole body tingles with excitement. There's nothing like it in the world!"

"So why fish in tournaments?"

"Combine the excitement that you feel when a fish suddenly blasts your plug, with the thought that you've got four-hundred-and-fifty dollars on the end of your line, and it makes for a thrilling time. You have to play the fish just right – have the drag set soft enough that the line doesn't break, yet hard enough to set the hook. Speckled trout have soft mouths, and if you try to horse them in, the hooks will pull out. But if you take too much time playing a fish, the hooks loosen and the fish can pry them out of their mouth. So it's a real balance, and quite a challenge to land a gator trout."

"What's a gator trout?"

"One that's graduated from the University of Florida." She didn't get the joke. Skip knew this woman hadn't spent much time in north Florida.

"What?"

"Just a joke. A gator trout is one that weighs over, say, five pounds. That would make it twenty-five or twenty-six inches long or longer."

"Oh." She stared out the window at a few scattered pine trees next to the road, whose straight, tall trunks held surprisingly few branches and pine needles for their height.

"It's amazing those pines can survive like that, isn't it?" Skip said, trying to draw her into conversation. He was curious to know this woman, and what she was doing, and why she was in the panhandle having come from Key West.

"What do you mean?" Claudia squirmed in her seat.

"Well, they're growing in soil that looks to me like it's nothing but loose, white sand. And they have so few branches and pine needles, yet they're huge and healthy. I heard once that the roots can go as deep as three times the height of the tree!"

Glancing at Claudia, another thing struck him – she was no gardener. Her nails were narrow and cut fairly short, but more pointed than round on the ends. Her hands, dotted with freckles, were soft and supple. From what he could see of her face under her fine, flowing hair, it seemed to have few signs of wrinkles. He gazed at her as often as he dare as she looked out the window. He did not want to make her uncomfortable. Her nose curved upward ever-so-slightly on the end, and her lips were less than full, yet perfectly formed; the top and bottom lips curving delicately toward the place they met. She held her chin high, giving her a determined look. He found her beautiful, not in the sense of women whose made-up faces appeared on the covers of glamour magazines, but beautiful in a glowing, healthy, natural way.

Claudia must have sensed Skip gazing at her. She turned, and just for a moment their eyes met. Her green irises had gold flecks close to her pupils, and she seemed to be sizing him up, which made him a bit nervous. Her mouth curled in a smile. He smiled back, but too late for her to notice, as she turned away. She stared straight ahead as they rolled along, as if she could make out the future in the distance where the heat shimmered off of the dark gray pavement.

The golden oldie song "I've Been Lonely Too Long" coursed through Skip's brain. He wanted to reach out and gently take her hand off of her knee and hold it his, then caress her fingers gently, one at a time, and massage each knuckle with his forefinger and thumb, then make soft circles in the palm of her hand with his middle finger. His pants became tighter, and he knew he had to change that chain of thoughts, or risk embarrassing himself if she noticed his arousal.

The truck slowed as it once again struggled up the incline of the bridge that climbed over the Apalachicola River. The bridge seemed to have been built by someone who had a desire for aesthetics rather than practicality, as the last quarter of the bridge swung high over the river at the same time curving down toward the quaint town in an arc that necessitated the road slanting so the traffic could handle the curve. It was the perfect place for a futuristic car to take wing and fly off into the setting sun.

"We're going over the Apalachicola River," Skip said "which, in some parts of the state, would mean it's an hour earlier than before."

"What do you mean?"

"I mean further north of here, once you cross the Apalachicola you change from Eastern time to Central time, and it would be 4:05 instead of 5:05."

"Oh! Great!" Claudia said. "Now it looks like I'll make it on time –"

"Like I was saying, further north of here, the time changes at the river. But they bent the time line, and Eastern time extends all the way to St. Joe near the coast."

"That stinks. Why did they do that?"

"The folks who settled St. Josephs were mostly from Apalachicola, and they wanted to be in the same time zone."

"Oh. How long does it take to get to the Treasure Bay Lodge from here?"

"Well, about thirty minutes, if I remember correctly."

"This sure is a pretty town and that was a beautiful river we just crossed."

"Beautiful but bloody."

"Why bloody?" Claudia asked.

Skip gazed inland up the coffee-colored Apalachicola River. "In 1513 Ponce de Leon landed near St. Augustine and was impressed by the beautiful native wildflowers on the east coast. He named the land Florida, after the festival of flowers in Spain."

"What does that have to do with the Apalachicola?"

"It was the beginning of Europe's encroachment into the territory. The beginning of centuries of bloody history as the old culture met the new. And few incidents in Florida's history can compare to the blood that was spilled on the banks of this old river in the early 1800s."

"Really?"

"Yes. British Colonel Nichols and company built a large dirt fort at Prospect Bluff on the Apalachicola about thirty-five miles north of where we are now. Helping build the fort was an international army he had assembled that consisted of British Colonial Marines, Chocktaw and Red Stick Creek Native Americans from Alabama, people called Maroons –"

"Maroons?"

"I think it came from the Spanish word Cimaroon, meaning wild people. They were Muscogee-speaking blacks born and raised in Seminole Indian country. Other French and Spanish speaking blacks also helped build the fort. In 1812, England ceded West Florida to Spain, which didn't sit well with Colonel Nichols. He and a Captain Woodbine remained in the territory as British spies, hoping to return West Florida to Britain. Most of the blacks disbursed and built scattered villages between the Apalachicola –"

"That's a pretty name."

"I think it means 'place of the enemy people'. Anyway, like I was saying, most of the blacks spread out and wound up living between the Apalachicola and the Suwannee rivers. But the Spanish speaking blacks from Pensacola, along with the Choctaw Native Americans, decided to stay at the fort, which became known as Fort Negro. About a hundred black and Choctaw warriors and two-hundred women and children made the fort their home. A mixed-blood black from Pensacola named Garcon was their leader. Having an allegiance to Britain, he declared that the lands along the Apalachicola River belonged to England. And he insisted on flying the British 'Union Jack' flag above the walls."

"Where'd you learn all of this?" Claudia asked.

"I got a minor in history from Florida State University. And I really enjoy reading books about Florida's past. Anyhow, as the young United States tried to expand westward, Ft. Scott was built some five-hundred miles north of Ft. Negro, on the Flint River, which flows into the Apalachicola, to protect farmers and trappers who were already spreading west and south from Georgia. The problem with Fort Scott was that it had to be supplied by the water route, as there weren't any good roads there at the time. Therefore, the only way to supply the United States' outpost was to bring munitions and goods up the Apalachicola River, which was in Spanish West Florida. So General Gaines, who was in charge of Ft. Scott, ordered two United States' supply ships and two gunboats to sail from Mobile to the mouth of the Apalachicola. Then he ordered Colonel Clinch to march south from Ft. Scott with one-hundred-and-sixteen soldiers to be sure Garcon and the residents of Fort Negro did not attack his supply ships. On his way south, Colonel Clinch joined up with William McIntosh, the leader of the White Stick Creek Native Americans. McIntosh and his band of White Stick Creeks were bounty hunters, who returned run-away slaves for a reward. They also captured Maroons and Seminoles and sold them into slavery. McIntosh deviously told Colonel Clinch that Garcon's men at Ft. Negro had attacked a small party of American sailors from the supply ship who were sent to look for fresh water. The scoundrel McIntosh claimed that several sailors had been killed, and the rest taken prisoner, then tortured and burned to death with hot tar. McIntosh produced a scalp he said was given to him by one of Garcon's men as proof of the story."

Skip paused to see if Claudia was listening, then went on. "Believing McIntosh, Colonel Clinch sent word for the ships to proceed up river. He and his men surrounded Ft. Negro. Garcon opened fire using large canons the British had left behind. A truce was called. Garcon made the fatal mistake of allowing McIntosh and several of his warriors to approach the fort. Garcon told McIntosh that he would not allow the U.S. ships to pass. While they were talking, McIntosh was looking around, and noticed a large number of unprotected powder kegs stacked inside the fort. He returned and told Colonel Clinch. Clinch ordered the two United States' gunboats to slip past the fort at night and take positions on the opposite side of the river. He told the crew to heat cannon balls in the ship's cooking oven until they were red hot. At sunrise, Garcon saw the ships and fired his cannons. Colonel Clinch, who was now aboard one of the gunships, ordered the crew to open fire with the red-hot cannon balls. On the fifth shot, they hit their target! A huge explosion was set off inside the fort, and no more gunfire came from within the walls. The United States' soldiers broke down the gate. Dead bodies lay strewn everywhere, some draped on the branches of the trees near the fort walls, cries and screams filled the air. Miraculously, Garcon and the chief of the Choctaws survived, and were captured. It would have been better for them had they died in the blast! Colonel Clinch turned them over to McIntosh and his band of White Stick Creek warriors, who put Garcon and the Choctaw chief to slow, agonizing deaths."

"Wow!" exclaimed Claudia. "Not a great time to be alive back then, eh?"

"No, life was hard. Bloodshed was pretty common. Sometimes when I think about how good we have it now, in 1999, I thank God he chose that I be born in this day and age. And I think about all those people who lived before us and contributed to making life what it is now for us."

Claudia looked around at the sights of downtown Apalachicola – the sprawling, manicured face of the Gibson Inn, and the beautiful restored homes along Highway 98 that had resisted the elements since being built in the late 1800s when Apalachicola was a booming, busy seaport. She knew he was right about having been born in a country where, in that space and time, knew peace inside its borders, and prosperity. But then her mind drifted forward to her current predicament, and she didn't feel so lucky.

"Are you sure you know where the hotel is?"

"Uh, huh. It's about a half mile before Presnell's."

"There aren't two near Pt. St. Joe, are there?" Skip could hear the tension in her voice as she thought of her rendezvous.

"Not that I know of. Port St. Joe is a pretty small town. I doubt there would be more than one. Who are you going to meet there?" Skip asked, hoping to hear that she was meeting an aunt or uncle, mother or father.

"Billy Bowlegs!" she said, as a smile spread across her face.

"Billy Bowlegs!" he repeated, laughing. "You're about one-hundred-and-fifty years too late."

She looked at him, a bit surprised. "You know about Billy Bowlegs?"

"Yeah, both of them."

"BOTH of them?" she asked, sounding astonished.

"I know about two of them – there were probably more. The first one I know about was William Augustus Bowles. His father had been a Tory during the Revolutionary War, and the people in their community treated the family so bad during the war, young Bowles joined the British army. They brought him down to, ah, Pensacola, I think. His enemy, a lieutenant or something, hated his guts."

"Why?"

"I don't know – maybe jealousy. I'm not sure. Anyhow, this lieutenant took a squad of men, including Bowles, in a launch from the fort they were building near the mouth of Pensacola harbor, into the town of Pensacola. He told everyone to be back at 2 PM in front of Bowles, then found all the others in town, and changed the time to noon. Bowles suspected something when he noticed all the other soldiers were gone, and ran back to the dock. He got there just in time to see the launch pulling into the harbor without him. When he realized he had been tricked, he ran as fast as he could to the west, scratching and clawing his way through dense underbrush, wading across tidal creeks, until finally, at dawn, he got back to the fort. But not in time. He was court marshaled, found guilty, and kicked out of the British army."

"And then he became a pirate?"

"Pirate? Not William Augustus Bowles. He had little interest in piracy. He tried to make his way back home to South Carolina, by going east, then north and east through the swamps and woods. He had nothing but the clothes on his back, but managed to survive on oysters he dug from the bays and berries he picked from the bushes. A tribe of Native Americans, including one who spoke English, found him. They took him back to their camp. Bowles trained them in the ways of British warfare, drilling them, and having them learn formations. When the news of the training spread to other tribes in the areas of North Florida, Alabama and Georgia, more warriors came to participate. To make a long, fascinating story short, he organized the Native Americans into a formidable army. He planned to create a union of tribes that, if they stuck together, would stop U.S. expansion to the west."

"How do you know so much about this guy?" Claudia asked in a suspicious tone of voice.

"As I said, I minored in history at Florida State. And I've been especially interested in the history of the Florida panhandle. Some fascinating things happened here. Let's see, where was I? Oh, yeah – so Bowles has a formidable Native American army. Under a flag of truce, the Spanish tricked him, and he was captured. They sent him to New Orleans, then shipped him to Spain, where the Spanish tried to get him to ally with Spain against England. Bribes and promises of wealth had no effect on him, and he refused to allow the united Native American tribes he led to cooperate with Spain. After a while, they sent him to Manila in the Philippines. Then back to Spain. But on the way, he managed to escape..."

"Escape? How?"

"He tried to organize the captives on board the ship to mutiny, was discovered, and locked in a cabin with one porthole. He saved small pieces of the salt pork they were feeding him, and saved it until he had enough to grease his shoulders, and wormed his way through the hole and dove overboard. Swam to an island, and evaded the Spanish so long, they finally gave up and left him. Somehow, he made his way to Sierra Leone, then to England. He was quite a man!"

"So then what happened?" Claudia asked. Looking at her expression, Skip could tell she was really interested in the Bowles adventure. "Is that when he became a pirate?"

"No. He was the toast of London because of his adventures and the sway he had over the Native Americans in Florida. Wanting the territory back from Spain, they gave him a British navy schooner named "Fox", loaded it with presents and supplies for his Muscogee Nation, and sent him on his way."

"And that's when he took to piracy?"

"No. He stopped in New Providence, Jamaica, got guns and ammo from the Miller, Dunmore Company, who wanted the lucrative pelt trade. He also offered the opportunity to privateers..."

"Privateers? You mean pirates?"

"Basically. He told them they could fly the flag of the Muscogee Nation, and prey on Spanish and American boats legally, and split the booty with his tribes."

"So that's when he became a pirate."

"No. Not Bowles. But the privateers did cause havoc – they were a bloodthirsty lot, and took a bunch of Spanish and American ships."

"Did he make it back to Florida?"

"Kind of. The "Fox" sailed into a hurricane, and was shipwrecked on St. George's Island. The Spanish had a fort at the mouth of the Apalachicola..."

"Didn't we just cross the Apalachicola?"

"Yeah. And the British company of Panton, Leslie, his enemies, had a trading post up the St. Marks River, so he built a temporary capital for the Muscogee Nation up the Ochlocknee River, right in between the Apalachicola and the St. Marks Rivers. But the Spanish sent a fleet there and wrecked it. So he and a band of Natives took the Panton, Leslie and Company post at St. Marks, and captured one of their ships."

"So that's how he became a pirate?"

"No. He wasn't a pirate."

"What was he then?"

"A British sympathizer who was pissed off at Spain for how they treated him and his Natives, and pissed off at the U.S. for taking more and more of the Indian's lands. He envisioned a united Native American nation stretching from Florida to Canada which would kick Spain out of the Americas and stop the U.S. from expanding west."

"He had high hopes! Then what?"

"Then the British signed a treaty that brought peace between them and Spain, and the Muscogee Nation lost their only hope of survival. They were relying on the British to supply them with guns and ammo and supplies. Messed up his whole plan."

"So he became a pirate?"

"No! He was never a pirate. He went home to his Native American wife and child..."

"You didn't tell me about that!"

"There's a lot I haven't told you about William Augustus Bowles. He also married the daughter of an Englishman and had a child with her."

"Turkey!"

"Back then I don't think it was illegal to have two wives."

"Tell me all about him, then." Claudia swiveled her legs toward Skip, totally engrossed in the story of Billy Bowlegs.

"It would take hours. He was an amazing man. So there he was, caught between a rock and a hard place..."

"How so?"

"The Spanish had a six-thousand dollar and fifteen-hundred kegs of rum bounty on his head. Panton, Leslie and Company, who were supplying the Native Americans with guns, ammo, food, and other essential supplies on credit, told them they would stop supplying them the necessities they needed to survive, unless they handed over Billy Bowlegs. It was a very harsh winter, and starvation reared its ugly head. The U.S. offered the tribes food, yearly cash, plows and spinning wheels if they turned Bowles in."

"So did Bowles go into hiding?"

"Not Bowles. He marched right into the Indian council meeting at Hickory Mound..."

"Where's that?"

"Near where Montgomery, Alabama is now. And tried to persuade the Native Americans that the U.S. was just after their land, and the Spanish were their enemies, and they could trade with other British companies instead of Panton and Leslie. He tried to get them to unite again, under his leadership."

"Did they?"

"Nope. The Seminoles and the Lower Creeks supported him, but the other tribes fell for the Spanish, U.S. and Panton and Leslie lies, and he was handed over to the Spanish."

"Surely they hung him."

"No. They took him to Pensacola, then to Havana, Cuba, to a place called Morro Castle. They say he died of a broken heart, being betrayed by his own people. He passed away in December of 1805."

"Wow! That dude had a rough life!"

"But think about it. What if he had succeeded? Who knows what this country might be like now? The Native Americans and the British might still be ruling part of what is now the United States! There could have been the Eastern United States, and the Western United States, or something like that."

"What if, what if. I don't spend a lot of time thinking about 'what ifs'." Claudia said, stretching.

"Right," Skip answered. "What if your parents hadn't made love the night you were conceived? You could go crazy thinking about 'what ifs'. You're smart."

"And you're just a wealth of knowledge." Claudia cooed. They smiled at each other.

Looking around, Skip realized that they were passing the cut-off to Indian Pass. A few more miles, another ten minutes, and they would be saying good-bye. One thing missing in Skip's life was the companionship and love of a woman, and he was very attracted to Claudia. He wanted to get to know her, and see what kind of a person she was. Not being good at social interactions, especially when it came to trying to get a date, he knew what he wanted to say but didn't know how to say it. Then he remembered that it might be useless anyway, as, for all he knew, she may have been on the way to meet a boyfriend in St. Joe.

"So, who are you really meeting at the Treasure Bay Lodge?"

"A friend."

"Ah, Billy Bowlegs, the pirate, I presume." He looked into her beautiful green-gold eyes.

"Of course," she said, nodding her head to the side, her fine light brown hair brushing off his inquiries like a broom. He realized he wasn't going to get any more out of her regarding the "friend" she would be seeing.

"Well," he began awkwardly, "I'd like to see you again and spend more time with you, Claudia."

Silence. That was as good as a "no" in his mind.

"Swing by Presnell's sometime over the next three nights – it's just a few hundred yards past where I'll be dropping you off. I'll be camping there. The campground is an open field by the marina, and you won't have any trouble finding me."

"Maybe," she responded half-heartedly. "I sure appreciate the ride and the story!"

"Sure. Stop by the campsite and I'll tell you about the other Billy Bowlegs, the pirate."

"I'd like that," she said in a sincere voice. Then, in a half-mumble, he thought he heard her say something under her breath, but couldn't make out what she mused.

"What?" he asked.

"Nothing."

He pulled into the hard-packed mud driveway of the Treasure Bay Lodge. Weathered brown wood railings ran around the piling-supported building, giving way in the middle to two stairways that curled down to the parking lot. Skip had never stayed there, but often thought about it as an alternative to camping at Presnell's fish camp. But he chose to spend any extra money he had on lures instead of comfort. The hotel overlooked St. Joseph's Bay, and little Black's Island. The island rose like an oasis in a desert of water, it's palm trees rustled by the sea breeze, pelicans gathered on her bare limestone rocks that jutted out of the water due to the low tide.

"Thanks again!" Claudia said as she hopped out of the truck.

"My pleasure!"

Skip watched as she picked up her belongings and headed for the stairs. Turning her head, she winked flirtatiously, and shouted, "Good luck in the tournament!"

Skip looked at Claudia as she climbed the stairs, wistfully thinking that he would love to get to know her better, spend some time in her company, and catch a glimpse of her soul. That's what he promised he would do before he got involved with another woman – catch a glimpse of her soul, and make the decision of whether to be in a relationship with that person from that perspective, rather than being blinded by looks, personality, or the infatuation that swells men's hearts when first dating an attractive woman. Twice in his life he truly believed he was in love. He felt the passion, saw the glimpse of a kindred spirit. Yet fate was hard on the relationships and both grew shallower rather than deeper with time. At last there was only the past that kept them together, and the past was not as strong as the promise of a future that held the possibility of developing a relationship with someone with whom Skip would be fulfilled, and spend the rest of his life loving. The hurt was etched in his soul, not only the hurt that he felt from falling out of infatuation, and what he thought was a deep love, but the hurt that his lovers felt as the relationships fell apart.

He restarted the noisy engine, put the truck in gear, and doubted that he would ever see her again. He took one last look at her as she walked across the wooden planks that lead to the hotel office, carrying her duffle bag, pocketbook, spade, tin and hat. As he turned away from Claudia, he noticed a new burgundy pickup with a familiar trailer that carried a shiny Grady-White parked at the far end of the hotel parking lot.

CHAPTER IV

SUNSET ST. JOE STYLE

A few minutes later Skip saw the large sign on the sloping grassy hill by the highway, "Presnell's Bayside Marina and Campground", in bold blue letters on a sun-faded white background. He recalled the original owner of the resort, now deceased. He was a tall, quiet man who didn't offer any advice on his own, but would answer any questions you might pose to him. Skip didn't remember ever seeing him smile, but his calm mannerisms indicated that old man Presnell was satisfied with his lot in life.

Pulling into the paved drive that led directly to the launch ramp, Skip was tempted to get the boat in the water right away, being anxious to wet a line, but knew that setting up the tent in the dark would be a problem. He parked the truck and trailer next to the lime green bait and tackle shack that overlooked the launch ramp. Jumping out, walking under the tin awning next to the canal, yanking the rough metal handle of the screen door, he stepped inside the dimly lit shop.

"Hey, Charlie!" he shouted to the smiling man behind the counter. Unlike old Mr. Presnell, Charlie engaged customers in small talk, and freely volunteered his wealth of knowledge about what the fish were hitting and where the biggest ones had been caught recently. A medium height man approaching forty, with a strong build, Skip envied Charlie and the life he was leading. Handsome and outgoing, he always seemed to be in a good mood. His wife Vonniciel seemed like a lovely lady, she was a full-figured woman with a beautiful face, and an even temperament. She handled the business when he wasn't around, and she was every bit as capable as Charlie. Skip hadn't seen much of Vonniciel lately, as she had recently given birth to their first child.

"Hi! How are ya, Skip?" Charlie extended his hand. His handshake was as solid as it was sincere.

"Great! What's fishing been like?"

"It's been good! Had someone bring in a five-pound two-ounce trout today."

"Really? Where did he catch it?"

"Just the other side of Black's Island."

"What did it hit?"

"A top water Mirror Lure."

"What color?"

"Pink and white, I think."

"Is that one of those with propellers on each end?"

"Yeah, like this one," Charlie came out from behind the L-shaped counter and pointed to a row of lures hanging from a peg board display.

"Jeez! What do fish think that is, anyway?" Skip asked, gazing at the lure that looked like a pink and white cigar with chrome propellers at either end, and three silver sets of rather large treble hooks.

"It's the commotion it makes that attracts them."

"Weird. How's Vonniciel and the new baby doing?"

"Fine."

"Got any campsites available?"

"Sure. How long are you going to be here?"

"Well, I'm fishing the tournament this weekend."

"Tournament?"

"The Big Bend Saltwater Classic. I've fished it every year now for the past 6 years or so."

"Oh, yeah. I forgot that it's this weekend. I think some other campers are entered."

"I'll need it through Saturday night. The tourney ends on Sunday at 2 PM."

"O.K. Pick a spot," Charlie said as he spread a map of the twenty-site campground on the counter. The campsites were in a level field nestled between the small marina docking area and the bay. A dirt road winded around in a circle through the grassy field. A dozen scattered sabal palms, also known as cabbage palmettos, provided what little shade the campground had to offer. The state tree of Florida, the palms offered limited shade from their fanlike leaves that sprouted from the top of the carrot-like trunk. Skip chose a location next to the canal that connected the marina to St. Joseph's Bay.

"Where's your fishing buddy?"

"Todd? He couldn't make it this year. Family commitments."

"And your son?"

"Benny? A bit too young to spend three days fishing in this hot sun. I'm gonna give him a couple of years before I bring him."

"How old's he now?"

"Six."

"Will ya be needing electricity?"

"Nope."

"Let's see – Thursday, Friday, Saturday – three nights at $14 per night, that's $42, and $3 per day to dock the boat. That's $54.51 with tax. Want to pay now or when you leave?"

"I'll pay now. I may need to rush out of here Sunday to weigh a big one in before the tournament ends."

"Wishful thinking!"

"Before we settle up, let me take a look around." In front of the bubbling tanks that held live shrimp sat an antique wood table, atop of which sat two large cardboard boxes. They were filled with lures that had been in the shop for a long time, and weren't selling. Skip loved to browse through the boxes, checking out each lure carefully. He found a small sinking Mirror Lure with two sets of treble hooks, in just the right colors - orange belly, yellow middle and green top. He also picked up a soft-bodied lure that he had seen before but felt it was too expensive. It had big white and black eyes painted on what felt like a rubber body. The two things he liked about the lure was that it had dark treble hooks rather than silver, and the green body had gold flecks in it. Looking closely at the lure, Skip was reminded of Claudia's eyes, and wondered what she was doing, whether he would ever see her again, and if Lucas and Buck were hassling her at the Treasure Bay Lodge.

"That's a Dusky Mullet," Charlie interrupted Skip's daydream. "And they were selling so well last year, I had a hard time keeping them in stock. But for some reason this year, I can't get rid of them. Funny how a lure's popularity comes and goes like that."

"Do they float or sink?"

"Sink. But not real fast. So they're easy to keep out of the grass."

Skip knew the ability to keep a lure above the grass on the flats was of utmost importance in choosing lures that would be effective for the speckled trout in St. Joseph's Bay. The trout inhabited the grass flats, and the grass didn't grow well in water over eight feet deep. And some of the biggest trout he had ever hooked had been in real skinny water, at a depth of two or three feet.

He bought two Dusky Mullets, one green and gold-flecked, one amber and gold-flecked, and the small Mirror Lure.

"I'm going to set my tent up and launch. Maybe I can find a hot area before the tournament begins tomorrow. Got any suggestions?"

"Well, try the other side of Black's Island where that five-pounder came from today. Then try to the north along the grass flats close to shore. Someone brought in a six-pounder last week from that area. He used a cast net to catch pilchards, and waded out by the mouth of the river by the paper plant."

"O.K. Thanks, Charlie!" Skip wanted to run, but restrained himself to a fast walk back to the truck. Judging by the sun, he figured he had no more than a couple of hours before it got too dark to be out on the water.

Skip erected his forest-green pup tent in five minutes, using ten-penny nails on the bottom peg holes, and yellow plastic stakes for the outside rope supports, as he had done hundreds of times before. He bought the tent for his twenty-second birthday with money given to him by his parents. It wasn't quite tall enough for his six-foot body to stand in, but it gave him enough room to stretch out on the floor. Each time he had occasion to set the tent up, he marveled at its durability, having had the lightweight tent for twenty-three years. It was ideally suited for Florida camping, with screening that ran around the sides, the front was all screening, and the back had a square window screen, so no matter which way the breeze was blowing, it would enter the tent. The roof overhung the screening on the sides, and flaps could be lowered over the front and back screens in case one of the frequent summer thunderstorms arose. The tent and the two aluminum support poles together weighed less than five pounds. The roof was waterproof if you didn't touch it. If you accidentally bumped the top with your head in a rainstorm, water would come through the fine mesh material. The tent was like an old friend, always there when needed.

Skip loaded the vintage Lancer skiff with his rods, over-sized tackle box, a once-white throw cushion with a slice in the dirty plastic cover, an orange life vest, two paddles and a rag – one of his old Fruit of the Loom briefs that had one-too-many holes to wear any more.

One of the nice things about Presnell's was that, whenever you launched, there was always someone there to help you. If not Charlie, then Vonniciel, or another young hired hand that occasionally worked weekends. Charlie assisted Skip in launching the boat by telling him when the truck was back far enough, and pulling the skiff off of the trailer with the bow rope. He secured it with a line that was attached to a cleat on the floating dock next to the ramp. Skip thanked him, and parking the truck at the campsite, trotted back to the boat. He hopped in and set about the frequently difficult task of cranking the old engine.

After the fuel line was connected from the six-gallon tank in the stern, and the bulb on the gas line squeezed to get gas into the carburetor, Skip braced his left foot against the rear gunwale, and pulled on the starter cord with all his might. Nothing. Then he remembered to pull out the choke. Another pull. Nothing. On the fifth pull, the engine fired, but didn't catch. Pushing the choke in, he pulled again. This time the engine started, but died right away. Again, he pulled the choke out. The engine started with the next pull, and he quickly pushed the choke in. Keeping a hand on the throttle of the outboard, he untied the one line that held the boat to the dock. Flipping the gear lever forward he gave the throttle a twist, and was off, careful not to leave a wake in the fifteen-slip marina. Skip turned and waved to Charlie, who stood in front of the bait shop by the fish-cleaning table. Charlie was making a motion with his hand from left to right, like he was shooing a mosquito away, and Skip couldn't figure out what Charlie was doing.

Crunch! The bow struck the end of a floating dock and glanced off. Using the throttle handle to correct his path and avoid any more embarrassing accidents, he looked back at Charlie, shrugged his shoulders as if to say "Oops!" Charlie waved again and, smirking, ducked back into his bait and tackle shop.

Skip made sure not to bump into anything else on his way through the little canal that leads to St. Joseph's Bay. The poured gray concrete walls of the canal were covered with barnacles, shell encrusted animals that feed off of the microscopic plankton that float by. Sharp as razors, they attract minnow-sized baitfish and blue-claw crabs. When Skip reached the first channel marker, he gradually opened the throttle until the engine was running wide open, and the boat planed off. As was his custom, Skip let out a loud "Yee-haw!" as the skiff skimmed across the near-calm water. He could feel ripples from the bay clack against the flat bow, the thrill of making his first cast only minutes away. Reaching the last channel marker, a plastic orange buoy, he noticed that it was leaning to the right, meaning the tide was still going out. Making a mental note of that, he knew that fishing the flats to the north, toward the city of St. Joe, on an outgoing tide, would not produce the same results as fishing that area on the incoming. But those flats were closer than Black's Island, and the sun was sinking toward the horizon. As fast as the boat was cruising, a good thirty miles an hour, Skip was aware that too sharp of a turn would capsize him. With a slight push of the throttle handle to the left, the boat made a wide turn to the right, heading for the north flats.

To the right lay a small island with a single palm tree. The water around that island was only inches deep, so Skip kept well outside of it. The water clarity made it fairly easy to navigate in the bay. Sand patches in the shallower water were a light shade of turquoise, and the sand patches in deeper water were a darker shade of green.

St. Joe Bay boasted the clearest, most beautiful water in the Florida panhandle, and being able to see the bottom in ten feet of water made fishing there all the more fun. Healthy waves of sea grasses (turtle grass, manatee grass, widgeon grass, star grass and Cuban shoal grass) grow in the shallows. They blanket the sandy bottom from one end to the bay to the other near the shores, and out in the middle of the south end of the bay, surrounding Black's island. The grassy areas are interrupted by sand patches, sometimes as small as a card table, other times as wide as a street and forty feet long. The grasses are home to a myriad of creatures large and small. As the water deepens toward the center of the bay and in finger-like troughs in the south end, the grass becomes sparse, until, at the depth of ten feet, the bay bottom turns to sand. Skip liked to follow that demarcation, keeping the boat on a path that paralleled the shore where the grass was sparse as the water became deep. To his left he could see the darker blue-green water that marked the edge of the flats. To his right, he kept a close eye on the light areas in the water, the sand patches between the thick beds of sea grass.

The wind blew gently from the east, the water close to the mainland was as smooth as a mirror and a slight ripple began fifty yards off shore where Skip's boat cut a wake through the crystal clear water. Here and there he saw a mullet's silver-sided body break the calm in an arching leap above the surface. Perhaps being chased by a predator, but more likely just enjoying a Summer afternoon frolic, the leaping mullet were a welcome sign that fish were active, and raised Skip's hopes of catching a few nice trout before dark. He had the feeling that the question was not if he would catch any trout, but how many and how large they would be, as St. Joseph's bay in the summer yielded abundant catches, being full of the feisty game fish.

A mile to the north of the island he had passed, Skip decided to try his first drift. With the wind blowing off shore, he nosed the boat toward a little bridge that crossed a narrow tidal creek. Skip liked to have a recognizable landmark in sight when fishing, in case the spot turned out to be a good one, and he wanted to find it again. A few hundred feet can make the difference in being an area that is chock full of fish, and one that is nearly barren. Just before the skeg of the outboard touched the bottom, he turned the boat parallel to the shore and went another fifty yards to be sure he did not drift over any of the water that he just disturbed. Turning the throttle grip all the way to the right, the engine sputtered and died. He chose this particular area because it had more sand patches amidst the sea grass than in other places, and through the fifteen years he had fished the bay, he found that type of bottom held the most fish. Speckled trout are ambush feeders, and hide in the grass next to a sand patch, waiting for their next meal to swim by. Quickly opening his voluminous tackle box, he selected a noisy top-water plug with an orange belly, yellow side and green top, the same color as the little suspending plug he had just bought from Charlie. It sported a rear treble hook that was disguised with white buck tail hair. He did not trust his ten-pound test line to hold up to a gator trout, so he tied the tiniest black barrel swivel he could find to his line, then attached a twelve-inch length of clear fifteen-pound test monofilament. Tying the lure on to the leader with a double-improved clinch knot, he set the spinning reel and rod in a rod holder next to him. Quickly grabbing another light spinning combo, he used the same leader set-up, tying the green Dusky Mullet to the end using a loop knot to give the lure more motion under water.

Finally the time he had waited for had arrived. He cast the top-water plug just beyond a sand patch, and it plopped in the still water over the sea grass. He let the lure settle for a while as the small concentric ripples caused by the splash disappeared. With a flip of the rod tip, he gave the floating lure a twitch. It made a popping sound, and minute waves were driven by the circular mouth of the lure toward the boat. Another twitch, and stop. Something swirled in back of the lure, and he twitched again. The fish teased Skip by swirling in back of the lure a second time. Skip patiently twitched and paused the lure until it was back at the boat.

The skiff drifted away from the shoreline, the water became deeper. After several more casts, the boat had drifted into five feet of water. He cast parallel to a sand patch, and began to work the lure along the border, the lure following the edge of the grass. Twitch, pause, twitch, pause, twitch, pause, SPLASH!!! The water exploded under the plug as a hungry trout tried to inhale it, but missed, throwing the lure a foot into the air! Skip let the lure sit still for a moment, then twitched it again, hoping the fish would return. Another twitch. Pause. Twitch. BLAM! The trout hit again, and again missed the lure. Skip tensed in anticipation of another strike. He twitched the rod tip and the lure popped on the surface. It was only fifteen feet away now, and he wondered if the fish would hit again, or be scared off by the boat. Twitch, pause, twitch, pause, WHOOSH! The water exploded for the third time, Skip pulled back, the rod bent and the reel's drag screamed as the fish made its first run. It swirled on the surface, and Skip could see the silvery side of a decent sized fish. After a strong first run, the fish tried swimming directly toward the boat, and Skip reeled as fast as he could. The trout veered off to the right, and took out more drag. Skip reached down and loosened the drag adjustment on the top of the spinning reel. He did not want to chance having the hooks rip through the soft flesh of the trout's mouth. The fish, feeling less pressure, made several more strong runs, pulling ten feet of monofilament off the reel with each burst of energy. Skip gained some line by gently pumping the rod and reeling. Nearing the boat, the fish tried to escape by dashing for the engine, and Skip had to dip the end of his rod deep into the water so the line would not scrape the skeg of the outboard and snap. The trout surfaced and made one last desperate jump, shaking its head. Skip saw the orange inside of its gaping jaw as it shook the lure in vain. Engaging the anti-reverse on his reel, Skip dipped his left hand in the water in anticipation of landing the fish, knowing the chances of doing harm to the beautiful creature was less if he held it with a wet hand while taking the hooks out. He applied even pressure, raising the rod tip up and back, easing the trout toward the boat. He could see dozens of black dots on the trout's dark green back, and the silver scaled sides of the fish clearly now. He quickly grabbed the trout behind the head and above the gills, and held it firmly, but not too tight. Lifting the fish's head above the water, he set the pole down, snatched the needle-nosed pliers from their place on the side of his tackle box, and gripped the rear set of treble hooks. Two of the barbed hooks were set firmly in the jaw. Skip pushed down, flicking his wrist, and freed the hooks. Easing the beautiful four-pounder's head back in the water, he held it loosely until the fish gave a shudder, and swam away to freedom.

Skip sat back in the swivel seat, took a deep breath, and looked toward the sun that was making its way toward St. Joseph's Peninsula on the horizon. He drew a deep breath, attempting to relax, his body flush with adrenaline. "Where in the world would you rather be?" he asked himself. And the answer was apparent. The here and now for Skip was a wonderful place.

He rubbed the slime dripping from his left hand on the plug and on the Dusky Mullet tied to the other spinning combo. Confident now that the top-water plug would be effective during the tournament, he picked up the other rod and began casting the soft-bodied green Dusky Mullet. He was amazed at how far he could cast, the aerodynamics and weight of the lure were ideal for flinging it far away from the boat. Retrieving it in a jerk-and-pause fashion, he was careful to keep it from sinking into the turtle grass. He watched the motion of the lure as it approached the boat, and was impressed at how much it looked like an injured mullet. The gold flakes of the Dusky Mullet reflected the waning sunlight, and it again reminded him of Claudia, and his thoughts drifted back to her. Was she thinking about him, he wondered, or was she dining with her lover somewhere? He cast again, marveling at the distance his arching line traveled before the lure came down with a splash.

Ah, Claudia! Mystery woman. Skip pondered on why she had brought that shovel with her. And what brought her to the shores of this peaceful bay. A sudden jerk of the rod sent a shock through his arms, and he reared back and set the hook. Another four-pound trout splashed at the surface a hundred feet away, and Skip knew he had found one more lure that would catch him some hefty trout during the tournament.

After landing and releasing the fish, Skip looked toward the shore to be sure he could find the productive area again. He was still directly south of the bridge. After a few more drifts in the area, catching and releasing several trout in the three-pound range, Skip headed back to the campsite, satisfied that he had found an area that would produce fish. The only question was whether any larger trout could be found there, because he knew that weighing in a fish under five pounds would be useless.

Backing off the throttle as he entered the canal, he looped the boat around and brought it to rest on the long, slanting PVC pipes Charlie had set in the water so boats would not get damaged scraping against the concrete walls. Skip noticed that someone had erected a pop-up dome tent in the space next to his. A charcoal colored four-wheel drive Ford pickup was parked in front of the black tent, but the person was not around. The truck had dents in the fenders and dried mud all over the sides. The bed held empty, bent beer and soda cans. Skip could see into the bed of the late model truck because the tailgate was missing, and had been replaced by a cloth-mesh net that boasted a smiling, urinating boy. One side of the darkly tinted rear window held a faded rebel flag, and on the other side bore a Jack Daniel's Whiskey sticker. In the middle was an OAR, Organization for Artificial Reefs, decal. The Big-Bend Saltwater Classic was an OAR event, and he wondered if the guy was fishing in the tournament. Skip had a bad feeling about the camper, and was not looking forward to making his acquaintance.

Laying out his sleeping bag on top of a thin blue egg-crate type cushion, he gathered his bathroom stuff and a change of clothes, and walked toward the cinder block bathroom. It had been painted to match the old bait house, a lime green, but the paint was peeling because of its exposure to the hot Florida sun. The men's side of the facility was closest to his tent. Pulling the screen door out and pushing the thin wood door in, he brushed by the dirty porcelain sink. To access the toilet bowl and shower, Skip had to close the shaky wood door that moisture had weakened and swollen through the years. He laid his clean clothes on the rickety wood bench in front of the tiny shower stall. Drawing back the cheap blue shower curtain, he laid his shampoo, conditioner and soap on the narrow plastic shelf inside the stall. Placing his contact lens case and solution on the toilet tank, he washed his hands in the sink, and removed his contact lenses.

Returning to his tent, Skip felt tired for the first time that day. He barely slept the night before, being so excited about the tournament. Reaching into his old red ninety-four quart cooler that lay on the rusty pick-up truck bed, he snaked his hand to the bottom though the food he brought, grabbed a cold O'Doul's from its resting place among the ice. He walked to the dock where his boat lay snug against the PVC pipes lining the sides of the canal. Skip knew the tide was as low as it was going to get for the night, so he did not have to loosen the docking lines. With feet dangling over the tranquil water of the canal, Skip unscrewed the top of his non-alcoholic beer and took a big swig. For some strange reason, his body had lost its tolerance for alcohol, and if he had so much as a real beer or a mixed drink, he would pay for it the next morning with a splitting headache. The sun was setting over the peninsula across the bay. The scattered palms in the campsite were still as the breeze had stopped with the setting of the sun. The water of the bay reflected the pink and blues of the sky, and Skip felt the calm summer dusk enter his weary body, and settle in a sweet and peaceful place in his soul.

As he lay in his sleeping bag, trying to focus on a plan to win the tournament, thoughts of Claudia returned, reminding Skip of the deep, pervading loneliness he felt at times, and how long it had been since he had been with a woman.

CHAPTER V
MISS ADVENTURE

C laudia struggled up the steps of the motel, wondering what kind of place that brother of hers had recommended they stay. Harris never did have a clue about the finer things in life, she thought, as she set her load down on the weathered wood deck. She knocked on the door with her knuckles, as there was no doorbell or knocker. The black plaque with white letters that read "Office" nearly fell, one of the rusty nails that held it gave way, and the sign swung down, suspended now by only one rusty nail. She took that as a bad omen. As the door opened inward, Claudia felt a rush of welcome, cold air.

"Yeah?" A middle-aged man with a white sleeveless T-shirt and beer-belly looked her up and down. She hated when men did that – it was so crass and obviously sexual, and she felt that she was being violated without even being touched.

"I have a reservation," she said, stepping back, hoping that she would not have to enter the office with him.

"Whassa name?"

"Claudia Kilmer. I made the reservation for two."

"Where's your pal?"

"My brother will be here any time now. Unless he has already arrived – his name is Harris Kilmer."

"Nope."

"Well, I'm beat and I'd like to check in." She noticed the tattoos on his sagging, once muscular arms and legs, and got the impression he spent time as a seafaring man. The anchor, dagger, sea horse and sailing ship on his arms were still recognizable, although from the shape of them she could tell his arms were larger when he was a young man. She couldn't make out all the shapes on his legs, but the one that caught her eye was a long-stemmed rose on his right thigh, because it was cut in two by a large, ugly scar. As he turned his back to her, she noticed that the back of his right leg opposite the scar on the front held a similar scar, as if a chain saw had tried to cut his leg in two from the front and from the back, but had stopped each time it struck bone. It sent a chill down her spine. She could see the head of a dragon, with its tongue sticking out, rear its fearsome head between his shoulder blades, but could not see the rest of the dragon hidden below his wrinkled, sleeveless shirt.

He returned with a set of keys, and said, "This way."

She picked up her belongings and followed him toward the back of the motel. She looked over the flimsy deck rails and was pleasantly surprised at the view. Turquoise and blue-green water sparkled in the bay like a mirage that invited her to dive into the refreshing coolness. A mile away from shore an island arose, beckoning her to its seemingly uninhabited shores, promising shade under the palm trees, and peace, and solitude. She wished she could take her room and move it out there, away from the man she was following down the deck, where she would be removed from all other people that might distract her from the quest she had undertaken.

"Here it is. Let me know if it suits your fancy."

Claudia walked into the room, smelled the musty air, and dropped her belongings on the floor next to the old air conditioner that was set below the plate glass window that looked out upon St. Joseph's Bay. She glanced at the living room/kitchen area, which comprised one half of the rental, then walked into the bedroom/ bathroom area to her left. She noticed it held two double beds in the same room.

"Do you have any with separate bedrooms?" she asked.

"Nope."

"Does the air conditioner work?"

"Yup."

"O.K., then, this will do. I'll need two sets of keys."

"Who are ya expecting?"

"My brother," she answered with a tone of voice that made it clear it was none of his business. He sneered, not believing that it was a brother that would be sharing the room. He thought to himself it was probably a married man, and they were having a sizzling affair. He decided to watch closely, and take down the license plate of this so-called brother. Perhaps this mystery man would be wealthy, and not want his wife to know of his weekend frolics.

"Be right back," he said, and sauntered off toward the office.

Claudia sighed, and walked out to the wood railing that encased the deck. In the backyard grew a handful of healthy sabal palms, their fronds softly whispering a welcome in the warm breeze. The bay shimmered as the sun reflected off the ripples on the clear, inviting water. She gazed at Black's Island, and wondered who owned it; a very fortunate person, or the state. She felt like an island herself, adrift in a sea of humanity, trying to keep herself above the crowd, and separate, very separate. She had little desire to mingle or socialize with anyone at that time of her life, and wondered if her attitude would change if she were to be successful in her search.

The manager came back with the second set of keys. "Here you go. Y'ever been to these parts before?"

"No."

"Well, Apalachicola's about 30 minutes east of here, and it's a quaint little place. Lots of fancy historic houses and museums and gift shops. Then the town of St. Joe is up the road apiece. But there ain't much there – fast food and convenience stores and a couple of restaurants. Let me know if ya need anything."

"Thanks." An uneasiness filled her as she watched him walk away, and she noticed a slight limp from the damaged right leg. Her intuition told her that he could not be trusted. But then again, she did not trust many men in her life. Some she had trusted wound up hurting her deeply. That's why she had asked her brother to help her. Even though he was a troublemaker, she felt she could trust him. And she knew how much he needed something to do to keep him out of jail again.

She turned and went inside the room, closed the door, turned the air conditioner on to its coldest setting, and had a closer look around. She opened the refrigerator door, and found a couple of open boxes of baking soda. The shelves looked like they had not been cleaned in a while, but the inside was cool, so she could tell it was working. She opened the freezer and looked at the three cheap blue ice trays. They had cracks in the top between the cubes, but were still functional, and already held ice. Pulling open a kitchen drawer, she found tarnished silverware, in assorted patterns and shapes. Probably bought at yard sales, she thought. Opening a cupboard door, she found plastic glasses and yellowed ceramic coffee cups. Under the sink was a frying pan with the Teflon coating in tatters, two tin baking pans with small sides and permanent stains burned in the metal, and one medium-sized aluminum pot with a lid.

She took her bags into the bedroom, and laid them on the bed next to the plate-glass window. Under the window was another air conditioning unit, and she opened the control panel. Turning the control knob to the coolest setting, she heard no click of the thermostat. Only warm air came out of the vents. "Great!" she exclaimed, and walked to the bathroom at the far end of the room. It was small. A plastic-walled shower stall was to her left, a sink that needed a serious scrubbing took up the wall in front of her, and a porcelain commode that proudly displayed the maker's name, "Wellworth" on the back of the bowl, sat to her right. The linoleum floor was cracked and buckled. White towels with a few small rust spots rested on the back of the toilet tank, along with one hand towel and a wash cloth.

Bang, bang, bang! She could hear the front door vibrate with someone's knocks. Shaking her head, she wondered if she would be getting any privacy at the Treasure Bay Lodge. Peering out the window in the living room, she saw two men there. She latched the safety lock, and opened the door a crack.

"Howdy!" bellowed Buck, his big body looming in the doorway. Claudia could see Lucas' smiling face over Buck's shoulder, his yellow teeth bared beneath his brown mustache.

"'Evening!" echoed Lucas, tipping the brim of his baseball cap.

This just keeps getting better and better, Claudia thought to herself. What did I do to deserve this?

"Can I help you?" Claudia asked.

"We're your neighbors!" Buck responded. "We just figured we'd say hi, and letcha know we're here. Wanna beer?"

"Ah, not right now, thanks." From their breath, Claudia could tell they had been drinking.

"Well, we got plenty of cold ones, and you're welcome to them anytime you want. You just let us know."

"You bet," Lucas chimed in. "We're fishin' in the tournament, though, so we won't be in most of the time."

"What a relief!" Claudia thought to herself. With any luck, she wouldn't run into them again. "I'll pass."

"You a football player?" Lucas chuckled. Buck and Claudia looked at him. "You did say you were going to pass...get it, pass – "

Buck smiled and put his elbow into his friend's ribs. Lucas stumbled backward, and hit the rail. Crack! The wood gave way, and Lucas hung on for dear life. Buck ran to his friend, grabbed his right arm just as the rail dropped off the deck. Lucas swung his left hand up and got a precarious hold on the next post. Buck lifted, heaving Lucas back to safety with such force that he sent Lucas flying toward the partially open door.

Claudia jumped back, as Lucas-turned-missile rushed toward her. Claudia instinctively closed the door. Crash! Lucas managed to get his hands out in front of him before making impact, slamming into the wooden door. Claudia opened the door again slowly, security chain still in place.

"You O.K.?" she asked Lucas, who was sprawled out on the deck. Buck helped him up.

"Sure," he said, brushing off imaginary dirt from his pants, shaking his head in disbelief. "Well, wish us luck in the tournament!" he added, slurring his speech.

"Sluck!" Claudia said, thinking that they would really need all the luck they could get if they were as good at fishing as they were at socializing. She closed the door and couldn't help but chuckle at the antics of the inebriated duo.

Hungry, Claudia decided to take a walk to the convenience store she saw on the way to the hotel. It was less than a mile away, and she knew her brother, who was supposed to meet her at 5 o'clock, would not be there on time. He never had been on time in his whole life. In fact, it would not have surprised her much if he didn't show up at all. His irresponsible ways had landed him in a lot of trouble – losing jobs, unable to find a woman who would put up with him, and even winding up incarcerated at times.

Although he was unreliable, he was still her younger brother, and she felt a responsibility to take care of him since their mother had died last year. Mrs. Kilmer focused all her energy on raising Claudia and Harris, as their father had tragically been killed in an automobile accident when they were just two and three years old. Harris and Claudia had been close as children. But as strict and protective as her

mother was with Claudia, or her "precious girl" as she was fond of
calling her, her mother had a laissez-faire attitude toward Harris, and
it served him poorly. She let him get away with anything, maybe feeling bad for him because he had no father figure to look up to. Harris always felt that Claudia was the favorite child, and took his anger
out by disobeying Mrs. Kilmer's every rule as a kid. Deep inside he
wanted to be punished for his misdeeds as Claudia would have been
had she committed them. That, in Harris' mind, would have proven
that his mother cared for him as much as his older sister. As a teenag-
er, he got in with a bad crowd, and ran afoul of the law even before
finishing high school. Ft. Lauderdale was a small town back in the
60s, and most of the folks there knew Harris as a troublemaker. So,
after graduating by the skin of his teeth from high school, Harris had
fled to the big city of Atlanta, where he could make a fresh start and
earn a decent living. Claudia had kept in touch with him now and
again, but the only time he initiated contact with her was for money to get him out of jail. Still, Claudia thought, he was her brother,
and their father would have wanted Claudia, being the oldest of the
two children, to take care of him. The memory of her father had long
since left her, but she kept her parent's wedding picture in a place she
would pass by often, to try and keep them both in her thoughts. She
had talked to her mother several times a week, and had cared for her
on her death bed.

 Harris, on the other hand, had little contact with Mrs. Kilmer
once he left for Atlanta, and felt she could care less if he lived or died.
He had arrived two days after she had passed away, leaving all the details of the funeral and burial to Claudia. Then he had the nerve to
demand his share of the inheritance. After selling the house, paying
for the funeral and burial, and paying off her mother's debts, their
inheritance came to around $5,000 each. Harris had accused her of
cheating him out of his fair share, which he had hoped would be ten
times that amount. And, when she finally convinced him that she

was not holding out on him, he took the check and headed back to Atlanta, not even thanking her for handling the details of the estate. And yet, Claudia thought, he is my brother, my closest living relative.

She hoped her search would pan out, and Harris would have the sense to make his share of the find last. That is, if he even showed up at all. And if he didn't, she thought of Skip, and how nice he had been to her. Although she wasn't crazy about his looks, she also wasn't unattracted to him, either. She had been very impressed by his knowledge of the area's history, and, he had peaked her curiosity. What did he know about Billy Bowlegs that she didn't? She figured he might be able to help, if her hapless brother never arrived. But that would take some doing, she knew, because of how excited he was to fish the tournament. The same tournament the two characters next to her were going to be fishing, she remembered. How very different those two were from Skip. Maybe she'd pay him a visit that evening, if Harris didn't arrive.

When Claudia was in high school, her mother had doted on her, and wanted to know everything she did and everyone she dated. When she was growing up in Ft. Lauderdale she felt so confined. Her mother's "precious one" was not allowed out past 9:00, even at the age of seventeen. All her friends made fun of her. It made her furious, and she couldn't wait to leave the nest as soon as possible. The day after graduating from high school, deaf to her mother's pleas and tears, she packed her stuff in the old Opel Kadett she had purchase with money she earned waitressing in the Route 441 Diner on weekends, and drove to Cocoa Beach. She shared an apartment with a friend who had graduated the year before, and who had moved there because she had a boyfriend in the area.

Cocoa Beach was a fun place for a young girl in the late 1970s. Experienced, attractive waitresses and barmaids were in demand, and she never wanted for a job. She learned to surf, and was exposed to all those things her mother had done such a good job sheltering her from at home: drugs, alcohol, sex and rock concerts. The church group in Ft. Lauderdale would never have approved. Her mother tried in vain to get Claudia to move back home, but Claudia would never have dreamed of it – she was on her own, and loving the freedom she found outside the prison walls her mother had so carefully erected to protect her from harm.

Claudia spent several wild years in Cocoa Beach, working nights as a bartender in a popular club by the beach, and hanging out with the surfing crown during the day. She fell for more than one fair-haired surfer boy, and had her heart broken twice. Finally tiring of the same old scene, and wanting to start anew, she drove her '72 Chevy Nova down to Key West. She did not want to be too far from her mother, nor did she want to be too close.

Key West was a spicy slice of life for Claudia. She was hired by a locally based air charter company, and served as a stewardess on flights from Key West to fascinating destinations in South America, the Caribbean, Central America, Mexico, and all over the United States and Canada. She got to meet some incredibly interesting people, even celebrities. She had been invited to parties at Jimmy Buffet's house and had made many friends in the Conch Republic, as Key West's residents are fond of calling their tropical paradise.

Mel Fisher, the treasure hunter, had been a frequent customer of Key's Air Charters, and Claudia had become friends with him and his wife. Mel's enchanting stories of sunken Spanish galleons and hidden treasure thrilled Claudia, and she even got invited to a dive site once.

The search for sunken treasure in Key West brought back memories of the man her brother was named after, her dear Uncle Harry. Uncle Harry had married a woman from Apalachicola whose maiden name was Gladys Johnson. Gladys was a cooky person, flighty and spirited, who the family all thought was in fleeting touch with reality most of the time. Aunt Gladys and Uncle Harry often drove from their Florida panhandle home to Ft. Lauderdale to visit Claudia, young Harry, and Mrs. Kilmer, Claudia's mom. Mrs. Kilmer was Harry's sister, and they were very close. Frequently during the visit, Aunt Gladys would rant and rave about her grandfather, and how he had been associated with the most evil of pirates, and had become a particularly close friend to one of them. Fascinated by the story of the pirate family, Claudia encouraged Aunt Gladys to tell the story over and over again.

Aunt Gladys recalled that her grandfather told a tale of this pirate's wife, a Native American, who loved her children dearly. Sadly, she died of yellow fever, leaving the four sons and two daughters to be raised by their sinister pirate father. Gladys would recount the tale with a twinkle in her eye, happy to have an audience. The old pirate's sons grew tired of living a life of poverty. They demanded their father allow them to dig up his buried treasure. But the father wouldn't let them, for fear of being hung for the bloody-thirsty deeds of his younger years. When his sons continued their demands, according to Gladys, the old pirate threw them out, saying that they cared more for the treasure than for their own father. The old pirate took ill, and, according to Gladys, her grandfather moved in with him, taking care of him until the pirate died in the mid 1800s. Gladys swore that the old pirate gave her grandfather, Nick Johnson, the only existing map of where a huge treasure lay buried. As soon as he had properly laid his pirate companion to rest, Nick Johnson set off with a group of three men to dig up the treasure. But when they got to the site, they found that it had been covered with fifteen feet of sand from a hurricane. In those days, Gladys said, they had no way to excavate the site and find the treasure. Claudia thought her aunt was crazy, and indeed Gladys never seemed quite in touch with reality. Claudia never believed the wild tale, but loved to hear her aunt tell it.

Her Uncle Harry passed away the year Claudia graduated from high school. Her aunt Gladys was so bereaved, she went further off the deep end and had to be committed to the Florida State Hospital at Chattahoochee, unable to care for herself anymore. Claudia wrote Aunt Gladys once a month, and had visited her once a year on the anniversary of Uncle Harry's passing. One day an official-looking letter arrived in her Key West P.O. Box. It was from an attorney in Sopchoppy, the little town where her aunt and uncle had lived in north Florida. Aunt Gladys had passed away without leaving a will. However, the attorney was in possession of Uncle Harry's "Last Will and Testament" in which he gave all of his worldly possessions first to his dear wife, and, secondly, to Claudia. The letter that came with the copy of the will mentioned that she had inherited a run-down house in Sopchoppy, a blink-and-you-miss-it town of the Florida panhandle between Apalachicola and Tallahassee.

Claudia packed up some clothes, and headed for Sopchoppy in her old Fiat convertible. She had to handle the details of burying Gladys by herself, having been told by her brother Harris that it was her responsibility because she was named in the will and he was not. But Harris told Claudia he expected half of it anyway. She told him in no uncertain terms to go to hell. Gladys' savings were barely enough to cover her funeral expenses. After a few weeks, Claudia managed to sell the property and the run-down house. Cleaning out the dusty and forsaken cottage, she came across bills for a safety-deposit box in the Wakulla Bank. She brought her power of attorney papers to the bank, and removed the contents of the box. She was surprised to find Uncle Harry's wedding ring, a deed for some undeveloped property on the Sopchoppy River, some costume jewelry, and a manila envelope with various papers in it. Among the old titles of cars long since junked, and boats long since sunk, was a wilted, cracked piece of parchment. Rather than looking at it closely with the bank clerk looking over her shoulder, Claudia raced back to her uncle's house in the Fiat, and carefully spread it out on the uneven dining room table. To her amazement she realized she was looking at a hand-drawn map of a coastal area with a peninsula that paralleled the shore, creating a bay. The bay had an island in it, and inside the circle that represented the island, "Black's" was written. The map showed an arrow that started at the end of Black's island and stretched across the bay, the tip of the arrow penetrating the peninsula. It pointed to a circle, and inside the circle she read "Indian Mound". Another arrow exited from the Indian Mound circle, and pointed to a poorly sketched tree. Above the tree was written "Live Oak". From the base of the tree, another arrow was drawn back toward Black's Island. A hash mark just below the tree was marked "9 ft." Claudia noticed that the bay was not named, nor was the peninsula. She jumped in her Fiat, and raced to Tallahassee, an excitement brewing within her that sent a thrill to every cell of her body. Could it be that Aunt Gladys, the former Gladys Johnson, wasn't totally crazy? Gladys' grandfather's name, Nick Johnson, was scrawled on the back of the map in shaky, fading cursive letters. Claudia vowed not to rest until she had done everything in her power to see if the map was real, and to try her best to recover the treasure.

At the Leon County Public Library, with its huge façade and daunting steps as wide as a three-lane highway, Claudia found an atlas of Florida, and quickly turned to the Northwest section, and searched the North Florida coastline for peninsulas. The first one she found was Alligator point, but its dots of islands were so small, none had a name on the map. But the second peninsula she came across was St. Joseph's peninsula, and there was Black's Island larger than life in the northern end of the bay. The bay was peculiar, because it occupied an indentation in the coastline. St. Joseph's Peninsula ran north and south rather than east and west. She noticed that the closest town was St. Joe, on the eastern mainland of the bay. She compared the crinkled map with the one in the atlas, trying to get an idea of where the treasure was buried, and found that it was probably near a cove on St. Joseph's Peninsula, in the southern part of the bay.

Now, looking out at Black's Island, she envisioned the imaginary line on the old map, and gazed across the bay beyond the island. She could barely make out a gray-green line of trees on the horizon, and knew that she would be toiling under a few of those trees for the next few days, or even the next few months, if it took that long. Recalling her aunt's story, at one point in time the treasure was buried under fifteen feet of sand. Yet she was determined to unearth it and run her hands through the gold doubloons and precious gems and pearl necklaces she imagined the chest would contain.

Looking back, the last time she yearned for something with such a passionate desire was when she was living with her smothering mother, and she longed for the freedom of life on her own. Yet even that craving did not compare with the one she felt now. Whereas the desire to leave home was a slow and steady flame, this obsession was much more intense, an urge to succeed in an adventure she knew would only come once in her lifetime. And she felt that this was the one and only chance fate would give her to become wealthy – independently wealthy. With success, her longing for independence could be satisfied. She would not need to rely on employers for sustenance. She would be free to pick her companions, and they could be from any social status she chose. Ah, and the exultation of not being bound by a job, to decide what you would like to do with your time at your whim! And she would not have to rely on any man for security. Yes, she wanted to find that treasure, and nothing, nothing was going to stop her from succeeding at this one golden opportunity to take complete control of her own life.

CHAPTER VI
THE WAY IT'S SUPPOSED TO BE

S kip woke up to the sound of an outboard starting in the marina. Dazed, he looked around the small tent, trying to orient himself. He had awakened from a bizarre dream. He was out in a boat in the bay, and Claudia was with him. The bay was very rough, and the storm was whipping the waves into frenzied white caps. In the dream, he and Claudia were hauling in a seine net. The net was filled with treasure, gold ingots and large coins and jewelry of every shape imaginable. He thought they would sink any second, as the harder they pulled on their ends of the net, the closer the side of the boat tilted to the water. Skip yelled to Claudia to stop pulling, or they would sink. But Claudia, eyes bulging, kept yanking on her end of the net. Then an even more bizarre thing happened - Jesus arose out of the waves! He held a book open, and revealed that it contained empty pages. Then Jesus beckoned Skip to come out of the boat, walk over the water to the land, and begin filling in the blank pages of the book with writing. Skip looked at Claudia, and back at Jesus, the waves calmed, and he was just about to step out of the boat and follow Jesus when the outboard engine woke him.

Inside the tent was damp and dark. The only light filtering through the cracks between the flaps was from a weak street lamp near the bathroom. Skip remembered the night before, how he had eaten leftover pepperoni pizza from his cooler, showered, and fallen fast asleep by 10 o'clock, only to be woken up an hour later as his rude neighbor's pickup truck came skidding to a halt near his front tent stake, radio blasting a country tune, bright headlights glaring through the once peaceful night. He had a hard time getting back to sleep after that, especially since his neighbor had turned on a Coleman lantern that seemed as intense as the sun itself. Skip wasn't sure what the guy was up to, so he peeked out of the tent and observed that the inconsiderate loon was refilling his reels with new line. Trying desperately to fall asleep again, he heard him sharpening a knife and hooks, then noisily reorganizing his tackle and equipment. Finally, after several hours, the lantern was turned off, and the racket stopped, and Skip began dozing off. But again he was awakened by a strange noise, one that pulsed rhythmically through the night air – the loud, obnoxious sound of a man snoring. Not just normal, run-of-the-mill snoring, but the kind of rip-roaring snoring that sounded like a gorilla was being strangled. Skip managed to ignore it long enough to fall asleep, and slept soundly the rest of the night, until awakened by his neighbor's outboard motor.

No glimmer of light shone on the eastern horizon. Gazing out the front of his tent south along the bay's shore, toward the hotel that sheltered Claudia, Skip wondered if she was still asleep.

Fumbling for his flashlight, he turned it on and looked at his watch. It was 4:45 AM, and he heard his neighbor's boat slipping out of the canal toward the bay. He heard the engine rev and the boat was off like a flash, probably waking everyone in the campground. Skip hoped to hear the angry whine of the outboard as it struck a crab trap marker or a shallow bar, but, wishing as hard as he could, he did not manage to make it happen. The engine noise drifted away in the morning dew, until it became barely noticeable.

Skip pondered the strange dream. Why was he out on the bay in a storm with Claudia, and what was Jesus trying to tell him? Was the empty book a symbol of the life Jesus wanted him to live in the future, the blank pages to be filled with good deeds to please God? Or was the book with empty pages just that – a book that Jesus wanted Skip to write, an unwritten story that might bring the morals of the 10 commandments to millions of readers? Claudia, in the bow of the boat, had her back turned to Jesus in the dream, but had turned to look at the savior with sad eyes. Would she have followed him, too? He wanted to go back to dreaming, and see how the dream ended, but couldn't fall back into that magic twilight state between waking and deep sleep. So he decided to get up and prepare for the fun day ahead. He knew the best odds of beating Buck and Lucas was to fish from dawn to dusk every day of the tournament.

Skip was thrilled, an entire day with nothing to do but fish. No one to tell him where to fish, no compromising as to how long to fish or whether to drift, troll or anchor. He was on his own, the angling day ahead of him a blank slate for him to fill however it struck his fancy.

Getting dressed, Skip took great precaution not to touch the tent top with his head, as the dew had settled thick on the roof, and even the slightest bump would send water through the thin fabric. Pulling a clean set of white socks and underwear out of his duffle bag, Skip felt two conflicting urges – he had to urinate so bad he could hardly keep it in, and yet his mouth was so dry, he wanted to guzzle some cool, refreshing water first. The need to relieve himself won out, as Skip knew that if he did not get in the bathroom right away before the other tournament fishermen got up, it could be an hour before he got his turn. And that delay was unacceptable to him, wanting to maximize his fishing time, especially during the peak fish activity hours near dusk and dawn. Stumbling in the half-light he opened the poorly fitted screen door of the men's room. The smell of stale cigarette smoke nearly choked him. He couldn't for the life of him figure out how someone could be so inconsiderate as to light up in the enclosed bathroom, forcing everyone that came later to have to smell that stench.

Back at the campsite he noticed a dark, slinking shape lurking under the picnic table. As the raccoon was doing no harm, Skip chose not to disturb the creature, and opened his cooler that lay in the bed of the pickup truck. Having filled four two-quart plastic juice bottles with water and freezing them the week before the tournament, he knew he would have enough to drink. The frozen blocks of ice inside the containers kept the food and other drinks cold, and, as they melted, provided a cold treat for a dry fisherman in the boiling hot days of June. With the temperature at seventy-eight degrees and no wind blowing, Skip knew the day ahead would be a sweltering one. He read somewhere that the best thing you can do when you get up is to drink a bunch of water. And he knew he had to be very conscious of not getting dehydrated on the water, baking in that summer sun.

Feeling through the three grocery bags of snacks he had, to the raccoon's disappointment, locked in the cab of his truck, he broke off a banana from the bunch, and thought about the superstition surrounding the fruit. A long-time charter boat captain told him that bringing bananas aboard a boat was bad luck. Skip pondered the origin of that superstition, and had a theory. The city of St. Joseph, first established by the French in 1718, once held the reputation of the richest and wickedest town in Florida. St. Joseph flourished, and by 1835, 150,000 bales of cotton each year were being shipped out of its protected harbor. With five thousand inhabitants, riding high on the wealth of trade and commerce, the future looked bright for the seaport. Then came the year 1840, and a ship bearing goods from South America brought with it yellow fever, and a plague swept the unfortunate city. Of the five thousand inhabitants, only three hundred survived. Skip thought that among the goods brought into the port along with the yellow fever were bunches of bananas, and hence the beginning of the superstition. Whatever the origin, the charter captain bought it hook, line and sinker. He even went so far as to warn the people who chartered his boat not to bring bananas aboard. Skip had heard a story of the captain anchoring over one after another of his favorite spots, only to be thwarted with no fish in the boat. Frustrated, he searched the lunch bags of the hapless clients, and found some bananas. In a tirade, he threw bananas as far as he could away from the boat, and, as the story goes, no sooner did they hit the water then the rods of the shocked fishermen come to life with grouper strikes. The party continued to catch fish until their arms were sore, and, never considered bringing bananas back aboard that boat again!

Choosing to leave behind only his sturdy "brown trout" rig, he extracted all 6 spinning outfits from the cab, grabbed his Empire State Building - sized tackle box, and loaded his skiff. He put the heavy cooler in the center of the boat for stability. Dressed to prevent sunburn, Skip wore an old pair of light green pants. To cover his arms, he had on a white cotton-polyester blended dress shirt that bore faded stains of spilled food and cut bait. Atop his head was a tan, round, safari-shaped cloth hat made of 100% cotton. The wide brim protected Skip's face and neck from the sun. A strip of leather circled the front of the crown, and disappeared on both sides of the hat through brass grommets that were green from exposure to the salty air and water. Skip tied a loose bow under his chin to keep the hat from flying off his head when the boat was under way, or when the wind whipped before a thunderstorm. Around the top, two on each side, were four larger grommet vents, bearing the same green corrosion as the smaller ones. Imbedded in the brim and over each ear were copper snap fittings, in case the wearer wanted to look cool and snap the sides of the hat up in cowboy-hat fashion. Skip was crazy about the hat, and managed to keep track of it for over five years now – a new record for him. His previous best was about a year, those earlier hats not having a way to be tied on. Friends used to tease him about a fishing trip not being complete until they had to turn the boat around and retrieve his hat from the water at least once.

Skip loaded a cream-cheese container full of squid, his landing net (a huge grouper-sized scooper with half the handle cut off – he was taking no chances), a grocery bag with crackers, a bait knife, cookies and suntan lotion into his boat. Checking the small compartment in the bow, he made sure he had his heavy-duty yellow rain suit, the first-aid kit and an extra anchor rope. Locking the pickup truck, tying the outer flaps of the tent together, and closing the rear tent window using the Velcro patches sewed into the tent wall, Skip was ready to go. Bracing his foot against the stern, he succeeded in starting the old eighteen horsepower outboard after only four tries. Looking around before untying, he noticed he had forgotten his life jacket. Hopping out of the boat, he ran as fast as his old sneakers would take him to the pickup, grabbed his bright orange life jacket and the dirty white throw cushion, and raced back to the boat. But the engine had cut off. Cranking it up again, ready to shove off, he realized he had forgotten the oars. Jumping back to the dock, he returned to the truck bed, grabbed two wood oars, and rushed back to the waiting boat, only to find the engine stalled again. For the third time he began to pull on the starter cord when he heard laughs in the dark, and a quiet craft gliding toward him. Looking up he saw the shape of a white Grady-White heading right for him.

"Hey!" Skip shouted.

"Damn!" Came an all-too-familiar voice from behind the center console of the menacing boat. "Almost ran over a minnow!" Chuckles cascaded over the gunwale of the larger craft as it slipped by inches away from Skip's skiff.

"Don't make fun of that minnow! He's going after the legendary brown trout, ya know!"

More laughter. Skip ignored the clowns and finally got his engine running, untied the docking ropes from the PVC poles, pushed the boat away from the bulwark with an oar, and engaged the engine. On his way to fish the bay of his dreams, he was determined not to allow anything or anybody to mess with his head on such a fine morning. The sun's first promise of light rose over the tree line to the east, and Skip envisioned Claudia stretched out on a comfortable bed, sleeping peacefully, clad in the skimpiest of night gowns, her small, firm breasts outlined in the silk.

What bound Skip's soul closest to the earth was fishing, and sex. He truly treasured the value of love for his son, his mother, his late father, and his close friends. He felt in his heart that those loves would transcend the earth, last beyond death, be taken as an integral part of his soul to the afterlife. But fishing and sex would be left behind.

Skip contemplated what bound other souls to the earth: material possessions – money, houses, property, cars, boats, computers and a myriad of other worldly belongings. He also thought about those who, after their spirits are lifted from the realm of physical being, will miss food more than any of the other treasures of the earth. Some will miss sports, some hobbies. Some will miss music, others theater and movies. Some will miss books, others TV. Many will miss their jobs. But not Skip. He would miss fishing all day on a pristine bay, full of speckled trout and redfish. He would miss a romantic night with a woman he deeply loved, one who cared for him in the same passionate way, and gladly shared her body with her lover. Skip considered himself a very lucky man, as God had been so gracious as to provide him with both experiences in life. He knew those wonderful times would remain etched in his memory as long as he walked the earth and had a sound mind. Perhaps, Skip thought, those memories would also transcend his body's death, if only as fleeting glimpses of times gone by. Oh, but what times! Peace, and passion. The peace of being gently rocked in the middle of a fish filled bay. The passion of expressing spiritual love in a physical way.

He felt the peace. And he yearned for the passion. Somehow, he knew he could not feel whole until he had both in his life again.

With the canal behind him, Skip opened up the engine and the boat flew over the calm water. The skiff was made of such light fiberglass it could go thirty miles an hour with one person aboard. Wind whipped through his uncombed hair and he let out a cry, "Yeeeeeeee-Haaaaaw!" Then he remembered there may be folks still asleep in the campground, and wished he hadn't yelled so loud. Looking south he could see the Grady-White's rooster-tail as it carried his rivals Buck and Lucas, making a beeline toward Black's Island. He wondered just where in the bay their honey-hole was, the one that produced those trophy trout year after year.

Skip gazed at the barely distinguishable form of the Treasure Bay Lodge to the left of Black's Island, and wondered what Claudia was up to on this fine morning. It sure would be nice to have her out with him, show her how to fish, and get her hooked on the sport, and on him.

Knowing that Buck and Lucas would think he was following them if he turned to the south out of the channel, Skip decided to head northwest, follow the shoreline, and find the place he fished the night before that had provided such action. But he decided not to fish that area too long if all he caught was small trout. He resolved once again to optimize his chances of showing Buck and Lucas up, and winning the tournament. When Skip set his mind on accomplishing something, he gave his all. His favorite saying in life was a quote from Calvin Coolidge, "Nothing in the world can take the place of persistence. Talent will not. Nothing is more common than unsuccessful men with talent. Genius will not. Unrewarded genius is almost a proverb. Education will not. The world is full of educated derelicts. Persistence, determination, and hard work make the difference."

Skip remembered that he had not said a prayer yet. Several years ago he decided not to pray at night any more, or at least not say his major daily prayer at night. That used to be his routine. But he found that he fell asleep in the middle of the prayer. He was not sure if God had caused him to doze off, or the nature of prayer made him conk out, but he did not think it was fair to either himself or God to fall asleep in the middle of a prayer. So he began to say the day's main prayer in the mornings. On his way to work, people in passing cars would wonder who he was talking to. But it didn't bother Skip – he didn't care a bit about what others thought of him – what mattered was how he felt about himself.

Starting the day off with a prayer, he found, reminded him of his morals, and set the tone for the day. It put things in proper perspective. It reminded him that his job and the material possessions of the earth were only trappings that disguised the real purpose of life – to interact as a loving, caring being with the people in his life, and to learn soul lessons that would be carried on to the afterlife. He considered the trials and tribulations he encountered learning experiences for his soul, and rationalized that, if life was a bowl of peaches and cream, his soul would not evolve one iota. His prayer ending, he sung "Amen" as he heard them do at church when he was young.

Backing off the throttle, the engine sputtered and stalled, as Skip glided into position for his first long drift. The wind was blowing out of the west at five knots, just right for trout fishing. It enabled him to cover a lot of territory, yet gave him enough time to cast in all directions. He began the drift three hundred yards from shore, guessing where the deep water ended and the grass flats began. The sun was just coming over the horizon and it would be another hour before he could clearly see the grass patches beneath the sparkling water.

Picking up his favorite rod, he began casting the orange and green top water plug, knowing that plugs that made loud commotions on the water worked best near dusk and dawn, and were less effective when the sun was high in the sky. He didn't get any action on the first cast, and he figured he was still out over the deeper water. To confirm his theory, on the second cast a fish sent his plug a foot out of the air, then hit it again as soon as it splashed back in the water. What looked like a baby tarpon two feet long began stripping out drag, jumping wildly out of the water like a mullet gone crazy.

"Ladyfish!" Skip said aloud, and watched the aerobatic display at the end of his line. After the sixth jump, the ladyfish spit the hook.

Realizing that he was over deep water, as ladyfish prefer that to the shallow grass flats, he picked up his pole with the red lead-headed jig and forest green plastic body. He thought about casting it the way it was, but decided to sweeten the offering with a strip of squid. It seemed that he got three times as many hits on jigs if he added squid or shrimp to the hook underneath the soft green plastic grub. Cutting the squid into narrow triangular squares, he hooked the thicker part of the triangle on the hook once. Dropping it in the water by the boat, he could see the squid strip flutter like the tail of a wounded fish.

Casting the lure toward the shore and the grass line, he waited until it sank to the bottom. He wasn't thrilled by the distance of the cast, which depends on the size of the eyes on the rod, the amount and diameter of the line on the spinning reel, the shape of the reel's spool, as well as the aerodynamics and weight of the lure. The aerodynamics of the jig and squid combination was not ideal, as the plastic jig body and the strip of squid caused wind resistance. Once he was sure the lure rested on the sand bottom, Skip twitched the rod to make the jig rise a few inches, then fall again. He was not sure if the fish thought the lure was a shrimp or a crab or an injured baitfish, but the technique worked well for flounder, trout and redfish. Hoping large flounder would swallow the offering, he tensed as he felt a bump. Letting the line go loose for a second, he noticed the line moving to his right. He took in the slack, and set the hook.

The rod doubled over and the drag sounded, and Skip thought for sure he had hooked a doormat summer flounder that would take first place in that division of the tournament. But then he did not feel the vibrating, stick-to-the-bottom run of a flatty, but a right and left dogged pull at the end of his line, and he was disappointed. His intuition was right, and after a few minutes he could see the hardhead catfish that had managed to swallow his jig. One of the slimiest fish in the sea, they are also the most dangerous when it comes to removing the hook. Three serrated barbs adorn the body just in back of the head, one hidden by each of the two pectoral fins, and one hidden by the dorsal fin. As the fish shakes its head, if you happen to be unlucky enough to be speared by a barb, the serrated edges rip your flesh as they are pulled out. But that's pleasant in comparison to what happens next. The catfish has some kind of chemical that makes your hand throb with excruciating pain for hours after the puncture. And the deeper the penetration, the more it hurts and the longer the pain lasts.

Skip, having experienced that twice before in his life, took no chances. He waited for the dangling fish to calm down, then quickly grasped the fish by the underbelly with his left hand, thumb under one pectoral fin and ring finger under the other. He found the fish became paralyzed when held in that fashion. With his right hand he grabbed the needle-nosed pliers from their resting place on the outside of his tackle box, and pried the jig from the back of the fish's mouth. Some blood dripped out the gills as Skip carefully lowered the catfish toward the water and, loosening his grip, yanked his left hand out of harm's way. Wiping off the slime on an old battered dishtowel, Skip decided he had had enough fun with catfish for the day, and went back to the top water plug.

He fished the morning in the north end of the bay, and caught several nice speckled trout, but none of them went over four pounds.

Skip knew it would take at least a five-pound trout to place third, and at least a six-pound trout to take first place, so he released them.

Tying on a size one bait-holder with small barbs on the shank that helped hold baits in place, he threaded a red and white Whiffle Tail plastic jig body on it. Casting it into the wind as far as he could, and letting out an additional thirty yards of line, he closed the bail and set the rod down in one of six rod holders. With the shaft of the hook buried inside the plastic body, the tail fluttered in the tide, as the drifting of the boat dragged the light lure near the surface. Skip had decided to eat lunch, and wanted to keep a lure in the water at all times as the boat drifted in the light, warm breeze.

Afternoon clouds formed over land; big, beautiful cumulous clouds that looked like giant puffs of cotton adhering to each other and combining into a fluffy whole. Awed by the sky, Skip was hopeful and wary at the same time. He hoped the clouds would bring some welcome relief from the blazing hot mid-day sun. On the other hand, he had to remember to keep an eye out for thunderheads forming. He had seen them form over land and blow over the bay with little warning. An unlucky fisherman who was not paying attention to the afternoon sky could easily be caught in a fierce lightning storm in the middle of the large bay.

Washing off his filet knife with salt water and a clean rag, he took a roll of summer sausage from his cooler. Cutting the plastic packaging with his filet knife, he sliced a dozen pieces of the spicy meat on top of his tackle box. Opening a package of round, salted snack crackers, he placed each piece of sausage on a cracker and began eating. It always amazed him how tasty that combination was, and how he would like to eat it more often. However, with the fat content of the meat and the nitrite preservative, he only allowed himself the treat once or twice a year – and always during the Big Bend Saltwater Classic. He washed the sausage and crackers down with a few slugs of a clear-colored sports drink, and then had a plum for desert.

"Ah, life is good!" Skip said to himself. If he wasn't so intent on winning the tournament he would have kicked back, dropped the anchor, taken a swim in the warm water, and napped while drying off. But Skip's desire to whoop Buck and Lucas, especially considering all the grief they had given him, made him focus on fishing. So he reeled in the Whiffle Tail lure and cranked the engine. Or, at least he tried. This time it took him fourteen pulls to get the engine started – it seemed the longer the old Evinrude sat, the harder it was to get it to turn over. Skip set a course south for Black's Island, as he knew a deep channel near there with fairly deep grass flats on either side that held large trout on occasion.

In the back of his mind he hoped he would catch a glimpse of Claudia at the Treasure Bay Lodge. He fantasized about seeing her in a bikini, sunning herself on a blanket in the grass, and inviting her to come out fishing with him for awhile.

Skip hadn't been on a date in nearly a year. Having been divorced three years now, he yearned to be in a meaningful, fulfilling relationship with a woman, someone he found attractive, with a sweet disposition. He missed the companionship. He longed for sex, it was such a deep-rooted compulsion in Skip. He wasn't sure if all men had the same sex drive. But his was so strong he could not stop his mind from wandering to sexual thoughts whenever he was in mixed company, and frequently when there were not any women around. He craved the excitement and thrill of making love, and he longed so desperately to feel that sensation again. He even considered answering personal ads in the Tallahassee Democrat, or going to smoke filled bars to try and meet someone. However, when he thought about the hurt surrounding his last long-term relationship, he always decided to take his time and find more wholesome ways of meeting women – ways that would better the odds of finding someone wonderful, both inside and out.

So he did some volunteer work, and went to friend's get-togethers where he would meet friends-of-friends, and he even tried having a friend fix him up with a date. But none of that worked, he was still unable to find the right woman, the one who he would want to spend the rest of his life loving. Where was the woman, warm and caring, understanding and fun that he knew must be out there? A woman who was not on an emotional roller coaster, sometimes full of joy, and other times full of anger or sorrow. He longed to find a mate with a big heart, one who was kind to everyone, and who treated all people with respect. He wanted to be in a relationship with someone who he could count on to be there when things got tough, as they always do at some point in everyone's life. His ideal woman would be as crazy about him as he was about her, and Skip told himself that if he ever did find her he would do anything moral to win her heart, and then treat her like a queen for the rest of their time on earth. As time went on, Skip wondered if he would ever find that woman – or, if a woman who met those stringent criteria even existed.

Daydreaming of meeting the woman of his dreams, Skip almost had a collision with an eighteen-foot Polar skiff that was speeding out of the channel of the marina. He swerved just in time, and the wake of the larger boat nearly capsized him. After gaining control of his boat, Skip looked up and saw a woman waving at him from the helm. To his surprise, it was Claudia. She slowed and turned back toward him.

"Sorry about that!" she yelled over the hum of the idling outboards.

"My fault!" Skip shouted back. A thrill went up his spine as he talked to her, a strange feeling of excitement not unlike the sensation he experienced when a big fish struck a top water lure.

"How's the fishing?"

"O.K., but I haven't caught the whopper yet. What are you up to, and where'd you get that fancy boat?"

"I rented it from Charlie – nice guy! But he looked a bit nervous about renting to a woman."

"Looks like you know your stuff – I don't think he has anything to worry about - "

"Yeah, right! I almost cut your boat in half! And I've only had it for two minutes now!"

They both laughed, and smiled at each other. Claudia had a feeling come over her that she couldn't explain – she felt that, somehow, she had known Skip for a long time.

"Where ya heading?" Skip tried again to find out what she was up to.

"Here and there. How about you?"

"Going to a hole I know near Black's Island that produces big trout sometimes. Want to come along?"

"Nah, fishing's not my thing. Thanks anyway. Maybe I'll catch up with you tonight at the campsite. I still want to hear the story of the other Billy Bowlegs."

"Great! I'll see ya around dusk then?"

"Sure." With a wave of her hand, and her light brown hair streaming in the wind, she was off. The skiff pointed to hurricane cut, south and east of Presnell's marina, on the other side of the bay. Skip continued to parallel the shore, on a southerly heading toward Black's Island.

The low tide exposed lime rocks around Black's Island's oval-shaped form, and pelicans perched on them, waiting for the tide to turn and begin its slow flow into the bay. The birds knew that the start of a tide, whether it was the beginning of the outgoing or, as in this case, the beginning of the incoming, caused a spurt in the activity of the baitfish that called St. Joseph's Bay their home. Schools of pilchards, menhaden and silversides ripple the surface of the smooth waters. Mullet go airborne with their arching jumps, and long, skinny needlefish scoot across the top of the water looking for little creatures to swallow. Skip counted four great blue herons wading in the shallows, their delicate legs carrying them slowly and noiselessly toward unsuspecting mud minnows and small crabs creeping in the shadows of the tall palms of Black's Island.

Skip slowed as he passed sandy patches between the sea grasses, and watched a huge spotted stingray glide across one open area. It was a beautiful sight, the brown body of the ray, speckled with white dots across its back, and the rapid rolling of the wings that propelled the fish swiftly through the water, kicking up little plumes of sand as it raced across the bottom. He noticed smaller stingrays and spiny puffers at the border of the sand and grass, and saw glints of pinfish darting through the clearings ahead of the boat. A pair of speckled trout streaked ahead of the boat, spooked by the noise of the engine. They were not very big, and Skip was looking for a gator-sized trout. The grass flat gave way to a deep channel fifty yards away from the island, the water turned a dark blue-green, indicating its twenty foot depth. Skip knew the channel wasn't very wide, so he stopped the engine and the boat slowed to a drift in the middle of the cut. Big trout and flounder frequent the border where the grass flat and the deep water met, camouflaged in the grass, waiting in ambush. They darted out to catch baitfish, crabs and shrimp floating by in the tide.

Skip chose to cast toward the deeper grass flats he had just passed, as he never had any luck fishing the ones on the side closer to the island, where the grass was only a foot or two below the surface at low tide. It seemed to him that the deeper the grass flat, the bigger the trout – at least in the summer months when the waters were tepid. The slight southerly breeze drifted the boat within casting range of the shelf, and Skip let fly a cast with the new plug he had bought from Charlie, the one with orange, green and yellow colors and two silver treble hooks. He let it sink close to the grass, and it came to rest on the sand at the edge of the channel. He twitched it to life, and retrieved it slowly back toward the boat with small jerks of his rod tip. After a few winds of his reel, he raced the plug back in, thinking that no trout would be in the middle of the channel, and the plug did not run deep enough to catch a flounder. The breeze blew him parallel to the channel edge, a perfect drift for the technique he was using.

He caught and released a small trout and a blowfish, and had a good feeling about the area that he was approaching, as he remembered catching some big fish there in the past. It was an indentation in the grass line, and the sunken cove had ten feet of water in it on low tide, and patchy grass on the bottom. He threw the plug as far as he could into the fishy area, and was bringing it back in when he spotted a large loggerhead sea turtle ahead of him. It was a beautiful sight, with four strong feet paddling the barnacled shell twice the size of a kitchen sink, the turtle's head the size of Skip's fist leading the way.

Then he saw it – a shadow behind the turtle, big and dark and gliding along in the shade of the turtle's shell. Skip tossed his lure well ahead of the turtle, gave the lure time to settle, and twitched it enticingly. The shadow darted out from under the turtle, and smashed the lure! Skip's heart pounded as he set the hook, his rod bent and the drag screamed as the fish raced away from the boat. Skip knew from the dogged, unrelenting run of the big fish that he had not hooked a trout, but something much, much bigger. Cursing the fact that he was using only 10 pound test, he kept an eye on the quickly disappearing line to be sure he didn't get spooled. He turned the knob on top of the spool clockwise, tightening the drag slightly in hopes of slowing the fish down. The rod bent more, and Skip was not sure if the rod or the line would hold up to the extra tension, but they did, and the fish slowed. Looking at the reel, he could see the core of the spool through the remaining line, and knew that if the fish didn't stop soon, the line would snap when it ran out. Skip heard a huge splash in the distance, and saw a big swirl two-hundred yards away from the boat, as the fish rose to the surface and shook it's large head, trying to dislodge the lure. That was a good sign, as it meant the first run was over.

Skip pumped and reeled, gaining some line back, then loosing it again as the fish took off in another direction. Skip thought he might have hooked a jack crevalle, a black-tipped shark or a cobia. He hoped his rod and line would hold up to the test, and allow him to get the fish close enough to the boat to see what he had hooked.

For twenty minutes, each time he got the monster within fifty feet of the boat, the fish would make one strong run after another. Skip was wondering if it would ever give up, and his arms were getting sore. The fish was slowly pulling the boat across the deep sunken cove a little at a time, sea anemone and sponges dotted the sandy bottom.

The sound of distant thunder caused Skip to look over the Treasure Bay Lodge to see ominous clouds rising, forming an anvil shape, white against the blue sky. It was only then Skip noticed that the wind had picked up and the once-calm bay was getting choppy. He was winning the battle with the behemoth on the end of his line, and hoped the tug-of-war would be over soon.

After another fifteen minutes, he had the fish beside the boat, and could see that it was a beautiful cobia, about three-and-a-half feet long. Skip estimated its weight at twenty to twenty-five pounds. In all the years of fishing the Big Bend Saltwater Classic, he had never seen a cobia place that was less than thirty pounds. Although, if he were to land the fish and weigh it in at Carabelle on this first day of the tournament, he would have a chance at the hundred-dollar prize for being the daily leader – but only if no one else brought in a larger cobia. He thought about it for a few minutes, going back and forth as to whether to kill the fish that had battled so well and with such strength. Looking at the large, prehistoric-looking head with beady eyes, its dark rounded body topped by a spiny dorsal fin, and it's large tail still kicking in an attempt to swim away, Skip's made his decision. Slipping a glove on his left hand, placing his thumb in the fish's mouth, griping the lower jaw, he said, "I'll probably regret this later, fella! But you put up a helluva fight!" Putting his rod down, he grabbed the fishing pliers with his right hand and pried the lure carefully out of its mouth, being careful not to inflict any more damage to the beautiful creature. Pulling the fish through the water, he attempted to revive it. Cobias are hardy fish, and before long it snapped its head away from Skip's loose grip and swam slowly away.

"Wow! That was fun!" Skip said to himself, wiping the perspiration from his brow with his shirtsleeve.

A westerly breeze kicked up, and reminded Skip of the storm that was brewing inland. Something felt strange, like static electricity in the air. His arm hairs were standing on end. He knew it was time to race back to Presnell's. He wondered why a storm approaching from the east gave rise to a westerly wind.

"Weird!" he said to himself, and noticed that the breeze and the fish had carried the boat across the sunken cove and he was approaching shallow grass flats ahead. Banking on the knowledge that it would only take him ten minutes to get back to the shelter of Presnell's fish camp, he decided to take a few casts in the shallower water he was approaching. After all, he'd heard it said that fish bite best before a storm, and Skip's past experiences had proven that to be true in the summer months.

In the distance toward the Treasure Bay Lodge, in the direction of the gathering clouds, he spied a large sandy area amidst the grass. His first cast fell short of the mark, and he retrieved it quickly so the plug would not get stuck in the grass. Deciding that the sandy area looked like an ideal hiding place for a large flounder, Skip picked up the rod that was rigged with the red lead-headed jig and forest green plastic body that resembled a shrimp tail. He hooked a strip of squid once on the hook so its long triangular shape would sweeten the presentation. As he had drifted within easy casting distance of the sandy area, he cast to the far end of it and allowed the jig to sink to the bottom. Thinking that the sandy swatch of bottom looked like a big smile, Skip grinned himself, and gave the jig a twitch.

A tap vibrated the top of his limber rod. Skip saw the line going slack as whatever had picked up the jig was moving directly toward him. "Hmm...very unflounder-like," he thought to himself. He reeled quickly, and when the line was taught, he set the hook with a hard flick of his wrist.

The fish reacted by turning and darting away from the boat. Skip saw a sparkle in the water and a long shape bulldozing toward the grass on the other side of the sandy area. His heart skipped a beat – this was no flounder! He could hardly believe his eyes. He had hooked into another large fish.

"Couldn't be a cobia!" he gasped. Then, as his drag screamed and the pole bent wildly, he saw the fish break water in a huge swirl, its head out of the water, its body thrashing the surface into chaos!

"That's the one!" Skip shouted as the fish plowed away from the boat into shallower water. Skip stood up to keep his line high and to prevent the lunker from diving into the turtle grass. The fish thrashed on the surface again, sending spray in all directions. From the feel of the fish and the surfacing, Skip knew he had hooked a trout – maybe the biggest trout he had ever hooked!

Lightning cracked the sky, as thunder vibrated the boat. Skip ignored it. He wouldn't have given up on this fish if a waterspout approached. This was the one he had dreamed of hooking. In the seven years of fishing the tournament he had never encountered a trout this size. He was shaking with excitement as the fish stripped more line off the reel. Skip resisted the temptation of tightening the drag, knowing speckled trout have very soft mouths.

Skip stood, letting the fish take line, and kept his rod high and reeled only when the fish wasn't running. He was sure it was a trout

– it had to be a trout the way it was fighting. But he had been fooled before. Couldn't be a catfish, couldn't be a Spanish mackerel... or could it? He hoped not, because a Spanish would part the line any minute with its sharp teeth. No, he had a glance at it in the sandy patch, and again when it first surfaced – it was a trout, he was convinced.

Looking around, he saw the large landing net draped on top of his cooler, where he purposely had put it for easy access. The rod he used to catch the cobia was precariously balanced on the front-seat of the skiff, the plug dangling inches above the water on the right hand side of the boat. Skip made a mental note to be careful not to tangle his line in that when and if the fish got closer.

The runs were less strong now, but the fish was nowhere near exhausted. Each time the water swirled and the fish splashed, Skip held his breath. He knew big old trout had a way of spitting hooks. The longer the fight lasted, the looser the hook set would become, as the hole that the hook made in the fish's jaw stretched. He wanted to get the fish to the boat quickly, but knew that extra pressure could pull the single-hook lure right out.

A lightning bolt cracked much closer this time, striking a pine tree in the yard of the Treasure Bay Lodge. Skip heard an eerie sound as a large branch broke off of the tree and fell with a thud in the soft grass. The storm had reached the hotel now, and Skip could see the gray sheet of rain advancing steadily toward him.

As if feeling the lightning strike, the big trout went wild on the surface, thrashing water in all directions - a beautiful display of strength and its will to survive. The big fish ripped line again from Skip's reel in a furious run away from the boat. But that burst of energy tired the trout. It swam parallel to the boat, as Skip slowly gained line.

The monster trout neared the skiff and caught sight of the hull, and again stripped line off the reel. Skip held the rod steady as the sound of the drag zinging out smoothly echoed in his ears along with the sound of the wind whistling as it blew through the tense line. The gator trout was now on its last legs, as it wallowed near the surface, making a slow circle around the boat. The fish swam on the side of the boat where his other lure dangled above the water. Skip reached for the net with his left hand, the reel in the anti-reverse mode. Grabbing the net, and watching the fish at the same time, Skip felt resistance on the net, yanked, and heard a splash. "Damn! Just what I need!" he shouted as he realized what he had done. The plug tied to his other pole was entangled in the net, and when he yanked the net handle he had sent the rod flying overboard.

A lightning bolt cracked as it lit up the sky on the shoreline. The fish, spooked by the vibrations of the lightning, ran toward the boat. Skip dropped the net and put his foot on it. Grabbing the reel handle he cranked frantically to keep up with the trout. It was heading right under the skiff!

Skip dipped his bending rod tip deep in the water to prevent the light line from being cut by the hull. He tried to turn the fish, but it took out drag in a last-ditch effort for freedom. The net slid out from under Skip's foot as the fish swam around the line from the sunken rod and reel. A sickening feeling hit Skip as his right hand strained to keep the rod tip deep enough to prevent the line from scraping on the hull, and his left arm jiggled the landing net trying in vain to get the treble-hook lure free. He was stretched to the maximum, one arm off the bow shaking the net, and his other arm by the stern, trying to keep the line from scraping the bottom of the boat.

The fish pulled harder, desperately trying to rip the hook free from its mouth. He could see the fish swim away from the skiff on the landing net side, then back toward the skiff. Skip knew if the line got wrapped around the line from the other rod and reel, it would part in a split second. Desperate to catch the trout, Skip's body shaking, he jammed the landing net into a rod holder, snatched the filet knife from the side of his tackle box, and slashed the line below the entangled plug. To his relief it parted. He could feel the extra tension on the rod disappear and the fish swam freely again.

But the behemoth was not ready to give up, and swam off the left side of the boat, then toward the stern. With the fish on one side of the boat, and his rod dipped deep in the water on the other side, the fish's maneuver spelled disaster. Any second the line would touch the sharp blade of the prop and snap. Skip dropped the knife he still held in his left hand, grabbed the back of the heavy old engine, and lifted with all his might. The shaft slowly raised out of the water, as the fish passed inches away.

Skip managed to turn the head of the fish back toward the boat, and it's huge speckled body dragged across the top of the now choppy water. Reaching for the landing net, the plug still dangling from its mesh, he eased it into the water in front of the prize fish. The giant trout saw the net and, with its last burst of energy, shook it's big head at the surface as if to say, "Noooooo!"

To Skip's horror the jig flew out of the gaping mouth and landed with a thud on the bow. Lunging with the net, Skip felt the frame hit the trout. His body stretched out over the stern, a wave broke over him and splashed into the boat. He lifted with all his might and felt the trout slip into the landing net. Grabbing the engine with his right hand to save him from falling overboard, the outboard tipped back down into the water. The top half of his body in the water, and his waist on the stern of the faltering boat, another wave broke over the gunwale and threatened to sink it.

Wedging his foot against the swivel seat, he gained enough leverage to swing the net closer to the boat. Pushing himself up with his left hand, crouching now in calf-deep water, Skip lifted the fish into the boat. He lunged, net in hand, to the front of the skiff to keep the stern higher off the water and prevent any more waves from washing aboard. Quickly, he grabbed the beautiful, powerful fish by the back of its large head, lifted the cover of the live well in the middle of the boat, and dropped it in with a splash.

"Yahoooo!" he shouted at the top of his lungs. There was no time to waste. The rain was beating on the water as it swept off the mainland toward him. The skiff rode low in the water, and would not be able to handle another wave over the stern without sinking.

Skip yanked hard on the starter cord once, twice, but the cantankerous outboard wouldn't start. His hand fumbled for the choke lever, and finally managed to jerk it to the open position. He gave another pull, his foot braced against the stern for extra leverage. Vrooom! The engine came alive and Skip slammed the choke lever in and jammed the gearshift forward before the motor could stall. The boat lurched forward, Skip accelerating as fast as he could in the turbulent water. When the skiff neared plane, Skip reached behind him and pulled the drain plug. Slowly the water drained out of the back of the boat, as he picked up speed.

In the excitement of the fight, Claudia and everything else in the world had left his mind. Now that the battle was over, Skip's mind drifted back to Claudia. He wondered if he would see her at Presnell's, taking shelter from the impending storm. He scanned the horizon for the white rental skiff with the blue Bimini top. Skip began to worry for her safety, as her boat was nowhere in sight. He was racing toward the safety of Presnell's, conjecturing that Claudia was not aware a storm was on its way. Realizing that she could get caught in its fury, he was torn by the need to get back to shelter, and the overwhelming desire to help Claudia if she needed it.

His son needed a father, he reasoned, and he'd better get back to Presnell's. Lightning kills hundreds of people in Florida each year, and he did not want to leave his son fatherless.

On the other hand, he could not stand the thought of Claudia being hit by lightning, or trying to make her way across the bay in the teeth of this storm nature had hurled their way. Many a boat has been capsized and the crew drowned when summer thunderstorms kicked the wind up from flat calm to forty miles an hour in the space of fifteen minutes.

Skip turned the bow toward hurricane cut, wind blowing at his back, the craft navigating a following sea.

"I must be crazy!" he said aloud, knowing that he would not be able to make it back to the safety of Presnell's now that he had committed to crossing the bay.

An inner voice reminded him that, if he did not look for Claudia, he would not be able to keep his peace of mind. Skip valued his peace of mind so much, that he made life-endangering decisions to keep it. He knew he would never be able to live with himself if something happened to Claudia and he had the opportunity to prevent it, and failed to act.

CHAPTER VII
BILLY BOWLEGS II

With adrenaline pumping through his veins from both the thrill of catching the big trout, and the danger of the storm that crept steadily toward him like a sky-born shroud, Skip changed course and headed into the waves toward hurricane cut. The bow slapped against the choppy seas. He could only run half throttle because of the size of the white-capped chaotic waves. He three-quartered the square front of the boat into the swells to avoid taking one over the bow.

Lightning struck a tree on Black's island, which was barely a hundred yards behind him now. Looking back to see the strike, Skip saw the gray sheet of rain pelting the water as it approached the island.

Turning to God as he had so often when he found himself in danger, he shouted into the wild wind "Lord, please help me get to the other side of the bay safely and find Claudia and bring her to shelter. And be with all those people around the world who are in danger and help them too in their time of need!"

He turned the throttle up with a twist of his wrist, taking spray over the bow. If he went too fast, he could capsize. If he went too slow, the driving rain and lightning would catch up to him. Skip knew he couldn't head directly to Hurricane Cut, as there were shallows that even his little skiff couldn't negotiate between Black's Island and that shore, so he headed due west. The course he set took him over the deep open waters of the bay. A wave broke over the bow and soaked him.

Looking toward Presnell's, he couldn't see the marina any more, as it was under the watery deluge of the storm. Glancing back toward the mainland, he hoped to see clearing sky behind the storm, indicating that it would not last too long, but the clouds were solid over the land and not a ray of sun shone to the east. He could turn back and be at Presnell's in fifteen minutes, but those fifteen minutes would be hell, and the chance of getting hit by lightning pretty high. His boat was the highest thing in the water for miles in that direction.

No, there was no turning back now. He had to make the other side of the bay and seek shelter there. In the distance he could barely make out the blue navy top of Claudia's boat bobbing in the water near shore as the wind rippled the canvas. That was bad news and good news. The bad news was that she hadn't seen the storm approaching, and had not made it back to the shelter of Presnell's. On the other hand, at least she was not now trying to cross the bay in the gale-force winds.

Bouncing along the waves, Skip kept one eye on the swells as he jammed the black rubber drain plug back in place. Most of the water that came over the stern had now drained out, and even some of the water that had splashed over the bow had returned to the bay. The design of the boat allowed water to drain from the front two compartments to the rear compartment through drain holes cut under the front seat structure and under the live well structure in the middle of the boat. Actually, the middle of the boat had not been designed as a live well. It was originally designed as a dry storage area. But Skip had drilled two holes in the hull, creating a live well.

The reason he was thinking about it now was because the boat had been touted as unsinkable by the guy who sold it to him. Skip wondered if it was still a positive floatation craft after the alterations to that dry storage compartment. He had plugs for the two holes he drilled in the live well, but they did not fit perfectly, and it would fill up after a while, so he seldom used them. He thought the boat might still remain afloat after filling with water, but also hoped he never had to find out. If the boat sank to a certain critical level, even if it didn't entirely submerge, the engine would flood and he'd be stranded.

What was Claudia doing on shore by hurricane cut anyway? The question brought back memories of the folding shovel she carried when they met. What on earth would she be digging for over there? Maybe she was an archeologist. Or maybe she was looking for a cache of buried pirate treasure that folks say is buried somewhere along this "Forgotten Coast". Or maybe she just enjoys camping and campfires. Skip's curiosity spiked. He desperately wanted to find out what she was up to. And he wanted to get to know Claudia better. He was so attracted to her looks. Having been divorced for years now, he was desperate for a woman's companionship. How he missed the warm touch and kisses of a lover! It was tough to go without that in his life, and he spent many a lonely night hoping to find someone again.

Yet at the same time, he was adamant about not getting involved with the wrong woman, and regretting it later. He was searching for a woman he could spend the rest of his life loving. Was Claudia that woman? Maybe. He was driven to find out.

Bearing slightly south and west now, the rain caught up to him. Although the temperature that morning had already hit the upper 90s, a chill shook Skip's body. Being thin, and having been acclimated to the humid heat of north Florida in the summer, he had a tendency to get cold easy. He was glad to have his fishing hat on, as it kept his head dry, and he knew that most heat was lost from the head in cold conditions.

Lightning cracked overhead, and Skip flinched. Looking toward shore, he saw Claudia emerge from the woods, shovel in one hand,

and a backpack in the other. She gazed up at the sky, then out toward Skip. He waved, and she waved back.

Damn it! Claudia thought to herself as she realized that she was about to get very wet. Seeing Skip heading her way was a puzzle, too. Why did he not seek shelter back at the marina? Surely, unlike herself, he could see the approaching storm and have enough time to get to a safe haven. What was he doing here? She had mixed feelings about seeing him. She did not want anyone snooping around and discovering what she was up to. On the other hand, he was a pretty nice guy, and didn't seem to be someone who would try to cut in on the treasure, or ridicule her for believing in it.

As the little skiff approached the shore, Claudia took shelter under the Bimini top of her boat. Skip pulled alongside, and said, "Are you O.K.? I was worried that you hadn't seen the storm blowing in."

"Yeah, I'm fine. Not really dressed for the weather, though!"

"Claudia, you'll get fried if you stay under there!" Skip yelled through the hard driving rain. His anchor's splash could hardly be heard through the sound of the wind in the pines and the lapping of the waves on the shore.

"You have some place better in mind?" she said with a hint of sarcasm in her voice.

"Yeah – that dock over there!" He pointed to the Forest Service dock down the beach. It was a sturdy structure with the planking laid very close together. The pylons were barnacle encrusted creosote-soaked pillars that supported the dock as it stretched like a tongue of the forest into the bay.

Claudia could see that Skip was right. The dock would afford some protection from the driving rain that was soaking her under the canopy of the boat – and, at the same time, be a good place to avoid a lightning strike. She left the spade in the boat, grabbed her backpack, and jumped into the shallow water. As they splashed to the shore a lightning bolt struck a tall pine nearby and they could see what looked like a ball of lightning sizzle to the ground.

They ran along the shore until reaching the relative safety of the dock. Finding a place where only scattered drops of rain leaked through the thick planking, they settled down on the sand. Skip had brought two saran wrap thin rain ponchos he kept in the top of his tackle box. He handed one to Claudia. The light blue plastic fluttered in the wind as she tried to find the arms and the head holes. Skip wasn't having much luck getting his on either, and they both laughed.

"Nice rain gear, ya got here!" Claudia teased.

"Only the best! Guaranteed to protect the wearer from lightning!" Skip replied, finally managing to get his over his head, and his arms through the correct holes. He reached over and helped Claudia with hers.

As he pulled the hood over her head, their eyes met and Skip's heart stood still. There was something about her eyes...something marvelous, attractive, sexy. At the same time they gave him the impression that she was self-confident, and could handle any situation. He wanted to kiss her, just put his arms around her and give her a passionate kiss, but didn't know how she would react.

Claudia smiled as if reading his mind. She could tell what men were thinking just by looking in their eyes, and from their body language. And she felt the warmth from his gaze, an unthreatening warmth that reassured her that she was in no danger.

"Why aren't you back at the marina?" she asked, her voice sounding like the purring of a kitten.

"I was headed that way when I realized you were still out here."

"I'm a big girl. I can take care of myself."

"Oh, I have no doubt about that. I could see by the way you handle the boat that you're no stranger to the sea."

Both sat silently looking at each other.

"So, what are you doing here?" Claudia asked.

"Like I said, I was worried about you. Thought maybe you were having engine problems, or didn't know the storm was coming."

"Thanks," Claudia said, not sure what to think of his motives. Was he really that nice of a person, or did he think like so many of the other men she had met, and hope to seduce her in this remote part of the bay? Her intuition told her it was a little of both.

"Which brings up the question – " began Skip.

"Of what I'm doing out here, right?" Claudia interjected.

"Right. But that's your business, so I don't really need to know. Just curious."

"Curiosity kills the cat, it's said." She raised her hand in claw-like fashion, scratching in the air. "Wrawr!"

Wanting to change the subject, Claudia asked "How's fishing?"

"Fantastic!" Skip looked down the beach to be sure his skiff was not floating away or sinking with that huge trout in its belly. "I caught the biggest trout of my life this morning! I couldn't be happier!"

"Do you think it will win the tournament?"

"Yeah, I do! It's a good 7 pounds. I haven't seen a trout that big weighed in since '95. It's gotta win! I hope."

Claudia felt the child-like innocence in Skip, and could see how thrilled and proud he was to have landed that fish. She remembered a time in her life when she felt that level of excitement, too. It had been during a dive trip that Mel Fisher had allowed her to participate in after he had located the wreck of the Atocha off Key West.

Seeing the far-off look in Claudia's eyes, Skip asked "Whatcha thinking about?"

"Trout dinner!" They laughed.

"Nope, that one's not going in to a frying pan. Not quite yet, anyway."

"I remember a time when I was as excited as you are about something. I've only felt that thrill once. I was living in the Keys, and was a waitress at one of Key West's fancier restaurants, and got to know Mel Fisher and his wife pretty well. Mel was quite the talker, full of life and loved to tell stories. I didn't believe half the tales he wove, but I loved to hear about ships sunk with riches aboard, and not yet found. I got to know him real well, he and his wife would come in and ask to be seated at my station about once a week."

"No kidding?"

"When the rumor circulated around Key West that he had really discovered the mother lode of treasures, I asked him about it. He swore it was true, and that if it was O.K. with his wife, he'd like to show me first hand. His wife was an angel, and said it was fine with her. So the next day, I met him and the crew of the Dauntless at the dock, and set off for the sight of the Atocha, a Spanish galleon that sunk in a storm in 1622 with tons of gold and silver aboard. He made me swear I wouldn't tell anyone where it was, and I agreed, and assured him I wouldn't be able to find it again anyway if I wanted to."

"So he took you out on his boat?"

"Yup! On the first dive of the day, something sparkled in the silt of the wreck. Moving a sea cucumber, I dug my hand down and pulled out a tarnished chain. It was covered with growths, seaweed and stuff, but I could see the glint of metal as I rose to the surface with it. On deck, they ran water over it and I could see the shape of jewels embedded in the chain. I'll never forget that dive, or finding that necklace!"

"Wow! That's a great story! What a find! What happened to the necklace?"

"They cleaned it off and restored it, and put it on display at the museum. It's still there today."

"So that's what brings you here, eh? The thrill of buried treasure?"

Claudia looked at Skip for a long time, her gaze seemed to penetrate his soul. Claudia wanted to tell Skip all about her quest. She wanted to share her excitement with him, and reveal all that she knew about Billy Bowlegs' treasure. But she was still not quite sure that was wise. She didn't think he would try to horn in on it, or anything like that, but she wanted to be sure that he would not tell anyone else.

"Don't you owe me a story?" she asked, as another bolt of lightning hit so close it made the ground shake.

"Yeah, I guess I do. Billy Bowlegs II, as I recall."

"Uh, huh."

"O.K. But somehow I have the feeling that you already know parts of this one."

"Maybe. Go on."

Lightning split the dark sky, and the rain was falling so hard that sheets of water poured off of the dock in places. The thin plastic rain suits protected Claudia and Skip from the wind, and kept them dry. The breeze, blowing the thick scent of the downpour and salty spray, continued to whitecap the water. Waves broke against the pylons of the pier, foam pushed by the wind drifted toward the end of the cove. The small inlet ended a hundred yards from the pier. After the last hurricane, St. Joseph's peninsula had been cut in two as the huge waves in the Gulf relentlessly blasted the sand from the area called the stump hole, and forced their way into the bay, washing out the road as if it were merely a path in the sand. But man had rebuilt the road, and built a fortress of granite boulders on the Gulf side of it, to withstand the next attempt of Mother Nature to restore the area to its natural state.

Skip looked into Claudia's beautiful green eyes. The gold flecks of her irises glistened like the raindrops dripping from the dock. His heart skipped a beat. The romantic, impetuous part of him longed to hold her, and kiss her moist lips, and feel her body pressed to his, and make sweet, passionate love to her. But the other voice, the voice of caution and reason, wanted to get to know her better, wanted to find out what kind of a person she was, whether she could be trusted with his affection, and whether she was interested in him the way he was interested in her. With these conflicting emotions churning inside him like the water churning in the bay, Skip began his story.

"Billy Bowlegs, the pirate, like Billy Bowlegs the British loyalist and Indian unifier, was not born with that name. Billy Bowlegs, the one I've already told you about, was born William Augustus Bowles. Billy Bowlegs, the pirate, was born William Rogers. I don't know about his earlier life, but he was an Englishman. He must have made a decent living in New Orleans, or inherited some money, because around the year 1810, he bought a plantation seventy-five miles outside the city. Then he married a Choctaw Indian, who bore him four sons and two daughters."

"What do you mean bore "him" four sons and two daughters? They were her children, too!"

"Of course. Just a figure of speech. Anyway, ol' William got fed up with life on the plantation, or maybe he just wanted to get away from all those kids for awhile. He wound up in Batavia..."

"Where's that?"

"South of New Orleans, I think."

"Oh. I didn't know there was anything south of New Orleans, except water."

"No, the delta stretches way south of New Orleans."

Claudia heard something in Skip's voice, deep, yet soft, that spoke of self-confidence without conceit. When she interrupted him, he didn't get annoyed. She liked men with patience. And she had great respect for people who knew history. She could listen to stories of days-gone-by for hours at a time, and never get bored.

On the other hand, she told herself to focus on her goal. Finding that treasure would allow her to be independent for the rest of her life. Independent from men. Independent the way she craved to be when she left her mother after high school. Free to do what she wanted when she wanted. She desired that with all her heart. When she felt independent, totally self-sufficient, then she could think about a lover. And not a minute before then, she told herself.

She noticed the size of Skip's forearms as he sat with his legs bent, his hands clasped in front of his knees for support. They were larger than she would have expected from someone as thin as Skip. His fingers were long, and well formed, and his skin tan. Aside from some small wrinkles that emanated from the corner of his eyes, his face was not weathered like a typical man of the sea. She found herself wanting to reach out and touch him, lightly run her fingers through the hair on his forearms. But she didn't want to tease him, and didn't want to give him the wrong idea about herself. So she gazed into his hazel eyes, and noticed for the first time that they, like hers, had some green in them.

"William got in with the wrong crowd – the notorious Lafitte brothers."

"What made them notorious?"

"They were outlaws. Smugglers. Suspected pirates. Bad news any way you look at it. But when they were needed to save the city of New Orleans, they came through. They took part in the battle of New Orleans, and fought bravely. Risked their lives to save the city, and were rewarded -"

"Who'd they save the city from?"

"The Spanish. They teamed up with the United States militia, and won the battle, saved the city! So the U.S. government gave a pardon to the Lafitte brothers and their gang of outlaws for defending the city. William Rogers, or Billy Bowlegs as his buddies now called him, somehow got a hold of three small ships. He sailed them to Santa Rosa Sound - "

"Where's that?"

"By Pensacola – you know where that is, right? Just east of the Alabama/Florida border?"

"Uh, huh – not far from where Jimmy Buffet grew up?"

"I guess. Anyhow, Billy and his colleagues in crime began a smuggling operation."

"What were they smuggling?"

"Not sure – guns to the Native Americans? Rum from the Caribbean? But that only whet their appetites. The smuggling was going so well, they decided to up the ante, and began to commandeer ships."

"Who'd they prey on?"

"At first, they set their sights on Spanish galleons. The Spanish ships carried bullion from Mexico and Panama and other places in South America to Spain, and the shipping lane was right off of the coast of Florida. Most of the time the plate ships were protected by heavily armed Spanish frigates, so it was not easy to attack one. So, getting greedy, they began to prey on British and U.S. ships too."

"Wow! The life of a pirate!"

"Wow nothing! You wouldn't say "Wow" about the life of a serial killer, would you? Billy Bowlegs was much worse! You know how most pirates boarded ships and stole the cargo, and maybe if they were mean, put the crew to sea in a lifeboat? Well, Billy and his boys were cutthroats. They burned or scuttled every ship they ever attacked, after taking everything worth anything. It was his policy not to leave any survivors that could testify against him. He killed sailors, women and children. Not a soul survived when he and his bloody crew attacked."

"Damn!"

"Billy Bowlegs and his men amassed huge amounts of treasure. As word spread of their dastardly deeds, British and U.S. warships began searching the Gulf coast for them. In 1838, afraid of being captured, knowing more and more warships would be sent to look for him, Bowlegs paid his fellow pirates their share of the treasure as he deemed fit, and told most of them to scatter. All that is known of the loot that he had accumulated from the Spanish, British and U.S. victims is that he buried it on the north side of a sandy island or peninsula."

"Has anyone found it yet?" Claudia asked.

"No. No one. No one really knows where it is."

"But the north side of a sandy island or peninsula – how many places could that be?"

"On the Gulf coast? Dozens! Literally dozens. Then, on the mainland, across the bay from his treasure, he is said to have buried two huge caches of minted coins."

"Oooh. I'd like to come across one of those chests."

"Bowlegs kept several hundred thousand dollars worth of coins on his ship, the one ship he kept, that is. It was ninety feet long and twenty-two feet wide. I read that it drew only six feet of water, yet had eighteen cannons. It was a fast ship with a lot of firepower. For two years, little was heard from him. He probably hid out in some out-of-the-way bay or uninhabited harbor or bayou. But I guess hiding got old after awhile, because a couple of years late, around 1840, he went back to his old tricks."

"Maybe he ran out of money."

"No way. He may have spent the coins buried on the mainland, but he never touched the treasure buried on the island or peninsula."

"It's still there?"

"You tell me. What do you think?"

Claudia shrugged her shoulders.

"Bowlegs decided to take one last pirate cruise before giving it up forever. Within several bloody weeks, his ship's holds were filled to the hatches with rawhide sacks bulging with gold ore, and chests filled with jewelry, and bags of gold and silver coins. Bodies of his victims floated over the Gulf waters or sank beneath the waves on their way to watery graves. But his ship had been damaged, too. Several spars had been shot away, there were jagged holes in the bulwark and hull where cannonballs had ripped through. The sails were torn to ribbons, and the ship was leaking badly from round shot that penetrated the hull."

"Darn. It's a wonder it didn't get sunk!"

"Yeah. He patched the ship up as best as he could, and was heading back to his hideaway when he was spotted by a British sloop-of-war. The pirate ship tried to outrun the sloop, but the British ship was seaworthy and fast, and determined to put an end to the bloody era of Billy Bowlegs and his gang."

"Did they?"

"They tried. A gale was blowing, and the seas were rough, as the British closed in on the pirates. Bowlegs' ship, slowed by all the booty in the hold and rough water, made its way toward an inlet, followed closely by the warship, which had nearly closed the gap. The British captain sensed victory, because it would only take a few minutes to be broadside of the pirate ship, open fire with his cannons, and sink it."

"Time for Billy to pay his dues?"

"Well, Bowlegs, knowing that his only chance of escape was to get to a place the bigger boat couldn't, steered his ship across a shallow sandbar that spanned the mouth of the bay. He had an advantage, because he knew those waters like the back of his hand. But he didn't make it across the bar. The mangled ship struck bottom. Wind raging, surf crashing over the deck, several pirates were washed overboard and drowned. The shock of striking the sandbar, and the power of the waves rolling over the ship wrecked most of her rigging."

"What about the loot?"

"Still in the hold. Meanwhile, the British were getting closer and closer. Billy Bowlegs was desperate to get the ship to the shelter of the bay, out of the furious surf and away from the British, who would hang him in a heartbeat if they caught him."

"Would serve him right!"

The waves crashing against the pilings made Claudia feel like she was in the middle of the saga herself. Thunder echoed like the sound of British cannons opening fire on the pirates.

"The British sloop-of-war, closing in on the stranded ship, began bombarding the pirates with their cannons, but the rough seas and the howling wind made it difficult to hit them. Bowlegs thought his days were through, when a sudden gust of wind and a surging wave pushed his ship across the sandbar. Tilting and taking on water, the pirate ship, pushed by the wind, floated away from the British."

"Damn, he was lucky!"

"I'll say! The British captain, determined to put an end to the bloody pirates, and realizing that the bar stretched across the entire mouth of the bay, steered his ship toward the deepest part. As fate would have it, the warship ran aground. The captain cursed furiously as the pirate ship drifted further and further away. The cannons continued to fire, but soon the pirates had drifted out of range. As soon as Bowlegs knew he was out of range of the British guns, he dropped anchor."

"Why?"

"I guess he wanted to get the treasure off the ship before it sank. The British captain, having sailed halfway around the world to capture Bowlegs, was not about to let him escape. Shouting orders to his crew at the top of his lungs, longboats were dropped over the side, and in minutes armed marines were rowing toward the crippled pirate ship.

"Bowlegs and what was left of his crew grabbed supplies, equipment, some cash, and one chest full of their bounty, and loaded it into their two lifeboats as the British approached. Heavily outnumbered by the British force, the pirates had no choice but to run for it. Just as they were abandoning ship, Bowlegs ordered the cannons to be fired through the hull, so the ship would sink with the rest of the treasure aboard so the British would not be able to recover it. The British fired their rifles as the pirates rowed for their lives toward the heavily wooded peninsula that formed the bay. Several more of Bowlegs' men were killed by the British bullets. But the pirates' lifeboats were smaller and lighter than the British landing boats, and pulling on the oars like their lives depended on it, the pirates beat the British to the shoreline."

"Damn! They got away?"

"Yeah. They abandoned their boats and scattered into the dense cover of the pine and palm woods. The British force knew better than to try and pursue them – the pirates would have picked them apart with ambushes. So, turning back toward the pirate ship, the British watched helplessly as the bow sunk beneath the waves."

"It went down with treasure in it?"

"Yup! The marines rowed back to the sloop-of-war, and had to face the captains' rage at their failure. He ordered them to return to the sight of the pirate ship's sinking, and check the depth of the wreck, hoping that they could reach some of the bounty. Sunk in five fathoms of water –"

"How deep is that?"

"Thirty feet. But they had no way to dive that deep, and couldn't raise the sunken ship. So the British gave up hope of recovering the stolen jewelry, gold, silver and money. Realizing that the pirates were familiar with the area where they had hid, and would never be captured, the captain sailed away empty-handed."

"What happened to the sunken ship with all that treasure?" Claudia asked.

"Good question. No one knows. When Bowlegs left the ship in such a hurry, he only took one large treasure chest, and a few thousand dollars worth of currency with him. He and the twenty-seven surviving pirates were elated to see the British ship rise with the high tide and sail away. Over the next several days they built flimsy shacks on the peninsula, hoping to salvage the rest of the bounty that lay at the bottom of the bay. But the ship was too deep, and try as they might, they couldn't dive deep enough to retrieve any of the booty left on the sunken pirate ship."

"You mean the Bowlegs' treasure is at the bottom of the bay somewhere?"

"No, not all of it – remember, he stashed away all that loot on the north side of a peninsula or island, several years earlier. When he and his men abandoned the ship, they took one large treasure chest with them. And then there was all those coins buried on the main-land, that he may or may not have spent."

"Oh, right!" Claudia didn't want the story to end, ever. She was thoroughly entranced by the tale of Billy Bowlegs, and feeling closer and closer to this odd sort of guy who knew so much about history.

"Don't stop now – what happened next?"

"I'm not sure of all the minute details, but as I understand it, Bowlegs left a Spanish pirate, Pedro Bogue, in charge of the encamp-ment, chose two of his best men, and made his way on land back to the plantation in Louisiana."

"He returned to Louisiana? Wasn't he afraid someone would rec-ognize him as a pirate?"

"He was paranoid of being discovered as a pirate, but he knew no one could prove that he was Billy Bowlegs or that he had taken part in piracy. Remember, not a soul survived any of Bowlegs' attacks – he put every single victim to death!"

"Bloody bastard!"

"That's being kind – he was the worst of the worst! So he and the two crewmen made their way back to the plantation in Louisiana. He sold the plantation, gathered his family and what equipment he could take, bought a trim little sloop, and sailed back to the pirate's hideout."

"Who was with him?"

"His wife, his four sons, two daughters, and the two crewmen. But Bowlegs was in for the surprise of his life!"

"He got captured?"

"Unfortunately not. When he returned to the encampment, he found that only four of the twenty-five men were left; Pedro Bogue, two other Spaniards, and the bo's'n Jim Kelly."

"What's a bo's'n?"

"I think it's short for boatswain."

"Great! Now what the heck is a boatswain?"

"He's the guy who's in charge of the sails, rigging, and anchors. He's the one who calls out "All hands on deck!""

"Oh. So what happened to the rest of the pirates?"

"Some died of yellow fever. Some, fearing capture or yellow fever, had deserted in the middle of the night. Others had been killed when a band of Indians attacked the encampment."

"Jeeze!"

"Yeah, and as if that wasn't bad enough, Bowlegs' wife contracted yellow fever and died too!"

"What about the rest of the treasure on the sunken ship? Did they ever get it?"

"After months of trying, Bowlegs quit. But he never gave up hope of some day raising that ship or salvaging the sunken loot. So he took his children to the mainland and began building himself a nice log cabin. The cabin is said to have overlooked the bay, and had a clear view of where his ship went down. He wanted to keep an eye on it to be sure none of the other pirates returned to take the treasure."

"Years went by. Bowlegs yearned to get at his loot. Pedro, who had built a cabin near him, passed away. Jim Kelly, the boatswain, married and raised a family. Then he, too, died a poor man. Bowlegs, in 1865, had finally run out of the money from the sale of his plantation, and spent the money he had taken off of the sinking ship. He was 70, and still in good health, and his sons had grown. His daughters were married."

"I thought you said he still had treasure buried on the north side of an island, or peninsula."

"He did. I'm getting to that. The sons, used to living the good life while their father still had money, and being greedy like their father, bugged him to dig up some of his treasure. The more they badgered him, the angrier he got. He became sick of their whining. After all, in his mind, it was his treasure, not theirs. And, if caught with that kind of wealth and no explanation as to where it came from, he was likely to wind up swinging by his neck at the end of a rope. The mystery of who Billy Bowlegs really was, and his whereabouts, was still talked about in taverns across the Gulf shores. I'm not sure about this, but I'd be willing to bet he witnessed men being hung for piracy after they drank too much and spilled the beans about their pirate days."

"Did the sons get their way?"

"No. In fact, the crusty old man, thinking that his greedy sons wanted the treasure more than they wanted their father to be safe, kicked them out of the house. He sent them away, disinherited them, and never said a word to them for the rest of his life. The bitter pirate, however, had formed a close bond with a nephew, who was taking care of him as he got older. As they grew closer in his final days, Bowlegs promised to reveal where some of his fabled treasure was buried to this dear nephew."

"What was the nephew's name?"

"Nicholas Johnson, I think."

Flushed with excitement, Claudia couldn't believe her ears! Could it be?

"What was his name?" Claudia asked again. Skip noticed that the color of her face had turned from cream to crimson.

"Are you O.K.?"

Claudia swallowed hard. "Yeah. What were you just saying?"

"You asked me what was the name of Bowlegs' nephew. And I said I thought it was Nicholas Johnson. Have you heard of him?"

"Yeah!" Claudia spurted out without thinking. "I mean, no!"

"Which is it – yes or no?" Skip already knew the answer.

"Well, it could be just a coincidence, but my late aunt's maiden name was Johnson."

"And what makes you think that your late aunt was somehow related to Nicholas Johnson?"

Claudia wanted to blurt out that she had a map of Bowlegs' treasure. The words ping-ponged around the inside of her head, desperately wanting to be uttered. But once uttered, they could never be taken back. Skip would have to be trusted. One side of Claudia said, "And why not? This guy braved a storm just to check on me. If I can't trust him, who can I trust?" The other side of her reminded her of how she had trusted men in the past, only to be disappointed.

Looking north east over Black's Island, Claudia saw the sky clearing over the mainland. She took it as a sign. As she stared off into the distance, rays of sun pierced the clouds and shone on the calming water. Were they pointing to the sunken treasure ship?

"Promise to keep whatever I tell you a secret?"

"I promise!"

"Good. Although, more than likely no one would believe it anyway. It's so bizarre!"

"Tell me."

"Everyone thought my aunt Gladys was a bit on the loony side. She was a bizarre woman. We thought she was prone to, let's say, be off the deep end at times. Well, one of the peculiarities of dear aunt Gladys was that she would mumble about her grandfather's map, and how she was going to be the richest woman in the world one day. I loved to sit and listen to her stories, especially the one about a pirate's treasure and how her grandfather had befriended an old pirate. We all thought she was in fantasyland, and, indeed, in the end, she was diagnosed with dementia and spent the last years of her life in Chattahoochee. When she passed away, I inherited all that she owned..."

"How'd that happen? Didn't she have any children?"

"No. No children. And no other family that we knew about."

"So why you? Was she fond of you?"

"Kind of. I always listened to her ramble on when no one else would. But her husband, my uncle on my mother's side, was very fond of me. In his eyes, I could do no wrong. I was an angel from heaven."

"Your uncle has good taste!"

"So he put me as second to inherit his property after his wife. He passed away first. Then, when she died, what little was left I inherited. A nearly worthless property in Sopchoppy, and a savings account that barely covered aunt Gladys' funeral expenses. Cleaning out the decrepit house, I found some bills for a safety deposit box. So, with my "Power of Attorney" paper in hand, I convinced the folks at Wakulla Bank that the contents of the box should be turned over to me. Inside the box I found some costume jewelry, my aunt and uncle's wedding rings, a deed to a small riverfront lot, and a manila folder with some papers in it."

"Ah, a map perhaps?"

"Right. I was shocked. It was drawn in pen on old parchment, and on the back was written the name of Gladys' grandfather, Nick Johnson."

"So that's why you nearly fainted when I said the name Nicolas Johnson!"

"Yeah! And now you know what I'm doing here."

"Damn! That's exciting!"

They looked at each other for a long time in silence. Claudia wanted to see his reaction, if he believed her, and if he would become greedy and try to talk his way into part of the treasure.

Skip could understand now the impact his story about Billy Bowlegs had on Claudia. He wanted to see the map, but did not want Claudia to think he was interested in stealing the pirate treasure. And now that he was close to a find such as this, he had mixed feelings. Ill-earned money was a curse, and nothing good ever came of it. He had known friends that had made a lot of money illegally – mostly smuggling pot into the country. And not one of them now had anything to show for it but poor health and time spent in jail.

"Are you sure you want to find that treasure?" asked Skip.

"Yeah, sure as I'm alive! Why not?"

"Oh, I don't know. I would love to discover a pirate's treasure, too. But keeping it? I don't know."

"Are you religious or superstitious?"

"Both. More religious than superstitious, though. And I don't want to put a damper on your adventure, but keeping loot that was stolen from people who were massacred..."

"Yeah, I know what you're saying. You think they'll be some kind of a curse -"

"No. Not a curse. That's superstitious. Karma is more like it. Bad karma."

"Bad karma. Bad karma. Hell, I can handle some bad karma to live the rest of my life high on the hog."

"I can't. I'd rather stick with good karma and live a life of poverty than deal with bad karma and wealth."

"Good," replied Claudia, genuinely relieved that she wouldn't have to deal with Skip wanting a piece of the fortune.

"Good?"

"Yeah, good. This way I know you're not going to want any of it when you help me find it."

"Oh, I'm gonna help you find it?" asked Skip.

"Yeah. Remember, you said you'd love to find a treasure, but you wouldn't want to keep it."

"So I did."

"Shake on it, then."

Their right hands met, and what seemed like an electrical charge, starting from their outstretched hands, filled their bodies with a sensation that neither had felt before. Skip wanted to shout "Did you feel that?" But if Claudia had not, he would have been embarrassed. Claudia wanted to ask Skip if he had felt that, too, but did not want to take the chance that he hadn't. Holding each other's hand, they sat looking at each other for what seemed like an eternity. Finally, Claudia broke the silence.

"The rain's stopped. Let's see the trout you caught!"

"Sure! I'll show ya the trout if you show me the map."

"Deal."

They held hands and ran along the narrow, hard packed white sand beach towards the boats. As they approached Skip's skiff, Claudia saw the tackle box and, pointing to it, exclaimed "What's that?"

"That's my tackle box."

"Hell, I've packed enough clothes for a three-day weekend in luggage smaller than that!"

Skip laughed. "I've got two more like it at home" he fibbed, "but I'm travelling light this trip. Only the most essential lures lie within that box. It's my idea of a treasure chest!"

"You don't need any life preservers with that thing on board. You could sit on it and paddle to shore! How heavy is that thing?" she said as she grabbed the handle and tried to lift it.

"Look out!" Skip shouted, noticing that, in his haste to retrieve the ponchos, he had forgotten to latch the top compartment. Claudia gave the handle a yank, and to her surprise, the top flew open and jig heads, spools of line, a disposable camera, truck keys, nail clippers, packages of hooks and unopened lure boxes spewed out into the boat, splashing down in disarray as they hit two inches of water deposited by the storm in the bottom of Skip's boat.

"Oooh! Sorry!" If this wasn't a true test of his patience, nothing was, thought Claudia as she surveyed the mess she had made. She began to pick things up.

"Don't worry about it," Skip said. "Instead of putting that soggy stuff back in the tackle box, I'm going to need to wash it down tonight when we get back to Presnell's in case there's any salt in that water."

Continuing to pick up the spilled contents, she asked, "Well, where do you want to put it? I'm really sorry! I can be a klutz sometimes."

Skip slipped his plastic poncho off, tied a knot in the hood end, and said, "Let's put it in here."

"Oh, no! I've ruined your camera!"

"Not to worry! It's one of those one-time use cheapies. I haven't taken any pictures yet, so no big deal."

Fishing out the spilled gear and dropping it in the makeshift bag, Claudia remarked, "I'm surprised you're not pissed off at me."

"I'm not. It takes a helluva lot more than a spilled tackle box to get me upset."

"How about having to look after a wild woman who doesn't have the sense to come in out of a storm?"

"That doesn't anger me a bit – I enjoy helping people."

"You must have the patience of Job!"

"Yeah, God's blessed me with patience. I'm pretty lucky."

"I think it's more than luck. Patience is learned, not something you're born with."

"Maybe so. Remember when you asked me if I was religious or superstitious? Being somewhat religious, I'd like to think I have a good grasp on what's important and what's not here on Earth."

Claudia looked Skip up and down. She didn't expect him to be a religious person. It surprised her. Religion held no special meaning to her. She wasn't sure if God existed. But she wasn't convinced that he or she didn't exist, either. Not enjoying the experience of being forced to attend Sunday school as a child, when she left home, she stopped going to church. Holy rollers made her uncomfortable, and she hoped that Skip wasn't one.

"Just how religious are you?"

"Well, I don't go to church on Sunday much. But, on the other hand, I pray every day. And try to do God's will."

"Do you think God would want you killing his fish?" she said with a smile.

"Actually, I've asked myself that question a million times."

"And?"

"And, I either come up with a good rationalization or think about something more pleasant."

"This oughta be good – what rationalization do you come up with?"

"First, that ninety percent of the fish I catch I release. So I'm not really killing that many."

"Yeah, and how about the ones you do keep?"

"It goes like this: in order for a fish to get to be big enough for me to consider keeping it for supper, it would have already eaten thousands of smaller fish and crabs and shrimp. So, I'm not doing anything to it that it hasn't done to all those other thousand creatures."

"Yeah, but you are consciously ending the fish's life. I doubt the fish is conscious of what it is doing."

"True. Maybe someday I'll stop keeping fish. And become a vegetarian. Maybe. But not today!" Skip held up the gator trout for Claudia to see. "Isn't it beautiful?"

"Huge!" Claudia was surprised at the size of the speckled trout. She had seen them before in fish markets, and even caught them before when she took a trip to Everglades National Park and fished with her former boyfriend in Whitewater Bay. She had never seen one even close to this size. "Nice fish!"

"Should win the trout division this year. I'd say it weighs about seven-and-a-half pounds."

"You'd better mark it."

"Mark it? Why?"

"What if someone steals it before the tournament is over?"

Skip hadn't even considered that. "Good idea. I know a couple of guys who'd love to get their hands on this monster."

Skip pulled his filet knife out of the salt-stained leather sheath, and, using the sharp tip, cut the tail lengthwise 12 times. When he finished you couldn't tell the fish had been marked, but, spreading out the tail, it parted into sections. "That should do it. Good thinking, Claudia! The weigh-in station at Carabelle closes at 7. I wouldn't want Buck or Lucas ripping this fish off if I don't get to weigh it in tonight."

Those two names rang a bell in Claudia's head, but she couldn't remember where she had heard them.

Curious to find out if Claudia really did have a map that could lead her to a treasure, or whether she was the victim of a hoax, he said, "Now, let's see that map."

CHAPTER VIII
CLOSER TO THE TREASURE

The afternoon sun in all its splendor shone down upon Claudia and Skip, at first feeling wonderful as it warmed them to the bone and chased the chill of the torrent away. As they began to dry, the heat of the sweltering north Florida summer rose to greet them. They looked across the bay toward Black's Island, through what looked like steam rising from the bay, and saw the white tails of boat wakes as anxious fishermen, determined to win the tournament, raced back to their favorite spots after the storm. Setting her waterproof backpack on the bow, Claudia slipped off her poncho and threw it over the back of the front swivel seat in Skip's skiff. Walking toward the shore, Skip remarked "Fish bite better before a storm."

"And afterward?"

"Not as active as before. At least that seems to be the pattern in the summer. They hit on a dropping barometer, and aren't as active on a rising one."

"Why?"

"Who knows? The great thing about fishing is that, even if you lived 1,000 years, you would never know all the secrets of fish. It's a sport that always holds a surprise. You can never even approach a state when you could say to yourself you know it all."

"Guess."

"Guess what?"

"Guess why fish bite better on a falling barometer."

"O.K. Maybe it reminds them of the fall, when the temperature of the water begins cooling down, like it does when a thunderstorm hits. The cooling of the water triggers their survival instinct – if they want to survive the winter, they will need to feed hardy before the bait gets scarce."

"Hmph! Why do they stay around in the winter when the bait gets scarce?"

"Some don't – the trout and the redfish head up into the spring-fed creeks and inland waterways that stay warmer than the bay in the middle of the winter. In fact, I don't think trout can survive in water temperature under sixty degrees."

"And where do the other fish go?"

"Flounder head off shore to spawn. Cobia either head out to deeper, warmer water, or migrate to the west, heading for the warmer waters of Mexico. Spanish mackerel and king mackerel go the other way – they head east toward the warmer waters of south Florida."

"And the baitfish?"

"Beats me! There must be a million pinfish on the grass flats in this bay alone in the summer time. Yet in the middle of winter there's not a one. I guess they go out into deeper water in the middle of the bay, or go off shore to deeper water. But I haven't heard of anyone catching one in the winter, so I'm really not sure."

"Well, you'll have to find out and report back to me!"

"Right! I'm sure you're dying to know!"

She smiled, and looked coyly at him. Skip's gaze was drawn to Claudia, and he noticed her nipples, still chilly from the drenching, taut and outlined beautifully by her thin blue bikini top. Noticing the direction of his glance, Claudia scooped up some water and threw it at him.

"Don't stop!" Skip taunted. "I could use a cold shower right about now!"

Claudia threw more water at him and, laughing, they flopped down on the find white sand shore of the bay. Skip drew a deep breath, feeling like he was in a dream. How lucky could one guy get? Catching what he hoped was the biggest trout in the area, being caught in a thunderstorm with a beautiful woman, and now sitting next to her on this pristine beach on the bay he loved so much. He took a mental picture of the whole scene, intending to store it in his memory for the rest of his life.

"Are you sure you want to see the map?"

"Yeah, I'd really like to see it."

"Promise that any of the treasure we find is mine?"

"Sure, what's not the state of Florida's is yours."

"What do you mean?"

"You know, like Mel Fisher. He wasn't able to keep the entire treasure he found, only a portion of it. The largest part went to the state."

"True. But what the state don't know won't hurt it."

"I'll never tell. But are you sure you really want to find it?"

"Of course I want to find it! Why wouldn't I?"

"Karma."

"Karma. Karma. Screw karma. Don't think I haven't thought about it. I have. And what you told me about Billy Bowlegs the pirate doesn't help matters any. But I'm not going to let an opportunity like this fly away because of some superstitious karma crap!"

"O.K. Just remember, I warned ya!" Skip said lightheartedly. Claudia didn't know whether he was serious or just joking. But she was a bit uneasy about the prospects of being in possession of stolen loot, and especially now, with the knowledge that not one of the owners ever survived the looting. On the other hand, she was bound and determined to find it, and finding it would be her key to an independent life – and she wanted that so bad she could taste it.

Reaching into her backpack, she pulled out a large ziplock bag. Inside the ziplock was another large ziplock bag, and inside that, a smaller ziplock with a paper folded to the size of a handkerchief. As she extricated the fragile paper from its well protected home, they heard the sound of a boat approaching. Looking up they saw Buck and Lucas heading right for them full throttle!

Claudia and Skip jumped up, as the boat veered suddenly, sending spray 15 feet in the air. As if in slow motion, the droplets descended toward the map. Claudia whipped herself around and bent over the map, Skip grabbed Claudia from behind in an effort to shelter her from the onslaught of the spray. Water broke on Skip's back like a wave from the angry Gulf in a storm. They stood frozen for a few seconds, letting the dripping water find its way to the ground. Claudia had zipped up the map in one of the large bags, and she felt Skip's arms around her waist. She at once wanted to turn and give those jokers a piece of her mind, yet at the same time, his embrace felt so good she didn't want to move.

"Did it get wet?" Skip asked.

"No. No thanks to those idiots. They friends of yours?"

"Not hardly! More like the bane of my existence, I'd say."

"Assholes!!!" Claudia shouted at the top of her lungs.

Buck and Lucas, grinning ear to ear, slowed their boat down to survey the damage they had just done. Skip's little skiff took a lot of water over the side from the wake, and they could see with pleasure that they had succeeded in soaking both Claudia and Skip.

"Now honey, that ain't no way to address your saviors! We was just coming to rescue you from that piece of trash there."

"Yeah, right! Get the hell out of here and leave us alone!" Claudia yelled.

But Buck and Lucas didn't have any intention of leaving. During the storm they had spent their time in Presnell's bait shop sucking down beers like water. They swung the boat around so quickly, they almost capsized. Claudia and Skip watched in horror as Buck aimed the bow right between their two boats. A few feet away from the imminent collision, he cut the engine. The bow of the large center console sport fishing boat crunched and squealed as it not-so-gently came to rest between the two anchored craft.

"Are you sure you don't need saving, Ms.? That's a nasty varmint, there by yo' side!"

"Bite it, Buck!" Skip yelled at the drunken fisherman.

"I don't need saving!" To Skip's delight, she grabbed his hand. The electric shock shimmered through both their bodies again, and they turned and looked at each other with astonishment. "So you two can go to hell!"

"Now, that's not nice, missus!" Lucas replied. "We was just trying to help!"

"Help! Help? You call sinking our boats and drenching the map help!" Claudia was furious. "I'll tell you what you can do with your help! Shove it up your ass!"

"Now, now, sister. Calm down," said Buck, a bit taken back by how angry Claudia was. "I don't let anythin' in my butthole, but what's there naturally. Brown trout! Ain't that right, son?" He chided with a big grin across his chubby, unshaven face. Lucas laughed so hard he nearly fell over the railing.

"Brown trout?" Claudia looked at Skip quizzically.

"I'll tell ya about it sometime," Skip answered, not wanting to get into an explanation any time soon.

"That's disgusting!" shouted Claudia. "And so are the both of you! Go away."

"What's that about a map?" Lucas said.

"None of your cotton-pickin' business!" Claudia roared.

"Hey, son! Did you catch any of them brown trout you was after?"

"Hell, yes! And you guys would give your left arm for the one I caught earlier today!"

"Yeah, right!" Buck answered defiantly. "Let's see whatcha got!"

"If I show ya, do you promise to leave us alone?"

"Sure!" Lucas and Buck said at the same time.

"O.K. then." Skip reluctantly let go of Claudia's hand and waded out to the boat.

"Skip..." Claudia called after him.

"Don't worry. These guys are harmless. Big idiots. But harmless."

"What's with her?" Lucas asked Skip as he approached the boats.

"She's got good taste in men, and she's smellin' something foul right about now," Skip replied with a smirk on his face.

"Serves ya right not using any under-arm deodorant!" Lucas retorted.

"You guys ain't gonna believe this," Skip said, as he reached into the live well and grabbed the gator trout by a large gill. Lifting it, he could see the expression of surprise on their faces.

"Damn, boy! You weren't kiddin'! That's a whopper!" said Buck in amazement.

"Hell, Buck! That fish is bigger'n the one you won last year's tournament with!" Seeing the big fish seemed to sober them.

"Yeah, but it ain't near the size of the one I won the tournament with in '97."

"True. Let's go get us one that'll make that fish look like bait."

Skip spread out the tail, showing the twelve slices. "Don't think of sneaking around tonight and making off with this beauty. I'll know it's mine by 12 slices in the tail."

"We may be mean and ornery, but we ain't cheats!" Buck said angrily. "Keep a civil tongue in your mouth, boy, and we might even let you get back to weigh that fish!"

Skip didn't like getting threatened, but he was in no position to do anything about it. He let the remark slide.

"See you guys at the weigh-in," he said, flopping the trout back into the live well, and turning his back on them. He heard the engine start up, and rev wildly as Buck accidentally raised it out of the water with the electric tilt control switch. He turned around to watch them pull away, not at all convinced that they wouldn't stoop to stealing his prize fish.

Back on shore, Claudia asked, "Where do you think they're off to now?"

"In search of the hole."

"What?"

"In search of the hole. They told me when we, uh, ran into each other on the way down here, that they knew of a hole in the bay that was full of gator trout."

"Oh. Well, then I guess we have something in common."

"Something in common with those two characters? I doubt it."

"Yeah, we do. I'm in search of the hole, too. In search of the hole that hides Billy Bowleg's treasure."

"Hmmm!" Skip reflected on that thought for a while. "I guess all four of us have something in common, then."

"How so?"

"Well, I'm in search of the hole, too."

"What hole?"

"The one that's spelled w-h-o-l-e."

"And what might that be?"

"Oh, I'll tell ya someday. But right now, I'd love to see that map."

Skip used the fine sand and salt water where the gentle ripples of the bay met the beach to scrub the fish slime off of his hand. Sitting down next to Claudia, who was slowly, carefully opening the delicate parchment of the map, Skip eased over to get a closer look. Their hips touched, and Claudia let her leg rest against Skip's. Being so close to Claudia brought a warm rush of blood to his already hot body. The breeze rolling off the water had little cooling effect, as he felt the sweat gathering in his armpit and beads of salty perspiration rolling down his side.

Skip gazed at Claudia's profile, and thought that every freckle on her face and chest was like a brown jewel set in just the right place by the most talented creator. The rise of her cheekbone and the set of her jaw spoke to him of strength, yet the length of her eyelashes and the softness of her skin spoke to him of tenderness. How he longed to hold her, and kiss her, and make love to her. But even if she were willing, which he doubted, that voice deep inside of him called out to be cautious. Slow down, it shouted. You don't even know this woman. You don't know if she's attracted to you or not. You don't know what she is really like. She could be a she-devil for all you know. Didn't you hear the way she cursed Buck and Luke out? She could unleash that anger at you. Is that the kind of woman you're interested in spending the rest of your life with?

The other voice inside him fought back: She lost her temper – so what? I could have done the same under those circumstances. Those fools almost ruined a map that was over a hundred years old, passed down from generation to generation. She had a right to be mad! And did you notice how fast she got over it? That should tell you a lot about her. Maybe she is the one. Maybe she is everything that you are looking for in a mate. Maybe she is a dream come true.

Their eyes met, the uncertainty in their gazes communicating without even the whisper of a word.

Dozens of mixed emotions filled Claudia at once. Who is this man? What am I doing showing him this map – the key to my future? I must be stupid, sharing this with him. I don't even know him. And, yet, there is a gentleness behind that rough exterior. The big arms and thin body are hiding a big heart. I can somehow see that just by looking in his eyes. I want to trust him. I want to get to know him better. I want him to be a part of this, a part of my life, even if only as a friend. But he could be more.

She dared not go beyond that thought for fear of where it would lead her. "What do you think?" she cooed as if unwrapping a masterpiece.

Skip had to tear his eyes away from Claudia's, he wanted to go on gazing into them for hours, but at the same time didn't want to make her uncomfortable or embarrass himself.

Studying the map, he was struck by the authenticity of it. He had never seen such an awe-inspiring piece of parchment outside of a museum before, and he reached out to touch it. Claudia pulled it back.

"It's very delicate!" she warned.

"I know. It's beautiful. I just had the urge to touch it, and feel the paper between my fingers. I can't explain it."

"No need. I know how you feel. Here." She put the map back in front of her, allowing him to reach out and caress it.

"Awesome!" Skip sighed, rubbing his fingers together on a corner of the map. He sensed that it was the real thing. A not-so-well preserved pirate map. The one he had heard existed, yet never thought in a million years he would ever live to see.

"Yeah. It's gotta be real," Claudia purred, as she caressed the opposite corner of the parchment between her thumb and index finger. "No one could make such an authentic looking reproduction. You can just feel the age of it, can't ya?"

"Yeah. I can." They gazed into each other's eyes.

"What I can't figure out," said Claudia, pointing to the oak tree on the map, "is where that live oak could be. I'm not seeing anything but pine trees here, and we seem to be in the area of the arrow." She swung her head around to look at the tree tops.

"Probably long gone."

"Long gone? But I thought those trees lived for centuries," Claudia said with a hint of disappointment in her voice.

"They do. But remember, this is a peninsula. And it's subject to the whims of nature. A tree could grow in this soil for 300 years, and in an instant be knocked down by the force of a hurricane or a tornado, spawned from a hurricane."

"What makes you think that's what happened to the tree?"

"I don't. It could still be here."

"But how can we find it, if it is?"

"See the Indian mound drawn near the tree? The arrow goes right along the far edge of it."

"Yeah, but I didn't see any Indian mound either, and I've been looking for hours."

"If it was a snake, it would have bit you!"

"What do you mean?"

"Look right behind you."

Claudia turned, a puzzled look on her face. "I don't see a thing."

"Look closely."

Claudia jumped up, and walked toward the woods. Only ten feet of beach separated the woods from the bay, and the sand rose slightly toward the trees. She kicked a white shell that protruded from the sand, and found to her amazement that it was an old conch shell.

"Hey, look at this! I found a conch shell! I didn't know there were conch in this part of the state."

"There aren't. But they used to be abundant here."

"Hey, there's more!" Claudia notice more bleached white crowns and points of conch shells beneath the roots of the trees that the wind and water had exposed.

"See how the land swells here? The rest of the forest is flat, but there's a little rise under these trees. That's your Indian mound."

"Jeez! I was looking for something twenty, thirty feet high. I would have never found this! How did you know?"

"A friend of ours took my son and I out fishing one day in his boat. He wanted to learn how to fish St. Joseph's Bay, so I agreed to teach him what I knew. When lunchtime came, we decided to go ashore, relax and eat. The fishing wasn't too good anyway. After we got done with lunch, we were walking down the beach and Benny..."

"Who's that?"

"My son. Benny said 'Look, Dad! I found a shell!' And I saw it was a conch shell. Our friend Steve noticed that the top had been broken out. Looking around, we discovered more shells, under the roots of the trees. That told us they had been there a long time, and then Steve noticed how the land rose up in this area. We were sure we had found a new Indian mound – one that no one had ever come across before."

"And..."

"The next day I called the Bureau of Archeological Research with the state of Florida, and got transferred a few times until I got someone in the Site Files section to talk to me. To my disappointment, we hadn't discovered a new mound. He even had a name for it – the Richardson Hammock site. I asked him if anyone had ever excavated it to see what was in it, and he said no – no one had ever done a dig out here that he was aware of. And, of course, he cautioned that I shouldn't either, because it is a jailable offense to mess with state historic sites."

"Bet you wanted to come out here the next day with a shovel, eh?"

"Yeah, kind of. I am really curious to see what else lays within this pile of discarded conch shells. But not curious enough to risk going to jail for it."

"We don't have to worry about that, we won't be digging in the mound. See how the line touches the edge of the mound, then ends at the live oak? All we need to do is line up this end of the Indian mound with the end of Black's Island, and continue in that direction until we find the live oak. Right?" Claudia asked.

"Yeah. Let's give it a try. If we're lucky, the tree will still be there."

Skip jumped up and, offering his hand, pulled Claudia to her feet. They stood there, face-to-face for a brief second, looking at each other. Skip thought about caressing Claudia and kissing her. As he hesitated, Claudia took him by the hand and led him into the scrub brush and pine wood forest. Skip felt the warmth of Claudia's hand. Her skin was soft, but her grip was strong as she walked with determined steps toward the treasure of her dreams.

Zigzagging along the edge of the mound, as the Spanish bayonets and other underbrush allowed, they came to the side that the imaginary line met on its way toward the oak tree. But they were too deep in the woods to see Black's Island.

Skip said, "I'll go back to the beach, and you shout from here, and I'll come back to you along the line from the tip of Black's Island, O.K.?"

"Sure," said Claudia. "But hurry! I can't wait to see if there's a trace of that tree left."

Skip picked his way back toward the beach the way they had come, then jogged up the beach until he was roughly in line with the end of Black's Island and where he left Claudia.

"Yo!" he yelled.

"Over here!" Claudia yelled back. Skip adjusted his position on the beach by a few feet.

"Yo!" he yelled again.

"Over here!" she shouted.

Then Skip heard Claudia scream at the top of her lungs! He ran toward her as fast as his legs could fly, jumping over Spanish bayonets and crashing through the dense vegetation. Thoughts of "What the hell are we doing trying to unbury a bloody pirate's treasure?" rushed through his mind, sure that it could only bring bad karma to them both. When he got to Claudia, she was rigid as a rock, and pale white.

A long, slick black snake slithered into a hole in the Indian mound between two ghostly white conch shells.

"That's a black racer," Skip said, an amused smile on his face. He looked down, and noticed his legs bleeding from the cuts and scratches he suffered thanks to the young scrub oaks, thorny black-berry vines and Spanish bayonets in the underbrush.

"Is it poisonous?" asked a still ashen Claudia.

"No. Can't harm anyone! Afraid of snakes?"

"No. At least, not non-poisonous ones. That one just spooked me and I couldn't tell if it was poisonous or not."

"You can tell which snakes are poisonous in these parts by look-ing at the shape of the head. If it's flat, look out. If it's round, don't worry about it. Except coral snakes."

"Coral snakes?"

"Yeah. Deadly poisonous. Will kill a person in a heartbeat. But you don't need to worry about them."

"Why not?"

"About the only way one can bite you is if you handle it. They have small mouths, and are as much afraid of you as you are of them."

"What do they look like – I'm not taking any chances."

"Banded. If the bands of black and yellow touch each other, it's a coral snake. If they are separated by another band, then it's a harm-less snake."

"And what kind of flat-headed snakes are there in these woods?"

"Rattlers, pigmy rattlers and cotton mouths. Just watch where you are stepping, and it shouldn't be a problem. A snake's got nothin' to gain messing with a person."

"That's comforting – not!" Claudia said with a scowl on her face. She reached out her hand for Skip. Somehow she felt safe with him nearby, and hated herself for it. Independence was what she craved. Being her own person, doing her own thing, whatever she wanted whenever she wanted. And yet, it felt good to have Skip along for the ride, and she was disappointed in herself for feeling that way.

Again they stood toe-to-toe, and Skip was dying to caress her and hold her, touch her perfect lips with his. Claudia gazed into his eyes and read the longing there. Not wanting to see his desire, she lowered her gaze and saw his leg wounds from running through the underbrush.

"Skip, you're hurt!"

"Yeah..."

She pulled him close. With her left hand on the back of his neck, she gently pushed his head down to her waiting lips. If this is going to happen, Claudia thought, I want to be in complete control. Their bodies entwined in a sweet embrace, their lips touched for a brief moment that neither would ever forget.

Claudia, using as much restraint as she could muster, eased away, still holding his hand.

"Come on," she said in a chastising voice, as if the kiss was Skip's doing. "Let's find that treasure!"

"You mean your treasure," said Skip softly. "I may have just found mine."

She nearly yanked his arm out of its socket as he stood there transfixed on her. They had only met yesterday, but he was finding himself drawn toward her like a bee to honey. No, that's not exactly it, thought Skip. More like a moth to a flame!

Time and time again he had promised himself that before he got involved with anyone else, he would take the time to find out who that person was inside – was her heart full of love and caring, tolerance and forgiveness, charity and inner peace? If not, he wouldn't pursue that relationship. He longed for the kind of person in his life that would be so much more than a sex partner. He wanted a soul mate. Not necessarily someone who enjoyed the same things he did. But someone whose kindness toward others and willingness to give of themselves matched his own. Could Claudia be that person? Only time would tell, if she were willing to give him that time.

"Treasure!" Claudia said again, bringing Skip out of his daydream.

"Right!" Smiling, they walked deeper into the forest, hand-in-hand.

CHAPTER IX
TWO LATE

Walking in as straight a line as possible, navigating their way around the briars, Spanish bayonets, pine trees and scrub oaks, they searched for the live oak pictured on the map. Forty minutes of scrutinizing the trees and, much to Claudia's dismay, they didn't come across a single live oak. Claudia began to doubt her ability to find the spot on the map.

Skip was content to wander the woods holding Claudia's hand, treasure or no treasure. But his faith in the map was dwindling. Claudia tripped, and would have fallen had Skip not been holding her hand.

"Damn!" exclaimed Claudia! "That was coordinated!"

Skip turned to see what Claudia had tripped over, and saw the gray branch of an old tree mostly covered by sand. As he turned to inspect it closer, Claudia yanked his arm again.

"Come on, that oak has got to be here somewhere."

"Wait. Check this out..."

Skip began kicking the sand away from the dead branch. "Maybe we've been looking up instead of where we should've been looking – down!"

Claudia knelt down and with both her hands, cleared away sand from the old branch.

"Live oak?" she asked.

"Looks it. Although it's hard to tell. I'm used to identifying live oaks by the shape of the tree and their enormous size, and their leaves. But if I'm not mistaken, it is the bark of an old live oak. See how it's courser and thicker than the bark on these scrub oaks?" He picked up a piece of the bark for Claudia to inspect.

Claudia's heart raced. She began scooping away the sand frantically, as if the tree was the treasure itself.

"Uh, Claudia," said Skip in a playful tone. "At that rate, you'll have the whole tree dug up in a couple of years!"

"The spade! Get the spade!" Claudia shouted excitedly.

"Where is it?"

"In the boat!"

"Uh Claudia?"

"What?" she responded, beside herself with excitement. Her whole body was shaking.

"With that spade, you'll have the tree unearthed in a year, max!"

"Wise guy! What do you suggest?"

"Well, since we're not digging for buried tree treasure, I'd suggest you save your energy for excavating the real thing."

"And how the hell are we going to find that now that we've located the tree?"

"Scienterrifically, my dear!" Skip answered in a Sherlock Holmes voice.

"Just get the damn shovel!" Claudia shouted, too excited to think clearly.

"Let's stop and think about what we're doing."

"I'm not interested in karma or superstition. All I'm interested in is finding the treasure!"

"I can see that!"

"So help me dig! Or better yet, get the spade!"

"Uh, Claudia..."

"What now?!"

"I don't think there's much of a market for old live oak branches!"

She stopped digging for the first time since they located the oak. Skip had a big grin on his face. And Claudia realized how silly she must look digging at the branch like a dog after a bone.

"Right!" she said, flopping down in the pine needle covered sand. "So what now?"

"If I had the money, I know what I'd do. I'd buy me one of them there fancy electronic treasure locators."

"You mean one of those things the retired folks with lily white legs carry along the beach looking for rings and things?"

"Yup! I think they work off of the same principle as a depth sounder in a boat. That disc on the end is the transducer, and it sends sound waves into the ground. Once it locates something solid, it beeps."

"Great idea! Where can we get one?"

"Maybe at the hardware store in Carrabelle."

"How far is that?"

"About an hour's drive. And I'm going there to weigh the fish in. The only thing is, we need to get to the weigh-in station before 7 PM."

"You'll take me, then?"

"Yeah. Sure. I'd love to. And if we get there on time, I should win a hundred dollars for having the heaviest trout of the day. I'll treat you to dinner."

"Sounds good!" Claudia looked at herself, sand clinging on her legs and arms. "I'll just go like this, if that's O.K."

"Works for me!" Skip chuckled.

He held out his hand, and she reached for it with both hands. But rather than allowing him to pull her up, she gave a sudden jerk, and Skip lost his balance. He nearly landed right on Claudia. Hitting the ground with a thud on the other side of her, their hands still intertwined, he rolled to break the fall, pulling her over him, and their momentum then carried him over her and he felt a sharp pain in his back. Claudia giggled like a child, pleased with herself being able to bring Skip down and rolling in the sand and pine needles. Skip smiled and shook his head. "Didn't know I was that strong, eh?" Claudia asked playfully.

"No. And I didn't know that you had your mind set on killing me, either!" said Skip in a lighthearted way.

"Well, the karma of the treasure's taken over!" she shouted and raised her hands as if to attack him. "The treasure's mine, all mine!"

Claudia noticed Skip grimacing. "What's up, sailor? Is my acting that bad?"

"No, kinda cute, actually. It's just this stick protruding from my back..."

Claudia turned him over slowly, and saw that he wasn't making it up. His back of his shirt was ripped, and blood stained the white cotton. She gently lifted it to see how much damage she had inflicted.

"Damn, Skip, I'm sorry!"

"I'll be alright."

"You've got a scratch about a foot long across your back, and it's bleeding. But not too bad. It's not very deep."

"That's comforting."

"Let's get back and clean it up. I'm sure in a few months you won't even be able to see where it was!"

"Wonderful!" Skip said with a laugh. "This treasure thing is really fun. There you are with sand all over you, looking like a model in a Sports Illustrated bathing suit issue, and here I am, bloody as one of old Billy's victims! We really must do this more often!"

As they walked hand-in-hand back to the boats, Claudia felt bad about what happened to Skip. She blamed herself, knowing that if she hadn't been quite as determined to unearth this treasure, Skip would still be in one piece. Maybe it was a sign for her to slow down. After all, if the treasure was still buried there, it wasn't going anywhere. And if she had learned one thing from the gurus on the streets of Key West, it was that the best times of your life are not in the past or in the future, but in the here-and-now. She squeezed his hand tighter, and smiled that charming smile she had practiced in front of the mirror as a child.

Skip smiled back, wondering what he had gotten himself into. He was so attracted to Claudia, so physically attracted to her that his whole body yearned for her. And he loved seeing her playful side, she seemed so childlike and innocent at times. But he also recognized that she had a temper. One that could ignite and send her into a flurry of cursing that would make a drunken sailor proud. The phrase "like a moth to a flame" echoed in his mind again.

He thought about what kind of influence Claudia would be on his son. He wondered if they would get along, and if the impatient side of Claudia would show itself around Benny, or the childlike playful side that he found so appealing.

His thoughts drifted to his bizarre circumstances. If someone had told him yesterday, before he met Claudia, that he would be combing the woods of St. Joseph's peninsula with an attractive woman who was hell-bent on finding a pirate's treasure, and who had just accepted his invitation to dinner, he would have thought them insane. But here they were. "Life's a trip!" He said half out loud, half to himself.

"What?" Claudia asked.

"I said, don't trip! We don't want to find any more live oaks. One's enough for today, eh?"

"Yeah. That's got to be the one, doesn't it?"

"Seems to be in about the right place, according to the map."

"What do you think happened to it?" asked Claudia.

"Got too close to that cursed treasure, I'd say. Probably touched it with a root!"

"No, really. How did it die? They are such hardy trees."

"Even the hardiest of trees can be humbled by the forces of nature; hurricanes, twisters, floods. Who knows what caused the downfall of that tree. Maybe Bowlegs came out here with an ax and chopped it down at just the right angle so it would fall on top of where he buried the treasure as extra insurance that no one would find it."

"I hadn't thought of that. This land has seen a lot – from peaceful Indians gathering conch to bloody pirates slinking through the forest."

"Yeah. But the worst is yet to come!"

"What could be worse than pirates?"

"Development. Indiscriminate development. Pirates took people's possessions. Even took their lives. In a few generations, no one will remember but the historians. But development rapes the earth of its beauty and its wildlife and its unspoiled character. And even after generations have passed, the scar will remain on the land. It will never be the same again."

"That's sad. But what about those folks who get to live and play by the sea? Don't they have a right to pursue their dream?"

"Yeah. I guess. But the folks who get to build where hammocks with shady red cedars once stood, where forty-foot dunes were not uncommon, have tons of money. The wealthiest people in society. I'd feel a little bit better about it if poor folks could enjoy it, too."

"Isn't that what state parks are for – so that everyone can enjoy the beach, and to keep it the way nature intended?"

"Yeah, but I still can't understand how rich people can develop pristine areas, like the west end of St. George's island, then close it off to everyone else. That's not right."

"They did that?"

"Yeah. They used to allow people to go in, for a fee, and fish at Bob Sike's cut, but now they don't even allow that any more. Something is wrong with a group of people telling the public they can't access a cut that was paid for with government money. It should be open to anyone who wants to wet a line there. Not just to those who can afford a house in the Plantation, as it's called. And not just to those who can access it by boat."

"But Skip, if someone offered you a house on the beach, wouldn't you take it?"

"I've thought about that – how nice it would be to own a house with the view of the Gulf. But I have mixed feelings. On one hand, I'd love to retire there, spend my days combing the beach, fishing in the surf, reading a book under a beach umbrella in my own back yard, writing a novel. Who wouldn't love that? On the other hand, what happens when all the dunes and natural areas disappear? Maybe the answer is a moratorium on new waterfront development. But then those dwellings that exist now will only get more expensive, more out of the reach of the common man. I don't know. It's a dilemma."

"Yeah. It sure was beautiful back in the woods!" remarked Claudia, as she stepped on the fine white sand bordering the bay. "I'd hate to see it developed."

"Me too!" said Skip, turning to pull her closer.

Claudia looked deep into Skip's eyes. Had she had found someone who she could trust? Someone she could rely on. Someone with whom she could share the secrets of her soul. But she had felt that before, and had been proven wrong. Remembering how those other men had wanted to own her, to control her, to have her all to themselves, she wondered if Skip would act the same way. She hoped not, but she was not about to take a chance – that had been too painful to endure, too much like her mother who wanted to control her every move. No, she would not get herself into that situation again. She was going to take her time, get to know Skip intimately, not physically, but know his mind and his true nature, before she got herself into another situation that would result in a broken heart. She had had enough of them for one lifetime. Three broken hearts was plenty.

Skip sensed that Claudia was feeling uncomfortable, and refrained from getting any closer. How he wanted to hold her, kiss her, feel her presence pressed against his body. But he knew that the flames of infatuation blinded even the most cautious man, and when those flames were ignited, there was no way to put them out. Only time could do that. And the more he held her hand, the more he looked into her eyes, the more he touched her sexy body, the more those flames ignited a passion that, like the breaking of a wave on the sand castle of his resolve, could wipe it away in one fell swoop.

"Race you back to the marina!" he said, knowing that his skiff was no match for her rented outfit.

"You ain't got a prayer, buster!" Claudia yelled, splashing her way toward her boat.

Skip checked his live well, just to be sure the monster was still there. It was, but it was no longer alive. The gorgeous, powerful fish laid on its side on the bottom, never to roam the bay she called home again. It saddened Skip to have killed such a pretty creature. At the same time, he was excited knowing that he would have an excellent chance of winning first place this year, and showing Buck and Lucas that he was as good a fisherman as they were. He desperately wanted to take that much needed money home, and buy Benny some of those things he wanted for his birthday. And buy him new clothes from a store rather than at yard sales. If his luck held out, and he caught a large flounder that placed in the top three, he could even win the tournament, and the fishing trip to Costa Rica. After all, he still had a full day and a half of fishing left. The tournament didn't end until Sunday afternoon.

Claudia had her anchor in the boat and was idling toward deeper water before Skip got the old Evinrude started. They raced off across the bay, Skip sweeping across the wake of the larger boat, crisscrossing back and forth in the man-made waves. Claudia kept the throttle half open so Skip could keep up. The world was the two of them, the bay, the seagulls, and the welcomed spray that splashed their faces. They skimmed across the surface like the gray-green dolphins they saw cruising in the glassy clear waters of St. Joseph's bay.

SKIP DROVE CLAUDIA back to the Treasure Bay Lodge, and promised to return in a half-hour to take her to Carrabelle. Back at the campsite, he put the gator trout in the bottom of his food cooler under what ice remained. Buying another ten pound bag of ice at the marina store, he dumped it into the cooler and lifted the cooler into the bed of his old pickup truck. He quickly shaved, took a shower, dabbed some cologne on his neck, and raced back down the road to the motel. Claudia was waiting for him, dressed in sandals, blue jeans, and a halter top. Her hair was still damp, and the scent of an exotic flower that Skip had never smelled before wafted in the air.

"You look great!"

"Thanks! You don't smell like fish anymore!"

"Nice of you to notice! How do you like my legs?" Skip asked. Not having any long pants with him, he had to wear shorts. "I cut myself shaving!"

"I hate when that happens!" said Claudia. "How's your back?"

"Sore. Best not to let anyone know about that deep scratch, though. They'll think we were doing something else in those woods instead of looking for treasure."

"I'm pretty excitable," cooed Claudia, "but I don't scratch."

"Darn!"

Laughing, Skip looked at his watch. "We only have 40 minutes to get to the scales at the Carrabelle Marina. I hope we make it."

"What happens if we don't?"

"Well, for one thing, I'm out a hundred dollars. For another thing, I've got to drag this fish around with me for another day, and think about whether I want to limit my fishing and run all the way back to Carrabelle tomorrow night to get there before the weigh-in is over."

"What time does the hardware store close?"

"I'm clueless. They don't stay open late, that's for sure. Nothing but the bars and restaurants stay open late in these parts."

"I hope we get there on time. And I hope they have a metal detector."

"Yeah. It sure would be the way to go."

"Are you going to help me find the treasure tomorrow?" Claudia said with sugar in her voice. "I don't know how I would lift a big chest out of the sand by my little old self."

"From what I've seen of your 'little ol' self', I'd say you'd manage just fine!"

"Really, I would like you there when I find it."

"Yeah, and I'd like to be there, too. But I'd also like to win this tournament. I want to see the look on Lucas and Buck's faces when they announce the winner. Benny and I could sure use the money. Best of all, the overall winner gets an all expense paid fishing trip to Costa Rica for two."

"Wonderful!" Claudia jabbed sarcastically. "Do they have any undiscovered pirate treasure down there?"

"Probably. Might even come across one of those dead buried trees you seem so fond of!"

"Great! Count me in!"

Skip's imagination ran wild thinking of five days and nights with Claudia in Costa Rica. That would blow his resolve big time. He would never be able to resist her given those circumstances. Oh, well, he thought to himself, chances are that he wouldn't win the whole thing anyway, but, if he did, he'd deal with that problem when it arose. His fishing buddy Todd would be disappointed not to be going to Costa Rica with him, but he'd understand once he saw Claudia.

The loud truck bumped down the road, engine whining as Skip pressed the accelerator close to the floor.

"Can't you go any faster?"

"No. I can't. Wish I could!"

"Piece of junk!" Claudia kidded him.

"Yeah, it may be a piece of junk. But it's a helluva lot faster than the piece of junk you own."

"Too true!" Claudia said, thinking about the Fiat she abandoned in Apalachicola. "I wonder if it got towed away yet."

"That'd be a blessing!"

"It's a fun car. But I can't seem to keep it running."

"Yeah. Don't feel bad. It's the nature of the beast. Not you."

Skip looked at his watch. "Damn! We're just approaching Apalachicola, and it's already 6:30 – I doubt we're going to make Carabelle by 7!"

Skip had gotten behind a large motor home that was cruising slowly down the road in no particular hurry to get to the next peaceful destination. Knowing the truck would struggle to accelerate and get around the large home-on-wheels, Skip dropped from 5th gear to 3rd gear, and raced toward the rear bumper of the vehicle. Checking the rearview mirror before pulling into the opposite lane, he noticed a dark-colored pickup truck catching up to him, travelling at a high rate of speed. Skip backed off the bumper of the RV, deciding it would be better to let the speeding pickup pass first. The driver of the pickup raced within inches of Skip's bumper before swerving recklessly into the left lane to pass both vehicles. He whizzed by the noisy pickup and was halfway around the RV when he suddenly slammed on his brakes. As the RV lumbered passed him, he swung the pickup in right behind it, narrowly missing a head-on crash with an oncoming car. Skip leaned on his horn, to no avail, and jerked the steering wheel to his right – it was his only chance to avoid a collision with the out-of-control truck. As Skip and Claudia skidded on the gravel in the parking lot of an abandoned seafood wholesaler, Skip noticed the rebel flag and a pirate's skull and cross bones decals on the rear window of the wild truck. The driver of the charcoal-colored truck gave them the finger.

Smash! Claudia's head hit the ceiling of the cab, as the right tire bounced over a piece of concrete in the pebble-strewn lot. Skip turned hard to the right in an effort to control the skid, and the truck teetered a second before responding and then tipped dangerously to the other side. Wrenching the steering wheel to the left, the truck straightened out and came to a screeching halt inches before slamming into the abandoned brick building.

"Are you alright?" Skip asked, aware that Claudia's head had hit the top of the cab as the truck bounced over what had once been part of the concrete parking retainer.

"I guess," said his visibly shaken passenger. "No thanks to that creep! That asshole nearly killed us!"

"Tell me about it! He must have been drunk, or something!"

"Are you O.K.?" she asked Skip.

"Yeah, but I think we have a flat!"

Hopping out, Skip ran around the front of the truck to inspect the right front tire, which was flat as a pancake. "Well, there goes any chance of getting that $100 for the daily leader prize."

"Hey, that's the least of our worries!" said Claudia, who had joined him in assessing the damage. "We could have been killed!"

"Yeah, and the jerk didn't even bother to stop to see if we were O.K. Wonder where he was going in such a hurry."

"Probably to weigh in a fish!" said Claudia. "He's probably one of those crazy tournament fishermen who would risk his life to get to the scales on time!"

Skip looked at Claudia sheepishly. "You mean kinda like me?"

"Yeah, kinda like you. 'Cept a bit more insane."

"Oh, so you think I'm insane, eh?"

"Uh, huh! When it comes to fishing, anyway."

"That may be so. But, then again, who was it today diggin' like a mad dog trying to unbury a dead tree?"

"O.K. So maybe I'm a bit touched myself."

Skip pulled the rusty four-way tire iron from the bed of his pickup and retrieved the jack from behind the seat. Cranking the spare down from its perch under the truck bed, he rolled it to the front of the truck. In a few minutes the tire had been changed, the flat was back in place under the truck bed, and they were on their way to Carabelle again.

"At least it won't be too late to get a metal detector from the hardware store, right?"

"If this was Tallahassee, that would be true. But this is Carabelle. And they just don't keep the same hours down here."

Skip had been driving slowly through the streets of old Apalachicola, still a bit shaky from the close call they had just experienced.

"Hurry up, then," pushed Claudia. "I don't know what I'll do if the store is closed and I can't get one tonight."

"You can kick back and relax and go fishing with me tomorrow." Skip suggested, knowing that would be the last thing Claudia would want to do, being hell-bent on uncovering her treasure.

"You know, I'd like to take you up on that offer some day. But first there's the little matter of silver coins and gold doubloons that I must take care of first, my dear!"

"Fine. Go ahead and pass up a beautiful day on the water for a day digging in the sand and getting your pretty self all dirty. See if I care!"

"I'd rather be sandy than smell like fish slime. Besides, the only dirty I plan on getting is filthy rich!"

"But who's going to protect you from the fierce black racer snakes?" Skip teased.

"I can take care of myself. No little snake is going to keep me from getting my hands on that treasure!"

The Tillie Miller Bridge rose above the tannic acid-stained waters of the Carabelle River. Skip looked at his watch. "Seven-twenty! Missed a hundred dollars by twenty minutes!"

As the pickup glided down the bridge into Carabelle, another pickup pulled out from the weigh-in area of the Carabelle Marina. It had a rebel flag decal on the left side of the rear window, and a skull-and-crossbones on the right side. "Damn!" yelled Claudia. "That's him – that's the jerk who almost killed us!"

"Geez! That looks like the guy who is camping next to me at Presnells!"

"Catch up to him! I'm going to give him a piece of my mind." Claudia yelled.

Skip had the urge to give the driver a piece of his mind too. He desperately wanted to tell him off. On the other hand, pickup driving men in small towns often carried guns, and he wondered how smart it would be to confront him. Especially if he was drunk. And, Claudia needed to get to the hardware store before it closed.

"Claudia, let's not."

"What? Why not? He almost killed us!"

"Yeah, I know. But let's save it for another time. Let's get to the hardware store before it closes. Besides, what if he's got a gun? It could be a bad scene."

Claudia hadn't thought about that possibility. She never carried a weapon. And she suspected Skip didn't either. The last thing in the world she wanted was to put Skip in harm's way again – she had hurt him enough already between the scratches on his legs and the scratch on his back.

"You're right."

"Do me a favor and take that tag down. There's a pen and some paper in the glove compartment."

"Good idea," Claudia finished writing the tag number down just as Skip pulled into the hardware store on the left. The parking lot was empty, and, looking at Claudia, he could see she was dejected. The sign on the front door indicated that they had closed at seven, and wouldn't open again until Saturday morning at eight.

"Hungry?" Skip offered, not knowing what else to say.

"Hungry? Hungry? No, I'm not hungry. Actually, I am hungry!" Claudia shouted. "I'm hungry for that treasure, and nothing's going to stop me from getting it."

"You're not suggesting we break in, are you?"

"No. I wouldn't go that far. Is there a phone number on the door in case of emergencies?"

"Yeah. Under the hours."

"I'll be right back."

Claudia hopped out, pen and paper still in hand, and wrote down the number. Pointing to the convenience store across the street, she said, "Meet me there!" and took off running.

By the time Skip got across the street, Claudia had already begun dialing the number. After a few minutes of conversation, she jumped back into the truck.

"Any luck?" asked Skip.

"Yes and no. They don't carry any metal detectors there, but they do at a store called the "Beachcomber" on St. George's Island."

"What time does it close?"

"The guy I talked to said he thought they stayed open until nine on weekends during the summer. We may be in luck. Where is St. George's Island?"

"Down the road apiece. Remember just before we got into East Point, that little fishing village we went through? There was a sign that said St. George's, and a bridge that crossed the bay."

"Tell you the truth, Skip, I wasn't paying attention. How far is it from here?"

"Not but thirty minutes away."

"Let's go. If we make it there before they close, I'll buy you dinner."

"Deal. On one condition."

"What's that?"

"We stop and see what the largest trout is on the Daily Winner's board at the marina."

"How long will that take?"

"Just an extra minute."

"O.K."

The board was full of daily winner fish weights. Every category had some fish weighed in except the flounder division. Skip was relieved to find that the largest speckled trout weighed in was five pounds, twelve ounces. He was sure his weighed at least seven pounds.

"Does the one you caught top that one?" Claudia asked.

"Easily."

"Do you know that guy?"

"Dennis Wade? No. Never heard of him. But if I can get back here tomorrow before seven, I'll have another chance to win the daily prize of a hundred dollars, and it will no doubt save a lot of trout's lives."

"How so?"

"Once folks know that a trout over seven pounds has been weighed in, and a five-pound twelve-ounce fish, any trout they catch not in that class, they'll probably release, knowing that it's not going to place."

"How many prizes are there in each category?"

"First, second and third. First place gets four-hundred-and-fifty dollars and a plaque, second two-hundred-and-fifty dollars and third a hundred dollars. Then the one with the most points overall wins the grand prize – that fishing trip to Costa Rica I was telling you about."

"Oh, yeah. The one you and I are going on, right?"

"Yes! Keep thinking positive, Claudia!"

As they crossed back over the Tillie Miller bridge heading west, the sky began to turn a pastel blue with hints of pink on the edges of the wispy clouds scattered on the horizon, promising a beautiful north Florida sunset.

"Did you say you were from Tallahassee?" Claudia asked after remarking how pretty the sky was becoming.

"You remembered."

"How did a city boy like you get into fishing?"

"City boy? Hell, I'm no city boy! Tallahassee's not much of a city. Well, at least it didn't used to be. Tallahassee was as pristine and quiet as this area when I was a boy. I guess that's why I love it down here at the coast – it reminds me of Tallahassee when I was a kid."

"I can't imagine Tallahassee ever looking like this!"

"It was all woods and water and creeks and fields – a young boy's paradise. I was born in a neighborhood that was mostly woods and greenery. It felt like I was in the country even though we were just a mile away from the capitol building. We used to find Indian arrowheads in the creek that ran through the woods. We'd run into all kinds of wildlife – turkeys, rabbits, foxes, hawks and owls and snakes. Indianhead Acres was a great place to grow up."

"You lived by a creek?"

"Right across the street from it, actually. My dad worked for the Department of Transportation, and my mother stayed home and raised us. On weekends sometimes, we'd drive down to St. George's

Island and spend the day fishing and swimming. I could never get enough of that when I was a kid. I was always bothering my folks to take us to the beach, even in the winter."

"Did they?"

"Sure. But not often enough for my liking. I guess that's why I'm so crazy about fishing now – when I was a kid and couldn't control what I did, I didn't get to fish as often as I would have liked, so now I'm making up for it."

"Hmm. Makes sense."

"My dad loved being out on the beach. He loved the bay, loved the birds that flew around him looking for scraps. Loved the fish that seemed to be everywhere in the surf and the inlets back then."

"Where's your dad now?"

"He passed away a few years ago. Cancer. He was a smoker."

"Oh. Sorry to hear that. I lost my father when I was three."

"What happened?"

"Car accident."

"My father was fifty-nine when he died. How old was yours?"

"I don't know. Maybe around thirty-two. Mother didn't talk about him much. I think she was angry at him for dying."

"Do you have any brothers or sisters?"

"One worthless brother. He's a year younger than me."

"Why worthless? Y'all don't get along?"

"It's not that. We get along O.K. It's just that he's in and out of jail. And I can never count on him for anything."

"Oh. And your mother?"

"Died last year."

"I'm sorry."

"How about you, are you an only child?"

"No. I have a younger brother and sister."

"Are they in Tallahassee too?"

"No. Scattered, like most families nowadays. My sister married and is living on Long Island in New York. My brother's married too. He lives in Ft. Lauderdale."

"See them often?"

"Once in a while. Every year or two they come to town to visit mom."

"Are you close?"

"Yes, we are. We get along well. I wish they lived closer and I got to see them more often. It would be nice for Benny to spend time with his cousins."

"How old is Benny?"

"Six. He's a great boy! You'll like him."

"I'm sure," answered Claudia, wondering how smart it would be to get involved with someone who had a child.

"And your wife?"

"Ex-wife. I've been divorced for three years now."

"Do you two get along?"

"Good enough. We cooperate well when it comes to Benny. But when it comes to money, there's a lot of friction."

"Any chance of getting back together?"

"Not in this lifetime!"

"Does she have custody of Benny?"

"No. It's split custody. We both have him half the time."

"Must be hard on the boy."

"Yeah. Sometimes. But he's getting used to it now. He'll love you."

"Why?"

"I just have that feeling that you two will hit it off. He's really fun to be around. Wait and see."

"How come you didn't take him fishing with you?"

"Too young. One day I will, but a full day on the water is a bit much for a six year old."

"What do you do for a living?"

"I work for the State. I'm in Public Assistance."

"Public Assistance?"

"Yeah, you know, Food Stamps and cash and Medicaid. I determine benefits for the clients."

"Sounds challenging."

"It is. Most folks are really nice. But there's a small minority that are a pain-in-the-ass. Then again, that's no different than the rest of society, eh? Most people are easy to get along with, but then there's that small minority that have to make life hard for everyone."

"I've met a few of those in my time."

Apalachicola Bay stretched east and west as far as the eye could see from the top of the St. George's Island Bridge.

"Lovely sunset!" Claudia remarked.

"I'll say! My father would have loved it. Reminds me of the day he died."

"How so?"

"He'd been in the hospital for twelve days, and I went to visit him each day. On the twelfth day he told me that, since the next day was Saturday, that he didn't want me to come visit him – he wanted me to go fishing down the coast."

"Did you?"

"I told him he was way more important than fishing. But he insisted. So I went. The Spanish mackerel were biting, and what had started out as a few hours of trolling turned into an all day fishing trip. The sun was setting before we got off of the water, and when I got back to town, and called the hospital, he had passed away."

"Sad."

"I shouldn't have gone fishing that day. Should have stayed in town."

Tears rolled down Skip's face. They had reached the top of the St. George's Island Bridge. Claudia wiped Skip's tears off of his cheek with the gentle dab of an old napkin she found on the seat, and squeezed his right hand. To the left and right the waters of the bay were calm, quiet, well protected this day by the barrier island. Pastels of blue and pink began to illuminate the lofty clouds, gulls circled and dove after a school of pilchards that dimpled the water's surface, and a pair of pelicans flew alongside the truck, then veered off toward the setting sun.

Claudia wasn't used to seeing a man show his emotions. She didn't remember her father at all, and her brother never allowed himself to open up to her. The boyfriends and lovers she had been with acted as if a man's job was to hide his feelings, so much so that she had begun to wonder if they actually had feelings to hide. This man was so different than others she had known. Rough and tumble on the exterior. Soft and caring on the inside. She liked that. She liked that a lot. She smiled at him, and he smiled back through his watery, blood shot eyes.

He wondered if he had told Claudia too much. Would revealing his vulnerable, soft side be a turn-off to her? Would she be less interested in him, knowing that he was divorced and had a son, and wasn't making a ton of money? What was he doing, anyway, sharing his past with someone who he barely knew? After all, she hadn't shared much of her history with him, yet.

But as if she read his mind, and wanted to dispel his doubts, Claudia again brushed the tears from his face. Held his hand. Gave him a look of understanding and empathy. Perhaps he had done the right thing.

"There's the Beachcomber," Skip said as they turned down a side street. "And it's still open."

The turquoise walls, large bay windows and white trim looked like an oasis in a desert to Claudia. She instinctively knew it could take months to located that treasure without a metal detector, and she hoped with all her heart that they still had one left.

"Today's your lucky day!" said the owner, brown Panama hat askew on his head, a smirk emanating from under the bushiest of mustaches. "I've got one left. It's a beauty. Sensitive yet rugged..."

"Ah – just like you, Skip!" she teased.

"You'd better jump on it then! Equipment that fine only comes once in a lifetime!"

"How much?" Claudia asked, holding the shaft, and examining the circular transducer at the bottom and the adjustable arm brace at the top.

"Hundred and fifty."

"Hundred and fifty!" she exclaimed, shocked.

"Yup. And I'll throw in the carrying case." He held up a black vinyl case with a shoulder strap.

"How generous!" Claudia said sarcastically. Reaching in her purse, she pulled out a wad of folded bills.

Thinking that he had underestimated her finances, Skip's mouth dropped. Then Claudia began counting out the proceeds of tips earned as a stewardess, in ones and fives. It cut the once bulky wad in half.

Back in the truck, Claudia beamed. "All right! Where do you want to eat?"

"I'm starving, but I'd like to treat you," said Skip, thinking that Claudia was about out of money.

"No way. First, I don't go back on deals, and you got us here before they closed. Second, I owe ya."

"How do you figure?"

"Hell, Skip – you gave me a ride when my car broke down, you came and checked on me in the storm this afternoon, protected me from those brutes, saved me from the "deadly" black racer, then drove me all over the coast looking for this metal detector. At least let me buy you dinner."

"Is that all the money you have left?"

"No. There's more where that came from – it's in the bank," Claudia lied. "Besides, what difference does it make? I'm going to be independently wealthy tomorrow!"

"Oh, right! I forgot. O.K. Let's eat in Apalachicola – I know a place there that's got great food and it's less expensive than the restaurants here on the island."

"Sounds good."

Crossing the two-span bridge back to the mainland, Skip and Claudia were mesmerized by the gorgeous sunset, now spread in full glory across the western sky. God had seen fit to fill the sky with hues of orange, pink, purple, red and blue. The beauty far exceeded anything any person had ever painted on a canvas. And no picture from any camera ever made could do it justice.

CHAPTER X
UMBRELLAS

The sign on Market Street read "Experience Seafood – BOSS OYSTER" above a picture of an oyster character working tongs aboard a red skiff named "Shut Up and Shuck". Skip couldn't find a parking space in front of the restaurant, so he parked on the street beyond the bar – a choice that was to benefit the two adventurers later that night.

Walking on loose, bleached oyster shells that comprised the parking lot surface, Claudia was reminded of Key West by the funky look of the building. It was lime green with fuchsia-colored posts, window frames and trim, and had a tin roof. Pastels were real popular in the would-be capital of the Conch Republic, and she missed the coconut culture of the wild city.

Fastened above the rickety door was a black sign with "Boss Oyster" written in bold white letters. Holding the door open for Claudia, Skip said, "I hope the no-smoking section is O.K. with you?"

"Sure. In fact, I'd prefer to sit outside, if that's possible."

"Yeah, this way," Skip took Claudia's hand and headed for the well-worn wooden stairs that led to the patio deck above. Claudia felt somewhat uncomfortable being seen in public holding Skip's hand, and didn't like being led by anyone. But Skip's hand was warm and strong and he caressed her hand rather than squeezed, and she had to admit to herself that it felt good to touch a man again. Maybe it had been too long since she had the pleasure of being with a lover. Perhaps, after the treasure was hers, she would indulge herself in the arms of a man once more. She noticed herself getting more comfortable being with Skip as she got to know him better. He eased her up the stairs like a prince escorting a fair maiden to the dance floor.

Rusty ceiling fans with white blades circulated the musty, thick air. The antique license plates on the walls spoke of earlier times, arousing Claudia's curiosity about the history of the town. The fishing nets draped from the ceiling and walls, the stuffed game fish, the antique fishing equipment and the pictures of Apalachicola residents long since gone filled her with a sense that she had walked into a museum of sorts. The stuffed fox stared at her, as the smell of beer and fresh shucked oysters awakened her appetite. The place was packed, due largely to the boisterous fishermen who traveled to the Apalachicola area to compete in the Big Bend Saltwater Classic. A few local women mingled with the fishermen, and some older couples squeezed themselves into corner tables so as not to be jostled by the rowdy crowd.

The music could barely be heard above the din, it was a Jimmy Buffet tune, and Claudia smiled when she heard the words "Yes I am a pirate. Two hundred years too late. The cannons don't thunder, there's nothing to plunder, I'm an over forty victim of fate. Life ain't so great, arriving too late." The song brought back memories of good times she had in Key West. The words also reminded her of the quest she was on, and aroused anxiety about the possibility that she would be arriving too late. She had spent little time thinking about the treasure having already been discovered. That would be a heartbreak!

Skirting the curved, mahogany-looking round bar, snaking their way through the crowd, they passed the partition that separated the inside patio from the outside patio, and found themselves overlooking the Apalachicola River. Upriver, large commercial fishing boats lay silently against the rickety old docks, unsure of whether the dock was holding them or they were supporting the docks. Moored at the docks in back of the restaurant were sport fishing vessels with their shiny white gelcoats, gleaming in the spotlights that hung from the sturdy poles that anchored the floating platforms of the boat slips. Charter boats boasted names such as *Thoreaully Peaceful*, *Reel Thing*, *Wet Dream*, *The Four Sea Sons*, *Love Ta Fish*, *Pharaoh Seas*, and *Playing Hookey*. The commercial boats were named *Day Star*, *La Mercedes*, *Little Bear*, *Buddy's Boys*, *Pappa Ronnie* and *Southern Lady*.

Skip and Claudia settled down at the only table that was not occupied. It was at the very end of the porch, and partially screened from the noise of the crowd inside by a hip-high wood partition and thick plastic strips that draped from the ceiling. The plastic prevented a driving rain from soaking the inside of the restaurant, and kept some of the air conditioning from escaping.

Claudia, having seen Apalachicola on the way through earlier in the day, had been fascinated by the small southern town. The antique stores, art shops and mom-and-pop restaurants were a nice contrast to the strip-malls and shopping centers of towns she had seen along the east coast of Florida. The city hall looked like it had been there since the turn of the 20th century, and some of the churches and Victorian houses looked even older.

"Tell me a story about Apalachicola."

"Not fair!" Skip replied with a smile.

"What's not fair?"

"Me telling all the stories."

"I don't have many to tell."

"There is one you know that I'd love to hear."

"Oh?"

"Yeah. The one about yourself. How about it?"

"What do you want to know?"

"The whole story. Where you were born and raised. What your parents were like. What you did before we met. That kind of stuff. The whole story of Claudia."

"It's really quite boring."

"I'll suffer through it."

"Alright. But then you have to tell me a story about Apalachicola. And it better be a good one!"

"You got it."

A harried looking waitress drawled "Y'all care for any drinks?" as she set menus in front of them. Her red skirt was neatly pressed and rose above knees that could have belonged to a maid. Her lacey white blouse seemed out of place, this restaurant not being the kind of place that would warrant such attire, and the strong arms of the waitress looked like they would be more accustomed to being clad in a T-shirt with the sleeves rolled up. It seemed to Skip there was not an ounce of fat on her body, and her ample breasts were pushed up by a bra designed for such feats. Tattoos of three crosses adorned the back of her tan right hand, reminding Skip of the crosses someone had placed on an oyster bar in the middle of Apalachicola Bay.

"I'll have a frozen daiquiri. How about you, Claudia? It's my treat, remember."

"I'll have a Chivas on the rocks," said Claudia, looking for a re-action on Skip's face. When she didn't get one, she thought he might have more money than she imagined.

As the waitress sashayed back to the bar, Claudia asked, "Are you sure you can afford this?"

"That four-hundred-and-fifty dollar first place is as good as mine!" Skip bragged. "There hasn't been a fish that big weighed in for three years. Guaranteed! Done deal! No one is gonna beat that monster!" Unfortunately for Skip, Claudia was not the only one listening to their conversation.

"I see you're not taking any chances. At first, I was wondering what you were doing when I saw you lift the cooler and lock it in the cab. Then I remembered that fish of yours. What makes you think someone would steal it?"

"I don't. But like you said, I'm not taking any chances. I'll rest a lot easier when I've weighed it in. Especially with characters like Buck and Lucas on the loose."

"I heard that asshole!" bellowed a deep voice from two tables down.

Claudia and Skip's faces turned beet red as they turned to see who had overheard their conversation. Buck was sitting with Lucas, and had turned toward the couple, his huge stubby middle finger raised in ire toward them.

"It's our lucky night!" shouted Skip. "Buy you two a drink?"

If looks could kill, Claudia would have done Skip in. "What the hell are you doing?" she uttered between clenched teeth. "Do you want them to join us?"

"Hell, no!" shouted Buck. Lucas was looking as embarrassed as Skip and Claudia. "We don't let no brown trout fishing city boy buy us drinks! It'd probably be one of them pansy-assed frozen drinks with a umbrella stickin' outta it!"

The waitress brushed by Buck carrying Skip and Claudia's drinks. To Skip's horror, his frozen strawberry daiquiri was sporting a paper parasol. "Frozen daiquiri and Chivas on the rocks?" the waitress said, setting the daiquiri in front of Skip and the whiskey in front of Claudia.

"Thanks!" Claudia exclaimed, way too loud, as she quickly switched drinks with Skip. "Bottoms up!" she said cheerily, smiling at him, and, pushing the umbrella aside, took a big gulp of the frozen concoction.

"Bottoms up!" Skip said in a hearty sailor voice, and chugged the whiskey. In his haste, some sloshed down the wrong pipe, and he started gagging. After a few very embarrassing seconds, he was able to clear his throat and announce "Swallowed another ice cube! I hate when that happens!"

"Y'all ready to order, honey?" The waitress asked, giving Skip an odd look.

Buck interrupted, "I hope you have a special on brown trout tonight, 'cause that's his favorite!"

The waitress, sensing trouble brewing, sauntered over to Buck. Grabbing his hairy left ear, she yanked his head around so he was looking at Lucas. "You just mind your own business, buster, and I'll mind mine. I'll letcha know when I need your help!"

Buck, for once in his life, was speechless.

"I'll make him behave himself!" droned Lucas, obviously drunk.

"Well, y'all ready to order?" asked the waitress again.

"Not quite. Can we get an appetizer while we're making up our minds?" Skip responded.

"Sure. What'll it be, sugar?"

"What would you like, Claudia? They have great oysters Rockefeller and fried calamari. You peel-em shrimp are excellent, too."

"I haven't had calamari in forever. Let's have that."

The waitress nodded. "And another round?"

"Not for me!" Skip was quick to answer.

"I'll have another one," said Claudia. "Minus the umbrella, and bring an extra straw, please."

"You got it." As she walked by Buck, she ran her arm across his muscular back. "Y'all behave, now."

Buck waited until she was out of sight before getting up and staggering to Skip and Claudia's table. "Son, I sure hope that little dingy of yours doesn't git in our way tomorrow. 'Cause if it does, we gonna see jus' how good a submarine it'll make – if ya catch my drift!"

As Lucas got up to leave with Buck, he nearly fell over backwards into the table behind him, spilling beer on an angry fisherman's lap.

"Watch it, buddy!" the man yelled at Lucas. Buck turned and walked back to the table that held the four fishermen, none the size of Buck, but all as rough and tumble looking.

"You got something to say to my friend, here?" he asked threateningly, putting an arm around his drunk companion.

Silence. The waitress rushed back, grabbed Buck by the collar, and pulled him into the covered part of the restaurant. "I asked you nice to behave yourself, now you're outta here!" She swung him toward the stairs.

"I was leavin' anyhow, missey! No need to be so rough!"

Claudia, looking in the direction of the commotion Buck had made, suddenly turned pale.

"You O.K.?" Skip asked.

"Yeah," Claudia lied. Thinking her eyes had deceived her, she looked again and confirmed who she thought she had seen.

"Looks like you just saw a ghost!"

"You might say that. A ghost from the past."

"Who?" Skip asked, turning to look.

"No one. Never mind."

Skip could see that he wasn't going to get her talking about what or who she had seen. But it made him uncomfortable. He sensed someone's presence there, somebody that was linked to Claudia's past. He had the feeling that somehow it threatened not only Claudia, but himself.

Thinking it prudent not to pursue the subject, Skip asked "If you've made up your mind what you are going to order, tell me about yourself."

"As I said, not much to tell."

"Tell me about your brother."

"Can you disown a brother?"

"Don't think so."

"If I could, I would. Although, he's had a tough life. Grew up without a father. Dad died when he was two, like I said."

"Car accident, right? How'd it happen?"

"I'm not real sure – my mother didn't like to talk about it much. She said he was a car salesman, and he was with a customer who was test driving a new Corvette. Anyhow, the driver was going way too fast. It was raining, and he slammed on the brakes. The car skidded into a parked truck. The crash killed both him and my father."

"Sad. I'm sorry. You said your mother took it pretty hard?"

"She was devastated. Faced with raising myself and my brother on her own. Dad didn't have a lot in the way of life insurance when he was killed, so it was a struggle to keep food on the table. She was working at a bank, we never had much spending money. But we got by."

"Where was that?"

"Ft. Lauderdale."

"Did you like the town?"

"Yeah, it was alright. The canals and creeks that came off the intracoastal waterway were fun to play in. They were full of fish and blue claw crabs back then. It was really kind of nice. Only thing was there were wealthy children, and the rest of us. The rest of us barely had a pot to piss in. The rich kids had everything you could imagine – cars, boats, and lots of spending money. Didn't seem fair they should have so much and us so little."

"And your brother?"

"He had it pretty bad. Mom always looked after me, kept me under her wing, wouldn't let me out of her sight most of the time. I hated that. But as protective of me as she was, she was a whole lot less protective of him. She said she saw a lot of my father in Harris, and I think deep down she was pretty angry at my dad for getting himself killed and leaving only her to raise us. She doted on me, and took a laissez-faire attitude toward him."

"He kept on acting up and misbehaving. My theory is that that was the only way he knew of getting her attention. The older he got, the worse his behavior became. Suspended from school, in trouble with the law for shop lifting and breaking and entering. Mother was at her wits' end with him, and just gave up. There's only so much a parent can do, I guess. She tried to talk some sense into him, but he never listened."

"Where is he now?"

Claudia looked toward the other end of the patio again, then back at Skip. "Don't know. Don't care. The last time I talked to him was the beginning of the week. Thought I'd do him a favor, maybe help him turn his life around. Asked him to come down and help me find this treasure. He had just gotten out of jail near Atlanta, and I thought if I could get him on his feet for once, he'd straighten out."

"So, is he coming?"

"No."

"Why not?"

"Don't know, and, at this point, it's hard for me to care. He was supposed to meet me at the Treasure Bay Lodge yesterday when you dropped me off. Never showed up."

"Was that yesterday?" Skip said in a daze. "Seems like last week for some reason."

"Yes. Yesterday. But true to form, he didn't make it."

Skip was relieved, on one hand, that it was her brother she was supposed to meet, and not a lover. On the other hand, Skip felt sorry for Claudia, hearing what a tough time she had in her youth.

"So what did you do after high school?"

"Got out of Lauderdale as quick as I could. Needed to get away from my mother. Lived in Cocoa Beach for ten years or so. Learned how to surf, met a guy, got a broken heart. Moved on."

"Moved on to where?"

"Key West. Learned how to dive. Met a guy. Broke my heart. Same old story."

"You said your mother passed away?"

"Died last year."

"Sorry to hear that."

"And now here I am on a wild goose chase after some buried treasure." She shook her head and smiled a sad smile. "Quite a life, eh?"

Skip held his hand out across the table, and Claudia lay her hand gently in his. "Quite a life, Claudia. But look at you. The picture of health. Most women would kill for a body like yours -"

"Oh, yeah. These breasts are special."

"I think your breasts are beautiful. Just beautiful," said Skip, glancing at the small breasts that pushed against her halter top in an enticing way. "And your eyes are gorgeous. Your legs are perfection."

"If ya like skinny."

"They're beautiful, Claudia." Something in the way Skip said it made Claudia realize that he really did believe she was beautiful.

"Most women would die for your waistline." He looked into her green, gold-flecked eyes. "And I do believe that you have the prettiest eyes I've ever seen."

Claudia blushed.

"Be all that as it may, though, I have the feeling that the prettiest part of you is inside. Where it counts." He wasn't a hundred percent sure that was true, but he sure hoped it was.

"Thanks. You're pretty sweet yourself. Tell me about that 'whole' you're searching for, now that you know about my treasure."

The waitress came back and took their order. Skip explained to Claudia that he ordered his oysters fried because he was afraid to eat them raw in months that did not have "r"s in them. Claudia ordered a platter that came complete with fried scallops, fried oysters, baked grouper, stuffed crab, hush puppies and coleslaw. Skip had a baked potato with his meal.

"I'll tell you about the 'whole' I'm searching for some day. But right now, if I'm not mistaken, I owe you a tale of Apalachicola."

"Right. Let's hear it."

"Apalachicola was caught between a rock and a hard place during the Civil War."

"How so?"

"When the war began, Florida Rebel troops wanted to occupy Apalachicola because of its location at the mouth of the river. But they were ordered by the Confederate authorities to abandon the town and head north to fight the Union soldiers. Most of the men living in Apalachicola went north, many hooking up with Robert E. Lee's army. That left mostly women and children in Apalachicola."

"Really? I'm sure they got along O.K. without the men."

"No, life was hard on 'em. They didn't have much to eat except fish and oysters and what little they could grow in their gardens. The problem was that the East Gulf Squadron of the Union Navy had the area blockaded, so goods that used to come in to the seaport no longer arrived."

"How did the Union Navy maintain a blockade so far away from the North?"

"They had a lot more ships than the South. And used the west end of St. George's island as a dumping ground for coal for the Union steamers. To prevent the Union Navy from travelling up the Apalachicola, Confederates put obstructions in the river. Then they tried to build a big gunboat to challenge the Union ships. They were building it in a little town called Safford. The ship was to be all black, so it would be hard to detect at night, and they called it the *Chatahoochee*. Meanwhile, other Rebels were busy building another gunboat at Columbus."

"Columbus, Ohio?"

"No, Columbus, Georgia. Columbus is on the Flint River, which leads into the Apalachicola just like the *Chatahoochee*. That ship was called the *Muscogee*."

"Did any of the South's ships try to run the blockade and make it to Apalachicola?"

"Some tried, but only a couple made it. The Union's East Gulf Squadron had seven warships armed to the hilt, and quite a few tenders..."

"What are tenders?"

"Those chicken strips you get at fast food restaurants!"

Claudia kicked Skip under the table.

"No, actually tenders are smaller boats that were used to take sailors ashore and bring supplies to the larger warships."

"Where did the Union sailors get their food?"

"Supply ships occasionally made it down from the north, but mostly they ate off of the land."

"What do you mean?"

"St. George's Island was used for raising hogs before the war, and there were thousands of them roaming wild. And one black bear. To the west of St. George's is St. Vincent's Island, which is even larger than St. George's in area, and covered with trees. St. Vincent's not only had wild hogs, but cattle roamed on it in those days. So the sailors had a ready supply of fresh meat."

"They should have shared it with the women and children in Apalachicola! Did they?"

"I'm not sure, but I don't think so. One thing they did share, though, was their medical doctors. Every once in a while they would send a doctor into Apalachicola to treat the sick."

"What did the Union Navy do, then – just sit there and prevent ships from entering or leaving Apalachicola?"

"They weren't just blockading Apalachicola. They blockaded the whole Gulf shore in this area. They raided small salt-making operations the Rebels had set up, hidden along the shores of the bays. The commander of the East Gulf Squadron was ambitious – he asked for more ships so he could sail up the Apalachicola, then up the Flint, and take Columbus."

"What happened?"

"The Union didn't like his idea much. So he took several ships up the Apalachicola anyway. He captured one of the South's ships that was running the blockade, a fast ship named *Fashion*. That angered the Rebels, who in turn tried to sail the *Chatahoochee*, which was now ready, down the Apalachicola to teach the Yanks a lesson. But the *Chatahoochee* only made it as far as Blountstown, because it couldn't get by a sandbar there. Giving up on that idea, or deciding to wait for higher water, they turned the gunboat around and were heading back up to Saffold, when the boiler exploded and sank the ship."

"Bad luck!"

"Yeah, but the Union Navy didn't get away scott free. A hurricane in May of 1863 sunk several of their ships."

"Wait a minute! I thought hurricane season began in June."

"So did they. Caught them by surprise, I guess."

"After the hurricane were more Confederate ships able to run the blockade?"

"No, the South was pretty devastated by that time in the Civil War. Civil War - kind of an oxymoron, eh? They were in such bad shape, in fact, that the Union reduced the number of warships to three in the area. But the Confederacy was not about to give up. Remember I mentioned that they were building a warship not only in Saffold, but also in Columbus?"

"No, but go on." Fascinated by the tale, Claudia gazed into Skip's eyes and felt like she was back in the late 1800s, hearing the latest news of the war.

"They were building a warship that they hoped would be able to whoop any of the Union Navy's ships. It was an ironclad, an armored ship that would be nearly invulnerable to shelling, and pack a powerful punch of its own."

"Did they succeed?"

"Yes and no. The ship turned out beautiful – a real fighting machine. The only problem was that it was so heavy, they couldn't get it to the river!"

"You're kidding me!"

"No, I'm serious!"

"They finally managed to get it launched in December of 1864, but the war was coming to an end."

"The South got their butts kicked, eh?"

"But they had some victories of their own. It was a bloody war, yet people romanticize it now. But if you ask me, it's horrible to think about all the carnage."

"You mentioned the South had some victories?"

"The East Gulf Squadron commander, frustrated that he couldn't navigate the Apalachicola and attack Columbus, decided to try and take Tallahassee instead. The plan was to send a group of soldiers up the east side of the St. Marks river by land, cross at Newport, and attack the Confederate fort at the port of St. Marks, where the St. Marks and the Wakulla Rivers meet. As the soldiers attacked the fort from the rear, the navy would send warships from the Gulf to attack it from the front. Then the Union planned to capture the Tallahassee to St. Marks railroad, invade Tallahassee, and take Florida's capitol."

"Did they succeed?"

"Here's what happened: Colonel Scott of the Confederate army tried to stop a force of about fifteen-hundred Union soldiers from crossing a bridge over the East River. He only had about sixty men and one cannon with him."

"Did he succeed?"

"No. But he slowed them down. Retreating to Newport, he met with other Rebel soldiers, and set the town on fire so the Union wouldn't get use of the facilities."

"I'm sure the townsfolk liked that a lot!"

"When the Union soldiers, who were travelling by land, got to the bridge over the St. Marks at Newport, they found that the Rebels, had gotten there first and burned the bridge. There was a battle, but the heavily outnumbered Rebels were dug in on the West side of the river, and held their ground."

"How bad were the Rebels outnumbered?"

"Something like fifteen-hundred to a hundred-and-fifty."

"Wow! Amazing!"

"The Union soldiers were determined to cross the St. Marks, so they marched north to a place where the St. Marks goes underground."

"The river goes underground?"

"Yes, at Natural Bridge. But by the time they got there, the Confederate army had about fifteen-hundred soldiers waiting for them."

"Where'd they come from?"

"Troops were rushed down there on the railroad."

"Oh. Good thing!"

"The battle lasted over eleven hours. The Confederates won. The Union invading force had to retreat."

"Did they try again?"

"Nope. The Union fleet picked up the survivors and sailed away."

"What about the gunships that were to attack the fort from the other direction?"

"They were unable to navigate the river – they never made it either."

"I bet the Confederates were proud of themselves!"

"Yeah. Tallahassee was the only Confederate capitol not taken during the war. But the victory was short-lived. With the war coming to an end, and the Union forces closing in, the governor of Florida, a guy named Milton, only twenty-six days after the victory at Natural Bridge, returned to his plantation, I think it was named Sylvania or something like that, and shot himself!"

"Jeez!"

"That happened April 1, 1865. Lee surrendered to Grant eight days later."

"But what ever happened to those two ships the Confederates were building?"

"Nothing good! The ironclad *Muscogee* was captured with the fall of Columbus, torched, and set adrift in the Flint. They say it was only two weeks away from being ready for battle. It came to rest thirteen miles south of Columbus. The *Chatahoochee*, the one that had caught fire, had been salvaged and repaired. But the Union lit it on fire and set it adrift. It came to rest twelve miles south of Columbus."

"And the war came to an end?"

"Yup. Florida surrendered in May of '65."

"Depressing story. But interesting. Thanks for sharing it with me."

"Sure."

They ate in silence, each thinking about the Civil War, and the men who lost their lives in battle.

"Who's the jerk you're with this time?" The slurred, course voice startled Skip, coming from over his right shoulder, along with the heavy smell of beer on the man's breathe. He turned to see a tawny, rough-looking character smiling with missing teeth at Claudia. Skip didn't like his tone of voice or his looks, and he could feel blood rushing to his face. It wasn't like Skip to get angry easily, but this guy's audacity and the irate, offended expression on Claudia's face got to him.

"I don't see how that's any business of yours," Skip said, getting up and taking notice of the tattoos on the man's arms. His right biceps had an anchor and rope on it, his left a rose and dagger.

The two men, face-to-face, stared with narrowed eyes at each other before the stranger looked back at Claudia. Skip was a little taller than the drunken intruder, but the man was not intimidated.

"This guy giving you a problem?" he rasped to Claudia, who had turned white as a sheet.

"Leave him alone. He's a friend of mine."

"Some friend. Looks like an asshole ta me."

"Why don't you crawl back under the rock you came from." Skip said with venom in his voice.

The drunk turned to his right like he was walking away, and like a flash spun and hit Skip with a right to his jaw. Fortunately, Skip had a feeling it was coming, and rocked back, minimizing the impact of the blow. He stood there, arms down, every muscle in his body tense, waiting for the second punch. As the drunk reared back to take another swing, Claudia leaped from her chair and caught his arm. He flung her back over the table, and plates and drinks flew across the room. Skip grabbed him from behind, locking his arms to his side with a hug so strong it took the breath out of the attacker. Skip's hands held fast to each other as the man struggled to free himself.

People scattered to get away from the fray. Somewhere from the inside of the restaurant he could hear the waitress yelling in an angry, panicked voice, "Break it up!"

Skip felt a sudden pain in his buttocks. Realizing that he had just been kicked hard as a mule, and his hands were slipping away from each other, he spun to see who had kicked him. He caught the blurred vision of a large, stocky man with a beard. Their eyes met. Cruel, viscous eyes locked on his briefly, then, as if in slow motion, Skip felt the huge man grip his right arm like a vice. Behind him the drunk was swinging at him again. Skip ducked, and the blow landed squarely on the rugged, bearded jaw of the guy who had a hold of Skip's arm. In a rage, the man flung Skip with all his might toward the edge of the balcony. Skip slid across the top of a table, smashed through the patio railing, and fell like a ton of bricks toward the diners below. Stretching out like a skydiver, Skip landed smack on top of a patio umbrella, and felt a searing pain in his side. He clutched at the canvas in a desperate attempt to break his fall. The entire table tilted, then fell to the ground, glasses, salt and pepper shakers scattering across the patio. Food splattered on the laps of two startled diners as Skip hit the deck. Rolling to lessen the impact of the fall, he lay there for a second, stunned, taking stock of himself. He reached down and felt his right side, which throbbed with pain from the fall. Blood stained his Big Bend Saltwater Classic T-shirt, as he lifted it to see the damage wrought by the tip of the umbrella. A ten inch red gash oozed blood, but to Skip's relief it wasn't very deep. Struggling to get up, a flustered Claudia grabbed him by the elbow and led him down the dock away from the chaos.

Brushing through the crowd of onlookers, she asked, "Are you O.K.?"

"It's only a scrape."

Claudia notice the blood stain on his shirt and lifted it to see the damage.

"How about you?"

"Right now, I'm happy to be alive. Let's get the hell out of here!" she said with an urgency that made Skip think the two assailants were hot on their trail. As they made their way down the dock, Skip looked back and saw the bearded guy pointing at them from the balcony. The thinner man with the tattoos was nowhere in sight.

Skip and Claudia cut through a sandy, weed-filled lot and came out on the street right by the pick-up.

"Who were those guys?" Skip asked.

"No time to talk! Get us outta here, fast!"

Skip unlocked Claudia's door, grabbed the cooler that held his prize fish, and flung it into the bed of the truck. Claudia hopped inside, looking over her shoulder. Skip jumped in and the truck's engine turned over with a loud roar. Tires spinning on the loose sand and gravel, the truck lurched into motion. Skip looked in the rear view mirror, and saw several cars on the road behind him, but, to his relief, they were not racing to catch up. Sirens blared in front of them, and a Sherriff's car passed, lights flashing, speeding toward the restaurant. Skip took a left to get back to Hwy. 98, and one of the cars behind him followed at a distance. Claudia, seeing the concern in Skip's eyes, turned to look.

"Do you think they're following us?"

"Maybe. Can't tell."

"Do you have a gun?" Claudia asked.

"No. I don't have a gun. Wouldn't use one if I had one."

"Why not?"

"Don't believe in them."

"Don't believe in them?" Claudia shouted. "You're nuts, ya know it?"

"Maybe. Don't believe in using guns, don't believe in fighting."

"Is that why you just stood there when you got clobbered in the restaurant?"

"Yeah."

"You are crazy!" she said, sounding annoyed. "What would it take to make you fight?"

"I'd do my best to prevent you or any woman from being harmed, and if that meant fighting, I guess that would do it."

"But you wouldn't raise a hand to protect yourself?"

"It's not my way."

"What are you, some kinda saint or something?"

"Not hardly. Just principled. Don't believe in fighting, don't believe in violence. Too much of that in the world as it is, without me
contributing to it."

"Is that car still behind us?"

"I'm not sure. Another car pulled out of that gas station in front
of them." Skip took a quick right turn, passing a front yard filled with
tall azalea bushes that fronted Hwy. 98. He turned off his headlights,
and immediately took another right. Then he took a quick left, and
another right. Convinced that there was no one behind them anymore, he turned his lights back on and drove back to the highway.

"Do you know those two guys?" Skip asked, hoping that one of
them wasn't someone she had been romantically involved with.

"I know one of them, though I wish I didn't."

"Where do you know him from."

"The past. The past. Let's just leave it at that, O.K.?"

Skip could tell that he wasn't going to get any more information
from her, and decided to wait for a better time to find out how she
knew him. Remembering the scene in the restaurant only too clearly,
he was sure the one she knew was the one who approached the table
first.

Skip looked at Claudia, and saw a tear running down her cheek.
He didn't know what to do, but realized that trying to talk to her
about it was useless. He reached over and squeezed her hand gently.
She turned, and smiled at him through the tears.

"Know what?" Skip said quietly.

"What?"

"We just got us a free dinner!"

They laughed, and shook their heads. Claudia dried her tears
with tissues from her purse, and glanced at Skip. His lips curled in an
understanding smile, and Claudia felt she could really trust him. She
didn't agree with his philosophy when it came to fighting or guns,
but she respected it. And she felt admiration for the courage it took

Skip to be true to his morals in a time when it would have been a lot easier to just deck that drunken bastard.

She reflected on her opinion of him when she first saw him, stopping to help her by the side of the road. She had pegged him as a crass fisherman-type, with no couth and less culture. It is easy to stereotype people you meet into neat cubbyholes that conveniently fit into your perspective of the way things should be. First impressions are deceiving, as Skip had proven. She was in awe of his knowledge of local history, and felt she could sit and listen to his stories of the past for hours without getting bored.

But was there a piece to the puzzle that she wasn't seeing? If this man is all that he seems to be, why is he divorced? What happened to that relationship to turn it sour? Is there a side of Skip that she had not seen yet?

She wished she could put his character into a man with a good taste in clothes and a large portfolio. One who drove a new car and whose finances were such that he could travel at will and enjoy life to its fullest. Then she wondered what it would take to change Skip into that vision of manhood that she wanted him to conform to – perhaps the wealth that would come from an incredibly large treasure chest? Like the one she was bound and determined to unearth. That pirate treasure was the key to her realizing the good life that wealth and independence would surely bring if she was successful.

"When are you going to tell me about your search? You know, the one you mentioned earlier?"

"Oh. The search for the whole?"

"Yeah."

"I'm not."

Claudia looked disappointed.

"Just kidding!" said Skip. "I've been reluctant to tell you about it because it's really personal. And I didn't want you to think I was crazy or something. But now that you know I am, I guess I can share it with you."

"Yeah, do. I won't think you're crazy. You don't think I'm crazy looking for buried treasure..."

"I don't?" Skip teased.

"What?" Claudia scowled.

"I mean I don't," he said.

"So what is the whole you're looking for?"

"It's not a material thing, it's a state of mind. Or, more accurately, a state of the soul."

"Really? And how do you get there?"

"Good question. Not sure about that. But I think for me it's a matter of achieving four things in life."

"Like what?"

"Like, first of all, inner peace. The kind of inner peace that comes with having faith in God, and doing his will."

"I didn't know you were that religious."

"I am and I'm not. I pray every day. But I seldom go to church. I live the way I think God would want me to live. But I don't go out and try to get others to change their ways. I try to keep love in my heart at all times. But sometimes I lose it."

"Lose what?"

"My patience. My focus on what's really important on Earth."

"What's really important on Earth to you?"

"Excellent question. One of the things that's really important to me on earth is also the second part of my search for the whole: Friends and family."

"What about friends and family?"

"I think in order to achieve the inner peace I'm looking for, I need to be at peace with my friends and family. Love them. Respect them. Treat them special. Be thankful every day for their presence in my life."

"What about people that don't have any family, or any friends either?"

"They aren't very happy, are they?"

"No, but it's not their fault."

"I beg to differ. We all have our opportunities to make friends. Most of us have families that we're born into. And when friends have been around for a long time, they become like family to us. You don't have to be blood-related to someone to consider them family."

"That's two of the four. What's the third?"

"Learning to love myself."

"What's that supposed to mean?"

"Taking care of my body. Being thankful for all the things, material or spiritual, that I have. Feeling joy just to be alive. Getting into a career or volunteer work that makes me feel good about who I am and what I'm doing with my life. Taking the time to smell the roses. That kind of thing."

"Kind of narcissistic, isn't it?"

"No. I don't think so. God gave us the gift of life. And the best thing we can do with a gift is to use it and appreciate it, right? So being happy that I exist and taking care of myself is, in a way, honoring God by making good use of His gift."

"You mean Her gift."

"Sure. Her gift. I'm open to that. But I think God is both."

"How can God be both?"

"Not sure of that, either. But I have the feeling I'll find out when I die. I think a lot of things will become clear to us once we leave this plane of existence."

"So you believe in an afterlife?"

"And reincarnation, too. Why not?"

"I don't know. Seems farfetched."

"Farfetched? It is. But think about nothingness. Then a little bit of matter comes along. Then there's this big bang or something. Then a big ball of just the right materials comes into orbit around a huge, gaseous fireball that provides it warmth. Then things become alive. And evolve. And people populate the ball, and here we are. Speaking of farfetched! If that can happen, and by looking around, I'd say it has, how unrealistic is it to think that there can be life on a different plane? And reincarnation into this life?"

"Hmm. Never thought of it that way." Claudia became lost in her thoughts for a few seconds, then asked "That's three – what's the fourth thing that would make you whole?"

"Someone to love. A companion to share all of life's victories and defeats. Someone who I could get so close to that I would no longer care what their outside is like because I am in love with their spirit. Someone I can hold in my arms, and just by touching them express the deep affection that I have for them. And someone who feels the same way about me – someone who sees the person I am inside rather than my appearance. Someone who loves me for my kindness and caring and capacity to forgive, rather than someone who loves me for my looks or my bank account or my position in society."

"Asking a lot, aren't we?" Claudia said with a smile.

"Yes. Searching for a lot. But I've already found three of the four." Their eyes met, and Claudia heard the unasked question ring in her head as if he were whispering in her ear, "Are you the one?"

Skip was thinking that. He was thinking, "Are you the one?" But his self-doubt soon turned the question into, "Does she think I'm crazy? Does she think I'm some kind of religious zealot? Did I share too much too soon with her, and scare her away?"

She ran the slender fingertips of her right hand over his knuckles, and again looked into his eyes.

Claudia unbuckled her seatbelt and slid next to Skip, resting her tired head on his shoulder.

Pulling into the pebbly sand patch that passed for the Treasure Bay Inn parking lot, Skip wondered if Claudia would ask him up to her room. He wanted her to – wanted desperately to make sweet love to her despite the burning pain emanating from his side – wanted to spend the night next to her so the pleasure he was feeling wouldn't subside until the dawn.

His desire was so intense, that his mind only reluctantly raised that thorny issue of his commitment not to sleep with anyone unless she was someone he wanted to spend the rest of this life with. Although his physical attraction to Claudia was undeniable and passionate, he realized he did not know her well enough to recognize whether she would be a fine person with whom to spend the rest of his life. And what about his son Benny? How would she treat him?

Yet the warmth of her body next to his, and the beauty he saw in her face, tempted him to make love to her and worry about the consequences later.

"I'm beat!" said Claudia, yawning. "What a day!"

"Yeah. What a day!"

"I bet you rue the moment you laid eyes on me!"

"No. Not at all! The fishing tournament has never been this exciting before!"

"Tomorrow, let's get Billy's treasure."

"You locate it, and dig it up. Meanwhile, I'll catch a huge flounder that will clinch overall first place in the tourney. Then I'll help you lift it out of the ground and take it back to your skiff. This way, we'll both have our treasures."

"Well, I want to share mine with you – you deserve a portion of it."

"Thanks, Claudia, but no thanks. Ill begotten riches don't do people any good. Just a superstition of mine."

"But this one's not ill begotten – it's not like I'm stealing it from anyone. It's just sitting there waiting to be discovered. Finders keepers."

"I know you won't have done much wrong – I say "much" because I doubt it's legal to be lifting things off public land and reselling them. But the way the treasure was accumulated to begin with – bloody business, you know?"

"But I didn't shed one ounce of anyone's blood – why should that affect me?"

"I don't know. But I really don't want any, thanks just the same."

"O.K. Have it your way. But you will help me get it?"

"Sure. I'd swim the ocean for ya, Claudia."

Claudia put her hand on Skip's cheek and they kissed. Claudia and Skip were totally in the moment, swept away, hearts pounding. Immersed in that tender embrace, it seemed time stood still. Tongues touched and sent ripples of desire through their longing bodies.

The cab brightened as if someone had turned on an overhead light. Parting lips, they turned in unison to see the glaring headlights of a pickup blazing though the rear window at them. The same thought came simultaneously to Skip and Claudia – the men at the bar. Adrenaline coursed through their veins as their minds scrambled to decide what action to take.

"Hot night at Treasure Bay Lodge!" They heard an all-too-familiar voice say. And, although they would have been upset hearing Buck's voice at any other point in time, they were relieved to hear it now.

"Shoudda pulled the curtains!" Lucas chuckled.

Skip adjusted the rear view mirror to shine the headlight beam back in their eyes.

He stuck his head out the window and shouted, "Don't you guys have anything better to do than harass us?"

"Nope!" said Lucas. "Didja weigh that fish in?"

"Got there too late!"

"Thassa shame!" shouted Buck. "But that don't matter 'cause we're gonna get a bigger one tomorrow anyhow!" Buck turned the lights off and pulled into the space next to his empty boat trailer.

Claudia and Skip kissed again, but it was a hurried, tentative one this time.

"See ya in the morning?" Claudia asked.

Skip couldn't tell if it was a question that meant, "Are you coming up to my room?" or "I'll meet you tomorrow at Presnell's."

"Sure. I hate to leave you, with those two jokers staying here too, and those idiots back at the bar on the loose."

"I'm a big girl. I can take care of myself. See ya in the morning."

"OK. But if you change your mind, you know where to find me."

"Uh, huh."

"Meet me around dawn?" asked Skip, wanting to get as much fishing in as possible to maximize his chances of catching that big flounder.

"Sure. And by noon we'll be rich."

"You'll be rich. And I'll have the tournament won!"

"Right! Goodnight."

Not trusting Buck and Lucas, Skip said "I'll walk you to your room."

"Thanks!"

Up the stairs and across the weathered planks of the motel, Claudia and Skip walked in silence, each deep in their own thoughts. Looking over the rail of the balcony they saw the light from the full moon dancing across the rippled surface of the bay.

"Look! The moon's rising over the treasure," said Claudia. "That's got to be a good omen!"

Skip didn't want to spoil the moment. So he didn't tell her that the moon was actually setting over the treasure, rather than rising over it. "Beautiful night!"

"Thanks for everything." Claudia whispered in his ear, and they embraced and kissed again; a long, passion-filled kiss, as moonlight reflected off of their snuggling heads, Claudia's long locks touching Skip's shorter, sun-lightened hair.

A loud belch from Buck and Lucas' room reminded them of where they were. Standing belly to belly, arms around each other, they looked into each other's eyes and out across the bay. There stood Black's Island, moonbeams glimmering from the dew on the palm fronds. Their dreams lay spread before them, Skip's dwelling under the sparkling ripples of the pristine bay, Claudia's hiding in the darkness of the pine and scrub brush forest beyond, both within reach, the possibility of realizing those dreams as bright as the moon over St. Joseph's peninsula.

"See ya in the morning," Claudia purred as she searched her small purse for the room key.

"Bright and early!" Skip reminded her, knowing how anxious he'd be to get on the water before the sun rose too high.

"Bright and early," Claudia agreed.

CHAPTER XI
SKIP'S TREASURE LOST

Having gone to bed with his hair still wet from the shower he so desperately needed the night before, Skip woke with his hair standing on end in places. Hurriedly pulling on a clean pair of light-cotton fishing pants, and last year's tournament T-shirt, he flopped his hat on his head, just in case Claudia was already there. Unzipping the screen mesh that kept him protected from the mosquitoes, he noticed the breeze carried the familiar odors of salt water and low tide. Skip loved that smell, and dreamed of the day when, retired, he could experience that every morning, living by the sea.

The scrape on his side painfully reminded him of what had happened the night before. He shook his head, thinking for a brief moment that Claudia was bringing all of this about by searching for that blood-stained pirate treasure. If that was true, he reasoned, and she had only been close to it so far, what would happen if she got her hands on it!

Noticing to his chagrin that the sun was already up, he looked at his watch. He was shocked to see that it was already 9:00. Where was Claudia? He wondered if she, too, had overslept, exhausted from the long day by the bay, and the eventful evening. Skip sat down at the picnic table with a large chunk of French bread, an unopened package of Muenster cheese, a bunch of seedless red grapes and a big cup of lemon-flavored Gatorade. Planning his day, he knew the first thing he had to do was buy a large bag of ice from Charlie, stay far away from the tempting fishing lures in the tackle shop, then, if Claudia still had not arrived, go wake her.

Looking across the bay, he could see a dozen boats drifting the flats in search of that monster trout – one like he had in his cooler. Returning what was left of the cheese to the ice chest, Skip marveled at the huge tail, cut in twelve slices, that lay flat against the inside end of the cooler. Pushing it gently, not wanting any slime to come off the fish, he eased the beautiful fish down into the cold water at the bottom of the cooler to prevent the tail from drying out. He had seen tournaments decided by a mere hundredth of an ounce before, and he was optimizing his chance of winning. Now all he needed was a doormat-sized flounder, and he would be a shoe-in for the overall prize, as well as first place in both the trout and flounder divisions.

Skip knew the bay held doormat flounder. Fishing with a teacher friend of his one summer, his friend had hooked a huge one, had gotten it up to the side of the boat in that crystal clear water, and it shook the hook just before he could net it. Skip knew the big flounder were there, and he had an idea how to catch one. He would cast a half-ounce red jig with a green and gold plastic body shaped like a shrimp. The finishing touch was a long, triangular strip of squid hooked once near the larger end. That piece of squid would ripple enticingly in the current, and few flounder could resist such a tempting morsel. The trick was to keep the ever-present pinfish off the lure, as they would steal that squid in a heartbeat if given the chance. Beginning his drift in one of the many channels that cut through the grass flats, he would cast as long as he could along the edge of the channel where it met the grass. That was the most likely place to hang a big flounder, as they were fond of burying themselves in the grass and darting out to snatch prey that came swimming by. Then, as the drift carried his small skiff over the deeper grass flats, he would accurately cast into the sand patches, and bounce the jig off of the bright white bottom, creating puffs of sand that would attract any predator that was waiting in ambush in the turtle grass.

Skip ambled up to the tackle shop, and greeted Randy, a guy in his early twenties, who Charlie and Vonniciel hired for the summer to help launch boats and sell bait, tackle and snacks from the shop when they couldn't be there.

Skip entered the store and tried to resist browsing through the bargain lure table, but the temptation was too great. He saw a surface plug, red head and white body, with a tail that sported luminescent clear and chartreuse nylon bucktail. The red and white color did not catch as many fish as the green, yellow and orange combination, but, for some reason, red and white caught larger fish. Skip rationalized that he could go ahead and buy it, since it was half price and since he wound up not paying for dinner last night. Reaching into his wallet, he handed Randy a five-dollar bill, and slipped the new lure into an over-sized pocket of his fishing pants.

Taking the ice to his camping area, he set it down on the truck bed and tilted the cooler, spilling cold, slimy water off the tailgate, carefully keeping enough to cover the speckled trout. He shifted the drinks and food to get another look at the trout's large head. Skip smiled with satisfaction in the knowledge that, even if Claudia did not find a treasure, and he did not catch a winning flounder, that he had the trout division won. He gently laid the long bag of ice over the contents of the cooler and securely shut the lid. Straining, he set the cooler down on the front seat of the pickup, cracked the windows to prevent it from getting too hot in the cab, and locked the doors. Looking around, there was still no sign of Claudia. Skip took his toothbrush, toothpaste and soap to the outhouse-sized bath room, cleaned his teeth, wet and combed his hair, took a dump, and washed his hands. Opening the bathroom door, he hoped to find Claudia waiting for him, but was disappointed. He put his toiletries back in the tent. Unlocking the driver's door, he jumped in and turned the key. As soon as the dashboard light went out indicating the glow plugs were hot enough, Skip cranked the engine. He thought how lucky he was the night before to have the engine start without the glow plug light going out when those two wild men were after them.

Pulling into the Treasure Bay Inn, Skip noticed with no surprise that Buck and Lucas' truck was gone, he was sure they were out on the back side of Black's Island trying to top his trout. Climbing the creaky stairs, he had a vision of Claudia's lanky body dozing peacefully on the bed, oblivious to the time of day, deep in a sweet dream of pirate's treasure. Walking quickly down the porch, his heart sunk as he reached the door of her room. The door was ajar, and, to his horror he noticed that someone had cracked the bay window, making a hole large enough to reach in and unlock the door! Skip let out an involuntary "Noooo!", fearing the worse.

"I shouldn't have left her!" he cried, as he decided to open the door to the dim hotel room. If she was inside, lying in a pool of blood, he would never forgive himself. He bit his lip and grasped the rust-pitted door knob. The hinges squealed as he opened the door. He walked in, caution to the wind, in search of the woman he had grown so fond of, the woman who had slowly come around to being fond of him - the woman with whom he might have spent the rest of his life. His stomach knotted as he stood, unable to breathe. The kitchen was in shambles, Claudia's clothes scattered across the floor as if a twister had entered the room through that cracked window. Her duffel bag lay on the floor half open and empty, as if in the midst of a scream. In the dim light, Skip saw no trace of Claudia in the living room, so he slowly walked into the kitchen area, looked around, and wheeled sharply as a sound came from the front of the room. Squinting, he could see the shape of a crow that had landed on the hole in the window, teetering, undecided whether to fly inside or fly away. As Skip walked toward it, the crow flew off. Skip turned to his right into the bedroom, hoping against hope that Claudia would not be there. Had the crow been an omen? Was Claudia's last moments alive spent in that little bedroom on the other side of the wall? He paused before opening the bedroom door, stopped in his tracks, folded his hands together in prayer, and said "Dear, dear God. Please help me in this my time of need! Please let me not find Claudia here, dead. And please, dear God almighty, please let her still be alive, and please be with her wherever she is now. And lead me to her right away, that no harm may come to her. I love you God! Amen."

Cautiously opening the door, it's oil-deprived hinges creaking in the half-light, Skip felt the door bump something soft, and his heart sank. Expecting to see Claudia stretched out, mortally wounded, he pushed a bit harder and realized that it was only a blanket on the floor. Shoving the door with his shoulder, it grudgingly opened to reveal an empty bed. Skip, looking to his right, noticed the door to the bathroom was partially open, and he could hear water running in the sink. Taking a deep breath, he started for the bathroom, stumbling on a bed sheet sprawled on the floor. Pushing the door open cautiously, Skip felt resistance. He stuck his head inside, half expecting to see Claudia's body crumpled on the floor. Fortunately, it was only a still-wet bath towel the door had met. To his left hung the shower curtain. What horror did it hide, he thought, as he grabbed it with his left hand and flung it open. Breathing a sigh, to his relief, Claudia was not there either.

Another fluttering sound came from the near the front door. Skip came out of the bathroom, back into the disheveled bedroom and into the living room to find the crow again perched on the hole in the window. This time, the crow flew off toward Black's Island, as if to say, "Follow me! I know where your love is. Follow me!"

Skip returned to the kitchen, and flung open all the cabinets to be sure Claudia was not there anywhere. When he was satisfied that she was nowhere in the room, he ran out the door and down the landing toward the main office. He banged on the door, and the manager answered, looking rough in a sleeveless shirt, faded tattoos on now loose skin. For a moment, Skip suspected it was he who broke into Claudia's room. But why would the manager have done that, Skip thought, if he had a key?

"Have you seen Claudia?" Skip asked, brushing the man aside and looking around the room. A cigarette smoldered in an ashtray full of butts near a lazy-boy, the TV showing scenes of a riot somewhere on the other side of the Earth.

"Hey, what do you think you're doing?" A stubby, callous hand grabbed Skip by the arm and jerked him back toward the door.

"Claudia's missing and her room has been broken into!" Skip shouted.

"Who the hell is Claudia?"

"The woman who rented a room from you Thursday night!"

"Oh. Well, let's go have a look-"

"You go have a look! I have to find her!" Skip yelled as he raced down the stairs toward his truck. He could tell from the expression on the manager's face that he had nothing to do with Claudia's disappearance.

"And when you get done having a look, call the police!" Skip shouted over his shoulder.

Skip rushed back to Presnell's, wondering who could have done such a thing to Claudia. He was sure someone had abducted her. Why else would she not have shown up that morning to get Skip to help her with finding the treasure? Why else would someone have forced their way into her room? And why else would her clothes and stuff be flung around the floor the way he found them? "God," he prayed again, "please help Claudia in this her time of need. Please let no harm come to her. And please guide me to her side. Amen."

Skip skidded into Presnell's on two wheels, almost turning the truck over on the steep gravel driveway. He slid to a stop outside of the tackle shop, and jumped out. Seeing Charlie, he shouted, "Have you seen Claudia?"

"Who?" answered Charlie, obviously annoyed with the way Skip's truck nearly hit the side of his shop.

"Claudia – the woman who rented the boat from you yesterday?"

"Oh, yeah. Her."

"Well, have you seen her?"

"Yeah, she left out of here in the boat a little before dawn this morning."

"Was she by herself?"

"No. She was with two guys."

"What did they look like?"

"Who knows? I couldn't see them too well in the dark. One big guy and one skinny guy. Come to think of it, they were acting kind of strange."

"How so?"

"She didn't reply when I said hello, and the men seemed to be in quite a hurry."

"Damn! Charlie, someone broke into her hotel room last night. She was supposed to meet me here at dawn!"

"Well, last I saw them they were heading thatta-way!" Charlie pointed in the direction of Hurricane Cut.

"Thanks!" Skip said as he jumped back in the pickup and sped toward his campsite.

"Do you want me to call the police?" Charlie shouted after him.

Skip raised his thumb, indicating that Charlie should.

The truck came screeching to a halt in front of his campsite. Skip noticed that his neighbor's boat was gone, indicating that he was on the bay somewhere fishing. Skip slammed the pickup door closed and ran as fast as his legs would carry him to his skiff. He untied the boat and shoved the dock to point the bow away from the bulwark.

He pulled and pulled on the starter rope, but the old engine would not start. He alternated choking it and not choking it, until, fifteen pulls later, sweat dripping down his brow in the hot morning sun, the engine finally turned over. Skip slammed the gear lever into forward, and the skiff lurched. Ignoring the "Slow, No Wake" sign, Skip opened the throttle, and aimed the bow toward Hurricane Cut.

Charlie gazed after him, watching the skiff speed away from the sun that shone over the roof of the old tackle shop, rising over the mainland from the east. He wondered if he should call the police, then get in his shrimp boat and follow Skip. Thinking about his wife and newborn baby, Charlie decided it would be better to let the police handle the situation. After all, he rationalized, he didn't even have a gun.

"St. Joe police station."

"Hello, who's this?" Charlie said urgently into the phone receiver.

"Dolores. How can I help you?" The police station operator inquired.

"Dee Dee! Get someone out here right away! Looks like we might have a kidnapping on our hands!"

"Out where right away, sugar?" said Dolores in no apparent rush.

"Presnell's! This is Charlie."

"Hey, Charlie! How're ya doin' this fine morning, sugar?"

"Dee Dee! I don't have time for chit-chat. Is Bill in the area?"

"Yeah. He's on duty. But he's a-investigatin' a burgulary right now."

"How about Sammy?"

"Sammy? He's somewhere, hell if I know where."

"Well, call him up and get him down here, will ya? This is an emergency!"

"What kinda emergency, Charlie?" she drawled.

"I just told ya – looks like someone's been kidnapped!"

"Does it look like someone's been kidnapped, or has someone really been kidnapped, sugar?"

"Kidnapped!! Now get Sammy on the horn and get his butt down here!"

"All right, all right! Don't get so testy!" Dolores said, agitated, as she hung up on Charlie.

"Kidnapped my ass!" Dolores said to herself as she picked up the mike to call Sammy.

CHAPTER XII
TO THE RESCUE?

O ne big guy and one skinny guy – Charlie's words echoed inside of Skip's head. Sounds just like Buck and Lucas. He scanned the horizon for their boat. Not seeing it added to his suspicion.

Then it dawned on him that the two characters he and Claudia ran into the night before could also be described like that. Where did she know the skinny one from? Why wouldn't she tell me? Skip's mind raced like the skiff that skimmed across the smooth water toward Hurricane Cut.

If they were after Claudia for some reason, why would they not have just killed her in the hotel room? Why take her to Presnell's and speed away in a boat? Whoever they were, they must have heard about the treasure. He wondered if Claudia had told anyone about the existence of the map. In the chaos back at the hotel, he didn't notice it among the items strewn around the room. But, he remembered, he did see the handle of the metal detector sticking out from under the bed. Claudia would never have gone back to look for the treasure without it. Treasure – pirate's treasure! Even getting close to it has affected their karma, Skip thought. Imagine what things would be like if they actually took possession of the damned loot!

One thing was for sure, Claudia was not going along on the ride of her own free will. Skip looked around the boat, hoping to find something useful in a confrontation. His filet knife's black plastic handle jiggled inside the leather sheath stuck in the oval slot at one end of the tackle box. Seeing his toolbox, he remembered a stainless steel steak knife inside, the entire knife, handle and blade, molded from one solid piece of metal. Then he remembered his flare gun that he kept under the bow in case of emergencies. He wondered what would happen if he shot the flair cartridge at someone.

With his mind racing a mile-a-minute, Skip drew from his basketball experience, took a full breath, and tried his best to focus. What exactly was he doing racing across a bay, risking his life for someone he had only met two days ago? What if it cost him his life? He couldn't imagine how broken hearted his son Ben would be when he found out his father was dead. Why put him through that? Why even risk putting Ben through that? Ben was the most important thing in the world to Skip, and he wouldn't do anything to cause him harm.

On the other hand, if he did not at least try to help Claudia, he would regret it the rest of his life. What kind of a father would he make, knowing that he had left a female friend in danger to save his own hide, no matter what the excuse. He was determined to help Claudia, and, at the same time, determined to do it in a safe manner so he could be there to watch his son grow up. To help Ben over life's hurdles. To be the best father he could possibly be.

"Dear, dear God!" Skip prayed out loud. "Please help me in this my time of need! Please help me to rescue Claudia, and please help me to survive so I can raise Ben to do thy will. Amen."

Thinking that Charlie had alerted the police of the situation made him feel a bit more secure and daring than he would have had he been completely on his own. Surely, if he got himself in trouble, the police would not be far behind. He hoped God would send someone to their rescue.

Trepidation turned to anger as he pictured Buck and Lucas harassing Claudia. If they raped her, he thought, it would take all his faith in God to resist trying to kill them. Morally, he knew he would not be justified in revenge, and killing was abhorrent to a kind and loving God. But as the anger welled up from deep inside him, Skip had to remind himself that it was not O.K. to kill. Not even those who do something as awful as Buck and Lucas may have done to Claudia.

Nearing Hurricane Cut, Skip saw the outline of Claudia's rental boat bobbing in the water near the shore. He remembered seeing it there the day before, and what a wonderful experience they had together, sitting under the dock in the thunderstorm. He recalled how amazingly concerned he felt when he heard Claudia screaming, and how he had run like a bat-out-of-hell to save her from what turned out to be a harmless snake. He recalled the electric shock he had felt as their hands met, shaking on their deal. And kissing her the first time, and the sensation he felt as their lips met – an earthquake that seemed to touch his soul. And he remembered holding her and looking into her beautiful eyes after Buck and Lucas had finally left them alone. What a contrast to today – yet in both cases, Skip was thrown into the circumstances in the same way, trying to protect Claudia from harm. Maybe today would turn out as well as yesterday after all, he hoped.

Buck and Lucas' boat was no where to be seen. Did they both abduct Claudia, and use her rental skiff to try and steal the treasure for themselves? And if they did, why was their boat not still in the parking lot of Treasure Bay Lodge? It didn't make much sense, but it was still a possibility.

Skip thought again about the two characters they had encountered the night before. Maybe they had followed in the distance, with their headlights off to escape detection. Maybe they had followed Skip and Claudia back to the Treasure Bay Lodge. Maybe Skip had led them right to where Claudia was staying unknowingly. He wished he had taken more precautions last night. If he had it to do over again, he would have taken another side road, turned off his lights, and waited to see if anyone was following them back to the hotel. But he had been distracted by the warmth and comfort of Claudia snuggling next to him on the ride home. He recalled her smell, the feel of her head on his shoulder, and the burning desire to make sweet, passionate love to her.

A pain in his side drew him back to reality. If it was those two blokes from the night before, there's no telling how far they would go to get that treasure. They didn't have any qualms last night when it came to getting violent. Surely, they wouldn't hesitate to go that route again today if it served their purposes. Skip's thoughts again returned to his cherished son, and he vowed to himself that he would be careful, and get to see his son's smiling face again.

Three-hundred yards away from Claudia's rental skiff, Skip motored slowly to the narrow beach. Backing off the throttle, the engine cut off. Tilting it out of the water, the momentum carried the skiff silently to the fine white sand. He tucked his fishing knife between his belt and his shorts. He used the shorter steak knife from his toolbox to cut the hard plastic wrap that covered the flare gun. Loading a flare into the barrel, he put the other two flare cartridges in the left pocket of his shorts, and shoved the flare gun into his right pocket. He slid the steak knife between his underwear and shorts, blade parallel to his backbone. As he stepped out of the boat, the blade of the steak knife stuck him in the buttocks. He pulled it out of its hiding place and, at a loss for how to carry it, he tossed it back in the boat.

Clank! The noise echoed through the still morning, and Skip realized he had made his first mistake. He stood listening on the beach for a second, and, not hearing anything, entered the woods. He planned to surprise whoever had abducted Claudia by sneaking up on them. A few seconds of hearing the dry leaves and sticks crunching beneath his sneakers was enough for Skip to know that he wouldn't be sneaking up on anyone that way, unless they had a stereo blasting.

Returning to the beach, he stealthily made his way toward Claudia's skiff. A plan began forming in his mind. Setting the flare gun down on an empty ancient conch shell, he quietly waded out to the anchored boat, unlatched the engine cover, and lifted it off of the engine. Disconnecting the spark plugs, and reconnecting them to the wrong spark plugs, Skip thought, would buy Claudia and him some time if he could somehow manage to get her away from her captors. As he carefully placed the engine cover back on top of the engine and closed the latch, it made a snapping sound. Skip froze. Looking around, he was relieved to find that he was still undetected. Slowly wading back to the beach, he picked up the flare gun, took a deep breath, and crept as quietly as he knew how into the woods and underbrush, heading for the downed live oak tree. He pointed the flare gun ahead of him, wondering if it would do any good. Maybe whoever had abducted Claudia would think it was a real gun, and let her go.

Passing the end of the Indian mound where Claudia had been scared by the snake, Skip began to wonder what was going on – he heard no voices, no digging – just the chirping of a cardinal and the cawing of a crow in the top of a palm tree. He wondered if it was the same crow that he had seen perched in Claudia's broken window at the Treasure Bay Lodge.

"What the hell ya gonna do with that flare gun, bozo?" a deep voice bellowed from behind him.

Startled, Skip wheeled around to see the angry face of a giant-of-man who he immediately recognized from the night before. A gun, a real gun, was pointed at Skip's head.

"Where's Claudia?"

"What's it to you?"

"She's a friend. Where is she?"

"What makes you think she's here?"

"That's her rental boat in the cove. I know she's here. Where is she?"

"None of your business, asshole! Now drop that gun before you set the damned woods on fire!"

Skip hadn't realized that he was still pointing the flare gun at the man. He hesitated, thinking a fire would alert the police to their whereabouts. Should he risk getting shot to maybe start a fire in the brush? Or should he aim for the big guy's eye and risk getting gunned down? He came to his senses and dropped the flare gun.

"Now back up!"

Skip moved back a couple of feet. He wondered what a kick in the face would do to the guy as the large man stooped to pick up the flare gun. Probably not enough to prevent Skip from getting shot. Anyway, he couldn't bring himself to commit such an act of violence. It just wasn't his nature. And, after all, the guy did not say anything about shooting him. Yet.

"Why don't you put that gun down?" Skip asked.

"I'll put the damned gun down when I'm good and ready. Shut up, turn around, and walk that way." He pointed to the path that led to the downed live oak tree.

As Skip entered the clearing, the first thing he saw was Claudia tied by a single length of rope to a tree. Holes had been dug along the length of the tree, several on either side, four feet deep.

"Fancy meeting you here!" Skip greeted Claudia.

From behind a tree the other man he had encountered the night before emerged. "Look what we got here! Another treasure hunter!" With venom in his voice, he asked "What treasure you after, buddy? The one that's buried or the one that's tied up?"

"I'll let you have the one that's buried if you'll let me have the one that's tied up." Skip looked at Claudia, and forced his lips to curl into a smile. Tears ran down Claudia's cheeks.

"Don't seem to me like you're in any kinda position to be bargaining, fool." The wiry man smirked, and dropped Claudia's shovel.

"Whatcha wanna do with 'em, Will?"

"Tie him up too."

"Where?"

"Well, seeing as how we only have that one dock rope, schmuck, I'd say with the girl. Unless, of course, you'd like to take a run back to the boat and get the anchor rope."

Claudia began sobbing. Skip's heart sunk seeing her in such misery. He knelt beside her and wiped the tears from her cheek.

"It's all my fault – I'm sorry!" she sobbed. Skip gazed into Claudia's eyes through tears of his own. Words failed him, and he brushed the hair softly from her forehead.

"Oh, that's touching," Will commented. "Go ahead and tie them back-to-back." His companion walked toward the couple.

Skip heard a crinkling sound, and noticed that the sinewy thief had stepped on an old piece of parchment, no doubt the map, on his way to tie them to the tree. That map, Skip thought, so old and so brittle. If it wasn't for that map, they wouldn't be in the jam they were in. But, then again, if it wasn't for that map, he wouldn't have met Claudia.

Wrapping the rope as tight as he could around Claudia and Skip, the scrawny man began to tie a knot by Skip's right arm. Skip could smell the pungent odor of the man's underarms, and his stale-alcohol scented breath. Skip, with his back pressed to the tree, turned his head the other way to avoid the stench. He felt the rope tighten as the captor wrenched it as hard as he could. But it loosened considerably as the man finished the knot.

"Not that way, idiot! Where the hell did you learn to tie knots, Bones? That ain't worth a damn!"

Will handed Bones the gun, untied the loose knot, made a loop in one end of the rope, put it back around the tree and the prisoners, and tucked the free end into the loop. The blue polyester dock line made a burn on the Skip and Claudia's arms, as the burly man put his sneaker against the tree trunk, and yanked with all his might. The rope was so taut it forced the air out of Skip and Claudia's lungs. Only when Will finished snugging the knot against the loop did the pressure on their chests slacken, allowing them shallow breaths.

"You O.K.?" Skip asked Claudia.

"Yeah," she rasped.

"Now get back to digging, Bones. That treasure's got to be around here somewhere."

"If someone hadn't already got it!" replied Bones, looking viscously at Claudia as he picked up the small spade and began a new hole.

"Shut up and dig. If they already found it, they wouldn't have been sticking around, would they?" Will said. He sat down on the opposite side of the clearing from Skip and Claudia, and laid the pistol down next to him on top of a red bandana.

Skip whispered, "What do you mean, this is all your fault? Seems like those two are the culprits."

"It is all my fault." Claudia whispered back.

"Why do you say that? You had nothing to do with these two showing up at the Treasure Bay Lodge, right?"

"Well..." Claudia hesitated.

"Well, what? Where do you know that Bones from anyway?"

"Let's just say a past life, and leave it at that, O.K.?"

Skip didn't answer.

Changing the subject, Claudia asked, "Skip, you know what you were saying about the treasure having a bad karma to it, because of the way it was plundered. I'm beginning to believe it. I mean, we haven't even found the damn treasure yet, and look at all the trouble it's caused us!"

"Yeah, I was thinking the same thing crossing the bay. If it's brought us this much pain just looking for it, imagine the fine time we'd have if we actually found it!"

"Look," began Claudia earnestly. "I don't know how all this will turn out. But I want you to know that I really am grateful for all you've done for me. If we get out of this alive, I'll make it up to you, promise!"

"I'm not helping you to get something in return, Claudia. I've been helping you because it's been the right thing to do. And, I don't know how to say this, but..." Skip fell silent.

"But what?"

"I'm crazy about you. That's what. And every fiber in my body is yearning to make sweet, passionate love to you. There – I said it."

"Skip. I knew that."

"Oh. But it's more than that, Claudia. I want to get to know you better than anyone else on Earth. I want to be your best friend and lover. I just get this feeling when I'm around you that..." Skip hesitated.

"That what?"

"That I could spend the rest of my life with you. That you are what's missing in my life. That your presence in my life would make me whole."

"Ah. Whole. The end of your search?"

"Yes and no. Being whole is not a state of mind that, once you're there, you're automatically there for the rest of your life. It's something that takes work. Like relationships. Takes a lot of work to maintain the state of mind, feeling whole."

"Might be a lot of work, with me. I'm damaged goods, you know."

"In what way? You seem pretty together."

"I'm not. I was hoping this treasure would help. I don't want anybody or anything to rule me. Understand? I have to be my own person."

"And how would the treasure have helped that?"

"I thought if I was independently wealthy, then I would be the captain of my own ship. Could go where I want to go, even be with who I want to be with, and not have to compromise. I felt it would free me from having to answer to anyone except myself."

"You know, being in a relationship doesn't mean being bound by someone else. To me, being in a relationship means being free to be who you are, and that you've found someone who knows who you are, respects that, and gives you the freedom to pursue whatever it is that interests you. Know what I mean?"

"Sounds logical. But I've never seen a relationship like that. Never."

"It's possible."

"We'll see," said Claudia, with doubt in her voice.

"I hope we get out of this mess to find out. Any ideas?"

"No. Yeah. Why don't you pray to that God of yours and get his help?"

"Actually, that's a great idea. I've already done some of that this morning."

"Maybe that would counteract the bad karma of the treasure."

"Dear God, please help Claudia and me in this our time of need. And all those people around the world today who find themselves in similar circumstances. Thank you God. Amen."

"Amen," Claudia chimed in. "Is that all you're going to pray?"

" That's all. God knows what we need, and he'll decide whether to help us or not."

"I thought God always answers prayers."

"I think he does. Only, sometimes the answer is no."

"Ah, how long does it take for God to answer you? I'm getting' kinda hungry!"

They both laughed.

Bones' shovel hit something solid, a dull thud echoed through the woods.

"What's that?" Will shouted, jumping up with surprising quickness for such a large man.

"Dunno!"

Will looked over the side of the hole Bones was digging. Bones hit the object again, and Will grabbed the shovel, pushing Bones away.

Claudia's eyes bulged with anticipation and Skip, who couldn't turn around to see the flurry of activity, kept his ears pealed.

Will flung dirt out of the hole with the shovel, like a dog looking for his favorite bone. Bones hovered around the side of the hole, straining his neck trying to get a look at what Will was uncovering.

"I'll be God-damned!!" Will shouted in glee. "It's a chest! An old chest! And I'll bet it's filled with loot!"

"Hot damn!" echoed Bones. Inching closer to get a look, Bones caused the side of the hole to cave in. Will glared at him.

"Numb nuts! Get the hell away from the edge!"

Bones stepped back, anger in his eyes. "Keep a civil tongue, Will. Without me, you wouldn't have even known a treasure was buried around here."

"Bite my ass, you little jerk! If I hadn't protected your butt in jail, you wouldn't even be alive today. Don't forget that."

"We'll be splitting it even, right? That was our agreement."

"We'll talk about that when the time comes. We gotta unbury this sucker first."

Bones gave a menacing look at his big bearded companion who was again shoveling like there was no tomorrow. Scraping sounds came from the hole as Will slid the spade across the top of the chest and along its sides.

"Get your ass down here, Bones! And don't cave in the sides this time!"

The scrawny man carefully jumped into the pit on the other side of the chest. He noticed the corroded, pitted brass fittings, and wondered if it would hold together. Grabbing the old rope handles, they strained to extricate the trunk from its dank burial ground. It broke free from the sand, and, as they were lifting it out of the ground, Bones' handle broke, and his end of the chest slammed into the bottom of the pit, popping the lid open. Jewelry that hadn't seen the light of day for over one-hundred-and-fifty years spewed into the sand, and an avalanche of coins followed.

"Damn!" shouted Will, mouth open in astonishment.

"Holy shit! We're rich!" screamed Bones, who had jumped back in the hole and was supporting the chest from underneath his end. Heaving the chest onto the forest floor, Will pried the lid open the rest of the way with his strong hands. Inside the chest lay British, Spanish and American gold and silver coins, gold bars, silver ingots and jewelry. Entangled jewelry of all kinds; priceless necklaces with emeralds set in gold, solid silver and gold chains. The silver was tarnished, but the gold shone like the day it was buried. Priceless pieces of jewelry, undoubtedly wrestled from some poor soul's neck before or after being savagely killed by Billy Bowlegs or one of his demonic crew.

Scrambling into the ditch, they quickly gathered the jewelry and coins that had spilled, and tossed them back into the chest.

"We gotta hide this now!" Will shouted.

"Why? Let's just haul it back to the boat and get the hell out of here!"

"In broad daylight? Fishermen all over the bay wondering what we're doing loading a big old chest aboard the skiff? Not too smart

Bones. Besides, we gotta take care of these two." Will pointed a long callous finger at Claudia and Skip.

"What do you mean take care of them? Just leave 'em tied up. They can't do us no harm. We'll take this treasure and be long gone before they get themselves untied or rescued."

"Pea brain! If you want to spend this treasure instead of more time in jail, we better do away with them. They squeal, and every law officer this side of the Mississippi will be after us."

"That wasn't part of the plan."

"Well, it is now. Help me hide this chest."

"I don't like it. It's one thing being caught with treasure you ain't supposed to have. It's another thing being caught after killing someone. I say we just leave 'em here."

"Just shut up and help me hide this damned box. I'll take care of them. It's obvious you don't have the stomach for it. We'll hang out in the forest until dark, then take this loot back across the bay."

Dropping the chest between two palmetto bushes, they piled pine tree branches and palm tree fronds on it until it was well hidden. Walking back to the two captives, Will took a seat on the log he was on when Bones hit pay dirt, and wiped his forehead with the red bandana. Picking up the gun, he waved it in the general direction of Bones.

"Gotta fill the holes back in before somebody gets suspicious. Leave two, though. After the sunsets, we'll make good use of them, if you know what I mean. Would nail them now, but the gunshot might draw some attention."

"I don't like it, Will!" Bones said in a wimpy and dejected voice. "I didn't come here to get a murder rap hung on my head. I came here for the treasure."

"You just get to covering up them holes you dug, and leave the thinkin' to me." He again waived the gun in Bones' direction. Bones wondered if he would be leaving with Will and the treasure, or wind up in one of the holes he had dug come nightfall.

Skip whispered to Claudia, "It doesn't look good. What now?"

"I was just going to ask you that. Maybe if we play Bones against Will, he'll help us out of this mess. What do you think?"

"I think if we do that, they'll be three bodies in these holes come dark. I was hoping the police or Marine Patrol would be here by now!"

"You called them?"

"No. I asked Charlie to."

"How're we gonna get out of this?" Claudia asked in a desperate, shaky tone of voice.

"I can't get this rope to loosen any – do you have any slack on your side?"

"No. In fact, it's killing me. I hate this. And I hate those two bastards. If the tables were turned, I'd be real tempted to blow them away!" Her panic and despair had turned to anger.

"Easy. Rage isn't going to get us out of this pickle. And if you would shoot them for vengeance or for the treasure, then you're no better than them, right?"

"Not from my point of view. They messed with us first. They deserve to die. Do you mean to tell me you wouldn't kill them if you had the chance, knowing that they're planning on killing us?"

"Right. I wouldn't. Against my morals."

"What would you do?"

"If the tables were turned, I'd do what I had to do to protect you. But I wouldn't kill them, or even harm them. Karma will take care of them in the end."

"Karma? Karma? How the hell is karma going to give them what they deserve?"

"I don't know. But it would. Always does. I'd just get us both to safety and forget them."

"You're something else! Why don't you try another one of your prayers?"

"Good idea. Dear God, please help us, as are lives are in mortal danger. Lord, please have mercy on sinners such as ourselves, and free us from captivity, that we may serve you the rest of our lives. Amen."

"Amen."

As Bones shoveled dirt, Will laid his gun on his bandana. Stretching his arms backward for support, Will relaxed while his companion worked up a sweat. Will felt something brush the back of his head, and he instinctively swatted at it. He felt it again, and turned his head. He found himself looking down the barrel of Buck's 45-caliber pistol.

"Well, what have we got here? More treasure hunters, eh, Lucas?"

"What's your problem?" Will said, secretly shoving his bandana and gun under the log he was sitting on with his right heel.

"You got our friends, here, in a bind. That's our problem."

Lucas came out from behind a tree on the other side of the clearing.

"Don't stand behind that guy, Lucas! I don't want to shoot you if he makes a move."

Lucas walked over to Claudia and Skip.

"Man, are we glad to see you!" Skip shouted.

Lucas shook his head as he began to untie them.

"We knew something was up when we spotted that wreck-of-a-boat of yours anchored down the shore. I said to Buck, somethin's wrong! There ain't any brown trout in them woods! So we figured either you was havin' an orgy with this foxy lady, or you was in some kinda trouble. Either way, we wanted to have a look."

"Thanks!" Claudia said sincerely, rubbing her arms where the rope had made indentations and burns in her flesh. "I didn't think I'd ever hear myself saying this, but I'm sure glad to see you guys!"

"Enough of the niceties!" shouted Buck, who had both Will and Bones sit side-by-side in an open hole. Will reached into his pocket. "Get your hands up where I can see them!" he shouted at Will. Will slid the boat key out of his pocket, and it dropped in the sand by his leg. He quickly covered it with his foot, grinding it out of sight into the soft sand.

Bones, visibly shaken, threw his hands into the air. "I wasn't gonna kill nobody," he squealed.

"Which one of you clowns has the key to the skiff?" Buck demanded.

"Go ask your friend over there – she's the one who rented it," Will replied.

"I ain't got it," whimpered Bones. "And we were gonna let them go."

"Yeah, right!" commented Skip, who was embracing Claudia.

"I don't have the keys to the skiff," said Claudia.

"Come here, Lucas!" Lucas walked over to Buck, the rope neatly coiled between his right hand and elbow.

Buck whispered something in Lucas' ear, and Lucas scurried off though the woods in the direction of the boats.

"So what the hell's going on here?" Buck asked Claudia and Skip.

"Claudia had this idea that there was pirate's treasure..."

Claudia gave Skip a sharp elbow in the ribs.

"...somewhere in these woods, and decided she'd try to find it. Then, this morning, when she didn't show up for our rendezvous, I went down to her hotel room and found that someone had broken the window and forced their way inside. And she was gone! I rushed back to Presnell's, and Charlie told me he saw her and these two characters heading toward this side of the bay. So I came here to try and save her, thinking that Charlie would call the police and they'd be here in short order. Guess Charlie didn't call them after all."

"Probably called them. But they're a sorry lot. I doubt they would have done anything 'cept wait for you all to return and sort it out then."

"We almost didn't return. These jokers were about to do us in!"

"Zat right, boys? Tsk, tsk! And all for the chance at a treasure that don' even exist."

Claudia, still in Skip's arms, snuggled against him, whispering in his ear, "Keep your mouth shut."

The sound of Lucas returning through the woods made Buck turn around. Bones leapt out of the pit and made a run for it. Buck fired a warning shot at his feet. Bones turned, and jumped back into the hole, looking as pale as a ghost.

Skip picked up Will's gun, and put it in his pocket, leaving the soiled bandana in the sand.

"Now everybody listen up!" shouted Buck. "Here's the plan. We're gonna escort these two lovers back to their boat, if you can call it that. If I hear you two following us, I'll fill the woods with bullets and ask questions later. Got it?"

Will and Bones reluctantly shook their heads.

"Then, once they're on their way, Lucas and I are going to hang out by your skiff until they're across the bay. Follow me so far? If you so much as stick your ugly faces out of the brush, I'm gonna blow them off. Understand?"

Two nods from the kidnappers.

"Let's do it." Buck said, and the four of them headed back to the boats.

"I owe ya, man!" Skip said, voice filled with gratitude as he slapped Buck on the back.

"Gimme that trout of yours, eh?" said Buck in a lighthearted voice.

"You want the brown one or the speckled one?"

"Neither. Just kiddin'. We're gonna catch a trout to make that one you got look like a minnow, right Lucas?"

"You got that right!" Lucas said, nervously looking behind him to be sure the two outlaws weren't following.

"Those two didn't rape you or nothin', did they?" Buck asked Claudia.

Skip heard the words and felt a deep respect for Buck, a brotherly sort of love that surprised him.

"No. They didn't rape me. But they scared the hell out of me, I gotta tell ya!"

"They must have broken into your room after we left this morning, or we would've heard them," volunteered Lucas.

Reaching the beach, Buck said, "You two get on outta here now. We got a surprise for those clowns when they get back to Charlie's boat."

"O.K. Thanks again, guys. You saved our lives!" Skip said earnestly.

"Yeah, thanks!" Claudia chimed in. "We owe ya big time!"

Running down the beach hand-in-hand toward Skip's boat, Claudia felt a sense of newfound freedom, the freedom she had been craving for a long time. That "I can do whatever I want now" feeling permeated her soul and filled her spirit with a lightness previously unknown. And then it dawned on her – the treasure. The one way out of dependency she wanted so bad was back there with those two outlaws. She stopped in her tracks.

"Skip – the treasure!"

"Yeah, what about it?"

"They'll take it and we'll never see it again."

"So?"

"So!? So I want it."

"Claudia, it's that damned treasure that got us into this mess and almost, if not for the grace of God and Buck and Lucas, got us killed. I don't want anything to do with that treasure."

"I do. I want it. Just as much as I've ever wanted it."

"Claudia, we gotta get out of here. Those guys back there mean business. We escaped with our lives this time. We may not be so lucky next time."

"I'm not leaving without the treasure. You saw it! It's real! There's millions of dollars worth of coins and jewelry there. And if we don't get it, they will! Give me the gun."

"No! Hell, no! You're gonna get yourself killed."

"Give me the gun. I'll take that chance."

Reaching into his pocket, Skip pulled the gun out by the barrel, and flung at as far as he could into the bay.

"Nooooo!" Claudia screamed, too late. "What did you do that for?"

"I probably just saved your life. Now let's get the heck out of here. If you really want the treasure, I have a better plan."

"Damn it! I can't believe you threw that gun away! What were you thinking?"

"I said, I have a plan, if you still want that treasure."

"What?"

"Simple. And no one gets hurt. We go back to Presnell's, call the police and tell them about the abduction, and say we want to press kidnapping charges against those two."

"Hell, Skip, they'll be long gone with the treasure before the cops get them. That won't work."

"Oh, yes it will! They're not going anywhere. I switched the spark plug wires around on Charlie's outboard. It'll be hours before they figure out why it's not starting."

"O.K. It's worth a try. But what if they get caught with the treasure?"

"That's the chance we'll have to take. But remember what they said before? Will doesn't want to be seen carrying that chest in the daylight. I doubt they'll be hauling it away just yet."

Buck and Lucas flew by in their fancy rig, probably on their way to that hole in the bay they depend on to harbor big speckled trout. They waved as they passed, the boat sending a wake toward the beach, rocking Skip's small skiff and lapping the white sandy shore.

CHAPTER XIII
THE ESCAPE?

Grabbing the anchor and tossing it in the front compartment, Skip gave the light boat a shove to turn the bow around to face deeper water. Claudia settled into the front swivel seat, and rowed with a wood paddle so Skip would have enough depth to start the engine.

Skip pulled and pulled on the starter cord, one pull with the choke in and the next with the choke out, until he finally got it to start. He pushed the choke flush to the motor cover and jammed the engine into gear. Claudia sat back and glanced over her shoulder to see if the two thugs were coming after them. To her relief, they were nowhere in sight.

Steering a course straight to Presnell's, Skip kept the engine at full throttle. He calculated that, with two people in the boat, it would go 20 miles an hour, and that would get them across the bay in about 15 minutes. In the distance, he could see Buck and Lucas drifting the deep grass flats, casting lures with the wind at their backs.

Steering a course that took them near the drifting boat, Skip slowed down. So overwhelmed with appreciation for what Buck and Lucas had accomplished, he just had to thank them again.

"Thanks, guys, and catch a big one!"

Lucas shouted back, "You don't have to worry about them catching up to you!"

"Why not?" asked Skip.

"Because I switched the spark plug wires on them!" replied Lucas proudly.

"Aaaah! You didn't!" exclaimed Skip.

"Yup! Sure did!"

"My idea!" said Buck with a smile.

"Damn! I can't believe it! I switched them around before y'all got there!"

Buck, Lucas and Claudia all said at the same time, "Uh, oh!"

Skip gunned the engine and made a beeline toward Presnell's. Claudia looked back to Hurricane Cut anxiously. Skip looked back on occasion hoping not to spot Will and Bones following them.

BACK AT THE SIGHT OF the treasure, Will and Bones were having a heated discussion.

"I say we haul it to the peninsula road and catch ourselves a ride," Bones suggested.

"That's freakin' brilliant! How the hell do we explain the chest? And who in their right mind is gonna give us a ride the way we look?"

"Got a point there."

"We don't have to be in any hurry to move that treasure. There's only two other people that know about it, and they're well on their way back to shore to call the police, I'm sure. What we need to do is stop them!"

"Stop them! Stop them? How the hell are we gonna do that?"

"Easy!" Will scrounged around in the sand at the bottom of the hole, and found the boat keys. "Let's go!"

"But those guys with the gun said they would be waiting for us if we stuck our heads out of the woods!"

"And you believed them? You're dumber than you look! They were bluffing."

"And what are we gonna do if we can catch up to them?"

"Shoot 'em, like we shoulda done before!"

"But they got your gun!"

"I never leave home without at least two! The other's on the boat. Good thing one of us got brains!"

"Here we go again with the shootin'! I don't like it. Why don't we just get the chest, load it up, and take off across the bay?"

"If those two make it to the other shore, I guaran-damn-tee you that this bay will be swarming with Marine Patrol and Franklin County Sheriffs after our asses. Kidnapping is a serious crime! Once we stop them from squealing, we got it made. Trust me!"

Jumping aboard the rental skiff, Will jammed the key into the ignition and turned it so hard it nearly snapped. The engine roared to life, Bones threw the anchor into the skiff, and shoved the boat into deeper water. Will slammed it in gear, and, kicking up mud and grass, clouding the pristine water, they raced after Claudia and Skip.

"You take the wheel!" shouted Will.

Bones drove the boat while Will rummaged through his duffel bag and located a Luger handgun. Positioning himself on the bow, Will pointed out the tail wake of Skip's boat with the gun, and Bones raced to catch them. The flat-bottomed rental skiff was powered by a 50-horsepower Yamaha, and was flying at thirty-five miles an hour over the rippled water, blue canopy top flapping in the wind.

THE PALM TREES ON BLACK'S Island danced in the afternoon breeze, oblivious to the drama taking place near her shores.

Buck shouted, "I'm on!" as his white Styrofoam float disappeared beneath the surface.

The huge sea trout had spotted easy prey in the wounded bait-fish, and hadn't noticed it was attached to monofilament line and a hook. She met the unfortunate pinfish head on, opened her gaping jaw, and sucked the morsel deep into her mouth so it had no chance of escape. She felt metal penetrate her jaw, and rose to the top, shaking her powerful head with fury, in a vain attempt to dislodge the hook.

The drag screamed on Buck's reel as he shouted to Lucas, "It's a monster! This is the one I've been waiting for! Money time!"

Lucas saw the big fish wallow at the top of the water, and shouted encouragingly "Get it, Buck! Keep yer line tight! Don't give it any slack. I think ya hooked a freakin' whale!"

The sound of a speeding boat distracted Lucas momentarily, and turning his head, he discovered the rental skiff racing toward Presnell's.

"Buck! Those two idiots somehow got that engine started! I must have put the plugs back where they belonged not knowing that guy had already messed with them! What are we gonna do?"

The fish took a second long run toward Black's Island, stripping more and more line off of the reel.

"They'll be O.K. – they got a good head start. They'll be back at Presnell's before those characters catch up. Besides, we've saved their butts once today! Ain't that enough?"

"Hurry up with that fish, Buck, I don't think they're gonna make it!"

Lucas could see Skip's skiff a good ways ahead of the pursuers, but also a good ways away from the relative safety of the harbor. "Sure would be a shame to have saved them, only to see 'em killed."

"Pay attention to what we're doing, Lucas! If this fish gets away, I'm gonna kill you. Are you ready with the net?"

"Get him in Buck, and let's see if we can't catch up. I got a bad feeling about this!"

"I'm not forcing this big boy trout! That hook'll rip right outta those tender jaws. They'll be plenty of time to catch up after I play this fish right. It's too late in the tournament to expect another chance at a fish of this caliber!"

"All right. But hurry up! What's more important anyway? That fish or that guy and gal?"

"Right now this fish! Then we'll tend to them. Anyhow, they can take care of themselves. He's got the varmint's gun, remember?"

"Oh, yeah! I forgot. That makes me feel better. Take your time and play that bad boy! Don't give 'em any slack."

"If you tell me not to give him any slack one more time, I'm gonna throw your slack ass overboard."

"Ah, shut up and land that fish, Buck!"

CLAUDIA SCREAMED AT Skip "They're catching up. Do something! What the hell were you thinking when you threw that gun away! Idiot!"

"Oh, shut up! Seemed like a good idea at the time!" Skip glanced over his shoulder. "I don't think we're gonna make it!"

"Throw that tackle box over!" Claudia shouted.

"No!" Skip instinctively replied.

"You want that tackle box more than you want me?"

"No! But it won't make that much of a difference!"

"The heck it won't! Get rid of it, Skip! Throw it over for me!" Claudia's voice had panic in it, and Skip would have run a marathon through the infernos of hell to save her from agony.

Snatching the handle of the huge tackle box with his free hand, he tried to lift it over the side, only to find that he had left the latch open. Out flipped lead-headed jigs and other loose tackle into the bottom of the boat. Latching the top, he heaved the bulky box overboard.

"There! Ya happy?"

"Yeah. Thanks! Now your rods and reels!"

"What?"

"Your rods and reels! We have to make this boat as light as possible!"

"Now you've gone too far!" Skip shouted, annoyed.

"Look!" Claudia pointed in back of the boat, to the rental skiff that was rapidly closing the gap. Skip saw the glint of the Luger in the setting sunlight.

"Damn! Alright!" He scooped up all his rods, three at a time, and tossed them over the side.

"I guess you'll want me to throw the gas tank overboard too, eh?"

"Can you?"

"No!"

Claudia began rifling through the bow compartment, flinging items over her head as she managed to extricate them from the small opening. A first aid kit ricocheted off of Skip's forehead.

"Hey, watch it!"

"Sorry!" Claudia shouted back, flinging rain gear high in the air. She could see the first channel marker that lead into the safety of Presnell's marina. Turning, her heart skipped a beat as she realized that they were not going to make the final two-hundred yards to safety. Will was taking aim at Skip's head, only thirty yards away.

Crack! Water splashed next to them as the bullet narrowly missed its mark.

"Duck!" yelled Skip.

Claudia curled up in the front of the bouncing boat, still flinging things randomly out of the bow compartment; spare spark plugs, old rags, stiff gas lines, a plastic container full of hose clamps, and a spare rope.

The nylon rope spread out in the air like a snake uncurling in the wind. It hit the water perpendicular to the fleeing craft.

Skip lifted his head momentarily to see if the prop of the rental skiff would wrap around the rope.

Claudia shouted, "Pray again!"

"What?"

"I said pray again! It worked last time." A bullet skidded off the top of the engine and Skip felt a burning sensation on top of his shoulder. A few drops of blood began seeping into his white T-shirt, but he dared not take his right hand off of the throttle to feel the damage, and his left hand wouldn't quite reach. He began zig zagging the boat to throw Will's shots off. Under his breath he whispered a desperate plea to God, "Dear Lord, thanks for getting us out of that last fix – please, please God do it again! We need you God. Please help us! Amen."

"Rrrrrr!" the pursuit boat's engine sang as it momentarily met the rope Claudia had thrown in its path. The skiff came off plane, nearly throwing Will head first into St. Joseph's Bay.

"What the hell?" shouted Will.

"Dunno!" answered a concerned Bones. He was wishing Will had been thrown overboard, wanting nothing to do with murder. Will turned the gun on him.

"You do that again, and you're dead meat!"

"I didn't do nothin' – we hit somethin'!"

"Get us off of it, then before I blow your head off!" Will shouted, aiming the barrel at Bones' scared, gaunt face.

Bones swung the steering wheel radically to the right, then to the left, and the engine regained its momentum. But Skip and Claudia were entering the mouth of the marina.

"Chase them – full speed!" screamed Will at the top of his lungs. "Ram them if you have to!"

Bones got the boat up on plane again and speeded toward the fleeing duo.

Skip turned to see the skiff gaining rapidly, and, ignoring the "No Wake" sign, he kept the throttle wide open. He hoped the bridge beyond the marina, that allowed the creek to go under the highway, was too low for the larger skiff to negotiate.

"Duck!" Skip yelled to Claudia, but in reality there was plenty of room for them to glide under the bridge. The wakes of the speeding boats made the other vessels in the marina bounce against the docks, and Charlie ran down the creek bank shouting, "What the hell are you doing?"

As if answering his question, Charlie's own rental skiff, outlaw at the helm, came speeding through the canal only twenty feet in back of the hunted couple.

Bones, seeing the low bridge, tried to distract Will in hopes that he could slam his big body into the concrete.

"Now what, Will?" Bones shouted. "You gonna shoot him too?" Bones yelled, pointing at Charlie. But his ploy didn't work. Will ducked just in time. The blue canopy top smacked into the bridge, and was torn right off the boat over Bones' head.

The creek narrowed, Skip raced under overhanging willow branches, then suddenly backed off the throttle.

"Why are you slowing down?" Claudia screamed.

"Hang on!" Skip turned the boat hard right, just as the creek forked.

Will ducked under the willow branches that obscured the path of the creek. Bones couldn't see a thing, the branches and Will blocking his view. The boat flew out from under the branches, and the bow of the speeding skiff slammed full speed into a cypress tree. Bones heard a sickening thud as he flew through the air toward the bank. Will's body, gushing blood from his crushed head, slid down the cypress trunk and settled in a lump on the muddy bank.

"Oh, God!" Claudia shouted, as she saw the skiff crash against the solid cypress.

Backing off the throttle, Skip winced. He couldn't bear to look at the crumpled body oozing blood on the bank.

"Please go back, Skip! Hurry!" Claudia screamed.

Skip, unclear as to why Claudia was so concerned about two people only hours ago she wanted to kill, spun the boat around and headed back to the accident.

"Where's Bones?" Claudia shrieked.

"What do you care?"

"Find him, Skip. Please."

"Why should I?"

Claudia turned to Skip, and he saw tears flowing from down her face.

"Because he's my brother!"

"What?"

"Yeah. He's my brother," she said forlornly. "And I'm afraid he's dead!"

Skip, too shocked to speak, navigated around the back of the wrecked craft, and landed on the muddy bank on the other side of the boat so they did not have to look at Will's lifeless, gory body again.

Claudia jumped out on the bank, sunk into the black mud to her ankles, and trudged into the overgrowth, Skip close behind.

"Why didn't you tell me he's your brother?"

"Do you think I'm proud of that fact? How would you have felt about me, if you knew he was my brother?"

"The same," Skip said, but was not sure that was true.

"Here he is!" Claudia shouted, a ray of hope in her voice.

They knelt beside the motionless tattooed body that was lying on its side. Skip picked up Bones' limp left wrist and checked for a pulse.

"He's still alive!"

"Thank God!" sighed Claudia. She gently rolled him over.

"Oh my God! His arm!" She turned her head unable to bear the sight.

Skip's stomach churned as he examined Bones' broken right arm. Between his elbow and shoulder, the arm was bent as if Bones' had a second elbow there. The broken bone bulged the skin, threatening to break through with any wrong movement.

"We gotta get him to a hospital right away!" Skip said, grabbing Claudia's arm and turning her toward her brother. "It's a bad break, and I don't know but I'm thinking he may have other internal injuries. And if he's bleeding inside, we don't have a minute to spare."

Claudia, pale as a sheet, felt her brother's neck to see if it was broken.

"What if his spinal column is broken, too? Are you sure we should move him?"

"If his spinal column is broken, we shouldn't. But if it's not broken and we don't move him he could very well die from internal injuries. He landed hard, and who knows what he hit flying out of the boat – he may have hit the windshield or the rail. But he's your brother. What do you want to do?"

"You're right – let's get him outta here!"

Skip grabbed Bones under his moist armpits, Claudia grabbed his legs, and they carried him as gently as possible back to the boat. They set him in the front swivel seat, and Claudia held him securely while Skip started the engine. He glanced once more at the wreck of Charlie's rental skiff. The engine had stalled with the impact of the crash, which was fortunate for Charlie, Skip thought, because the momentum of the heavy outboard had cracked the transom and the cover was in the bottom of the hull, as the propeller reached for the sky. Skip was reminded of pinwheels he had as a child; the prop seemed to be waiting for a breeze to come along and set it in motion.

Motoring back under the bridge, Skip saw the blue navy top that had been ripped off of Charlie's skiff floating in the water, an air bubble caught in the canvas preventing it from sinking. Having no way to get around it in the narrow canal, he turned the engine off, tilted the outboard's skeg out of the water, and glided over the obstacle. Skip cranked the engine several times, but it was in one of its moods, and wouldn't start again. He grabbed the oar and paddled the last forty feet to the launch ramp.

Charlie shouted from the floating dock where he awaited them "What the hell happened?"

"Call the police, Charlie!" Skip shouted. "That guy who was shooting at us is dead!"

"What about my boat?"

"Bad news! It's wrecked. The engine may be salvageable, though."

"Where's the nearest hospital?" Claudia shouted, visibly irritated that they were discussing boats and her brother was perhaps mortally wounded.

"It's in St. Joe – Gulf Coast Hospital. They have an emergency room." Vonniciel said, as she stopped the bow before it scraped on the concrete launch ramp. "What's wrong with him?"

"Aside from a broken arm, we don't know," replied Claudia. "Maybe internal injuries."

"He was the one driving my boat, wasn't he?" inquired Charlie. "He's going to be responsible for the damage!"

"He's not going to be responsible for anything if he's dead!" shouted Claudia. "How about helping us get him out of here while Skip gets his truck?"

Skip jumped out into the calf-deep water, somewhat surprised to hear Claudia issuing orders. "How far's the hospital?"

"A few miles up the road," Vonniciel offered, pointing toward the city of St. Joe. "Maybe I'd better call an ambulance!"

"We don't have time to wait for an ambulance! Skip, do you know where it is?"

"I think so."

Skip ran to the truck, fumbling in his pocket for the keys. Unlocking the passenger door, he flung the cooler with his prize fish in it into the bed of the pickup. He wondered if that fish Buck was fighting would compare to his gator trout. Waiting for the glow light indicator on the dashboard to go out before starting the truck, he heard Claudia scream from the dock, "Hurry!"

Backing quickly through the camping area, and down the launch ramp, Skip hopped out and opened the tailgate.

"Set him in there," he suggested.

"No. In the front seat," Claudia insisted.

"O.K. Where exactly is the hospital, Vonniciel?" Skip asked.

"It's right off of Highway 71."

"Where's that?"

"That's Fifth Street. It's the one by the first light. Take a right off of 98, and the third left."

"O.K. Thanks!"

Claudia and Vonniciel gingerly set Bones in the middle of the cab. Claudia jumped in and supported his limp body. Skip spun the truck tires in the loosed gravel, and they sped toward the road that led to town. As they ascended the drive that opened on State Road 30A, a Gulf County Sheriff's car with its siren blasting and lights flashing pulled in, nearly sideswiping the pickup. Skip hesitated, thinking the Sheriff could get Bones to the hospital quicker.

"Keep going!" shouted Claudia in a panicked voice. "Get the hell out of here!"

"But..."

"But nothing! Let's go! If that Sheriff gets Bones, he'll be charged with kidnapping. And I don't want the authorities to know that we found that treasure!"

At the word treasure, Bones stirred and groaned. He mumbled "Treasure. Go back for the treasure. Leave them! Go back for the treasure."

"Oh, great!" exclaimed Claudia. "Everyone at the hospital will know about the find."

Driving into the sunset, blues, pinks and shades of orange spread upon the sky like a painter's canvas, and the trio fell silent.

"That's an awesome sunset, eh, Claudia?" said Skip, finally breaking the silence. But Claudia's mind was across the bay.

"Skip..." Claudia purred.

"Uh, huh?"

"Skip, we gotta go back there tonight and get it."

"No we don't. I've had about as much fun as I can handle in one day, Claudia!"

"Skip, if you love me, you'll do this for me."

"Love? Did I say anything about love?" he asked playfully.

"I can see it in your eyes when you look at me."

"I am taken with you, Claudia. I am totally, heads-over-heels crazy about you! But love? We only met the day before yesterday. Let's call it runaway infatuation."

"Whatever."

"Though I do believe that once I get to know you, I mean really know you, I'll love you like no other woman in the world. Seems to me you're the person I've been searching for all my life."

"You mean, like the fourth piece of your cosmic quest?"

"The one piece I'm missing in my search for the whole."

"So I'm your whole, eh?"

"Yeah."

"Never thought I'd be proud to say that about myself!"

They laughed.

"Then you do love me, admit it."

Skip thought about that, and had no answer.

"Please, Skip, let's go back and get it tonight. It could be gone by tomorrow."

"No it couldn't. Of the four people who know where it is, three of us are right here, and the fourth is dead. It will still be there in the morning."

"Skip, please. I'm not going to be able to sleep knowing that it's lying out there unprotected. We'll drive around the peninsula in the truck, walk to it from the road, and find it using flashlights. How about it?"

Silence.

"For me, Skip?" she gave him such an endearing look that Skip would have jumped over the Empire State Building to please her.

"Let's deal with your brother, first, then discuss it over dinner."

The road merged into Hwy. 98. Passing two gas station – convenience store combinations and the Burger King, Skip took a right on Hwy. 71, and the third left. Several blocks later, they arrived at the tiny hospital.

"Damn!" Claudia remarked. "I've seen doctor's offices bigger than this!"

Parking the truck under the eaves of the entranceway, Skip helped Claudia carry Bones in. Still unconscious, Bones mumbled an unintelligible word now and again, but showed no other signs of waking up.

"What happened to him?" a nurse asked curiously as she wheeled a gurney toward them.

"A boating accident." Claudia replied.

"Oh. This is the one Sheriff Thompson was talking about."

"What do you mean?" Claudia asked, concerned.

"He said for y'all to stay put – he's on his way. Called me from Presnell's."

Skip and Claudia glanced at each other.

"Well," said Claudia nonchalantly as they set Bones down on the gurney, "I see he's in good hands here. We're starving – we'll be next door getting a bite to eat." She grabbed Skip by the arm and walked out into the twilight.

"We gotta get out of here, now!" Claudia exclaimed.

"Why? You're not in any trouble."

"Not yet. But what if Charlie is holding me responsible for what happened to his boat? I am the one who rented it, after all."

"I don't think he'll hold you responsible -"

"And how are we gonna explain what happened without spilling the beans about the treasure? Let's get out of here, Skip! Please."

Slamming the door of the truck behind her as she got in, Claudia slunk down so she couldn't be seen if the Sheriff pulled up. Skip drove out of the parking lot, heading away from Hwy. 71. He heard the siren of the law officer in the distance. Accelerating, he felt like a criminal leaving the scene of a crime. He turned left on a side street that led back to Hwy. 98, just as the Sheriff turned onto the street behind them. Once they were out of sight of the hospital, Skip stopped the truck.

"That was close!" said Claudia.

Simultaneously, they both said, "What now?"

Claudia gave Skip another one of those looks that melted him. Scooting over next to him, she kissed his cheek. Skip turned and they kissed passionately, arms flung around each other with abandon.

After several seconds, Claudia pushed away and whispered, "Let's get out of here before the Sheriff finds us." Taking a left, Skip got on the two-lane Hwy. 98 heading back toward Presnell's.

"You mean finds you, right. Because he doesn't have any reason to be looking for me."

"Oh, I wouldn't be so sure of that."

"What do you mean?"

"I mean, like, leaving the scene of an accident. Speeding in the marina. Aiding and abetting a criminal."

"Nah," Skip said, doubt in his voice. "It's your brother they're after, for sure. You, maybe. But not me."

"I wouldn't bet my life on it. One thing is for sure, Skip. We can't use this truck to carry the loot, the Sheriff will have a description of it. Any car rental agencies here?"

"Oh, yeah!"

Claudia looked relieved.

"Yeah. Right next to the Hilton and the airport!"

"Very funny. Do you think Charlie would let us borrow his car?"

"Sure. He'd be glad to. We've only wrecked one of his boats so far today. Maybe he'll throw in a free trip to the Bahamas, too, while he's at it!"

"Point taken, wise guy. What do you suggest?"

"I suggest we find a place to hide this truck. Get something to eat. Then walk back to the campsite and sleep in my tent tonight. Just before dawn jump in my boat and cross the bay as the sun rises. What do you say?"

"That sounds like a good plan. They have showers at the campsite?"

"Naw. Fisherman don't take showers, I thought you knew that!"

"Oh, that's why you guys smell so bad, eh?"

Chuckling, Skip took a right off of 98 on an unpaved side street with a run down, abandoned warehouse on one corner and a Hungry Howie's pizza shop that was still open on the other. Travelling several blocks, he parked the truck in the midst of other vehicles that were in bad shape, in back of an auto body repair business. His beat up truck blended in with all the other dented, rusty cars and trucks that were in the lot.

CHAPTER XIV
PANHANDLE NIGHTS

Walking hand-in-hand toward Hwy. 98, the flashing lights of the Sheriff's car lit up the night as the officer cruised slowly along the highway looking for Skip's truck. Claudia flinched and pulled Skip toward the back of the pizza shop.

"What are you doing?" he asked Claudia. "That Sheriff doesn't know what we look like..."

"Wanna bet? He's had Charlie and that nurse at the hospital to question about what we look like – I bet he has a good description of us by now."

"Yeah, maybe you're right." Ducking out of sight behind the pizza shop, they kissed again.

"This is kind of exciting!" Claudia said. "I've never been wanted for questioning before. It's sort of cloak-and-daggerish, eh?"

"I guess. Being close to you is great. But running from the law is not what I'd call fun. My idea of a thrill is watching my topwater plug chug along on top of the water, and expecting an explosion any second. See, when I'm out there on the water, totally focused on fishing, I am living in the moment. There's no past and no future. My whole being is right there, right then. It's a great way to spend time."

"Well, maybe we should focus on this moment."

"Great idea. I'll try. But with the police cars with their lights flashing, your brother in the hospital ready to tell the whole world about the treasure, and wondering how on Earth I'm gonna get back to Carabelle tomorrow to weigh my fish, it's a bit of a challenge."

"I know. But after tomorrow, when that treasure is mine, we can both relax and kick back for awhile." Trying to change the subject, Claudia asked, "Are there any other places to eat in Port St. Joe, other than this pizza place?"

"Yeah. The Burger King. And the Great Wall of China. Unfortunately all the mom-and-pop restaurants close around eight o'clock on Saturday nights."

"Hoppin' town, eh?"

"Oh, yeah! The life of the panhandle!"

As the Sheriff's lights faded, Claudia and Skip ventured into the eatery. Rather than having pizza, they each ordered a pasta dish with salad, and large lemonades. Skip insisted on paying the bill.

"Once we get the treasure tomorrow, how will we get it out of town without using your truck?"

"I don't know. And how am I going to get to the weigh-in tomorrow? The deadline for weighing fish is 2 PM, and I have to be in line with my trout by then."

"How about if we just take your boat to Carabelle."

"Right!" Skip said sarcastically. "Might as well be the moon. First of all, there is no inland way that I know of to get there from St. Joe Bay, except up the inland waterway via Lake Wimico, into the Apalachicola River, down into Apalachee Bay, and across the bay to the mouth of the Carabelle. That would take us all day in my boat. Besides, I don't have enough gas."

"What about going out into the Gulf and back to Carabelle?"

"Not a chance. Even if we had perfect weather, by the time we went north far enough to get around the peninsula, we'd only have enough gas to get to Indian Pass. And that route would take us most of the day, too. Just can't do it in my small skiff."

"Hey, I have an idea. Let's steal a car!"

"What?"

"Just kidding! Do you know anyone else who is fishing in the tournament and would be willing to give you a ride?"

"Only that jerk next to me in the campsite, and I don't trust him. He's the kind of person that throws beer cans out the window, flicks lit cigarette butts on the street, and could care less about anyone else but himself. No, I wouldn't ask him for a ride if he was the last person on Earth."

"I know two other guys who will be going to the weigh-in!" exclaimed Claudia.

"Buck and Lucas! They might do it. Maybe we can find them in the bay tomorrow and ask. What do you think?"

"I think it's a long shot. But what else could we do?"

"Paint the truck," Skip said in jest.

Claudia looked up from her cheese ravioli. "Of course! Why didn't I think of that?"

"Ah, I was just teasing."

"No. I think it's a stroke of genius. They're looking for a guy and a gal in a tan and brown pickup. What if we painted it red, or green?"

"Or fuchsia?"

"No, really, Skip! Let's do it. I'll get you a good paint and body job when we get back to town. We'll buy a couple of cans of spray paint and have at it!"

"Claudia!"

"Come on, Skip. For me?"

Sandals off, she ran her foot up Skip's leg under the table, and gave him a seductive smile.

"Claudia. I'm putty in your hands. I do believe, for a hug and a kiss, I'd wrassle a shark if you asked me to."

"Then you'll do it?"

"No. We'll do it. But I choose the color. And everything's off if those two convenience stores across the street don't have any spray paint, deal?"

"Deal!" Claudia beamed.

"This is getting wilder and wilder!" Skip lamented.

"Bet you didn't bargain for this much fun when you left Tallahassee last Thursday, eh?"

"Nope. Didn't expect to be returning without my tackle box or any of my good rods. Didn't expect to be going back in a different color truck."

"Didn't expect to be returning with a woman who was filthy rich, either, did ya?"

"No." The thought of Claudia returning to Tallahassee with him and his son the next day after the weigh-in was thrilling to Skip. Treasure or no treasure, Claudia could be the woman his heart had been longing for all these years. The one he could spend the rest of his life with. The one who would love him and his son, come hell or high water.

Entering the first convenience store, Claudia and Skip split up to cover the store, in search of spray paint.

"Nothing here," Claudia reported disappointedly from the isle that contained hardware and auto supplies.

Walking with Claudia to the only other open convenience store, a Texaco station, Skip wondered how he got talked into spray painting his truck. True, it was rusty and the current paint job left a lot to be desired, but, on the other hand, it did match his boat.

"Hope we find something here," Claudia said, as Skip opened the door for her and a rush of cold, air-conditioned breeze escaped. Skip noticed only one clerk behind the counter. He was always amazed that one person could keep track of eight gas pumps, run the register, and chat with the customers, all at the same time.

"Got it!" Claudia shouted, as she held up a can of black Rustoleum spray paint. How many cans do you think it will take?

"I don't want black, Claudia. Black absorbs heat, and it gets awfully hot here in the summer."

"It's black or gray, love."

"Black. I like gray even less. It's the same color as the road, and people sometimes don't see ya coming."

"Black it is then. Five cans do?"

"Might as well get all six, just in case," Skip replied.

They got in line in back of a stooped woman with gray hair and a wrinkled face, a loose fitting smock draped lazily across her gaunt shoulders. Wheeling an oxygen tank behind her, she asked the clerk for a carton of Virginia Slims cigarettes. Turning, she noticed Skip and Claudia holding the cans of spray paint.

"Oh, paintin' the town tonight, are ya?" she cackled.

"Yup. Havin' the time of our lives!" Skip told her.

As he was paying for the spray paint, Skip asked the clerk "Have you heard the weather forecast?"

"I hadn't heard it myself, but I overheard some customers saying tomorrow was not going to be a good day to be out on the water, whatever that meant."

"Thanks!" said Skip, helping the clerk put the cans into a plastic bag. Outside the store, Skip looked at the sky and noticed there were no stars.

"Sure hope it doesn't rain!"

"What makes you think it might?"

"Oh, just not seeing any stars in the sky. Did you notice any storm clouds as the sun set?"

"No, but, then again, I had my mind on other things. I wonder how my brother is doing."

"Why don't you call the hospital. Surely they'll let you know."

"Good idea. Got thirty-five cents?"

"Sure."

Claudia looked the number up in the thin phone book that was attached to the open payphone canopy by a metal chain.

"Hello? I'm calling about the guy who was dropped off there about an hour and a half ago. How is he doing? Have you found out what's wrong with him?"

"Who is this, honey?" said a suspicious voice on the other end of the line.

"It's his sister. The one who dropped him off."

"Didn't I tell you that the Sheriff wanted a word with you? He left here all in a huff looking for you, gal."

"Ah, yeah, we talked," Claudia lied. "How is my brother doing?"

"Mighty groggy, right about now."

"What are the extent of his injuries?"

"We're transferring him to the hospital down the road in Apalachicola."

"Why? What's wrong with him?"

"I'm not a doctor, but if you ask me he's got himself one mean concussion. And that broken arm."

"Anything else?"

"Not that I can tell. What happened to him anyway?"

"Boating accident," Claudia replied. "Thanks!" She hung up the phone, shrugged her shoulders, and repeated the nurse's answers to Skip.

"He's a lucky man if all he's got is a concussion and a broken arm. Could have been killed!"

"Yeah. But I wouldn't call him lucky. He's had a pretty rough life."

"Shoot! I forgot to get ice for the cooler. Don't want that monster trout to go bad."

Inside the store, Skip asked the clerk if she had any block ice for sale, but she didn't. "Cubes, only, honey. Sorry!"

"O.K. I'll take two bags then."

Crossing the street, Claudia carried one bag of ice, Skip carried the other bag of ice and the bag holding the paint spray.

Reaching the rusty pickup, Skip unlocked the passenger door and pulled the cooler out. He opened the valve on the bottom of the cooler to let some of the excess water drain, but not all of it. He thought that keeping the trout submerged in water would at least keep the weight the same as when he caught it, if not increase it some. Dropping one bag of ice on the pavement to separate the cubes, he opened the top of the bag and poured the loose ice cubes into the cooler. He caught a glance of the side of the trout, still silvery and speckled, fresh enough to eat. He couldn't wait to weigh the behemoth. He knew it was the largest trout he had ever caught. He put the cooler back in the cab so it would not get black paint on it.

"Hey, maybe this will make the old truck last a few more years, eh?" Claudia consoled Skip as she shook a can of the rust inhibiting spray paint, getting it ready for use.

"Maybe. But I'm gonna remember what you said about a paint and body job when we get back to Tallahassee. I'm not riding around sweating in a black pickup in the summer without air conditioning."

"O.K."

Skip got into the truck and moved it to the end of the line of damaged cars, parking it far enough away from the last one so the spray paint wouldn't get on any of the other vehicles. Skip sprayed the driver's side of the truck, and Claudia painted the passenger side of the truck in the dim security light the business owner had left on in the back of the shop. Skip found some old newspapers in the cab of his truck, and they used them to cover the windows and windshield when they sprayed. They eventually ran out of paint before they could do the bed of the truck. Skip was relieved, because he didn't want to put his cooler on wet black paint, nor did he want to have to move the other stuff left in the truck bed, such as the extra gas can, and his only two remaining rods; the heavy duty rod he always brought along in case he decided to try for a cobia, and a back-up light tackle rod with a closed-faced spinning reel on it, that he only used if one of his other rigs had broken down and he was desperate. His son had won it the year before fishing a junior tournament, and he reckoned it was only worth about ten dollars, but it meant a lot to Benny.

"How long do you think it will take to dry?" asked Claudia, a worried look on her face.

"With or without rain?"

"Without."

"Normally it would dry to the touch in six to eight hours. But with this misty sea breeze blowing, it may not dry until noon tomorrow."

"What the heck are we going to do?"

"I have a plan – walk back to the campsite, buy gas for the outboard on the way. Get up before dawn, pack the tent and take it with us in the boat. Cross the bay and get the treasure. Then, instead of going back to Presnell's, we'll just motor into the town marina – "

"What marina? This town has a marina?"

"Not exactly. It has a public launch ramp and a dock."

"Where?"

"About two blocks thataway," Skip pointed back down the street toward the village green.

"Then what?"

"Get the pickup. Then we'll go back to Presnell's with the truck, get my boat trailer, pick up the boat, and head off to Carabelle."

"Do you think we'll have time to get to the weigh-in?"

"Shouldn't be a problem, if the weather cooperates."

Claudia held up an empty spray can and gave a mock toast, "Here's to calm seas, pirate treasures, and winning the fishing tournament!"

"Amen!" Their empty cans clinked together in the night, but toasting with empty glasses seldom produces the desired results.

Locking the truck and grabbing the upright blue plastic gas can, Skip asked Claudia to carry his son's rod and reel, and they headed back toward Hwy. 98. Skip bought two-cycle oil at the Texaco station, and poured ten ounces of it in the gas can. Knowing how heavy six gallons would be to lug all the way back to Presnell's, and thinking they only needed enough gas to get across the bay and back to the ramp in town, Skip pumped four gallons. Walking on the bay side of the highway, traffic having dwindled to a car every five minutes or so, Skip mulled over why Claudia didn't want to talk to the police just yet.

"Run it by me again why you don't want to talk to the Sheriff, Claudia." Skip said, swatting the occasional mosquito and no-seeum gnat off of his arms and legs.

"First of all, I don't want to risk revealing anything about the treasure."

"Why would he ask you about that? He has no clue what you were doing across the bay."

"Maybe he does and maybe he doesn't."

"One thing's for sure, Will didn't tell him anything!"

"True. And I know my brother would have kept his mouth shut if he had his wits about him. But, then again, he might have told the Sheriff the whole story, in that semi-state of consciousness he was in. I can't take the chance."

"Even if he did tell the Sheriff about the treasure, the Sheriff wouldn't believe him, I bet. I don't think you have anything to worry about."

"What about leaving the scene of an accident? And, maybe even evading a police officer? Remember, he told that nurse he wanted to question us. And we high-tailed it out of there."

"You don't have a criminal record, do you? Something you want to hide?"

"Hell, no. I've never been a wanted woman before. At least, not in that way!"

As they veered off of Hwy. 98 onto 30A that followed the shoreline of the bay to Presnell's, Skip walked in silence, wondering if he could be arrested for leaving the scene of an accident and evading a police officer too. It sure wouldn't look good that he had painted his truck black.

"Gorgeous night, eh, Skip?" Claudia purred, in an attempt to lighten the conversation. A cool breeze rolled across the calm bay, ruffling Claudia's silky hair. Between clouds patches of stars shone brightly now that they were away from the lights of town.

"Yeah. Beautiful. Almost as pretty as you, Claudia."

"Skip, how sure are you that there's a God out there?" Claudia asked, looking up in the sky.

"I'm sure. I'm as sure of the existence of God as I am of the existence of those stars that we can't see tonight because of the clouds. You can't see them, but you just know they are there."

"What makes you so sure God's there?"

"I really feel like, if he wasn't, I'd be dead now."

"How so?"

"I've been in life-threatening situations, and called on Him, and He's always seen fit to save my sorry self. It's amazing. By the odds, I would have been dead a long time ago, if it wasn't for God."

"You really believe, don't you?"

"Yeah. You?"

"Sometimes. Sometimes not. I just don't know. You mentioned you prayed every day. What do you say to God?"

"Wow. That's personal! I've only shared that with two other people in my whole life, my son and my ex-wife. Oh, yeah – three actually. A close friend of mine."

"I'd really like to know. Please share it with me."

"Well, it's kinda convoluted, but it comes from my heart."

"I'd love to hear it."

"O.K. I start off by thanking God for -"

"No, don't tell me what you pray for, actually say the prayer so I can hear it."

"Thank you dear God for the love in my life from Thee, my family, friends and son. Thank you God for my health; mental, physical and spiritual. Thank you Lord for being with me in times of need and for answering my prayers. Thank you dear God for my food and shelter and clothing, and my material possessions and my job. Thank you Lord for having so much patience with a sinner such as myself. Thank you God for the sky above, and the atmosphere, and all the lands and all the waters, and all the plants and animals and insects and microbes, and for the good people of the Earth; for those who are kind and considerate and friendly and helpful and caring. Thank you God for those folks. Thank you dear Lord for those who have come before us and taught us love, and those among us who are teaching love, and for those who are struggling for the environment, or peace, or to feed people, or for human rights."

"Seems like you have a lot of things to be thankful for."

"Yeah. I do."

"Is that the end?"

"No."

"Well, let's hear the rest of it.

"Please help all those people today who are on their deathbeds, sick, scared, sad, worried, in pain, insane, alone, hungry or homeless. Please comfort them with thy faith and help them, and help us to help them. And Lord please fill the hearts of all those people today whose hearts are filled with anger or hatred or nationalism or jealousy or zealotry or vengeance or prejudice or greed or cruelty or vanity or untruthfulness. Please purge those things from their hearts, and fill their hearts instead with kindness, and love, and joy, and peace, and forgiveness, and open-mindedness, and charity, and humility and pluralism and tolerance and truthfulness, that all the wars may cease, that there may never be another war, and that wherever humanity spreads may be a beautiful place to live. And Lord, please forgive me my sins, for I have sinned and I'm sorry for my sins. And Lord, please help all those people today whose lives are affected by war or hunger or disease or corruption. And Lord please comfort them with thy faith, and help them, and help us to help them. And please end all wars, and end corruption, and help us find a cure for diseases that plague mankind, and that we will disseminate those cures throughout the entire world in short order. And please help those people around the world today, who are trying to feed people, to do their jobs, that no one may go hungry and no one may starve. And Lord please help (and then I list all the people I know who have cancer) in this their time of need. Please cure them of what ails them and bring them back to health. And Lord please prevent the cancers from returning to their bodies. And Lord please help those people around the world today who are struggling for peace through peaceful means. Please comfort them with thy faith, and help them, and help us to help them, that they may succeed, and the Earth may know an end to war, and an end to violence. Thank you dear God for this beautiful, beautiful day and this beautiful Earth, and all the blessings in my life. I love you, God. Amen."

"Geeze! What religion is that?"

"It's not any one particular religion. It's just me talking to God."

"It's beautiful. Do you think he hears you?"

"Yeah. I do."

"And do you think it was God who got us out of the mess we were in yesterday – being tied to the tree and Will wanting to kill us, and then shooting at us on the bay?"

"Like I said, I really believe that if it wasn't for God, I wouldn't be alive today."

"You owe him."

"We owe him."

"And what do we do to pay him back?"

"Do justice, and love kindness, and walk humbly with your God."

"That's from the Bible, isn't it?"

"Yeah. I guess. The idea is to do his will here on Earth. The golden rule, and one step more."

"What one step more."

"Go out of your way to help others."

"Oh. Makes sense."

"And one other thing."

"What?"

"Forgive those who you are angry with."

"Tough order."

"It's not easy. But it will set your soul free."

Walking in silence, Skip took a big breath of the salty sea air and exhaled, letting go of all the embarrassment he felt in sharing his personal prayer with Claudia. He speculated that she would either think that he was crazy, or understand and accept him the way he was.

Crossing a bridge over one of the many lazy tidal creeks along the shore, the wind-swept clouds parted slightly, allowing beams of moonlight to break free and scatter shimmering crystals across the bay. For a second, Claudia could see the peninsula, its dark outline rising from the other side of the illuminated, tranquil water. She reached out for Skip's hand, and squeezed it.

"You will share the treasure with me, won't you?"

Skip smiled, and said "I just did."

"You know what I mean. Billy Bowleg's treasure."

"No."

"Why not?"

"Call me superstitious, but I don't think anything good is going to come to anyone who takes possession of that loot. I just have that feeling. Look what happened to Will. And your brother."

"Then why are you helping me get it?"

"Because it's the right thing to do. I'm not gonna judge you, or try to impose my beliefs on you. I can see how much it means to you to get that treasure chest. I'll help. But I don't want anything in return."

"Not even one gold bar?"

"Not even one gold bar. Just a thank you will do fine. And maybe my truck painted to match my boat again."

"You know, Skip, if I didn't see it yesterday, I'd still have my doubts that the treasure even existed. God bless old aunt Gladys! She wasn't as crazy as everyone thought. Damn, Skip! I'm so close to being rich. And independent. Independently wealthy! And it's lying there across the bay just waiting for me to scoop it up. I can't wait until tomorrow!"

As Claudia finished the sentence, the moon slipped behind the clouds again.

"Well, I hope I'm wrong about the treasure carrying bad karma. Maybe Will took it all with him to the other side. I hope it turns out to be everything you've dreamed it will be. I really do."

"Thanks."

As they walked across the bridge that had taken the navy top off of Charlie's skiff in the chase, neither spoke. The cacophony of a hundred cicadas echoed from the swamp, interrupted occasionally by a bullfrog croaking. Mullet splashed, reentering the water after acrobatic dashes into what must feel like the nothingness of air to them, playing in their borderland of life and death: Death if they remain out of the water too long, and death if they remain in the water too long as they are being chased by predators. Not all of their leaps are forced by fleet enemies. They play, when the mood hits them, night or day, and delight in their ability to soar through the air. Skip could never explain the logic of the mullet landing on its side as gravity pulled it back down to its watery home. Maybe there was no logic to it. Maybe landing on its side made a bigger splash, and that was more fun than to ease back into the waves silently. Maybe it just flat-out felt better. Maybe, that twist to the side was only the beginning of a complete spin that finished beneath the waves. So many mysteries in the sea, so little time to solve them!

CHAPTER XV
CLOSER AND CLOSER

Half running, half sliding, Claudia and Skip made their way down the dewy grass slope into the campground. Walking as quiet as possible across the pebbles and oyster shells in front of the launch area, Claudia whispered, "Do you have any clothes I could borrow?"

"Let's see – there's the blue jeans I fished in yesterday, and that T-shirt with the catfish slime on it."

"Yuck."

"Just kidding. I've got a tournament T-shirt from last year that's clean. It's really nice – each year it's different, the artwork on the back of the shirt is beautiful. And I've got an extra pair of shorts..."

"And a belt, I hope."

"Yeah, and a belt. And an extra pair of underwear."

"Clean or dirty?"

"Clean."

"Joy. I got the shower first, I call it." Claudia said to Skip as they walked across the grass toward the tent.

"Shhh! Let's not wake our neighbor." They could hear snoring from the tent next to them. Skip noticed quite a few more empty beer bottles in the back of the pickup than the first day he laid eyes on it.

Untying the tent flaps, Skip unzipped the mesh, and emerged a few seconds later with the fresh clothes for Claudia and a white bath towel.

"Where's the shower?" Claudia whispered.

"In that building." Skip pointed to a cinder block building that looked more like an overgrown outhouse than a bathroom and bath facility. The look on Claudia's face reflected her impression of the accommodations.

"Is it clean?"

"Oh, sure," Skip teased, grin on his face. "Clean as a whistle! Only dainty fisherwomen use the ladies side."

"There's a ladies side?" Claudia's outlook brightened.

"Yup! And I guarantee you'll want to use that rather than the men's area."

"I'll be back in a bit," she said, sauntering quietly away. She stopped, and turned to Skip. Skip's heart stopped momentarily, thinking she was going to ask him to join her. But to his disappointment she said, "Is there hot water?"

"What do you want, everything? Come back, I forgot to give you the shampoo and conditioner and soap. Yeah, there's hot water. But as hot as it is tonight, we won't be using much."

Ducking back into the tent, Skip returned shortly with the plastic bottles of shampoo, conditioner, a bar of soap wrapped in a paper towel, an unused toothbrush he got every year in the tournament bag with "Quill Turk, DDS" stamped on the handle, and a large tube of toothpaste.

"Don't forget my slippers, dear!" Claudia cooed. Skip fantasized about what Claudia would look like naked in the shower. His pants bulged at the thought of her au naturale, dripping wet, hair hanging down over her bare shoulders.

"Ah, if you, ah, need someone to wash your back, I'm available."

"No thanks. But I'll take you up on that some day soon."

Skip shook his head and smiled. His infatuation with Claudia was at a new high. The part of his mind that said, "Not yet!" was getting blown away by the part of his mind that was screaming "Please, please, please make love to her!" It was a losing battle, but one that was not over yet. Skip was still determined, although half-heartedly, to wait until he was sure of what Claudia's soul was made of before doing anything foolhardy.

He reasoned that she was still concerned about her brother, even after the things he put her through. Surely that showed her compassion and capacity for forgiveness. She voiced concern over Skip's affairs, and was not just focused on her own needs; that showed she was not self-centered. And she seemed to have an adventuresome outlook on life. Skip found that refreshing. So many of the women he had met were reluctant to take chances of any kind. Was she the one to complete him? Did she have the ability and desire to love him as much as he wanted to love her? Only time would tell, he told himself, as he ducked back into the tent to gather fresh clothes and wait for her to return with the toiletries. "What would she look like, braless, in his T-shirt?" He couldn't help but wonder, unintentionally getting aroused by the thought.

He wasn't disappointed. As Claudia waltzed back into the campsite, Skip stood up intending to get the bathroom stuff and towel from her. Walking daintily through the wet grass with bare feet, Claudia stepped on a shell and stumbled. Skip caught her and prevented the fall. They looked at each other in the darkness. Skip smelled the cleanliness of Claudia's sleek body, felt her breasts and hips pressed against him. Gently, his lips touched Claudia's, and Skip took a mental snapshot of the moment, it was so good to hold this intriguing woman close, caress her strong, sinewy body, and feel her melt in his arms. Skip's desire was fanned like a wild fire out of control. Claudia breathed deep and Skip could feel her heart pounding. Cupping his cheek in her hand, she slowly withdrew, and sighed.

"You're turn."

"Uhhh, yeah. My turn." Skip said breathlessly. "I'll be right back."

Exchanging the toiletries, Claudia eased her lithe body into the cocoon of the tent. Its upside down v-shaped roof reminded her of a picture she had seen in a book of fairytales, perhaps the gingerbread house. Inside, she fished around in Skip's duffel bag until she came across a comb, and sat in the middle of the spread-out sleeping bag combining her fine, wet hair.

Skip, half way to the bathhouse, realized he didn't have a change of clothes, or his toothbrush with him. Returning to the tent, he said softly, "Claudia, I forgot something."

She drew back the screening and Skip crawled in.

"What did you forget?"

"Oh, nothing important. Clothes. Toothbrush."

"Not preoccupied, are we?"

"Just a bit." Rummaging through the duffel bag, Skip found a clean set of clothes, his toothbrush, and floss.

"Got some floss here, if you'd like some," he offered.

"Yeah. Break me off a piece, please."

Handing her a foot of floss, Skip said, "See ya in a few minutes. I'll smell a whole lot better when I come back."

"You don't smell bad." Claudia called after him as he made his way out of the tent.

Setting a new personal record for taking a shower, cleaning his teeth and flossing, Skip walked silently back to where Claudia waited. Still torn as to how he would react if she wanted to make love, he took a deep breath, and crawled inside. Claudia sat cross-legged, still running the comb through her silky hair. As Skip turned to fasten the tent flaps in place, he noticed his hands shaking. Securing the flaps in the open position to keep the breeze flowing through the tent, he zipped the mesh screening closed. As he sat back, his hand accidentally landed on Claudia's.

"Oops. Sorry," Skip said softly. Claudia smiled in the darkness of the tent, her nervous grin slightly illuminated by the sparse light from the bathhouse.

"Skip..." she began, at the same time Skip said "Claudia..." An awkward moment of silence followed.

"Skip," Claudia began again. "I know how much you want me. And I want you, too. I really do. I want you more than any man I've known for the last ten years."

"But?" Skip could tell by the tone of her voice that she was leading up to telling him she would not make love with him that night. Feeling disappointed, yet, in a strange way relieved at the same time, he encouraged her to elaborate. "Go on."

"Well, I want the first time we make love to be something really special. Something wonderful, like when a princess and prince make love in a fairytale."

"You mean my tent isn't your idea of romantic?"

"Not exactly. And it's so hot tonight. And all I can think about is what's across the bay. I feel so out of sorts. As much as I want to make love to you, tonight's just not the ideal night for our first time. I want the first time to be magical, wonderful, fulfilling..."

"I get the picture. And I'm O.K. with that, Claudia. I am," Skip tried to convince himself.

"And besides, Skip. There are practical matters too. I don't want to get pregnant. And I don't want to catch any disease. Do you have any disease?"

"None that I care to share, darling. Actually, no, I don't. And I gave blood a few months ago, so I know I'm not carrying the AIDS virus. How about you?"

"No. Thank God!"

"Claudia, I really appreciate you being up-front and honest with me. I want you so bad, I could scream. But I hear what you're saying. I understand. Thanks for telling me how you feel."

"You're not angry?"

"A little disappointed, maybe. But I can handle it."

Kissing, Skip eased Claudia's head toward the back of the tent and gently lowered it on the only pillow he had packed.

"Good night, sweet lady!" he whispered in her ear, and lay down beside her. Pulling his shorts off, and taking off his button down shirt, he laid them back in the duffel bag.

Claudia could see in the dim light the bulge in Skip's underwear. She rolled over on her side toward him, and lightly laid her hand on his chest. She felt his heartbeat quicken, as she slowly and gently ran her fingernails through his chest hair. Gradually, at a snail's pace, she moved her hand lower, now caressing his strong stomach.

Skip lay perfectly still, his heart racing as Claudia's touch lifted him to higher and higher levels of arousal. His mind silently screamed, "Don't stop. Please don't stop!"

The tips of Claudia's fingers eased tantalizingly into his curly bush, and back to his stomach. Claudia could see Skip's erection propping up his underwear, like the tent pole taught against the tent roof. She heard his breathing and could barely discern a low, soft moan issuing involuntarily from somewhere deep within him. Her own juices welled in response to the erotic sight of having full control over his masculine, tense body. She ventured her index finger below the shaft of his penis, and ran it tantalizingly slow across his scrotum, then followed the same path, the same speed, with each of her other fingers.

Sweat poured from Skip's brow as he felt Claudia's deliberate and painfully gradual advances. He wanted to take her hand and wrap it around his throbbing penis, but he knew that doing so would spoil some of the pleasure Claudia was so selflessly bringing him.

Skip had never had such an intense sexual experience before. He thought he was going to faint at the height of his pleasure. Veins in his neck seemed to be at full capacity, ready to burst any second.

He lay there, exhausted, satiated. Claudia had recognized his burning need, and, rather than ignore it, had graciously satisfied him. It would have been easy for her to roll over, and leave him alone, yearning for her touch.

But she took care of him, and, to Skip, that meant a lot. The fact that she had not wanted to take the chance of getting pregnant, or catching a venereal disease showed him that she was responsible, too. He was surer than ever that Claudia was the woman he would spend the rest of his life loving.

Claudia wiped her hand on Skip's cotton underwear, and lay back on the pillow. She felt her body's desire to have its own needs satisfied, peaked as they were by her erotic performance. And yet, her mind, which could not seem to think about anything but the shining bounty that was so close at hand, would not cooperate in relaxing and enjoying the physical thrill of this man she had come to trust.

Skip discarded his underwear, and turned toward Claudia. "Thanks."

"My pleasure." Claudia purred.

Lifting her hand, he kissed it, and lay back, wondering if Claudia wanted him to return the favor. Laying his hand lightly on her stomach, where the T-shirt had ridden up to expose her navel, he could feel the soft, invisible hairs on her delicate skin. Beginning to make small circles on her flesh, the upward path nearing her breasts, the downward path nearing her pubic hair, Skip could feel Claudia begin to breath deep.

"Skip."

"Yes, Claudia?"

"Skip, I appreciate what you're doing. And it feels really good. But my mind's racing a mile a minute; the treasure and the police and my brother - I can't seem to slow it down..."

"I understand."

Sweeping away silken hair from her face, Skip kissed her softly, and briefly, first on her sleek neck, then on her cheek, then, on her lips ever so lightly and affectionately.

"Good night," he whispered in her ear, lying down on his back. "If I snore, just poke me."

"Good night, Skip. Thanks for all you've done. You're a great guy."

Skip no sooner closed his eyes than his weary mind drifted off to sleep. Claudia's mind raced on until well after midnight, when, it too drifted off in a world of slumber, filled with discovery, treasure, chases and love.

CHAPTER XVI
TROUBLE ON THE HORIZON

S ammy Coombs couldn't sleep that night. Cruising the streets of
Port St. Joe in his Sheriff's car, white with green lettering, he
contemplated how he could put this whole affair to rest. The scrawny
guy with the tattoos in the hospital was of no help at all. Finding his
identification in his wallet, Sammy had run an interstate check to see
if he was wanted on any charges, and found that, although his past
was mired in arrests, they were mostly for petty offenses, and he was
not a fugitive from the law. The stubborn, seedy character would only give his name and ask if the man he was with in the boat had survived. Sammy related the story of how they had to pry Will's battered
body out of the mouth of a ten-foot long gator, who was in the
process of dragging the hulk into the waters of the swamp. The Sheriff thought Harris had seemed relieved to find that his acquaintance
had perished, which was surprising to Sammy. Why would this Harris Kilmer be pleased that his accomplice had been killed? It didn't
make sense, unless this ragged stranger planned to blame the entire
incident on the dead man.

Knowing that his only chance to discover what happened on
the bay and in the swamp yesterday was to question the couple that
were being chased, Sammy doggedly cruised around the quiet, sleeping town, hoping to get a glimpse of their pickup. He drove slowly

through the campsite several times, not realizing that Skip and Claudia were inside the tent, because their vehicle was not in sight. If only he could question those two and get some answers, he would be able to write a report and put the entire incident to rest. He reckoned Harris would be charged with some kind of crime, since he was in the boat that was giving chase to the couple's boat. Unless, of course, the man and woman being chased had perpetrated a criminal act against the two men who were chasing them. No. Highly unlikely, he thought. After all, Charlie had rented the skiff to the woman, and they had somehow taken it from her and were after her when the accident occurred.

Still, he mused, if it turned out that there was a valid reason for chasing them, Will's death could be construed as manslaughter of some kind, he thought, but, by the looks of the two characters that had wrecked Charlie's skiff, it was them who perpetrated a crime. But what crime? Kidnapping, as Charlie had suspected earlier in the day yesterday? He had not taken the report of a kidnapping any more seriously than had Dolores, the dispatcher. Sleepy Port St. Joe didn't have much history of violent crime, like kidnapping. The last time a kidnapping had been reported it had turned out that the tantrumming child was being taken to the dentist by his grandparents. That's why he was yelling "You're not my mom and dad. Let me go!" Stopping the aged couple for kidnapping was an embarrassing situation for Sammy, and he vowed to be more careful next time. If only he had taken Charlie's report more seriously the day before, perhaps he could have unraveled the mystery before anyone got hurt. Now Sammy was hell-bent on getting to the bottom of the story and unearthing the crime that he just knew someone had committed.

SKIP SLEPT LIKE A ROCK all night, exhausted by the lack of sleep and the wild activities of the two previous days. He probably would have slept through sunrise, if Claudia hadn't shaken him awake at what he figured was about 5 AM.

"Wake up, Skip!" he heard someone say from the haze of a deep dream.

"Huh?"

"Gotta wake up now!" Claudia whispered urgently. "We need to get out of here before anyone else awakes, or the Sheriff comes by looking for us." She had slept intermittently during the night. The only dream she remembered was shocking to her, and she was jolted awake by the vision of the treasure sifting through her outstretched hands and into the Gulf of Mexico.

"Right!" Skip responded reluctantly. He thought how anxious he was to have this nasty business behind him, to go to the weigh-in and collect his winnings, and be on the road back to Tallahassee with his son and hopefully, Claudia.

"Did I tell you..." a gaping yawn interrupted his sentence, "that my ex-wife was bringing Benny down to meet me at the weigh-in? She does that every year, so I can hang out with him on Father's Day."

"Yeah, you mentioned that. At the time, I didn't think I'd be there with you to get to meet him, but, with any luck, I will. I'm sure he's an angel, if he's anything like his father."

"He's a great kid. The apple of my eye."

"If we don't get a move on, we may both wind up behind bars instead of at the weigh-in."

"I hear ya!" Skip begrudgingly dressed. While Claudia sneaked quietly to the bathroom, he rolled up the sleeping bags, and put them along with his duffel bag on the dew-dampened picnic table. Taking down and packing the tent was a breeze for Skip, even though it was still dark, as he had done it a hundred times before. Loading the tent, sleeping bags and duffel bag into the middle section of the boat, he unscrewed the gas cap of the nearly empty six-gallon tank on board, and poured the gas-and-oil mixture from the plastic carrying can into it. Hoping that the engine would fire up quickly, he squeezed the bulb on the gas line, forcing fuel into the carburetors.

Throwing the toothbrush and toothpaste in the boat on top of Skip's gear, Claudia untied the bow as Skip untied the stern. Silently they pushed off the concrete dock, the boat gliding into the middle of the canal. Slowly rowing the skiff until they were a hundred yards away from the campground, Skip engaged the choke, and attempted to start the old eighteen-horsepower Evinrude. After only five pulls of the starter cord, the engine sputtered to life, the noise echoing off of the bait shop and bulwark in the still of the pre-dawn morn. Barely discerning the channel markers, which were white PVC pipes whose tops protruded from the water like drinking straws from a glass of iced tea, Skip aimed the bow south and slightly east toward where he knew Hurricane Cut lay.

Well away from the campsite now, Skip let out a "Yeee-haw" at the top of his lungs, as the small boat sped across the flat bay. To Skip's surprise, Claudia took the Big Bend Saltwater Classic T-shirt off and waved it in the air like a flag. Feeling that nothing could separate her from the treasure now, she was overcome by a sense of exhilaration. Skimming over the water topless, waving her flag of freedom in the air, hair blowing in the wind, she experienced a high in her life unlike any she had ever known before. The closest she had ever come to it was on her first jaunt over the islands of the Bahamas as a stewardess working for a small airline in Key West. The pilot had let her sit in the copilot seat, and she watched the sunrise over the horizon, the islands looking like oases in the crystal-clear azure seas.

Promising to rise over the Treasure Bay Lodge, the sun shed pink light over the tops of the palms on Black's Island. As they approached the landing site on the beach near the Indian mound, Skip slowed the skiff to a crawl, and shouted to Claudia, "Can I ask a favor of you?"

Slipping back into the T-shirt, Claudia turned her head toward him curiously. "What?" Skip could tell by the tone of her voice that she was anxious to get her hands on Billy Bowlegs' booty.

"Benny's rod has a lead-head and jig on it, and there are a few strips of trout belly in the live well. Would you mind if I took about a dozen casts under the forest service dock?"

"Why?" Claudia was obviously not thrilled with the thought of anything delaying her gaining possession of the treasure.

"Think about it – if I can catch a big flounder, that will place in the flounder division of the tournament, I have an excellent chance of winning the grand prize. And I know there are flounder hanging around that dock – I've caught them there before."

"What's the grand prize?"

"Remember I told you a few days ago – a five day all-expense-paid fishing trip to Costa Rica! I'll take you with me! How about it?"

"Costa Rica, eh? Any hidden treasure there?"

"Maybe. Ya never know."

"O.K. I'm game. But only a dozen casts, right?"

"Right."

Cutting the engine off a good ways from the dock, Skip rowed the skiff into a position that allowed him to cast along the front and side pilings of the dock.

Softly, Skip said, "Slip the anchor over the side of the boat."

Claudia picked up the anchor and tossed in nonchalantly overboard, being preoccupied, thinking how close she was to the treasure chest.

Splash! The anchor hit the water and its impact disturbed the quiet Skip had been so careful to preserve. Stealthily sneaking up on fish in calm water is essential to not spooking them, especially in a clear water bay such as St. Joseph's.

"Thanks," Skip sarcastically murmured. "Tie it off now."

Reaching into the live well, Skip scooped a short, triangular piece of cut bait and threaded the wide part of the strip on his hook, so it fluttered in the water like the tail of a bait fish. The green soft-plastic body of the jig, shaped like a shrimp, added to the enticement. His first cast was along the pilings at the end of the pier, which is where he thought he had the best chance of hooking a big flounder. He let the bait sink to the bottom, and checked the drag on the closed-faced reel to be sure it was on the right setting – not too loose, which would prevent a good hook set, yet not too tight, which could cause the line to snap if a big fish was hooked. Twitching the rod tip, Skip skillfully bounced the jig off the sandy bottom, letting it settle again several inches closer to the boat. Accurately placing his second cast under the dock between the first and second sets of pilings, Skip twitched the rod slightly as he felt the jig hit the bottom. Reeling in the slack, he twitched the rod tip again, but the jig didn't move. Not sure if he was snagged or had a hit, Skip raised the rod in the air and jerked back. The limber rod bowed, and Skip could feel a quivering at the end of the line, and he knew he had hooked a flounder.

"I'm on!" Skip shouted. Looking around the boat for his ever-present net, he realized it had been tossed overboard during the chase.

"Costa Rica, here we come!" he prophesized, fighting the fish with the light tackle. Soon, he had the flounder near the boat, and realized, to his disappointment, that the fish would not be winning any prizes. It was about 15 inches long, and weighed a measly pound. The smallest flounder that had placed in the past several years was over 3 pounds. Skip's beating heart slowed down, but he could still feel the adrenaline coursing through his veins in the excitement of hooking a flounder.

"It's a postage stamp," he remarked to Claudia.

"A postage stamp? Looks like a flounder to me!"

"That means it's a small one."

"So what's a big one called?"

"A door mat."

"Well, catch a door mat next cast."

"Right."

Leaving the fish mostly in the water, Skip carefully and delicately removed the hook from its mouth. Replacing the torn strip of trout belly with another one, he commenced casting along the other pilings of the dock.

"What's that on the back of your lure?"

"A strip of trout belly."

"What a waste of good fish."

"Not at all. It's full of bones, and I cut it off of trout carcasses that the guides leave by the side of the fish cleaning table."

"Oh."

After a while, Claudia asked, "Can we go now?"

"One more cast."

Skip cast parallel to the side pilings of the dock, maximizing the potential of a strike from any fish lurking under the pier awaiting a meal. Unfortunately, no flounder cooperated, so, disappointed, he hooked the jig on an eye of the rod and set it next to Claudia in the front of the boat, not wanting it in the way as he attempted to restart the motor.

Claudia pulled up the anchor and set it at her feet. Skip yanked and yanked on the starter cord, but the old engine would not start. Sweat formed on his forehead and in the hair on his upper lip as he struggled to start the fickle motor.

Claudia picked up the rod.

"How do you cast this?"

"It's easy," Skip said, out of breath from the pulling on the starter cord. Just push the black button in, and, as you bring the rod over your shoulder, release it.

Pressing the black button on the back of the reel, she drew the pole over her shoulder, released the button and swung the rod in the direction of the dock. The jig flopped into the water behind her.

"Not exactly like that," Skip said with a smile in his voice. "You have to release the button later – after you swing the rod forward."

Trying again, the lure slammed into the water two feet in front of Claudia.

"O.K. That was too late. Now, right in between those times. Let go of the button when the rod is about eleven o'clock in the air."

Claudia followed Skip's directions, and the lure sailed toward the pier.

"Clack!" It hit the deck and skipped across the top of the wooden structure.

"Now what?" she asked, pleased that she had been able to cast, but annoyed that it had landed on the dock.

"Just give it a little pull. And, by the way, your left hand goes on the rod handle and you use your right hand to reel with these closed-faced spinning reels."

Winding slowly, Claudia tightened the slack in the line. She gave a slight pull and the lure dropped over the side of the dock, and landed right next to a piling.

Amused, Skip said, "That's actually the perfect cast. If there's a flounder around, it's sure to be there."

"What do I do now?"

"Just flip the rod tip slightly, and slowly work the jig back to the boat, making sure it stays near the bottom."

With a flick of her wrist, Claudia bounced the jig along the bottom once, then remarked, "It's stuck!"

"Give it a good yank," Skip advised.

Pulling back hard on the rod, Claudia felt the line move the other way, and Skip heard the drag being pulled out.

"Reel, Claudia – I think you got one."

Claudia could feel the power of the fish as it tried to run back under the dock to safety. She reeled as fast as she could, pumping the rod in the air.

"Give it steady pressure!" Skip advised. "Don't jerk your rod like that. Keep the line tight, don't let it have any slack!"

The fish turned and ran toward the shore, the drag on the little reel whirring as it begrudgingly released line.

"He's running away from the dock!" Skip shouted, as excited as if he was the one with the big fish on. "Keep reeling steady and don't give him any slack!"

"Damn!" Claudia exclaimed. "It's a big one!"

"Probably a redfish!"

"Skip, this is fun!"

"That's what I've been telling ya!"

Getting tired from reeling, Claudia paused for a second.

"Keep reeling if you can, Claudia. If that fish gets a chance, it will spit the hook in a heartbeat!"

"I'll try!" Renewing her efforts, Claudia began gaining line on the big fish.

"Now you can start pumping the rod some, Claudia. Reel fast bringing the rod back toward the water so you can gain more line."

The fish was directly under the boat now, and was still fighting with dogged determination.

"Keep the line away from the boat!" Skip yelled, as the fish swam further under the skiff.

"How?" Claudia asked in a panicked voice.

"Hold the rod tip out away from the boat as far as possible."

Stretching, Claudia nearly fell over the side. The fish continued its run toward the other side of the boat, then swung toward the engine. Skip moved fast, yanking the top of the motor as hard as he could. The foot of the outboard swung out of the water just in time!

Pulling with renewed vigor, the fish headed off the stern into deeper water.

"I'm getting tired!" Claudia gasped.

"Hang in there. With any luck, you'll have him up in a couple of minutes. Unless, of course, you want me to cut the line so we can go get that treasure!"

"No. It can wait."

"Pump and reel, Claudia!"

Limber rod bending under the weight of the scared fish, Claudia persevered. Sweat beaded upon her forehead and upper lip, and she could feel drops running down her side. Pink and hot, the sun rose over the pines at the other end of the bay, promising another sweltering June day. The fish was again under the boat, and Claudia dutifully kept the rod stretched out so the line would not touch the hull. Staring into the water anticipating being able to see the creature who was giving her such a hard time in this tug-of-war, Claudia saw a glimmer of brown in the water.

"What is it?" she asked. When Skip didn't answer immediately, she glanced at him, and found that he was nearly in a state of shock.

"It's...it's...I can't believe it!" Skip stuttered. "It's the biggest damn flounder I've ever seen in the Gulf of Mexico!"

"Oh, Skip, get it!" Claudia shouted as the fish neared the surface.

"Get it? Get it! I threw the net overboard with the rest of the stuff yesterday!"

Eyeing the boat, the fish took out more drag and headed for the bottom. But Claudia had tired it, and she eased it back up to the surface.

"What are we gonna do?"

"Bring your rod tip toward me, but whatever you do, don't try to lift the fish out of the water!"

Following Skip's instructions, Claudia moved the fish closer to the back of the boat. It was on the surface now, and a flip of its tail sent water splashing in Claudia's face. Skip slid his hand expertly down the thin line and grasped the lead head of the jig firmly with his right hand. Splattering water in a last ditch effort to escape, the big fish angrily shook its muscular, flat body in a frenzy of power. Gripping the jig head with all his might, Skip hung on for dear life. When the tantrum eased, he lifted the head of the fish with a death grip on the jig head and, striking like an osprey setting his talon into a fish, his left hand shot out, fingers and thumb tightened over the flounder's gills. Lifting, Skip looked at Claudia as he strained to bring the big fish over the gunnel.

Eyes wide with excitement, hands trembling slightly, Claudia cried out

"Wow! Skip, look at it – it's huge!"

Turning the thirty-inch fish around so Claudia could look at the markings on the brown side, Skip agreed, "Yeah! Huge!"

"Oh, Skip, it's beautiful! I've never seen a prettier fish!"

Circular dark brown shapes and freckle-like marks adorned the dark side of the flounder. The other side was as white as a lily.

"And I've never seen a flounder this big in the Gulf. They grow this big regularly on the east coast, but not here. What a catch!"

"Skip, do you know what this means?"

"Yeah, you're one helluva fisherwoman, Claudia! Nice catch!"

"Can you say 'Costa Rica'?"

Dejectedly, Skip answered, "No."

"No? Why not? You told me if you had a prize-winning flounder along with that trout, you'd take me to Costa Rica!"

"I can't do that Claudia. You caught the fish, not me. That would be cheating."

"No one would know."

"Yes. I would. And I wouldn't do that to myself. I'd lose that inner peace I've been struggling so hard to maintain. Not worth it."

"Not worth it?"

"No. Not worth it. Not worth a thousand free trips to Costa Rica."

"Hmpph! O.K. Well, what are we going to do with it, then? Can we let it go?" she asked, running her hand down the handsome back of the now sedate fish.

"Yeah. If that's what you want to do with it. She's yours – you caught her."

"Would you be angry? I know how good they are to eat..."

"Angry? Hardly. Delighted would be more like it."

"Delighted? Don't you like to eat fish? What's the sense in fishing if you're not going to eat 'em?"

"I think you know the answer to that now. Hold out your hand."

Claudia hand trembled as she stretched it out.

"See how it's still shaking? That's not from strain – that's from the excitement of playing this big fish."

Holding the fish next to the rod, Skip made a mental note of how far it stretched from the tip of the rod to the center eye, intending to measure the length when he got back to Tallahassee. Gently, Skip eased the fish back in the water, holding it delicately in his hand, moving it forward and back, until, with a burst of energy, it came to life and darted off toward the bottom.

"Pretty exciting. Gotta admit!"

"Uh huh. Quite a treat, isn't it? I've been catching fish since I was three, and it's still a thrill to hook and play a big fish. I don't think I'll ever get bored with it in this lifetime."

"I can relate, now. Just like I won't get bored finding treasure. I've been thinking. If Billy Bowlegs' loot is still there, think of how many other sights might hold hidden treasure. Not to mention all the ships at the bottom of the sea around here that are loaded with valuables. Think about it!"

"I guess that taste of Mel Fisher's fortune and now finding this chest, have gotten you as addicted to treasure hunting as I am to fishing, eh?"

"Addicted. Totally. Now let's go feed my addiction, now that you've shared yours!"

"Right!"

Unable to get the motor to start, Skip just gave up. He and Claudia rowed to shore. He was glad, in the frenzy to lighten the boat yesterday, Claudia had not thrown the wood oars overboard.

"Remember where it is?" he shouted to Claudia as she tromped up the narrow white sand beach with the anchor. Setting the flukes firmly in the sand, she rose to her full height, and scowled at Skip. She stood there, proud and tall, fine hair hanging down to her freckled shoulders, looking like a dream come true.

"What kind of a treasure hunter would forget where they set the treasure chest?"

"Just checking. Let's get it and go. Maybe we'll have some time to do a little more fishing before the storm hits."

"What storm?" Claudia said, alarmed.

"Pink sky at night, sailor's delight. Pink sky at dawn, sailors be warned," Skip recited.

Cumulus clouds shone pink and white over the western horizon, reflecting the rays from the sun that was now fully visible to the east. Claudia surveyed the bay, noticing rooster tails of fishing boats screaming toward their favorite spots, the last few hours of the tournament dangling in the dew of the morning.

"What makes you think those clouds are coming this way?" Claudia asked, eyeing the beautiful piles of cotton puffs in the western sky."

"Two reasons. One, the clerk in the store last night said she overheard some customers saying the weather was going to be bad today. Second, storms typically move from southwest to northeast this time of year. They build over the open Gulf waters, and roll northeast. Except for years when we're in a draught, thunder showers will arise somewhere in the panhandle every afternoon in the summer."

"I'm not worried about a thunder shower!" Claudia replied.

"See those clouds that are forming anvils there?" Skip pointed to some already ominous clouds rising on the southwestern horizon, over the warm offshore waters of the Gulf of Mexico. "Thunderstorms in this area of the Gulf have been known to turn a perfectly flat sea into fifteen-foot waves in less than half an hour!"

"But we're in the bay. No way the waves are going to get that bad here, right?"

"Probably not. But with the wind blowing from the west, this peninsula isn't going to shelter us much once we get to the middle of the bay. Let's get going, I can already feel the breeze picking up."

CHAPTER XVII
THE CROSSING

Rushing through the underbrush, like a moth attracted to a flame, Claudia made a beeline toward the treasure, with Skip close behind. He marveled at the graceful strides Claudia displayed as she weaved around the palmetto bushes, Spanish bayonets, scrub oaks and blackberry vines, under the canopy of Sabal Palms and towering pines. His infatuation with her seemed to build with each passing hour. He was totally taken with both her looks and what he had so far seen of her character. Falling head-over-heels for Claudia was both exhilarating to Skip, and scary. Exhilarating, because he felt thrilled just to be in her presence. Scary, because he knew his infatuation was overwhelming the logical side of his brain, which was still shouting, "Be careful! You don't really know this woman! You just met her a few days ago!"

He wanted to stop her, spin her around, throw his arms around her and kiss her passionately. But that would have to wait, now, as Claudia was hell-bent on recovering the treasure and getting it to safety. It was comforting to know that she wanted to share it with him, even though he was not interested in possessing any of the bloody loot.

Turning to see if Skip was still behind her, Claudia tripped on a pine root and landed on her hands and knees. Her face brushed a saw palm frond, which scratched her cheek.

"Are you alright?" Skip said, grasping her outstretched hand and hauling her to her feet. She felt her cheek, the blood on her hand evidence that she had broken the skin.

"It's just a scratch."

Skip pulled off his shirt and dabbed her cheek, a slight bloodstain appearing on the shirt.

"Now you've done it." Claudia smiled at him. "Ruined another Big Bend Saltwater Classic T-shirt."

"Who cares? Remember, I bloodied the new one last night, you're wearing last year's, this one is from the year before, and I still have some at home from earlier years," Skip said, looking down at the shirt. Pulling the shirt over his head, he looked up again. Claudia was racing through the underbrush.

"Hey! I guess you are alright!" Breaking into a run to catch her, and pulling the T-shirt over his head as he ran, Skip managed to tuck enough of the shirt into his shorts so it wouldn't fall out, hoping to prevent chigger bites that are so common in the deep woods.

"Are we going the right way?" Claudia shouted.

"Yup! We're almost to the spot where the snake ambushed you."

"I'll step on him today if he gets in my way!"

"Just be sure it's the same snake, Claudia. There are rattlers in these woods!"

Claudia came to a halt. "Say," she said in a coy voice "why don't you lead for a while!"

Skip jogged around her and said, "Great idea! Us men have a better sense of direction, anyway!"

"My ass! That's an old wive's tale!"

"Your ass? It's not that old! And I didn't know you were married!"

Sprinting, Claudia pushed Skip from behind. His legs made funny, awkward circles preventing him from falling into the brush.

"Hey, is that any way to treat your guide? Better tuck your shirt in – there are chiggers in these here woods."

"Great! Now you tell me! I didn't get any yesterday."

"Me neither. Guess we were just lucky."

Passing the Indian mound, they were closing in on the place where they had last seen the treasure, when Skip noticed that things were awful quiet in back of him. Turning his head, expecting to see Claudia, he was puzzled and somewhat shocked to find she wasn't there.

"Claudia!" he called.

No answer. Skip began to retrace his steps, keeping a sharp ear out for any noises that could give him a clue to what happened to her. Walking cautiously, he bent down to pick up a thick fallen pine tree branch, just in case he needed a weapon. Rounding a blind area in the path created by a huge pine tree on the left and a mature palmetto bush on the right, Skip tried to walk as silently as possible on the pine straw and scrub oak leaves that littered the trail.

"Booo!" Claudia burst out from behind the palmetto bush, scaring Skip half to death. He had the branch raised over his head to strike before he realized that he had been the object of a practical joke.

"Very funny!" he said nervously, adrenaline pumping through his veins. "You scared the hell out of me! Thought I'd lost ya again!"

"Nope! Not gonna lose me again, if I can help it!" she said with a smile, that melted Skip's heart.

"Come on! There's treasure a-waitin'!" Claudia shouted, and dashed down the narrow path that led to the fallen oak.

Skip followed, still clutching the makeshift club, a smile on his face. "Well," he said to himself "now I know life with Claudia will be anything but dull!"

Streaking through the more familiar part of the woods, Claudia bounded toward the treasure, like a doe flushed from her hiding place and sprinting through the woods. Skip saw her fly over the downed ancient oak tree in one graceful leap, and enter the woods on the other side of the clearing.

"Skip!" she shouted. "It's here! It's still here! I can't believe my eyes! Thank God it's still here!"

Catching up, Skip bent to help her lift the lid of the trunk. Layers of jewelry, some dull from being buried, some gems still sparkling like they just came from the jewelers, covered the top of the treasure. Scraping aside the necklaces and broaches, gold and silver coins lay scattered among the remnants of cloth and leather sacks. A few of the cloth sacks had split along their seams, spilling their contents of coins. But the leather sacks were still intact. Claudia untied one and reached inside. Her hand emerged with shiny Spanish gold coins. Skip lifted several leather bags chock full of doubloons and pieces of eight. Below them he could see that the bottom of the trunk held several gold and silver bars.

"Oh man!" Claudia gasped. "Pinch me, Skip! Is this real or am I dreaming?" Her face was flush from the run and the excitement of rediscovering Bowleg's treasure. Skip thought she might pass out.

"Hey – are you O.K.?"

"Just a bit dizzy..."

"Sit over here for a minute." Claudia grabbed three ornate necklaces, threw them over her head, and sat down beside Skip.

"Put your head between your legs if you're feeling faint."

"No. I'm fine. Really. I'm just a bit flabbergasted, you know? I've never experienced anything like this before. My God!!!" She gave Skip a hug that nearly broke his ribs. Kissing passionately, breathing heavily, Skip and Claudia were in seventh heaven. Claudia had her treasure, her independence, a friend she could rely on, and perhaps spend the rest of her life loving. Skip had this wild, attractive woman holding him like there was no tomorrow, a woman who he was sure would be the love of his life, the companion he was missing to complete his cosmic whole.

Thunder boomed across the bay, like an alarm clock going off in their ears, interrupting the sweetest of dreams. The noise brought them back to reality.

"We either need to get this back to the boat and get the hell out of here, or hang out under the dock again until that storm blows through."

"But what if the storm lasts all day? Let's make a run for it. I don't want to take the chance that someone will discover us with this treasure and tell the authorities, or try to take it. And those Sheriffs are still looking for us. Let's just go."

"I don't know, Claudia. I mean, I'd swim through a swamp full of 'gators for you, but I have to think of Benny, too. He needs a dad, and I'm gonna be a lot more use to him alive."

"You worry too much! Let's go!" she said, having made up her mind not leave the treasure again.

"Alright," Skip said, against his better judgement. "But we need to hurry!"

"Right!" Claudia sprung to her feet. A crow had alighted on the chest, and was pecking at the sparkling jewels.

"Shoo!" Claudia yelled. The startled crow grabbed an old emerald necklace and, flapping strong wings, made a whooshing sound as it carried off its prize to the lowest branch of a nearby pine.

"Give me that, you dirty bird!" Claudia, arms flailing in an attempt to get the crow to drop the jewels, rushed toward the thief. But the brazen bird, just out of her reach, perched there with the heisted trophy firmly clenched in its beak, seemingly grinning at her.

"I've seen that bird before!" Skip called as he closed the lid of the trunk.

"Where?"

"In your room back at the hotel. Oddest thing. Scared me a bit. Your room was in shambles, and I heard this noise. Looked around to see the crow sitting in the hole they punched in your window when they broke in. Flew away toward Black's Island...or, more likely, toward here, when I approached. Bad omen."

"Oh, you and your omens. Pretty superstitious for someone who's so religious. And how do you know it's the same crow?"

"I don't. And you're right. Just superstitious. Let's get out of here."

"Amen."

Thunder rumbled through the air like God playing giant, deep-sounding symbols in the distance, the vibrations resonating in Skip and Claudia's chests. Straining to lift the heavy chest, Skip advised her to bend her knees and lift with her legs. Claudia was able to lift it, legs wobbling, to her hip. Resting it on her hipbone, she began walking unsteadily through the woods. Skip walked backwards, keeping both hands below the trunk. He easily kept pace with Claudia, who was straining under the heavy load. She glanced back to see if the crow had dropped the necklace, but the stubborn bird was still perched in the tree, watching the two of them inching crab-like along the path, the large trunk swaying slightly as they walked.

"Damn!" Claudia exclaimed. "Why couldn't this chest be filled with currency instead of all this heavy stuff?"

"There's a good reason for that. Bowlegs and his gang took the currency with them. They couldn't have been very inconspicuous walking around with all this jewelry, coins and bullion."

"What are we going to do" Claudia panted "if there's someone near the boat? We can't let anyone see us with this."

"I don't think that's going to be a problem, dear. No one in their right mind would be in harm's way of this storm that's brewing. They're all heading back in by now, I'm sure."

"No one in their right mind, you say? I know a couple of fishermen who don't fit that category."

"Buck and Lucas?"

"Yes. Seems like you guys get so caught up in fishing, you don't think about anything else."

"Us? Fishermen? Never! Why, I can count on one, maybe two hands, the times I've been caught out in a storm."

"See. I hope they had the good sense to head in."

"Me too. Fish bite better before a storm in the summer. Wouldn't want them to catch a bigger trout than mine!"

"Do ya think you'll have time to weigh that fish in before the tournament ends?"

"God willing! The gun sounds at 2 PM, and you have to be in line with your fish, but it's only about 11 o'clock now. It shouldn't take us more than an hour to drive to Carabelle from St. Joe."

"I know how much you want to win the trout division, especially with Buck and Lucas giving you so much crap."

"Yeah. Can't wait to weigh that fish in! And see the look on their faces when the winner is announced. Brown trout!"

"What? Did you say brown trout?"

"Uh huh. I'll tell you the whole story sometime."

"Can't wait," Claudia said sarcastically. "Can we rest?"

"O.K. But not for too long. Feel the breeze picking up?"

"You worry too much!"

"True. But I'm still alive. Some who worried too little aren't."

Perspiration dripped from Skip's forehead and armpits as he sat next to Claudia on the old chest. He ran his fingers up the back of Claudia's neck to the top of her head, then backwards through her hair until the tangles stopped his stroke.

"Have you thought about how you're gonna cash this loot in? I mean, it is illegal to take artifacts from state property – how are you gonna get around that?"

"Oh, that shouldn't be a problem. I know a guy down in Key West who makes his living selling black-market treasure to rich folks around the world. He'll be able to sell this stuff in no time."

"You planning on selling it all?"

"No. Just enough to get by for a couple of years. Then I'll sell off some more."

"How about putting some of it back in this trunk, reburying it, and then calling the State Division of Historical Resources and reporting your find. They'll be thrilled to hear about treasure being found – you'll be famous..."

"Famous and poor. They would take the bulk of the bounty and not even leave me with enough to live on for a year, no doubt. Nah, I might do that just before I die, but no time soon. This treasure is going toward something that I really crave – my independence. Financial. Social – I won't need to rely on anyone to help me make ends meet. I'll be free as a bird!"

"Of course, on the other hand, if you get caught with it, you'll be as free as a jail bird!"

"Don't even say that!" Thunder boomed and lightning streaked across the sky in the distance, and the air grew rife with the smell of rain-on-its-way.

"We're out of here!" Claudia jumped up. "Get a move on, boy – if we get away with this I'll buy you a boat so big you won't have to worry about a little storm!"

"That big doesn't exist. No matter how big a boat is, Mother Nature is bigger."

Bending and lifting with their legs, the trunk rose again from the sand it had known so intimately over the past hundred-and-fifty-nine years. Making their way around the Indian mound, Claudia's thoughts were buried deep inside her newfound trunk. Skip thought of the native Americans who so long ago had called this site home. How they had waded into these same shallows and returned with

conches for the village to feast on. There must have been tons of
them in the bay at that time, by the looks of the mound. Skip had only seen a couple of live ones in the bay since he had been fishing there.
He wondered if the natives had over-harvested the easy prey, or if
modern man had somehow altered the environment, killing off most
of those remaining marvels of the sea. So majestic in their turret-
like hard shell fortresses, few predators other than man could pose a
threat.

"How ya doin'?" Skip asked Claudia, noticing that she was
stooping more than before, struggling with the weight of the treasure.

"I can make it. Let's keep going."

"Are you sure you want to cross the bay? We may be better off
waiting for this storm to blow by."

"Look, Skip, I'm a bay crossing away from being a rich woman.
And you are a few miles away from winning that first place prize –
I know how much that means to you, and by now, you know how
much this treasure means to me. Let's do it and get it over with. I
don't mind getting wet -"

"Gotta tell ya, Claudia. It's against my better judgement. And if
it comes to making a choice between winning that the trout division
and being around to raise my son, I'm gonna go with being around
to -"

"Damn it, Skip! Let's give it a whirl. If it gets too bad out there,
we can always turn back, right?"

"Maybe. Maybe not. Lightning doesn't give second chances."

Skip could see by the determined look on Claudia's face that
he was not going to change her mind. His options were to flat-out
refuse to go, and risk alienating the women he had come to adore, or
try to cross the bay and hope for the best. As much as he cared for
Claudia, he couldn't stand the thought of his son growing up without a father.

Stumbling across the last of the twigs and brush, Skip and Claudia dropped the chest next to the anchor on the sun-bleached sand of the narrow beach, nearly exhausted from their efforts.

"Look, it's not that bad," she said, hoping that Skip would agree.

"It's not that bad because we're inside Hurricane Cove." Turning to the north, Skip saw the outline of Black's Island in the distance. The water of the bay was turbulent, white caps cresting one after another.

"I don't know, Claudia – look at the bay – it's awful rough out there."

"Come on, I'll save you if you fall over. We can make it, Skip!" Claudia pleaded.

Skip gazed anxiously toward Black's Island and the mainland beyond. A bolt of lightning shot to earth somewhere on the western horizon where the clouds grew ominous, threatening to turn day into night.

"Maybe it will stall. If it gets too bad, we can always stop on the island," Claudia suggested.

"But if we go toward the island, it will take us forever to get back to the truck. The fastest way is straight across the bay toward St. Joe."

"O.K., captain. Let's go!"

Shaking his head, Skip waded out to the boat, rearranged the camping gear to the front and rear sections of the small skiff. Claudia drew the boat toward shore, pulling on the anchor rope. When the bow brushed against the beach, she dropped the anchor into the front, compressing the tent bag.

Skip helped Claudia lift the trunk. Wading, they deposited the heavy load in the middle compartment. The weight of the chest nearly tipped the skiff over, and the gunnel came dangerously close to taking on water. Skip held the side of the boat while Claudia pulled the chest from the other side, using part of the handle that was still attached. Skip pushed against the lid as Claudia yanked with all her might. The chest, begrudgingly scraping the bottom of the boat, inched its way toward the center.

Lifting himself carefully over the side, Skip settled into the swivel seat. He pulled the choke lever, and, bracing his left foot against the stern, yanked on the starter rope. The old Evinrude sputtered and stalled. Pushing the choke lever back in, he tried again, and the outboard came to life. Pushing the boat into deeper water, Claudia hopped aboard, lifting her long legs over the side. Grasping a front cleat for stability, she settled into the seat, turned, and gave Skip a sweet smile and thumbs-up.

The boat rode low in the water, making Skip even more uncomfortable. The protected cove was still calm as the old eighteen-horsepower engine screamed in response to Skip giving it full throttle with the twist of his wrist. Rounding the shoreline toward the open bay, his heart skipped a beat – the entire sky to the west was black as coal, and he could see the occasional bolt of lightning tear through the darkness toward the sea below. The first white cap slapped the bow, sending spray flying over Claudia and the treasure chest. Undaunted, she spun in the swivel seat to face Skip, and placed her feet on the tarnished lid.

Skip slowed down to prevent the waves from crashing over the bow. He knew that burying the bow in a wave would spell disaster for them, especially since Claudia had thrown the life jackets overboard when Will and her brother were in pursuit. Although the south end of the bay was a series of shallow grass flats separated by an occasional channel, the rest of the bay was thirty to thirty-five feet deep, the only shallow areas being near the shores. Steering the left edge of the flat-nosed skiff into the waves, Skip knew he would take on less water than if he rode directly into their fury. The waves came at them in sets; when smaller Skip could pick up speed, but when a larger set was rolling toward them, the crest white with foam, he had to slow almost to a stop. Rising with the powerful wave, the little vessel slapped down the other side, only to be lifted again, spray soaking Claudia, Skip and the trunk. Taking his eyes off the waves for a second, Skip checked the water in the rear compartment behind him, where the gas tank lay. It was filling up rapidly, covering half of the grimy tank.

"Claudia!" Skip shouted above the din of the crashing sea and the whine of the engine. "Reach into the live well and throw me that plastic cup!" Seeing the puzzled expression on her face, Skip pointed to the plywood cover on the live bait well between him and the chest.

Claudia stretched and managed to lift the lid. Skip took his eyes off of the oncoming waves for a second, the boat veered slightly off course, and a wave hit them hard broadside. Claudia fell out of her seat, and nearly over the side. Her weight on the starboard caused the right side of the boat to tip precariously near the water. Quickly, Skip threw himself out of his seat and leaned his weight over the port side, and the skiff righted itself. Claudia recovered her balance, and reached into the livewell, fishing around for the plastic bailing cup. Finally finding it, she tossed it to Skip. The wind caught it in flight and Skip lurched to try and catch it. The errant cup bounced off of his outstretched hand, hit the rail and was heading overboard as Skip took one last grasp at it. He caught it in midair, just before it hit the water. His sudden movement caused Claudia to lose her balance again, and she wound up on the bottom, squashed between the heavy chest and the gunwale. Skip had to throw his weight back to the port, but doing so caused him to lose the grip on the throttle, and the boat turned sideways into the waves. A large wave crested over the side, nearly capsizing them, and sending gallons of water into the already-too-heavy craft. Skip regained control of the motor and quartered the bow into the waves. Left hand on the throttle, right hand scooping the rising water and tossing it over the side, Skip managed to keep them going toward the landing at St. Joe. The boat was going too slow to pull the drain plug and allow the water to drain, so their only chance of staying afloat was to keep bailing. The drain holes under the front, middle and rear compartments of the boat allowed the water to accumulated in the rear compartment where the gas tank now floated.

Claudia's face was ashen-white as she surveyed their situation.

"Are we gonna make it?"

"Can't say!" Skip shouted above the din of the waves breaking, the wind whipping across the now treacherous bay, and the peals of lightning that kept getting closer and closer.

"I can't see shore, Skip! Are you sure we're going the right way?"

"The heading's O.K. But if this sea gets any rougher, we're in big trouble!"

"Let's abort – can you run with the waves back toward Black's Island?"

"Don't know! If a wave breaks over our engine, we've had it."

"Where are we?"

"Smack dab in the middle of the bay!"

"Do something!" Claudia half cried in a panicked voice that Skip had not heard from her before.

Unsure whether to keep the bow quartered into the waves and hold course, or to turn tail and run with the waves, Skip turned to God. "Dear God, please help Claudia and me and anyone else who's caught out in this hellish storm. Please guide us to safety, God. Amen."

"What?" Claudia shouted, trying to make out what Skip was saying.

"Just a prayer!"

"Say one for me, too!"

A rumble like neither Skip nor Claudia had ever heard before vibrated the turbulent air, so low in pitch it was barely audible at first. Expanding, the noise drew closer and closer to the vulnerable craft.

"Sounds like an airplane!" Claudia yelled, hoping Skip would have an explanation.

"Sounds like a train, to me! You know what that means?"

"Water spout?"

"Yup!"

Straining their eyes to see through the driving rain and salt spray, Skip and Claudia stared in the direction of the fearful noise, which seemed to be coming from the west. The waves grew angry and intense, and Skip knew he couldn't keep the bow faced into them any longer. The dread funnel cloud appeared to the left of the boat, the noise now sounding like a giant vacuum cleaner gone mad.

"Skip!" Claudia screamed in desperation as she spotted the twister, her hand pointing it out, trembling in fear.

Skip waited until he was in the trough of one of the angry waves, which had built to six feet now, whitecaps flying off the crests, and spun the boat around. Skip knew that taking a heading that would quarter the stern to chasing waves was his only chance to stay afloat. Pointing the boat in the direction the waves were flowing would ensure disaster, a wave would break over the engine and stall it out, and fill the back compartment with water, or the bow would submarine. The gas tank floated on oily water now, as Skip continued to bail with all his strength.

"Claudia!" Skip shouted in desperation, as a wave crested over the rear port, causing the boat to sink a little lower.

"What?"

"We have to lighten the boat!"

"How?"

"I think you know!"

"Oh, God, no, Skip!"

"We're in big trouble! Gotta do it!"

"No, please!" she pleaded, tears running down her face.

Crash! A bolt of lightning struck feet from the little skiff. Both Claudia and Skip felt a shock jolt them from the electricity carried through the moist air.

"Ahhhhhhh!" Claudia screamed at the top of her lungs.

At first, Skip thought she had been electrocuted, but then saw her lunge for the side of the chest. He waited until they were down in a valley, and lunged for the other side. Together, their adrenaline going wild from the near miss of the lightning and the waterspout in the distance, they lifted the heavy chest and set it on top of the port gunwale, where it rocked, unsure of where it was heading, back in the boat or over the side. Skip felt Claudia's hand next to his as he shoved the end of the chest - she was pushing too. The chest tipped and slid into the sea, the massive treasure sank out of sight in seconds. Another wave broke over the stern, and the boat settled in the water as if to say it had had enough. Only inches separated the gunnels from the bay. Bailing with his right hand and steering with his left, Skip managed to scoop enough water out for the boat to ride out the next wave. Without the weight of the heavy chest, Skip had the boat riding higher than it had been the entire trip as the next wave tried to come aboard.

A ray of light appeared ever-so-briefly over Claudia's head, in what Skip thought was the direction of the Treasure Bay Lodge.

"Did you see that?" he yelled to Claudia, who was gazing forlornly over the side of the boat. For a second, he thought Claudia was going to jump in after her lost treasure.

The rumbling of the waterspout grew fainter, and Skip could no longer see the outline behind them. The waves continued to push them in the direction of Black's Island and the shallows. He knew that if they could get to the safety of the island, they would survive – something he was not sure about only a minute before. He kicked himself for agreeing to try and make it across the bay in the face of that storm. How stupid he felt to have risked Claudia's life! And how irresponsible he felt for letting himself get charmed into a situation that could have ended with Benny having no father to raise him. The dream of having Claudia in his life had thrilled him so much that it affected his judgement. He swore to himself that he would never let that happen again.

Claudia continued to gaze at the water, as if staring hard enough would bring the treasure floating back up to its rightful owner. Tears streamed down her face and dripped in the topsy-turvy water that rolled back and forth across midship. Her hand, still shaking, covered her delicate lips. Skip pictured her mouth, hidden by Claudia's beautiful fingers, agape with the horror of what had occurred.

"We had to, Claudia!" There was no response. Skip thought she might be in shock.

"We had to, or we would have died!"

Claudia's head rose slowly. Looking at Skip with the saddest eyes he had ever seen, she lowered her hands and felt the necklaces that remained around her neck, the only remnant of what had been a fabulous treasure. Her lips trembled, as if trying to say something, then she bowed her head again, rain and sea spray dripping down her fine hair, mingling with her tears in the bottom of the boat. Skip worried that the lightning might have damaged her hearing, or that the trauma of losing the treasure crushed her soul.

A few minutes later, Skip spied the top of a fluttering sable palm, a sight for sore eyes, if ever there was one. Continuing to steer in the direction of Black's Island, the island itself came into view. Yet Skip knew they were not quite out of danger. The bay surrounding the island was shallow, and limestone outcroppings could rip the skiff's hull and hurl them overboard. He had to make his way down the deep channel that cut through the grass flats, and approach the island from the protected side.

The engine whined as the skeg flew out of the water behind the boat. He had misjudged where the channel cut through. A wave pushed them into shallower water, the bottom of the skiff scraping the tops of the turtle grass. Skip strained to hold the outboard up so the prop was barely in the water, and headed toward where he thought the channel lay. The boat hesitated momentarily as they struck bottom again, and a wave crashed over the side. The force of the wave pushed them over the shallow knoll, and a few feet later Skip found the deep channel. The rain was slowing down. Thunder cracked a long way away, like the distant memory of a bad dream, as the boat glided into the calm waters behind the island.

"Claudia. Are you O.K.?" Skip asked as the flat bottom boat skidded to a halt in the shallows.

"Claudia?"

She drew a deep breath, and a sigh emanated from her throat. Tears continued to roll down her high cheekbones, careening off the three old necklaces. The once ivory whites of her eyes were now red from crying and the stinging salt spray. Jumping out of the boat, Skip grabbed the anchor line and pulled the skiff until the bow caressed the safe sandy shore of Black's Island.

Holding his hand out for Claudia, she daintily held it, and allowed herself to be pulled up and out of her seat. Wrapping his arms around her waist, Skip lifted her over the side and gently eased her into the ankle-deep water. Looking at Claudia, and giving her a reassuring smile, Skip was saddened to see her respond by looking down at her feet, as if ashamed to be seen in such emotional turmoil. Squeezing her hand, Skip slowly led her to shore. The wind was dying down, and light appeared on the western horizon, signaling the passing of the storm. The drizzle was hardly noticeable to them now, being soaked to the bone by their ordeal.

Turning Claudia toward him, caressing her face as if handling the most precious jewel in the world, Skip looked deep into Claudia's eyes as if to say he knew her pain, and loved her deeply.

Claudia broke the silence. "You heard them, too, didn't you?"

"Who?" Skip responded, relieved that Claudia was not in such a state of shock that she couldn't communicate.

"The voices."

"What voices, Claudia?"

"After the lightning hit so close to the boat...those voices."

"No. I didn't."

"You're lucky. I wouldn't wish that on anyone."

"What did they sound like?"

"Oh, Skip!" Claudia began sobbing again. "It was horrible! Horrible!"

"Tell me, love."

"I heard the owners of the treasure – the ones who Bowlegs and his gang murdered – screaming, pleading, crying out in pain as they were put to death. Horrible. Just horrible."

"Are you sure it wasn't the lightning causing your ears to ring?"

"Positive. I heard what I heard. It was them, Skip. Screaming, crying out in agony! The sound was coming from the chest."

Skip looked appraisingly at Claudia, wondering if she had gone mad.

"Honestly, Skip! I heard them. And when we threw the chest overboard, the voices stopped. Just like that. I think the ghosts of those poor lost souls wanted to give me a taste of what it was like to be pirate's victims. I'll never forget their cries. Never."

"I believe you, Claudia."

Leading her to a limestone rock, they sat down together, facing the brightening western sky.

"You saved my life, you know." Skip whispered to Claudia.

"Saved it? I almost took it, with my greed. I wanted that treasure so bad I was willing to risk anything - and anyone, to have it. I'm sorry, Skip."

"Claudia, if you hadn't been willing to give that treasure up, we wouldn't have made it. Do you know that?"

"No. I hadn't looked at it that way. Thanks. You're the nicest man I've ever met."

"Thanks."

Embracing, cheek to cheek watching the rays of the sun break through the trailing edge of the storm clouds, Skip took a deep breath.

"I know I've only known you for a few days now, but.... I don't know how to say this, so I'll just say it. I love you."

Tears welled up in Claudia's eyes again. Skip couldn't tell if they were tears of joy or sadness. He didn't want Claudia to tell him that she loved him too. That would have felt as if she said it to be polite, or because he deserved to be told that. He just hoped and prayed Claudia would be receptive to his love, and accept it, and learn to love him, if she didn't already.

Claudia's hands grasped the hair on the back of Skip's head so hard, he thought she might pull it out. Turning his face to hers, she pressed her lips on his so hard it would have been painful had Skip been able to feel anything but her passion at that moment.

Suddenly, she broke away from the embrace. "It's not too late!" she shouted, as if a revelation had just occurred to her.

"Not too late for what?"

"For you to win that prize!"

Skip smiled ear-to-ear. Claudia was O.K. She was back to her old self again. And she hadn't rejected his love.

"We'd better get a move on, then, if we're gonna get there before the gun sounds!" Skip shouted, sprinting down the beach to pick up the anchor, Claudia at his heels.

Uncharacteristically, the old outboard started on the first pull, as if sensing the urgency of the situation. Bow pointing toward the deep cut, throttle fully open, Skip steered a course in the direction of downtown St. Joe. The skiff sped, light as air now, toward the sunny side of the bay. The bay that held such an abundance of life, whose waters were so pure and clear. The bay that Skip treasured and admired with nearly the intensity of the affection he felt for the amazing woman he had met. That bay he adored, much like Claudia, had almost cost him his life.

CHAPTER XVIII
RUSH TO THE FINISH

Wiping the moisture off his watch, Skip was heartened to see that it was still only 12:10. Knowing that he could make the weigh in if he left St. Joe by 1:00, gave him hope that the first place speckled trout prize would be his.

Going over in his mind things that could stand in the way of reaching Carabelle on time, he remembered the precarious situation they were in with the police. Would they have located his pickup truck yet? Did Claudia's brother spill the beans about the treasure? Was there a warrant out for their arrest? How many police were on duty Sunday, and had the local police notified the State Troopers to be on the lookout for his pickup?

Reaching behind him, Skip yanked the black rubber drain plug out of the stern, as they were going fast enough to drain the water that remained in the boat after the storm. The rain had ended, and scattered, white fluffy clouds inched across a baby blue sky overhead. The seas were considerably calmer now, but an occasional swell sent spray flying over the bow, misting them both.

Skip lifted the gas can by the handle, which was the only way he had of telling how much was left, as the gauge had long since broken. To his consternation, there was barely a gallon left. Fighting the seas during the storm had cost them a lot of fuel, and he was not sure if

289

they had enough to make the launch ramp at St. Joe. Skip thought about praying, but decided he had already imposed on God enough that day, and would save his prayers for more dire circumstances.

Claudia's hair was drying despite the occasional shower of salt water that cascaded down on her when the bow smacked an oncoming wave. It floated in the air behind her head as if she were sitting in front of a huge fan. Skip couldn't resist reaching out and feeling the ends brush his open palm. Claudia turned and smiled.

"Are we going to make it to the weigh in on time, Skip?"

"Maybe. It all depends on whether we have enough gas to get us back to the town launch ramp. It's going to be close!"

Skip had noticed Claudia searching the water, even though it was over thirty feet deep where they were cruising, hoping to see any sign of her lost treasure. All she had left of the loot was the three necklaces draped around her pretty neck, bouncing on her freckled chest as the boat skimmed across the bay. They were the remnants of a treasure that now, rather than being buried in the sand, lay buried beneath thirty plus feet of water, God-only-knows where.

Skip wondered if she would attempt to recover it, knowing that she was an accomplished diver, or whether the voices she heard would sour her on the pursuit of that dream she had held so dear. He also wondered, since the treasure had seemed to bring such near fatal events down upon them, whether those three remaining necklaces around her neck would bring them more bad luck.

Rather than making a beeline for the launch ramp in town, and taking the chance of running out of gas in the middle of the bay, Skip steered a course toward the shallow grass flats of the northern shore beyond Presnell's. He knew if they ran out of gas there, the road was not far away, and they could walk back to the truck, and still have a chance of making the weigh-in on time.

Claudia slumped down in her seat, her head coming to rest on the curved plastic of the backrest, her long legs stretched out in front of her, feet propped against the small storage compartment in the bow. She braced herself for the waves, which were mere ripples now that they had reached the shelter of the northern shore, with her hands flat on the bench that supported the swivel seat.

Closing her eyes, she envisioned a gold coin sinking slowly in the clear water of the bay, rocking back and forth as it traveled toward the sandy bottom. Finding herself in a dream world, she blew air out of her snorkel, took a deep breath, and dove to the bottom of the bay. There lay her treasure chest; jewelry and bullion and coins gleaming, half hidden in the white sand at the bottom of the bay. Struggling to reach them, she ran out of air and had to surface or drown. Rising reluctantly to the surface, she encountered a strong rip tide that pulled her away from the treasure site. She awoke to the sound of the engine sputtering and uttering its last gasp, as it ran out of gas.

"Damn!" Skip shouted. "I should have lugged six gallons back to the campsite last night! Damn!"

Claudia, looking around her, realizing that they were close to town and in shallow water, shouted, "We've come too far to stop now! Let's go!" Jumping off the bow, landing in waist-deep water, she began pulling the skiff toward shore, as Skip raised the engine to decrease the drag.

Joining her in the shallow grass flat, feet sinking ever-so-slightly in the soft sand underneath the turtle grass, Skip took Claudia's free hand and pulled her along.

"Jeeze! I can't believe I let this happen!"

"Don't beat yourself up about it, Skip. Remember, if I hadn't insisted we cross the bay in that storm, we wouldn't be walking now."

"True. But if I had had the good sense to tell you no when you wanted to try and cross in that weather, we wouldn't be walking now either."

"There's always plenty of blame to go around. But that's the past. The future awaits with open arms, and dares us meet its challenge!"

"When did you start to get philosophical?"

"Oh, there's a lot you don't know about me, Skip."

"Don't tell me your parents were aliens!"

"Shucks, how d'ja know?"

"It was the feeling I get when I look at you – like you're too wonderful to be real."

"Well, I'm real. And one of the things you don't know about me is that, once I make up my mind to do something, I go all out to get it done."

"Duh!"

"What's that supposed to mean?"

"Like I didn't already know that about you!"

"O.K. Here's something you didn't know about me – I sometimes have a hard time expressing my affections."

"And..."

"And, I guess I just want to say that, well, you're, uh...my kind of man."

"Yeah?"

"Yeah!" she said, yanking on his arm suddenly. Skip lost his balance and fell backward in the water. Claudia dropped the rope and ran toward shore. Skip tackled her half way there, and they rolled over and over in the shallows.

"Ouch! Skip leapt to his feet, an anemone stuck to his back.

"What's wrong?"

"Look!" He turned and Claudia saw the anemone. She picked up a scallop shell and gently pried it out. Skip turned, brushed the hair from Claudia's face, and kissed her. Claudia squeezed him so hard it took his breath away.

"Hey!" Claudia exclaimed, breaking the embrace. "We've got a tournament to win!"

"Let's do it!"

Running hand-in-hand back to the boat, they both grabbed the anchor line attached to the bow, and splashed their way toward shore. A tidal creek, emptying its brackish, tannic acid stained water into the bay, wound like a snake through spartina grass covering the muddy bank. They pulled the boat as far as they could into the grass near the bridge, then Skip hoisted the anchor and stuck it into the marshy ground to prevent the tide from floating the boat out to sea.

"What time is it?"

"12:35."

"Does that give us enough time?"

"Maybe. But only if we get back to the truck and leave by 1:00. I think we can make it if we run."

Jogging down State Road 30A toward town, Skip and Claudia were both thinking the same thing.

"Hope the Sheriff doesn't drive by!"

"Maybe he'll think we're joggers." Claudia offered. "Remember, he still doesn't know what we look like, exactly."

"I hope you're right. We're not dressed like your typical jogger. And there's no place to hide off of this road if we see him coming."

"Don't worry, Skip. We're gonna make it."

Skip wet his lips and they tasted like salt. He wasn't sure if it was from the bay or perspiration. Evaporating water on the warm pavement rose above the road in a barely visible, steamy cloud.

The humid air felt thick as he sucked it in his windpipe, lungs beginning to work double-time. He was surprised to see that Claudia wasn't breathing as heavy.

"You're in pretty good shape!" Skip said, huffing and puffing alongside Claudia.

"Thanks, but I'm really not. When I was in Key West, I could run five miles without hardly breaking a sweat."

Approaching town, where State Road 30A merged with Hwy. 98, Skip and Claudia spied a little girl alongside the road selling lemonade. At first, Skip thought it was a mirage, just wishful think-ing. Then, as they got closer, he realized it was real; a little girl in her pink Sunday dress sitting pretty as a doll on a kid's sized chair. In front of her was a card table, draped with a white sheet that hung down to the ground. As if a picture from a Currier and Ives book had come to life, upon the table sat a small cooler, and a pitcher of ice cold lemonade, drips of water gliding down the thick glass side. The sign, obviously created by the five-year-old, bragged "Best ised tee in town, 25 sents" in bold, crayoned letters of every color.

"Oh, she's adorable!" Claudia exclaimed as they neared the stand. "I wish we had time to stop."

"Amen. I would give ten dollars for a cold, tall glass of that lemonade right now!"

"Let's get to the truck first, and see if we have time to stop on the way to Carabelle," Claudia suggested.

"Hi!" Claudia and Skip echoed as they approached the young entrepreneur.

"Hi!" The little girl's melodic voice answered them. "Want to buy some lemonade? It's really goooooood!"

Hearing a car, Skip looked up and froze. Grabbing Claudia by the arm and stopping her in her tracks, he swung her down to the ground behind the stand. A Sheriff's car was making the turn toward them from Hwy. 98. He whispered in her ear as the little girl, delight-ed in their unseemly behavior, giggled.

"Whatcha doin'?"

"We're, ah, gonna buy some of your lemonade, but ah, our mon-ey fell under the table!" Skip lied, pulling Claudia under the card table with him.

Giggling, the girl lifted up the sheet to see what was going on un-der there, as the Sheriff pulled up at the curb.

"I'll give you all the money we find if you keep quiet about us be-ing under here – oh, look, another quarter! O.K.?"

"Goody!" she giggled, as Sheriff Thompson got out of the patrol car.

"Hi, Missy! How's business?" His booming voice seemed to carry in the afternoon breeze.

"Not so good until just now!"

"Oh, well, then I'm glad I stopped. Sure could use a tall glass of your delicious lemonade right about now!"

"That will be twenty-five cents." Missy collected the money from Sheriff Thompson. Still giggling, she poured lemonade in a large red plastic cup, spilling some in the process. Skip and Claudia, sweating profusely, breathing as quietly as possible, remained motionless under the table.

"I'm gonna have lots of money today, Mr. Sheriff!" Skip and Claudia looked at each other.

"I'm sure you will, Missy! You're momma's lemonade is the best in town."

"Yeah, and my two friends are finding money for me, too!"

"They are?"

"Yup! And they're gonna give me all of it!"

"How nice!"

"Wanna meet them? They're funny!"

"Ah, not today, Missy. Maybe some other time. I'm real busy. You're mom and pop keeping a good eye on you?"

"Sure are." Missy pointed across the street to the one story brick house, neatly landscaped, the white lace-curtained windows allowing a good view of the lemonade stand and the bay.

"Hey, come out and meet the Sheriff!" Missy shouted, lifting her side of the bed sheet. Skip, index finger to his lips, shook his head violently.

"Who're you talking to?" Sheriff Thompson asked.

"My funny friends!"

"Oh. Well, don't you go crossing the street without your momma or poppa, ya hear, Missy."

"Yes, sir. Don'tcha wanna meet my funny friends?"

"Some other time, sugar. Gotta go now. Bye."

"Bye, Sheriff!" Missy waved.

"Thanks for the delicious lemonade!"

"You're welcome!"

As the sound of the patrol car faded in the distance, Claudia and Skip emerged from their hiding place, hugged Missy, and headed off down the road.

"I found so many coins, I'm gonna have to get a bag to give them to you, Missy! We'll be right back!"

"Aw right!" Missy responded cheerfully in her innocence. "See ya!"

"See ya, Missy!" Claudia shouted, still shaking from the close call.

"Wow, what a sweet little girl!"

"I'll say!" Skip answered, also still jittery from the close shave with the law.

"I want one just like her, Skip!" Claudia looked with loving eyes at him, and Skip smiled.

He felt delighted, on one hand, that Claudia seemed to be implying that she wanted to settle down and have children, and her look told him that he would be the lucky man. The other part of his mind shouted, "Oh, no! Another child? At my age!" But if that's what Claudia wanted, he knew he would go along with it. Calculating how old he would be when a newborn would graduate from high school, Skip thought about being the oldest parent to attend the ceremony. Looking at Claudia, and her jaguar-like gait as she cruised down the sidewalk as if running on air, he realized that there weren't too many things in the world, short of compromising his morals, he wouldn't do for this delightful woman.

"It's funny how adults don't take kids seriously."

"A good thing for us they don't!" Skip replied.

"But not a good thing for the children, eh?"

"No. Not a good thing for the children," Skip agreed.

Reaching the truck, Claudia braced herself on the tailgate, out of breath from the run. Skip immediately unlocked the passenger door of the truck, opened the cooler, and grabbed two cold sodas. Glancing at the bottom of the ice chest, he could see through the fruit and drinks the assuring speckles on his gator trout, and he felt a strange comfort knowing that it was still there.

Popping the top of a Publix ginger ale for Claudia, he walked to the back of the truck. As he handed the drink to Claudia, she took her sweaty hands off of the tailgate to accept it. But Skip quickly pulled it back.

"Ugh! Claudia! Look at your hands!"

Turning palms to her face, Claudia was shocked by the sight.

"Oh, no! The paint's not dry!"

"Damn!" Skip exclaimed. "What else could go wrong?"

He gave her a rag from the bed of the pickup, and poured some outboard motor oil on it, thinking it would help remove the black paint from her hands. Although it did not get all the paint off, it did get most of it. Claudia and Skip guzzled their cold sodas. Skip lifted the cooler out of the front seat and into the bed of the truck, placing it in back of the cab so the top would not fly off. Hopping in and buckling their seatbelts, Skip turned the ignition key one notch to warm the glow plugs. Then, as soon as the light on the dashboard went out, he cranked up the old diesel engine and backed out of the parking lot, and began the road race to Carabelle.

"Now how much time do we have?" Claudia asked anxiously.

Skip looked at his watch and grimaced. "It's 1:05 – we're gonna have to scream down the road to make it!"

"How much time does it usually take to get to Carabelle?"

"On a normal Sunday, a good hour. But today, it could take longer going the speed limit, because I suspect they'll be more traffic from the tournament."

"Well, go for it!"

Skip pushed the pedal to the floor and accelerated as fast as the old truck would go down the pebbly road. Once they reached Hwy. 98, Skip turned to the east. He was pretty sure that there would be no police around, as the Sheriff had headed east from the lemonade stand, and he didn't think both of St. Joe's Sheriffs would be working on a Sunday.

"Reach in that glove compartment, Claudia. Pull out the zip lock bag with all those coins in it."

Claudia fished around and found the bag, which held a bunch of quarters, nickels, dimes and pennies.

"There must be ten dollars in here, Skip."

"As we go by Missy's stand, throw it to her."

Skip swerved onto 30A, hit the brakes, and slowed in front of the lemonade stand.

"Here ya go, Missy!" Claudia shouted, and threw the bag of coins on the grass beside the stand.

"Wow!" the child exclaimed as they drove away. "Yowza!"

Claudia looked back to see Missy bent over examining the bag with wonder in her eyes, just like Claudia had done when she first laid eyes on the contents of Billy Bowlegs' treasure chest.

"But what about your boat?" she asked Skip.

"Don't worry. It's in a safe place, and not much in it to steal. I'll come back tomorrow, get gas on the way down, pick up my trailer from Presnell's, drop the gas can off at the boat, and drive to the town launch. Then I'll walk back to the boat, fill the gas tank, and motor back to the launch."

"Aren't you afraid someone will steal it?"

"Ha! It's not worth much, and is out of gas."

"And while I'm down here tomorrow, I'll see where they towed your car to..."

"No way, Skip!" exclaimed Claudia. "That hunk of junk was on its death bed when it broke down, it's not worth whatever the towing charge would be to get it."

"Whatever," Skip replied. "It's your car."

Claudia unbuckled herself from the shoulder harness, slid over, strapped the middle seat belt on, and put her arm around Skip. The truck sped toward Carabelle along Hwy. 98, shaking in protest, as the speed approached eighty miles an hour.

"Can you go any faster?"

"Nope. Didn't know the truck could go this fast! It's the first time I've run it in fifth gear with the pedal all the way to the floor."

"Do ya think it will hold up?"

"Maybe. Maybe not. It's nineteen years old, but the engine is running fine. This might destroy it, but we have to make up time wherever we can, and we can't go speeding through Apalachicola or East Point."

"St. Joe isn't a very big city, is it?" Claudia asked, noticing that the houses stopped less than a quarter mile from the lemonade stand.

"Used to be!" Skip replied.

"Sounds like there's a story here. Tell me about it."

The diesel engine whined and complained in a throaty roar as Skip raced to make the 2 PM deadline. Claudia kept a nervous eye on the road, as Skip recalled what he knew of old St. Joseph. His deep voice resonated above the noise of the truck as the wind rushed through the open windows.

"How far back should I go?"

"All the way!"

Skip looked at her with raised eye brows.

"Native Americans lived there at one time – I don't know a lot about their culture or customs, but you saw the pile of conch shells they left."

"Yeah. The bay must have been full of them."

"Native Americans?"

"No! Conches!"

"Right. Then this guy named Vespucci came along, only seven years after Columbus discovered the islands in the Caribbean, around 1498. They think he sailed into the northern Gulf."

"How do they know that?"

"There's a Spanish map dated 1513 that shows a B.S. Joseph on it."

"What does B.S. stand for?"

"Bull shit."

"No, really."

"And Bay of Saint, as in Bay of St. Joseph."

"So Vespucci was Spanish."

"Not really. He was from Florence, Italy. But I guess he got the backing of the Spanish monarch for the expedition. Not sure about that."

"So, did Spain settle the area?"

"Not right away. Don Trist de Luna set out from Vera Cruz with thirteen ships in 1559, thinking that St. Joseph's Bay would be a fine place to set up colony."

"Did they make it?"

"Oh, they made it there alright. Built a settlement toward the end of the St. Joe peninsula. Always wanted to dig there and see what I could find."

"What happened to the settlers?"

"Nothing good. That September, they got blasted by a powerful hurricane that lasted twenty-four hours. Lost seven of their ships.

One was blown hundreds of feet into the forest by the gale and waves!"

"How did they get it back to the water?"

"I don't think they did. The survivors, totally defeated by the elements, left. When others heard the story of the furious storm, it discouraged them from trying to colonize the area."

"Then what happened?"

"Next thing I know about is a Spanish mission, sometime around 1600. The territory went back and forth between the British, Spanish and French. In fact, in 1717 the French began building a fort near present day St. Joe, on the mainland. They called it Crevecoeur, or Broken Heart."

"Why?"

"I don't know. Maybe because the French government forbid the growing of grapes there."

"Why did they do that?"

"I guess because they thought the land was well-suited for grapes, and the grape growers in France didn't want the competition."

"Weird."

"History is weird. The next year the French began building a settlement in New Orleans. The commander there sent his brother Lemoyne de Chateaugue to complete Fort Crevecouer."

"Did he finish it?"

"No. The attempt to finish the fort only wound up pissing off the governor of Spanish Florida, who was in Pensacola. He planned to send an army to attack it. When Lemoyne de Chateaugue and his troops heard that the Spanish were coming, twenty-five of his soldiers abandoned him, and headed to St. Augustine. So he and the rest of the men burned what had already been built, and left."

"Then what happened. Seems like no one stayed in St. Joseph very long!"

"I guess it just wasn't meant to be settled. When the Spanish got there, they built a fort on the site of Crevecouer, Fort St. Joseph. But Spain was so intent on taking back the territory around Santa Rosa to the west, that in 1722 they began dismantling Fort St. Joseph and bringing the materials and men back to the Pensacola area."

"Jeez! Then who settled St. Joseph?"

"Hardly anyone, until 1821. That's when Florida was deeded to the U.S. by England. In the 1830s a road was built between Marianna and St. Joseph and Apalachicola. Old public road number 64 – I suspect we're riding on it right now. That's when the place finally began being developed."

"And the rest is history?"

"Not quite. Mother nature was still not ready to give in and let man settle the area in peace."

"Oh, no! Not again!"

"Yup. Things were going really well for St. Joseph. Folks from Apalachicola, were ticked off by a Supreme Court decision in 1835 that upheld this huge company, the Apalachicola Land Company's claim to most of north Florida, including Apalachicola. They were made to pay this Apalachicola Land Company for the land they were on. So they came up with the idea to make St. Joseph a rival port, by digging a canal that would link the Apalachicola River to St. Joseph's Bay, via Lake Wimico, which is just north of St. Joseph and is accessible from the Apalachicola River."

"That was ambitious."

"Indeed. But digging the canal proved more of a task than they had imagined, and it failed. Still determined to make St. Joseph a port city and take the cotton and lumber trade away from Apalachicola, they devised another scheme."

"What made them think they could take the trade away from Apalachicola?"

"St. Joseph's Bay was deeper and did not have the oyster and sand bars that were so hazardous to ships in Apalachicola Bay. So they decided if they couldn't dig a canal, they would run a railroad from where they had begun the canal on Lake Wimico to St. Joseph, which was only eight miles."

"Dreamers!"

"In 1836, two steam engines arrived by ship from Philadelphia, and they began building the first steam railroad in Florida."

"What about that one you told me about that ran from Tallahassee to St. Marks?"

"That was the second one in Florida. I'm impressed – you have a good memory. So they laid the track and built a long, sturdy wharf in the bay, and got eight steam ships to agree to bring cargo down the Apalachicola to the landing on Lake Wimico."

"How did that work out?"

"Not so good, actually. Even though they dredged Bayou Columbus, they were constantly running aground because Lake Wimico was shallow and the channel was narrow. They wound up abandoning the railway line in 1839."

"Is St. Joseph ever going to catch a break?"

"Kind of. A few years earlier, realizing that the first plan was flawed, they began building a railroad line, the St. Joseph and Iola railroad, that ran from St. Joseph 28 miles north to a place called Tennessee Bluff near the town of Iola on the Apalachicola. It was quite successful. The wharf was expanded, and was three-quarters of a mile long and sixty feet wide! Ships from South America, Europe and the East Coast tied up to both sides of it. St. Joseph's population swelled to six-thousand, which made it, at the time, the largest city in Florida. In fact, in 1838, Florida's Constitutional Convention was held there. It began getting a worldwide reputation."

"So what happened? Everything was going so well."

"The Saints, as the citizens of the town were called, thought so too. Only nature decided she was not quite ready for that part of the world to be citified. And this is where the story gets really ugly."

"Tell me."

"Some say a ship from South America docked there early in the summer of 1841. Aboard was a deadly disease that would bring St. Joseph to its knees."

"What kind of disease?"

"Yellow fever. People got sick, began throwing up, and died within days of catching it. It ran rampant through the town. They say it killed three out of four people living there! The dead filled three cemeteries and the survivors began digging trenches for the bodies. The residents who could, fled. Ships stopped arriving. No physicians remained in the damned city. It must have been hell."

"How many stayed after that?"

"By the end of August, 1841, only about five-hundred folks remained!"

"What a disaster! Were they able to rebuild?"

"They may well have done that, if they had been given the chance."

"What do you mean?"

"In September of the same year, 1841, as if the people hadn't been through enough already, a huge hurricane hit. The wharf was destroyed, and the spirit of the town was broken. Folks fled, and that Fall, fire ravaged what was left of the city and the surrounding forests."

"St. Joseph crumbled like Sodom and Gomorrah."

"Yeah. The few residences and hotels that were left standing were dismantled and rebuilt in Apalachicola. And it's a good thing, too. Because three years later another powerful hurricane hit. The waves were so huge, they swept right over the peninsula, and knocked down any remaining buildings in the city. A handful of fishermen who had taken shelter in a place called Shipyard Cove survived the storm."

"Could anything else go wrong?"

"Sure. A few years later, 1847, I think, the lighthouse at the far point of St. Joseph's peninsula had to be abandoned because of erosion. Another one was built at Cape San Blas Point, further to the south. That didn't last but four years, when it got destroyed by a storm. By the year 1850, not a single person remained in St. Joseph! And it pretty much stayed that way until around the turn of the century."

"I can understand why, given that history!"

"And that's a good thing..."

"Oh, not again!"

"Yup! The summer of 1856 saw a hurricane so violent it caused an eleven-foot tide swell, and lasted six days, if you can imagine that! It must have stalled just off the coast. The worst day of the storm was the last one."

"I bet you could have bought land pretty cheap there, eh?"

"Oh, man! Not a place I would have wanted to invest in. So, then came the Civil War. After the war, a guy by the name of James Bennett Stone got himself a deal – he bought over six-thousand acres of land, the mainland from around Black's Island west including all of what is now the city of St. Joe, for a whopping one-hundred-twenty-five dollars and seventy-four cents!"

"No way!"

"It's true. Imagine buying even one acre of land today on the shore anywhere in Florida. The tract he bought was all along the shore, and ran a mile to a mile-and-a-half deep!"

As Skip told his tale of St. Joe and Claudia listened intently, they did not notice the rain cloud building over Apalachicola. The anvil-shaped cloud formation was a typical occurrence during the hot, steamy summer afternoons of the Florida panhandle.

"So what did he do with the land?"

"I'm not sure. Probably cut what lumber he could, or used the pines for the turpentine business. It wasn't until 1902 that a log home was built there by Terrill Higdon Stone."

"How do you remember all of these names and dates?"

"I didn't used to remember them, but each time I tell someone the story, I go back and find any names that I couldn't remember, and any dates I couldn't remember, and the next time I tell it, I remember more."

"Where do you find them?"

"After reading about the area in history books, I wrote a little history of the area myself, only touching on the highlights. So I look in that."

"I'd like to read that some day."

"Anytime."

"Then what happened to unlucky St. Joseph?"

"What do you think? Another hurricane hit in 1906."

"That town seems to be in the path of quite a few hurricanes!"

"True. But fortune smiled upon the city when the Savannah and Southwestern Railroad Company built a three-hundred-and-fifty mile railroad line that began in Savannah, Georgia, went through Apalachicola, and ended in St. Joseph. Three years later, the Port Inn Resort was built, right on the bay."

"I guess they didn't know about St. Joseph's history."

"The legislature, wanting the new town to succeed, changed the name of the city from St. Joseph to St. Joe."

"Why?"

"I don't know - maybe to distinguish it from the old St. Joseph that got blasted by so many disasters."

"Did that help?"

"Yes. For a time, anyway. St. Joe thrived as a tourist destination because of the beautiful bay and Gulf beaches. It also prospered due to the lumber industry."

"Then what?"

"Things went well from 1910 to 1930, then the Great Depression hit. There went the tourism industry. And the lumber industry, having cut down trees and not planting any new ones, burned itself out."

"You mean they ran out of trees?"

"Pretty much. They didn't bother to replant after cutting, and a lot of land was cleared to make room for cattle grazing and small farms. So the town shrank again, if I remember correctly there were only about eight-hundred-and-fifty people left by the end of 1930."

"Did those folks catch a break?"

"Sure did. In 1933 the federal government bought three-hundred-thousand acres and created the Apalachicola National Forest. They replanted pines, cut roads in the forest to within two miles of any point, and hired forest rangers to manage the land and put out any fires that started."

"So how did the folks get back on their feet again?"

"The next year, a guy name Alfred I. Dupont..."

"Of the Dupont chemical family?"

"Yes. Seeing the potential of the area, and wanting to help people who were affected by the depression, he invested $1,500,000 dollars in St. Joe. Rebuilt the wharf, repaired telephone and telegraph lines, and got the Apalachicola and Northern Rail Road functioning again."

"How did he manage all that?"

"He took over the St. Joe Land and Development Company, and appointed his brother-in-law Ed Ball as President. The public works projects begun by the federal government to get the nation out of the

Great Depression helped St. Joe, too. Beginning in '32 and ending in '35, the Gulf Coast Scenic Hwy. was completed."

"Where's that?"

"We're on it. Hwy. 98. It linked Panacea with St. Theresa with Lanark with Carabelle with East Point with Apalachicola with St. Joe, and continued west through Mexico Beach to Panama City, Destin and Pensacola."

"So that opened things up for St. Joe economically?"

"Not really, but it helped. What gave St. Joe a kickstart was Ed Ball investing $7,500,000 of Dupont money, building a paper mill in 1935. That wound up employing about a thousand people in the mill where they manufactured liner board for paper containers. Another two-thousand people gained employment in the timber industry. Then Ball bought 145,000 more acres in Gulf, Franklin, Calhoun and Bay counties."

"Who owns all that land now?"

"St. Joe Paper Company, the company he formed in '35."

"So it became a booming town again. Why is it not still prosperous?"

"I really don't know. Two other companies, chemical companies, I believe, located in St. Joe and are still there. But the paper mill is shut down. St. Joe's economy was very dependent on the mill. But tourism is increasing as the as the peninsula gets developed, and that's helping people find jobs."

Drops of rain hitting the windshield brought Skip and Claudia back from their contemplations about St. Joe.

"I don't know about you, but I've had about enough rain today as I can handle!" Claudia sighed, rolling up her window.

"This won't last long," Skip answered. I can see blue sky over East Point from here.

Claudia gazed to the east as the wipers swished away the raindrops. But she couldn't see very well.

"Man, your windows are filthy, Skip!"

"That's funny. They weren't before it started raining."

"Maybe it's raining dirt!"

"That's a first in these parts!"

Skip put his arm out the still open window to feel the rain, and drawing it back in again exclaimed, "Oh, no!"

"What's wrong?" Claudia demanded. Looking at Skip's arm, she noticed what looked like black mascara on his wrist.

"We're melting!"

"We're what?"

Skip wiped the smudge off of his wrist on a napkin he found in the glove compartment.

"That's paint, isn't it?" Claudia's face mirrored the concern on Skip's.

"Uh, huh! Could anything else go wrong?" Claudia removed the three old necklaces from her neck, and put them in the glove compartment.

A lightning flash appeared in the sky and thunder pealed through the afternoon shower.

"Ahhhhhhhh!" they shouted simultaneously at the top of their lungs. Looking at each other, they began to laugh. Softly at first, then louder and louder. Skip had to hold his stomach, it convulsed so much it hurt. Tears of laughter rolled down Claudia's cheeks. There they were, riding into Apalachicola, dripping beads of black paint behind them as if shedding the bad luck that had plagued them and the folks of St. Joe.

CHAPTER XIX
WEIGHT ONE MINUTE!

"**S**kip, if all this paint comes off, we're in big trouble. The Sheriff will spot us!"

"Not to worry! St. Joe is in Gulf County. And we're now in Franklin County."

"Does that mean there won't be any Gulf County Sheriffs here?"

"Hmm! I don't know. I'm thinking they won't cross the county line, but I'm not sure. I've never been a wanted criminal before."

"I bet they stop at the county line."

"I hope you're right!"

The steep incline of the John Gorrie Bridge that spans the Apalachicola River slowed the pickup to a snail's pace. The old engine whined as Skip dropped it down to second gear.

"What time is it?"

"1:30."

"Are we gonna make it, Skip?"

"Only if I speed."

"Well, speed then!"

"I'm trying!"

Reaching the apex of the span, Skip wound through third and fourth gear, racing the engine to the max before shifting into fifth. The brown-green waters of Apalachicola Bay below shimmered in the afternoon light. As the sun came out again, the droplets of paint rolling across the hood and onto the windshield slowly decreased until they were hardly noticeable. Turning off the wipers, Claudia and Skip rolled down their windows to cool off the cab, but Skip didn't dare rest his arm out the window for fear of getting wet paint on himself again.

As the bridge ended, Claudia read the green sign welcoming them to East Point.

"How did East Point get its name?"

"I don't know."

"I thought you knew everything about the history of the Big Bend."

"Wrong. Only what sticks in my mind. But I have an idea how it got its name. Apalachicola was settled first, and the closest land to the east was -"

"Called East Point."

"Right. A ferry used to take folks back and forth between East Point and Apalachicola before the bridge was built."

"Why did anyone want to live in East Point?"

"It's kind of a bizarre story. Before the turn of the century, around 1896, there was this Farmer's Alliance, a socialist group, who were also known as Populists. Travelling from Nebraska to Georgia, they bought a thousand acre plantation east of Columbus. One of the well respected members, a David Brown, had been to Apalachicola and East Point looking for a possible site for the cooperative before they chose the Georgia location. The community in Georgia wasn't very accepting of these socialists, and made it clear to the newcomers that they and their commune were not welcome."

"That's rude."

"You know how ignorant people have a hard time with anything they are not familiar with, whether it be a new life style, religion, or race. So in 1898, five families and two single men constructed a couple of thirty-foot house barges, purchased another smaller barge, and thirty-one members of the Farmer's Alliance shoved off heading for Apalachicola via the Chatahoochee River. The Chatahoochee flowed into the Apalachicola River."

"What do you mean, flowed. Doesn't it still flow into the Apalachicola?"

"Not like it did back then. Now it flows into Lake Seminole, and below the dam that forms the lake, the Apalachicola River begins. Anyway..."

"What does this have to do with East Point?"

"I'm getting to that."

"Oh."

Claudia noticed the tiny Big Top grocery store on her left, and the bay on her right. Along the shore were cozy mom-and-pop restaurants, wholesale and retail seafood shacks, and small, one-person oyster boats anchored in the cove behind the businesses. Piles of oyster shells sat abandoned in the empty lots between the disorderly array of buildings.

"Floating down the river, the large barges tied end-to-end with the smaller barge tied alongside, came this hopeful group of socialist farmers, carrying farm equipment, chicken, ducks, and a pair of turkeys. It must have been quite a sight!"

"Really!"

"Eleven days later they reached Apalachicola. Local businessmen got together, and somehow helped them cross East Bay with their barges."

"How did they do that?"

"Probably gave them directions and fashioned push-poles out of pines. East Bay, the one we're crossing now, real shallow. They landed at a place called Godley's Bluff, where they disassembled the barges and used the wood to build their homes."

"Resourceful lot!"

"Indeed! This guy named Vrooman arrived the following year, and, along with Brown, set up a cooperative colony, naming it the "Co-Worker's Fraternity". Although Vrooman and Brown put the emphasis on production, they also organized religious, spiritual and philosophical study groups."

"What's the difference between religious and spiritual study?"

"Not sure. But just because you consider yourself a member of a religion, does not necessarily mean that you are a spiritual person. They opened up the membership to anyone who wanted to join. The fee was either a hundred dollars, or a year's work. Individuals owned the land they worked, but everyone split the profits."

"Profits from what?"

"They grew and sold stuff to the folks in Apalachicola; onions, strawberries, turnip greens, sweet potatoes, satsuma oranges and muscadine grapes. But their most lucrative business was from Bay Croft brand syrup, made from sugarcane."

"So what happened to the coop – is it still here?"

"No. They did quite well for a while, branching into the fishing and lumbering industries. But look around. The soil is poor and there is no river for shipping like there is in Apalachicola and Carabelle. So the town didn't grow very fast, and eventually they disbanded, I guess."

"Now what time is it?"

"1:40."

"Are we gonna make it?"

"Only if I speed."

"Seems like I heard that before. Go!"

"I'm speeding, I'm speeding already!"

"Where is the weigh-in?"

"Carabelle. Just the other side of the Tillie Miller bridge."

"Carabelle? Must be a story behind that name!"

"Of course. See across the bay. There's St. George's Island right across from us. The next island to the east, that's Dog Island. Dog Island is across the bay from Carabelle. We're getting close!"

"So tell me the story about Carabelle."

"Around 1900, the settlers who lived by the mouth of the river, having debated what to name their little hamlet, and not being able to come to an agreement, decided to have a ho-down. They chose a non-biased panel of judges from Apalachicola, and the idea was that whatever couple won the dance contest, got to name the town. They had an abundance of good food and liquor, and three bands, one made up of local folks and two from Apalachicola who came over on the ferry with the judges. The couples got to dancing, and drinking, and whirling up such a storm on the wharf, that one of the dancers, a Cara Belle Jones, got flung right off the dock and into the river! Never to be seen again!"

"No!"

"Uh-huh! So shocked and dismayed was the crowd, that, in a unanimous vote the next day, they decided to call the town Carabelle."

"That's amazing!"

"Yup! Amazing. If only it were true."

Whack! Claudia punched Skip in the arm so hard that the graze from Will's bullet opened up and began bleeding.

"Ow!"

"Oops! Sorry." She slipped a napkin up his sleeve and patted the wound to soak up the blood. "But you deserved that!"

Skip chuckled. "I did, didn't I?"

"Dearly. Now tell me how the town was really named. And don't tell me you don't know."

"O.K. The founder of an organization called Patrons of Husbandry..."

"Patrons of Husbandry? Stop fooling around, Skip."

"I'm not, it was really called the Patrons of Husbandry. Some people also referred to it as the Grange. Anyhow, the founder's name was Oliver Kelley, and he was from Minnesota. Somehow, he got quite wealthy through his business dealings, and bought about 2,000 acres of land at the mouth of the river from a Benjamin Curtis, who also owned Dog Island. Being a shrewd investor, Oliver Kelly saw the potential in the land – a deep harbor surrounded by pine forest and a bay full of oysters, shrimp and fish."

"When was this?"

"Oh, around 1877. He built a large sawmill, then a hotel that he named Carabelle. Just kidding. He named the hotel Island House. He talked his favorite niece, Carolyn Arabelle Hall, into managing the hotel's operations for him. She also happened to be a national officer in the Grange, and was known locally for her beauty, and a wonderful Boston brown bread recipe that she served at the hotel. Under her management the business did well. So pleased and grateful was Oliver Kelly, that he named the burgeoning town Rio Carabelle, presumably a creative combination of Carolyn Arrabelle. Then, in 1893, a railroad was completed that linked the village with Talla-hassee. When they incorporated the town, Rio was dropped and the official name became Carabelle."

"Are you pulling my leg again?"

"Darling! Would I do such a thing to you?"

Claudia kissed Skip's ear, then reached across him, turned his wrist to see the watch face.

"Ten minutes, Skip!"

"We can do it!"

Approaching the Tillie Miller bridge over the Carabelle River, Skip and Claudia saw the tell tale signs of the tournament – pickups and vans with boat trailers attached were parked on both sides of the bridge, and all the way as far as the eye could see down Hwy. 98 in front of the Carabelle marina.

"Skip, how are we gonna park and get your fish to the weigh-in line on time?"

"Watch me!" Skip remarked confidently, having been in this predicament before. He pulled into the marina driveway, which was guarded by Franklin County Sheriffs, directing traffic away from the festival. Pulling up alongside a Sheriff's cruiser, Skip hopped out of the truck. A rugged, tanned Sheriff standing over six-foot tall and weighing close to three-hundred pounds waved at Skip to get back in the truck and drive on.

"Howdy, Sheriff! Got a big one in the cooler! Mind if I drop it off here, then find a parking spot?"

"S'O.K. by me. Just make it quick. The gun'll be soundin' in eight minutes."

"Thanks!" Skip signalled for Claudia to join him. They each took a handle of the cooler, flung it over the side of the pickup truck, and carried it toward the barrier that prevented cars from driving toward the stage. Wheelbarrow-like carts were inside the barrier to help fishermen get their catch to the weigh in line. Skip and Claudia set the cooler in a cart.

"I'll be right back! Be sure to get on line in the next few minutes, eh?" he shouted to Claudia as he rushed back to the truck.

"What do you mean, get on line?"

"Wheel the cart down there." Skip pointed at the stage, banners and leader boards set up at the edge of the parking lot.

"Me?"

"Sure. I'm gonna park."

Claudia begrudgingly set off with the cart toward the hustle and bustle of the tournament headquarters, people passing her from both directions. Feeling kind of embarrassed, yet anxious to get to the weigh-in line on time, she hit a rock and nearly dumped the contents of the cooler on the pebble-strewn ground.

"Hey, now!" She heard an all-too-familiar voice call to her.

"Did that cad leave you to drag his fish to the weigh in?" Buck chuckled.

"I recon he's got himself a whole cooler of brown trout there, Buck!" Lucas added, laughing at his own cleverness.

"Why I'd be glad to help ya out carrying that load, miss." Buck offered.

"I got it, thanks anyway."

Buck and Lucas continued to walk with her, one on each side when room allowed.

"I thought you two would be weighing a fish in too. What happened?"

"Oh, we got here an hour ago, and already weighed in that gator trout Buck caught. See the leader board. Buck's in second place."

"Second place. Too bad. When Skip weighs this one in, he'll take over first place and you'll be bumped to third." Claudia bragged.

"I doubt that, missy," Buck argued. "That fish in first place weighs seven and three-quarter pounds – I don't think even that trout Skip caught weighs that much. It may weigh more than my seven pounder, but it ain't no eight pounds, I'll tell ya that. There hasn't been an eight-pounder weighed in at the Big Bend Classic ever!"

"Well, there's always a first time," Claudia replied.

Buck and Lucas pointed to the end of the weigh-in line, and Claudia stopped the cart there, amidst stares from those already on line.

"Whatcha got there, honey?" the grizzled old fisherman ahead of her in line inquired.

"A pair of jokers and a big trout," Claudia remarked.

"Where I come from, jokers are wild."

"They must be from the same place, then!"

All four laughed.

"Can I getcha a beer?" Lucas asked Claudia.

"No. I'm starvin'. If I drank a beer now, I'd likely pass out."

"Then how 'bouts a grouper sandwich? They're mighty good."

"You'd do that for me?"

"Sure. Be right back."

Running, Skip swerved past onlookers until he approached the weigh in line, beads of sweat running down his forehead. Seeing Buck talking to Claudia made him uneasy.

"Well, look who's here!" Buck shouted as Skip approached. "Ya leave this fine young lady to lug your fish, and ya come around all sweaty lookin' like it was you doin' the work!"

"Hello, Buck! I guess we made it on time," replied Skip.

"Yup!" said Buck, pointing at the leader board for speckled trout. "But look at that. Some guy named Dennis Wade got him a seven-and-three-quarter pound trout."

"Damn! That's big. That may be the biggest trout ever weighed in at the Big Bend Classic, eh?"

"That's right. How do you think your fish will compare?"

"I don't know. But I gotta tell ya, it's awful big – you and Lucas saw it that day in Hurricane Cove. What do you think?"

"It sure is big – let's have another look at it."

"Here ya go!" Lucas beamed as he handed the styrofoam plate holding the savory grouper sandwich to Claudia. Looking at it, she wondered how she'd get her mouth around the sesame seed covered bun, lettuce spilling out the sides.

"Thanks, Lucas!"

"Thought you might need this to wash it down." Lucas handed her a cold lemon-and-lime soft drink in a green can.

"You're all right, no matter what Skip says about you!"

"Let's take a look at that trout," Buck repeated. Skip had ignored his first comment, hoping he wouldn't bring it up again.

"I'd rather not take it out 'til we get to the scales, Buck. I want all the slime and water to be on it when it's weighed." Claudia stuffed the grouper sandwich in Skip's mouth, and he instinctively took a bite.

"Man, that's good!"

"Ya don't need to take it out. Let's just have a look at it again. Maybe we can get a better idea how much it will weigh."

Skip opened the top of the cooler. All the ice had melted, but the water filling the bottom was still cool. Pulling some soft drinks out of the cooler, he brushed aside the remaining fruit and bread wrapper that hid the fish.

"Nooooooooooooo!!!" Skip screamed at the top of his lungs. The crowd got quiet and everyone looked at him.

Claudia gripped his arm. "Take it easy. What's wrong?"

"That's not my trout!" Skip shouted, panicked. "My trout was twice that size!"

Claudia, Lucas and Buck gazed into the cooler at a medium sized speckled trout that might have weighed four pounds at the most.

"Maybe it shrunk!" Lucas quipped.

Skip turned a stony glance at him. "Did you guys take my fish?"

"No!" Buck and Lucas said in unison.

"No way!" Buck continued. "Like I told ya before, we may be rude, but we ain't thieves or cheats."

"Yeah," Lucas agreed.

"Where the hell did it go then?"

"That definitely ain't the fish you showed us in Hurricane Cove the other day," Lucas commented. Reaching down, he spread out the tail.

"And its tail ain't cut in twelve pieces like that other one, either."

"Whoever took my fish replaced it with this one, hoping that I wouldn't notice until now."

"Right!" Lucas agreed. "Maybe we can get his fingerprints!"

Buck shoved Lucas. "Have another beer, buddy."

"No sense in weighing this fish in," Skip moaned, looking at Claudia.

"Jeez, Skip, I'm sorry! Running and racing to get back here on time, and we don't even have the fish to weigh in. Is our luck ever going to change?"

Skip looked at the three necklaces around Claudia's neck that she had put back on. Claudia read his mind.

"You don't think..."

"No. No. I don't think it had anything to do with that."

"To do with what?" Buck inquired.

"Never mind." Giving up hope, Skip sat down on the cooler.

"One good thing about it," Lucas commented to Buck, "your fish gets to stay in second place."

"True. Better luck next year, you two." Buck nodded his head sideways, signaling to Lucas that it was time to go. "Let's get closer to the stage, Lucas."

Skip and Claudia sat on the cooler, sharing the grouper sandwich.

"My son and ex-wife should be here soon."

"I'm looking forward to meeting your son. Can't say the same about your ex-wife."

"Don't worry. She won't hang out. This crowd is not her type, and this festival is not her idea of fun."

Claudia wondered what she could do to cheer Skip.

"Don't look so down." She slid her arm around his waist. People crowded around them, trying to get a better view of the stage, seemingly oblivious to the two sitting in their midst.

"You're right, it's not the end of the world. I have a wonderful son. And a new, beautiful best friend." He pulled her close and kissed her cheek. "But I'd like to catch the cad who stole my trout!"

The last fish was dragged dripping off the scale, tagged, and thrown into the refrigerated truck along with the rest; those unfortunate cold creatures of the sea unlucky enough to be unusually large for their particular species, who, having elected to eat what they thought was an easy meal, wound up hooked, then netted or gaffed, and flopped inside a boat, destined to spend the last few minutes of their lives out of the watery habitat they knew so well. This was the only part of the tournament Skip disliked – the taking of so many fish. Even though the ones that were not claimed were given to charity, and eaten, Skip wished there was a practical way to evolve the contest into a catch-and-release event.

Tournament volunteers, teenagers in slime-and-fish-scale coated T-shirts, adjusted some names on the leader board.

The president of OAR, the Organization for Artificial Reefs for the Big Bend area, Kenneth Johnson stood tall on the stage. Distinguished looking with his gray hair and neat appearance, he sported a new Big Bend Saltwater Classic T-shirt and cap above his woven khaki pants and expensive Sperry Topsider boat shoes. Grabbing the microphone like a politician about to speak to potential voters, he announced loudly over the racket of the crowd, "Now's the time y'all have been waitin' for!"

"Free beer!" yelled Buck from his ringside seat.

"No. Not free beer. It's the presentation of the awards and the crowning of the champions!"

The crowd whistled, cheered and applauded.

Sitting on the cooler, Skip shook his head in dismay. He had been so sure he would be invited to the stage to receive his first place check and trophy, and pose with his gator trout. He was really looking forward to finally getting the better of Buck and Lucas, especially after the brown trout fiasco.

"Come on, Skip! Snap out of it. I know how disappointed you are. But let's make the best of it. You don't want to look so down in the mouth when your son comes, do ya?" Claudia put her arm around his shoulders.

"Hi, Dad!" a cheerful voice from behind them shouted. Skip jumped up and wheeled around just in time to catch six year old Benny as he leapt on the cooler top and into his arms.

"Yowza!" Skip hugged the boy tight, their affection for each other evident to everyone watching. "Am I glad to see you!"

"Wish I could say the same!" quipped a curt voice. Skip had heard that sarcastic voice before, and it still grated on him.

"Hey, Melissa! How are you?"

"I'd be a helluva lot better if you had been somewhere I could see you. We've been searching for you for fifteen minutes!"

"Sorry. Melissa, this is Claudia. Claudia, Melissa."

"Hi!" Claudia responded in a friendly tone. "And who's the big guy there?"

"Claudia, meet my wonderful son Benny. Benny, say hi to Claudia."

"Hi! Are you my Dad's new girlfriend?" Kids cut right to the chase!

"Uh huh!" Claudia answered unhesitatingly, looking at Melissa for her reaction.

"Good luck!" Melissa said coldly.

"That's something Claudia and I haven't had a lot of the past few days!" Skip tried to change the subject. "And how've you been, Ben?"

"Fine. Show me the fish."

"There's a fish in the cooler, but I'll be darned if I know how it got there and who caught it."

"You caught it," guessed Benny.

"No. The one I caught was way bigger than that!"

"Yeah, right!" Melissa chimed in. "Your father's about to tell another one of his fish tales. I'd better be going. Give me a hug, Benny."

"Why don't you stay for awhile?" Claudia suggested.

"Nah. I'm not real fond of gawking at dead fish standing in the hot sun."

"Mom, the dead fish don't stand in the hot sun!"

"I know, I know. You're as bad as your father!" Shaking her head she added, "Give me a hug and a kiss!"

Melissa held Benny for an embarrassingly long time, then kissed him on the cheek, leaving a mark from her bright red lip stick. Perspiration dripping down her temple looked like milk drops because of the makeup she caked on her face.

"Nice meeting you!" Claudia called as Melissa began to make her way through the crowd.

Skip and Claudia positioned the cooler closer to the action, and Benny stood on it, marveling at the big fish the winners of each division brought with them to the stage as their names were called out. Kenneth Johnson, beaming with enthusiasm, read the names of the third place, second place, then first place winners of the amberjack division. The first place winner was a woman, Claire Steele, and she had to have help lugging the large amberjack to center stage for the presentation and pictures. Kenneth gave the third place contestant a check for $150, and the second place contestant a check for $250. The first place winner was handed a check for $450, and a tall but inexpensive trophy with a fish on top. Pictures were taken for newspapers and inclusion in the tournament guide the following year. Only the first place winners got to pose with their catches, as the volunteers had a hard time finding the tagged fish strewn on the refrigerated tractor trailer's slippery metal floor.

Between divisions, Claudia bought Benny a shaved-ice lemonade, his favorite drink. Benny, standing tiptoe on the cooler, wrapped his arm around her neck and kissed her cheek. Skip smiled. It was heartwarming seeing Claudia and Benny getting along so well. He wasn't sure how Claudia related to kids, and now, to his delight, he knew.

Kenneth Johnson began announcing the winners of the speckled trout division; Harlan Barineau, third place, Buck Quigley, second place. The crowd cheered – it seemed everyone knew Buck. He held his hands clasped above his head, looking over the crowd. Then the first place winner was announced, Dennis Wade. Dennis bounded up the steps to a round of applause from the crowd. Skip strained to see the man who had managed to strip the speckled trout crown from Buck and Lucas.

"Damn!" Skip yelled at the top of his lungs as he recognized Dennis Wade as his camping neighbor at Presnell's. Dennis held the fish high for the audience to appreciate.

Kenneth Johnson boasted, "First place trout weighs a whopping seven-and-three-quarter pounds! It's a new tournament record! Let's have another round of applause for Dennis!"

As the crowd cheered, Skip shouted to Claudia, "Watch Benny!" Nudging, bumping and wiggling his way through the throng, Skip finally reached the steps of the stage. Kenneth had given the third place check to Harlan, and the second place check to Buck, and was in the middle of presenting Dennis Wade with his trophy when Skip burst onto the stage shouting.

"Hold everything! That's my trout!" Grabbing the fish by the gills, he tried to yank it out of Dennis Wade's hands. But Dennis would have nothing to do with it.

"Get yer damn hands offa my fish!" For a few seconds there was a tug of war, and a Franklin County Sheriff rushed up on the stage to subdue Skip. Before he knew what was happening, the burly Sheriff had Skip handcuffed. The noise was deafening as the crowd cheered the tug of war between Dennis and Skip, and jeered the Sheriff as he attempted the arrest.

Kenneth Johnson had turned pale and frozen, caught totally by surprise at the turn of events. The Sheriff started toward the steps with Skip in tow, when Buck reached out and grabbed his arm with his right hand, and ripped the microphone out of Kenneth's hand with his left.

"Y'all quiet down now! Quiet down! Hush!" Buck bellowed, the magnitude of his voice over the PA system shook the ground.

As the noise faded, the shaky voice of the Sheriff drifted above the crowd. "Let go of my arm, Buck!"

"Not until we get somethin' straight here, buddy!"

Dennis Wade, standing next to a stunned Kenneth Johnson, yelled, "Get these guys off the stage, Johnson! They're ruining the whole ceremony!"

Ignoring Dennis, Buck continued, "Saturday, Skip, here, showed Lucas and I a speckled trout he caught over by Hurricane Cove in St. Joseph's Bay." The crowd listened intently. "Lucas will vouch for what I'm sayin'. The boy was so worried that Lucas or I would try and steal it from him (which, of course, we would never do) he put twelve slices in the tail as we watched. Now I recon, if Dennis Wade here actually caught that trout, he'd be O.K. with us takin' a gander at that tail right how, eh, Dennis?"

"You're crazy! I caught this fish!" Dennis protested, a panicked look coming over his face. Buck reached out and pulled one end of the tail, spreading it out for the whole audience and the Sheriff to see. It was easy to detect that tail had been sliced twelve times.

The fish hit the stage with a thump, as Dennis wheeled and ran right off the back of the stage, the Sheriff in hot pursuit. The crowd went wild, the uproar so loud that Benny had to cover his ears.

"That's my Dad's fish! That's my Dad! Benny screamed. Claudia picked him up and put him on her shoulders so he could get a better view.

Skip grinned ear to ear, standing there on the stage, still handcuffed.

"I owe ya one, Buck!" he shouted over the din.

"Yer damn straight, boy!" Buck handed the microphone back to Kenneth Johnson. "Take it away!"

Rattled, Kenneth Johnson took the microphone with shaking hands.

"How about that?" he exclaimed to the crowd, as they erupted into more cheers, catcalls and whoops.

"Now, to the real winner of the Big Bend Saltwater Classic sea trout division, I present a check for $450 and this well-deserved trophy!"

Ben continued to shout, "That's my Dad! That's my Dad!" from his perch on Claudia's shoulders.

The applause from the crowd was deafening. It turned from clapping to laughter, as Kenneth stood there trying to hand Skip the trophy and check, and Skip stood there with his hands still shackled by the handcuffs, grinning ear to ear. Claudia quickly lifted Benny off of her shoulders, and began making a beeline toward the stage, pushing and prodding people in her hurry to get there, Benny barely able to hold on to her hand in the melee.

Claudia bounded up the steps to the stage, with Benny stumbling behind her, still shouting "That's my Dad, that's my Dad!" Claudia held Benny's shoulders in front of Kenneth, to the delight of the crowd. As Benny accepted the check and wrapped his little arms around the trophy, the crowd went wild again. Claudia embraced skip with a hug so strong they both nearly fell over. Benny set the trophy down, turned to the appreciative, laughing crowd, and bowed as if it was he who had won the trout division. Flashes of light showered the stage as people took pictures. Tears of joy welled up in Skip's eyes.

The official tournament camera person hopped on the stage, a young woman sporting a Big Bend Saltwater Classic T-shirt and a bikini bottom, which gave the impression that all she had on was the T-shirt. Arranging Kenneth, Harlan, Buck, Skip, Claudia, and Benny on the stage, she didn't need to tell anyone to smile. Skip held his elusive fish, Claudia had her arms around Skip and Benny, and Benny hugged the trophy like a long lost friend. The photographer snapped a picture that was destined for the cover of next year's tournament guide, and the front page of the *Tallahassee Democrat* the following day. Skip held up the elusive fish. Tears of joy flowed from Claudia's eyes as she posed, one arm around Skip, one around Benny. A tear dropped on one of Billy Bowleg's necklaces which gleamed in the sun.

A very sweaty Sheriff leapt on the stage to the renewed applause of the audience, and unlocked the handcuffs. Skip thrust his arms in the air, and the crowd roared their approval. Benny handed Skip the check and trophy, and Skip handed Benny the fish, which was nearly as long as he was tall. Skip and Claudia embraced, and Claudia kissed him passionately, eliciting cat calls from the crowd. Benny strutted back and forth on the stage, straining to keep the trout in the air. When a tournament volunteer bounded on the stage to take the trout back from Benny, he refused to give it up, and dodged her to the amusement of the audience.

"It's O.K., Benny!" Skip beamed. "They're just gonna keep it cold for us. We'll pick it up later."

Reluctantly, Benny handed the gator trout to the volunteer, who raised it in the air, and spread the tail fin out again so the crowd could see the twelve cuts that identified the fish as being Skip's.

"Did you catch Dennis Wade?" Skip inquired of the Sheriff.

"Nope. But we will. We know his name and address from the tournament roster. If we don't get him before he leaves Franklin County, they'll pick him up tomorrow in Wakulla County. I'll need you to sign some paper work for me so we can issue the arrest warrant."

"Nah. Let's just skip it."

"What! After what he put you through?"

"Yeah. If you can't forgive someone who did you wrong, how can you expect God to forgive you? Let's just forget it."

"He'll get away scot free!" growled the Sheriff.

"Not really. First, he was totally humiliated before hundreds of his neighbors. Second, he won't be allowed to enter another Big Bend Saltwater Classic for the rest of his life, according to tournament rules. Third, and worst of all, he has to live with himself knowing what he did. That's punishment enough, as far as I'm concerned."

"Whatever." The Sheriff stomped off, shaking his head.

CHAPTER XX

DARKNESS, MOONLIGHT, LAUGHTER, TEARS

A gaunt figure sauntered toward the Tillie Miller bridge from the west. Beginning his ascent, keeping between the concrete abutment and the parked cars, trucks and boats, he moved in slow motion. Stopping to gaze toward the Gulf, as if it held an answer to his dilemma, he shook his unkempt head at his predicament. As if in a daze, he continued walking up the bridge, looking into the vehicles and boats he passed, in case something of value had been left unlocked. He kept a wary eye on the traffic to be sure no policemen had spotted him.

"I'M STARVING!" SKIP said to Benny and Claudia. "And darnnear tuckered out! Let's sit down at the Shrimp House and spend some of this prize money, eh?"

"Sure! I could eat a horse!" Claudia replied.

"Eeeew! Dad, does she really eat horses?"

"No, Benny! That's just an expression."

Walking hand-in-hand on the gravel, passing the booths that were selling food, drinks, jewelry, art and more, Skip saw his fishing buddy approaching. "Todd!" he called out.

"Hey! What's happening? Hi, Benny! Did your dad win the tournament?" he asked, rubbing Benny's curly head.

"Sure did!" Benny shouted.

"Nah," Skip corrected him. "But I did win the trout division!"

"No way!"

"Yup! Todd, this is Claudia. Claudia, Todd."

"Pleased to meet you!" Todd grinned at Claudia, then at Skip.

"Pleased to meet you," Claudia responded.

"So, you don't fish the tournament with me, and look who you wind up with! Do you fish, Claudia?"

"Skip kinda taught me, but, no, I'm not a fisherwoman yet."

"Well, watch him." Todd teased. "If he buys any more lures, there won't be room for either you or me in the boat!"

"Y'all don't have to worry about that anytime soon, eh, Claudia."

"Nope. I flung his tackle box overboard!"

Benny looked up, not knowing whether to be angry or amused.

"You what?" Todd asked.

"Yeah. I chucked it!"

"It's a long story!" Skip said. "How about joining us at the Shrimp House, and I'll fill ya in?"

"No, thanks. Just ate. And I want to see the rest of the awards ceremony. Man, I wish I could have fished this tournament with you! That would have been my trout in first place! How big was it, anyway?"

"Seven-and-three-quarter pounds!"

"Damn! That's gotta be a tournament record!"

"Yeah. Quite a fish!"

"Good job! Well, you look hungry. Maybe I'll meet you over there later for desert. If not, I'll give you a call at home, and you can fill me in on all the fun details."

"The details weren't all fun," Claudia moaned.

"Catch you later," Skip said. They crossed Hwy. 98 and walked down the street toward the bridge to the Shrimp House.

A FRIENDLY WAITRESS seated them a table next to the window that had a view of Hwy. 98 and the bridge. Waiting for their food to arrive, Skip noticed Claudia looking melancholy.

"Anything wrong, Claudia?"

"Yeah."

"Thinking about the lost loot?"

"Lost loot?" Benny was all ears.

"No. But I'm bummed out about that, too."

"What is it?"

"Harris."

"Harris?"

"Uh huh. I know it's silly after all he did, nearly getting the both of us killed and all."

Benny's eyes lit up. "Killed?" he squealed.

Claudia ignored him. "But he is my brother. And I'm worried about him."

"Sure. I can..." Skip's eyes grew large, and his face paled.

"What is it?" Claudia asked, and turned to see what Skip was looking at out the window.

"Speaking of the devil," Skip whispered.

Claudia saw the solemn figure, arm in a sling, walking along the highway, and couldn't believe her eyes. "Skip!" she cried. "It's him!"

"I know."

"What do we do?"

"Don't know. What do you want to do?"

"Hell, I don't know. One part of me wants to hide! The other part wants to run out there and hug him."

"Well, it's your call."

"Who's that?" Benny asked.

"Claudia's brother."

"Oh! Cool!" Benny jumped out of his chair and ran out the door before he could be stopped.

"Hey! In here!" he shouted, waving at the stranger. "Your sister's in here!" Skip grabbed him by the shoulder. Harris looked at the child, then at the window of the restaurant, where Claudia sat staring out at him.

Skip walked Benny back inside and sat down. Claudia continued to stare at Harris as he began crossing the street. Narrowly avoiding a speeding car, Harris made his way down the grass embankment, across the pitted parking lot, and opened the front door of the Shrimp House.

"Hey, Sis!" he shouted.

"Hello, Harris."

"Hello, Harris! Hello Harris?" Is that all you can say to the brother who saved your life?"

"Saved my life? 'Bout got me killed is more like it!"

"You don't think that Will smashing into that tree was an accident, do ya?"

"Yes, I do."

"Well, it wasn't! I had plenty of time to miss it!" The other diners gawked at the scene, as Harris raised his voice. "That bastard –"

"Watch your language!" Skip shouted, glancing Benny's way.

"Will had that gun aimed at me, too, you know! If I didn't chase you, he'd a blown my head off!"

"Sure."

"Why do you think we never quite caught up to you? I didn't have the throttle open all the way!"

"Seemed to me like you were as hell-bent on killing us as he was!"

"Killing you? I'm the one saved yer life!" Harris pulled a chair to the table and sat down. Folks in the restaurant continued to stare.

Skip looked at Claudia. He could tell by her expression she wasn't buying Harris's story. Skip slid a menu across the table. "Order anything you want. It's on me."

"Now that's more like it!" Harris grinned, revealing several bad front teeth.

"Dad, he hasn't been cleaning his teeth!"

"Benny, hush! Is that a nice thing to say?"

"No, sir."

Claudia welcomed the silence that had come over the table. The other diners went back to their meals, and the waitress took Harris's order.

"Dad, how'd you get that shiner?" Benny asked.

"Ask Harris," Skip replied. Claudia gazed out the window.

"Harris, how did my dad get that shiner?"

"I reckon I gave him that."

"Why?"

"Cause I was drunk, and he was messing with my sister."

"I wasn't 'messing' with your sister," Skip said. "We were eating dinner."

"Looked to me like you were messing with her."

"So you hauled off and socked him?" Benny asked.

"Yup. Sorry about that. Like I said, I was drunker than a toad. No hard feelings, eh?" His right hand reached out to Skip.

Skip shook his hand reluctantly, noticing the scorpion tattoo on the back of his hand.

Claudia didn't have the appetite for desert, but Skip and Benny were eating chocolate brownies with vanilla ice cream and chocolate syrup and whipped cream with a cherry on top, as Harris finished his seafood platter. Suddenly, Todd burst through the door.

Spotting them, he shouted, "You won!"

"I told you that," Skip replied.

"No! I mean you won the whole damn thing!"

"How can that be?"

"Garrett Collins was the only one who placed in more than one category. He had two third places. That only adds up to two points! And all the first place winners get three points."

"So. That would mean a ten-way tie."

"Right! And they decide the tiebreaker by which fish is the largest percent heavier than the second place fish in that category! And you won!"

"No way!"

"Way!"

"Eeee-haw!" Skip shouted, jumping up and giving Todd a high-five.

Claudia got up and Skip hugged her. "We'll be a-going to Costa Rica!" Squeezing Claudia, he looked at Todd.

Neither Claudia nor Todd knew if the "we" Skip referred to was them. They looked each other quizzically. Both were too polite to open that discussion in the restaurant. Everyone's attention was riveted to their table again.

"My dad won! My dad won!" Benny exclaimed, jumping up and down. In his excitement, he leaped on his chair, and right onto the tabletop before Skip could reach him, spilling drinks.

Skip whisked Benny off of the table, and into Claudia's arms. Harris seemed oblivious to the whole scene.

BENNY SNUGGLED BETWEEN Claudia and Skip on the way home, fast asleep. Harris leaned his head on the cooler, which he had propped up against the cab, his tired legs stretched out on the bed of the truck.

Clouds covered the moon, but Skip could see tears rolling down Claudia's cheeks as headlights of passing cars momentarily filled the inside of the truck with light. "I feel so torn, Skip!"

"Tell me."

"One part of me wants you to let me out right here and now. Go my own way. Be completely free." Skip caressed her hand.

"Another part of me wants to stay. Be your lover. Benny's step-mom. Harris's support. Take you all under my apron strings."

"Claudia, I know this sounds strange, after only knowing you for a few days, but... I do love you."

"Don't – "

"I do. It's crazy, I know. But that's me."

Claudia squeezed his hand.

"And because I love you, Claudia, I want what's best for you. Whatever that is."

"Even if it's not you and Benny?"

"Yes." Tears filled Skip's eyes.

"You wouldn't be angry?"

"Heartbroken. Not angry," Skip's voice cracked. "I'll understand."

"Then I'll give it a try. No guarantees."

His heart skipped a beat. "There are no guarantees. Not in life. Not in relationships."

"True," Claudia agreed.

The moon broke through the clouds, subtle at first, then in full glory.

"It's a gorgeous night, eh?"

"Beautiful, Skip. Just beautiful."

"For a while there I was thinking it was going to rain again."

"And you know what that means," Claudia said, grinning.

"Another black paint shower!"

"Oh, yeah!"

Chuckling turned to laughter, which turned to near hysteria. Benny stirred.

"What a mess!" Claudia blurted out between breaths.

"And what a blessing." Skip ran his fingers through her fine hair.

Claudia brought his hand to her lips and kissed it. Her tears reflected the moonlight.

"One thing's for sure," Skip said.

"What's that?"

"We'll never forget the last few days."

"Never."

Don't miss out!

Visit the website below and you can sign up to receive emails whenever Bob Hoelzle publishes a new book. There's no charge and no obligation.

https://books2read.com/r/B-A-DKCM-JFWIB

BOOKS 2 READ

Connecting independent readers to independent writers.

About the Author

Bob Hoelzle lives on Alligator Point along Florida's Forgotten Coast. He fishes local tournaments, and walks the white sand beaches of Alligator Point peninsula on Turtle Patrol. This is his first novel.

Read more at https://forgottencoastbobphotos.com/.

CPSIA information can be obtained
at www.ICGtesting.com
Printed in the USA
LVHW021102070821
694354LV00004B/15